P9-BTO-859

THE DEVIL AND WEBSTER

ALSO BY JEAN HANFF KORELITZ

NOVELS
You Should Have Known
Admission
The White Rose
The Sabbathday River
A Jury of Her Peers

FOR CHILDREN
Interference Powder

POETRY
The Properties of Breath

THE DEVIL
AND
WEBSTER

A Novel

—∞—

JEAN HANFF KORELITZ

GRAND CENTRAL
PUBLISHING

NEW YORK   BOSTON

Property of
FAUQUIER COUNTY PUBLIC LIBRARY
11 Winchester Street
Warrenton, VA 20186

WITHDRAWAL

This book is a work of fiction. Names, characters, places, and incidents are the product of the author's imagination or are used fictitiously. Any resemblance to actual events, locales, or persons, living or dead, is coincidental.

Copyright © 2017 by Jean Hanff Korelitz
Cover design by Kimberly Glyder. Cover copyright © 2017 by Hachette Book Group, Inc.

Hachette Book Group supports the right to free expression and the value of copyright. The purpose of copyright is to encourage writers and artists to produce the creative works that enrich our culture.

The scanning, uploading, and distribution of this book without permission is a theft of the author's intellectual property. If you would like permission to use material from the book (other than for review purposes), please contact permissions@hbgusa.com. Thank you for your support of the author's rights.

Grand Central Publishing
Hachette Book Group
1290 Avenue of the Americas, New York, NY 10104
grandcentralpublishing.com
twitter.com/grandcentralpub

First Edition: March 2017

Grand Central Publishing is a division of Hachette Book Group, Inc. The Grand Central Publishing name and logo is a trademark of Hachette Book Group, Inc.

The publisher is not responsible for websites (or their content) that are not owned by the publisher.

The Hachette Speakers Bureau provides a wide range of authors for speaking events. To find out more, go to www.hachettespeakersbureau.com or call (866) 376-6591.

Library of Congress Cataloging-in-Publication Data

Names: Korelitz, Jean Hanff, 1961– author.
Title: The devil and Webster / Jean Hanff Korelitz.
Description: First edition. | New York : Grand Central Publishing, 2017.
Identifiers: LCCN 2016023354| ISBN 9781455592388 (hardcover) | ISBN 9781478934868 (audio book) | ISBN 9781478934875 (audio download) | ISBN 9781455592395 (ebook)
Classification: LCC PS3561.O6568 D49 2017 | DDC 813/.54—dc23
LC record available at https://lccn.loc.gov/2016023354

ISBNs: 978-1-4555-9238-8 (hardcover), 978-1-4555-9239-5 (ebook)

Printed in the United States of America

LSC-C

10 9 8 7 6 5 4 3 2 1

For
Ann Dorothy Zabin Korelitz,
Nina Ann Korelitz Matza,
and
Dorothy Aoife Korelitz Muldoon

This, Sir, is my case! It is the case not merely of that humble institution, it is the case of every college in our Land...of all those great charities founded by the piety of our ancestors to alleviate human misery, and scatter blessings along the pathway of life...Sir, you may destroy this little institution; it is weak, it is in your hands! I know it is one of the lesser lights in the literary horizon of our country. You may put it out! But if you do so, you must carry through your work! You must extinguish, one after another, all those great lights of science which for more than a century have thrown their radiance over our land!

It is, Sir, as I have said, a small college. And yet there are those who love it!

Daniel Webster, 1818

A SMALL SCHOOL IN THE WOODS

At the exact epicenter of the Webster College campus, which was also the exact epicenter of the open rectangular space known today as the Quad, but formerly (and still formally) as the Billings Lawn, a large and unlovely stump protruded from highly tended grass. The stump was a lonely vestige of the great elms that once loomed over Webster's buildings and walkways, and filled the forests of New England in general before Dutch elm disease arrived, a half-century earlier. But this particular tree—this particular stump—was not a victim of that arboreal catastrophe; it had been chopped down many years before the first fungus-bearing *Scolytus* elm-bark beetle had met its first North American victim. That stump went back to the very beginning of Webster's story and it was a beloved symbol of the college to its graduates. Everyone else had to have it explained to them, but wasn't that what it meant to be an insider?

The stump had a proper name, naturally—it was "the Webster Elm"—but nobody used that; everybody just called it the Stump. As in: "We'll meet at the Stump at ten, okay? We can walk over *from there." Or: "Join us every Sunday at eight for sunrise yoga at the Stump!" Or: "Take Back the Night will leave from the Stump at midnight." And of course there had been protests at the Stump. Many protests, over the years. Many sit-ins and vigils. Webster was populated by students who cared deeply, passionately about things, who thought globally and acted locally, and who had been admitted to Webster, now one of the most selective colleges in the nation, for precisely those reasons. The Stump was where they went when there was something they wanted, or wanted rid of, or when something terrible happened, on campus or in the world—safe spaces for women, dodgy institutional investments, more choices for vegetarians (back when "vegetarian" was radical enough; no one had even dreamed of "vegan"), the raging (sometimes drunken) Indian who once served as the college's mascot (a slap in the face to those Native American students the college began to recruit in the '70s), or the disasters—man-made or natural—the wrestling coach actually struck by lightning on the golf course, the student killed in a driving accident while on a study abroad program in Peru, the fall of the Berlin Wall, the fall of the towers, the basketball player dead in his bed from a drunken aspiration of vomit, and once, long ago, when a freshman from the Midwest who turned out to be black arrived on campus to matriculate, an actual encampment at the Stump for nearly a week. So many petitions and expressions of solidarity and rallies and moments of silence! So much empathy and outrage and passionate youthful idealism! But whatever cause or grievance brought Webster students to the Stump, what happened once they got there was always pretty much the same: a clear statement of purpose, a plainly identified leader, and lines of communication smartly established with Webster's president, whoever he was at the time, after which that president would at least pretend to consider the students' demands or sympathize with their feelings. But then, once the protesters had picketed a trustees' retreat or a commencement to emphasize their point, the students would always just . . . go away. Had they graduated? Or transferred? Had Mom or Dad or whoever was paying Webster's tuition read them the riot act? It didn't really matter. The students of Webster College had convened, raised their voices, made their points, been heard . . . and then, having accomplished these things, they had departed, after which Buildings and Grounds would come along to clear away anything left behind. Then the area around the Stump would be reseeded and fenced off to give it a chance to recover. And that would always be the end of that.*

Exactly none of these prior protests, therefore, would have offered any guidance to Naomi Roth.

Naomi Roth, who'd arrived at Webster as its first dedicated professor of feminist and gender studies and then became its dean of women's affairs, and ultimately its first female president, and whose experience at Webster that awful year would come to seem . . . well, many things: inevitable, unforgiving . . . tragic, obviously. There were no crucial lessons in the college's past, no kernels of sage advice from those former Webster presidents still living. It was all a new terrain, baffling and undiscovered, and once the thing began there seemed to be no way of stopping it, at least no way beyond the many ways she did try, and despite how sincerely she offered negotiation, then—to be blunt—capitulation. Nothing worked, and it even occurred to her that what began at the Stump that fall was not so much a protest in the way that she, a former student activist herself, had always understood "protest," but rather an undefined compulsion to exchange ideas about what was wrong with Webster and wrong with the world. It was almost as if each of the students at the Stump encampment had come with some personal grievance, and in the airing of these grievances there emerged a general, generational, miasma of discontent: about Webster, the country, the way things were, that simply hung over the Billings Lawn and the campus itself, and represented, as Betty Friedan might have said, a problem that had no name. But, it was still Naomi Roth's problem: first ignored by her, and then irritating to her, and then alarming to her, and then, all at once, intractably complex and a threat to everything she had done at Webster, and everything she was trying to do.

It was Naomi herself who noted the deference paid to one young man, a dark and slight kid in a brown hoodie and heavy rubber boots, caked in November mud. And it was Naomi who asked who he was and began to wonder, possibly aloud, whether he would like to represent the group and talk with her in a calmer way about what was at issue here, and how the administration—how she, Naomi—could begin to make it right.

And so: Naomi found him. She appointed him—you could make a case for that. And everything that happened later, to the college, to Naomi herself, but mostly, of course, to him, was her fault. You could make a case for that, too, and even if you couldn't, Naomi herself could. She always would.

His name, it would emerge, was Omar, and he was a sophomore from Oklahoma, though he was not, of course, really from Oklahoma. He was from Oklahoma the way someone with an Irish name was from Massachusetts, or someone with a Swedish name was from Minnesota, only not even that, because the Oklahoma address on his Webster application just happened to be that of the foster family he was living with at the time, after earlier stints with other foster families in Milwaukee and Houston. Why Oklahoma? It was one of those questions you sensed there was no point in asking. Why Milwaukee? Why Houston? Why America in the first place?

Another question not worth asking, but for the opposite reason.

America because, as Omar would later tell it—to his

comrades in the finally named movement, Webster Dissent, to the earnest student journalists from the Webster Daily and the alternative Webster Contra, the Webster Tonight host on the college radio station, the Yale Daily News reporter and the Hartford Courant reporter and the AP reporter and the extremely famous reporter from NBC News and the also extremely famous host of Today—America had been his dream, for so many years in the refugee camp, far away in his cherished, blighted land.

His dream among open sewers and plastic bags flapping in the dry air and the sacks of grain from World Concern and the brave little soccer skirmishes on the broken ground under the lights of the perimeter fence...far, far into the distance. The sorrow and boredom and filth, the anguish of watching his loved ones taken, one after the next until he was alone, the ache of wasted time as other boys in other countries got to study, dream, plan, move forward into their futures while he could only sit still: immobilized by frustration, tormented by longing.

Such a terrible story. Such a terrible wonderful story because...look how Omar had journeyed from there to here, from that terrifying sad place to this lovely safe campus: buildings of gray stone, pretty fluttering trees, straight walkways to guide your footfalls as you progressed from destination to destination, and that single, misshapen stump left over from the past, to which you might tie yourself as to the mast of a listing ship. You couldn't save everyone in the world, of course, but wasn't it nice to think that a smart boy from such an awful life, burdened by so much suffering, so many losses, might still, incredibly, find himself at a place like Webster College?

Webster College. Once a school of the richest, the WASPiest, the most loutish and most conservative of American men, and then later, after its extraordinary transition in the 1970s, the

*institution of choice for creative and left-leaning intellectu-
als of all genders and ethnic varieties. "A small school in the
woods, from which, by the Grace of God, we might know His
will" had been its motto in the early days, when Josiah Webster
hacked his way north from King's College (later Columbia) to
establish his Webster's Indian Academy beneath the towering
elms. Two centuries later, with nary a Native American student
in nearly that long, those words—like so much else about
Webster—had been revised: "A small school in the woods, from
which, by scholarship and thoughtful community, we might
know the Universe."*

*That was how things stood when Naomi Roth became the
college's seventeenth president, and Omar Khayal, a sophomore from Oklahoma, Milwaukee, Houston, and a refugee
camp under Palestinian stars, its doomed and mystifying icon.*

PART I

ASSEMBLE

CHAPTER ONE

NAOMI ROTH'S DEFINING MOMENT

W hat happened at Webster that year was harrowing, but it wasn't the first harrowing scenario Naomi Roth had faced, either as Webster's president or, indeed, in her prior roles at the college: professor, dean of women's affairs, and reluctant member of the search committee for the very job she'd end up occupying herself.

That earlier skirmish (later she would think of it as a baptism of sorts) had been the Radclyffe Hall mess a decade earlier, more or less concurrent with the announcement that Logan Coulson, Webster's sixteenth president, intended to retire. Radclyffe Hall had brought the college, and Naomi as its situational spokesperson, the kind of attention that generated snark on Weekend Update and the gleeful nastiness of right-wingers everywhere. It also brought figures from Naomi's life in its many phases—her New York childhood, college in upstate New York, the years in northern New Hampshire (first as a VISTA volunteer then as a leftover from some nonexistent social revolution), and later graduate school and academia—poking back into her life, with emails to her Webster address, messages on her office phone, and a deeply unwelcome letter from her ex-husband, enclosing three glossy photos of himself with wife number 2 and kids (which went straight into the garbage, but which having been seen could not be unseen). There had even been one painstakingly written note on pink paper from a third cousin in Florida (the envelope containing a folded AP clipping from a Fort Lauderdale weekly that made Naomi look very old and grievously fat) admonishing her to do something about her hair, because she had been "such a pretty girl when you were little." The whole crazy—and crazily overblown—thing, Naomi now understood, had utterly changed her life.

The incident began, as these things so often did, with a whimper, not a bang, and that whimper took the form of a Webster room selection in accordance with a sophomore's designated lottery number, an enviably low number, as it happened. The sophomore's choice of dwelling had been a single room on the third floor of Radclyffe Hall. Radclyffe was one of a number of large, once private homes that had been converted to themed residential housing when the college embarked on a wave of new construction—Science Complex, Language Cluster, Arts Neighborhood—in the '80s. They ran in an opulent line down Fairweather Road, which was just beyond the athletic center and bordered its fields. First off the corner was the Co-Op House (genially socialist, with rotating food preparation, but not outright hippie), then the French House, then the German House, then the Sojourner Truth House, then the Gandhi Collective Center (those were the hippies), then the First Nations Center (Native American students in the '80s had preferred this Canadian moniker, for some reason, and it had stuck), and then Radclyffe Hall, after which fraternities and sororities stretched to the end of the block. Radclyffe Hall, a squarish three-story structure, vaguely Queen Anne in style, with shared public rooms on the ground floor, was named not for the lesbian novelist but for a gruff 1908 graduate named James Radclyffe, who'd made his pile the old-fashioned way—by inheriting it—and would have been horrified, *horrified*, at what his namesake building had become. The "Hall" was added eventually, as must have seemed inevitable, and after a few years people just assumed that the name was a kind of pun about *The Well of Loneliness*, even though not all of the women who lived there were gay. Gay wasn't the point; *female* was the point. "A living environment for women within the Webster community," ran the description in the Webster Housing Handbook. Translation: *Women Only*.

The sophomore, whose name was Nell Jones-Givens, would later claim to have been surprised by the impact of her room selection, which bubbled and brewed for a few weeks before, just prior to midterms, two women who lived at Radclyffe came to the dean of students' office with an official objection. The dean, a perpetually irritated man named Bob Stacek who had been at Webster since his own undergraduate days, had swiftly dropkicked the matter to Naomi, whether as chair of the Women's Studies Department or as dean of women's affairs she was never sure. Not that it mattered. Bob's distaste for the situation was plain; indeed, he acted as if he'd been personally asked to dig bloody tampons out of the Radclyffe Hall toilets. And Naomi, who until that time had been so underinvolved in matters of college administration that she routinely spent her time in meetings surreptitiously making to-do lists, understood that this particular bell was tolling for her. And she had to admit: No one on campus was remotely as well prepared to address the issue at hand as herself, a tenured professor of women's studies and gender studies, and author of the respectably read (for academic nonfiction) *Divide and Conquer: Femaleness and Feminism in the Women's Movement's Second Wave*.

Nell Jones-Givens, the sophomore with the enviably low housing lottery number, had by her own account (published eventually on *Slate* and later wildly misquoted by Laura

Ingraham and other right-wingers) been grappling with gender dysmorphia since early childhood, and by the age of twelve had accepted that she was essentially a male person misplaced in a female body. Her efforts to delay menses and mash her breasts flat against her rib cage, her unsuccessful attempt to run with the men's cross-country team at her suburban Illinois high school, and her attainment of peace within her family on these issues had also been the subjects of her admissions essay to Webster. Hence, though Admissions did not routinely share such material with the administration, the college could not claim to have been ignorant of the implications of Nell's housing selection.

Over the summer that followed her freshman year, Nell had legally changed her name to Neil in her home state of Illinois. Official gender designation was a bit thornier, which only added to the mayhem once the whole mess began to roil. She was a woman, genetically. She was a man, spiritually. She had been admitted to Webster as a woman. She was a man by temperament, by choice, by fate, by all that was holy—except to those few poor evangelical Christians on campus, who asserted that whatever else she was, she was far from holy. She was a member of a gender designation that had expanded beyond patriarchal structures to assume a spectrum of identities, of which Neil's was simply one among so many. She was a knowing invader of the only female-designated safe space on campus, and a debaser of femaleness itself, due to the incomprehensible fact that she had been given the gift of being female and had chosen to decline it. She was . . . well, at the end of the day, what she was mattered far less than what she was not. She was not a woman, by her own account. She was also not remotely ready for what was about to happen to her. Webster was not ready. And Naomi certainly was not ready.

It had been a slowly unfolding, lovely, and uneventful fall. That hadn't helped.

All began well enough at Radclyffe Hall. Neil had made a friendly announcement about his new name at the first sharing circle meeting in September, and generally assumed his uncomplaining share of the cooking, cleaning, and upkeep of the house. He prepared exotic teas for his housemates from a large personal collection and frequently loaded the dishwasher, even when it was not technically his turn to do so. He tutored two of the women on his floor who were struggling in Japanese (Neil was fluent, having spent a gap year in Kyoto) and maintained the Radclyffe Hall Facebook page, soon to be inundated with vitriol from the world at large. But slowly, the situation began to fester.

There were the hormones: little ampules of injectable testosterone in the first-floor bathroom (for one junior girl in the house, the needles themselves were triggering traumatic flashbacks to a childhood bout with leukemia, but that was a separate issue). There was the clomping presence of an increasingly hairy, increasingly muscular person in the hallways and on the stairs, "taking up space," said the needlephobe's roommate, in that indefinable yet obvious way men did *everywhere in the world*. And finally, there was the boyfriend, a slim-hipped fiddler who claimed to have dropped out of Webster because it wasn't academically rigorous enough, and who now worked at one of the coffee bars downtown. And this, Naomi would come to understand, was the most incendiary of all the resentments engendered by Neil Jones-Givens. Had Neil actually become a man only to sleep with other men? In which case…what was the point of that? If he'd wanted to sleep with men, why not just remain a woman?

Calm, Naomi told the delegation from Radclyffe, on their first visit to her very small office in Crump-Eustis Hall, where the English and Comp. Lit. departments were based. *Calm, calm.* Let's remember that we're talking about young people— people learning who they are. Let's remember that we're talking about a college housing assignment, and working out how to live with people who don't fall in with every one of our beliefs, predilections, innate prejudices, or tastes in junk food was one of the little challenges of life and a test of civilization in general. The women—four of them—did not nod. They did not smile. The needlephobe, who headed the campus LGBTQ political action committee, was sitting in one of Naomi's visitors' seats, a Hitchcock-style wooden chair, not very comfortable, with the college crest stenciled on the back in bright blue and green. She had her hands wedged beneath her thighs, and she leaned forward, mashing them down against the wood, as if she was scared they might escape her control and do something terrible.

"No," said her roommate, a basketball player from Florida. "No, we won't be 'calm.' Would you tell us to be calm if we were being threatened with rape?"

"Absolutely not," said Naomi, straining for composure. "But I don't think that is what is happening here."

"I don't see a difference," said one of the others. This one Naomi knew. She had been in Naomi's First Wave/Second Wave seminar the previous spring. "This is a case of male penetration of a designated women-only space."

Penetration, thought Naomi. *Oy.*

"Designated by whom?" she said instead.

"By...the college," the girl sputtered, outraged.

But in fact there was no official Webster designation for Radclyffe Hall, Naomi would discover when she looked into the matter. There was nothing there at all in the way of official rules or bylaws. Radclyffe Hall, like the other houses on Fairweather Road, had attained its distinction of habitation through a phenomenon far more subtle than official language, a phenomenon that would return to bedevil her life again and again over the following years: institutional tradition.

Tradition! Fine for a Broadway musical about a shtetl on the

Russian steppes, fine for the shtetl itself (like the one Naomi's own great-grandparents had long ago fled, in that classic, crushed-in-amber American story). Fine for a class prank or a holiday ritual. Fine, even, for the Webster seniors' own smashing of their ceremonial clay pipes against the Stump on the eve of their graduations—the ritual that most Webster alumni associated with the Stump—or any of the myriad other Websterian rituals. Not so fine for gender designations in the swamp of ideological ferment that was American higher education (subdivision: Liberal Arts), New England, circa 2006.

No wonder this would become Naomi Roth's defining moment, and the thematic overture to what came later. No wonder it would focus attention on her, just at the delicate moment when President Coulson announced his retirement and commenced a yearlong victory lap of alumni gatherings and honorary degree ceremonies, as a committee of trustees, consultants, and faculty members convened to begin thinking about a successor.

When Naomi, to her great chagrin, found that she was expected to serve as a member of the search committee (this news was delivered without fanfare in an email from Dean Stacek), she imagined she'd be able to wiggle out of it without much difficulty. She was already teaching her usual First Wave/Second Wave seminar that fall, and co-teaching a literature/history course on feminist utopias, and she had agreed to take over a freshman seminar on Ann Bannon for a queer theorist on maternity leave (an offer she regretted almost immediately as she reread the Bannon novels for the first time in years, finding them far less compelling than she'd remembered). Also: She had a ten-year-old feminist of her own at home that year, who furthermore was entering a phase in which all topics, from the profound to the banal, must be argued as a point of principle, which was exhausting. Also: The Radclyffe Hall situation was taking more

and more of her nonexistent free time. But when she phoned
Bob Stacek to explain—with appropriate regret—her situation,
the bastard declined to excuse her.

"You were requested," he said bluntly, managing to communicate that Naomi's participation had been neither his idea nor his
preference. "I'm afraid we'll have to insist."

Requested by . . . ? By one of the trustees, she was told, though
Naomi was not to know which for some months. This person
had read the previous week's *New York Times* article about what
was happening at Radclyffe Hall. Attention was being paid,
Stacek informed her, somewhat tersely, to how things were being
"handled."

How Naomi was handling things, at least thus far, involved
pretending that every interrogator who came to her about Radclyffe Hall was a fellow intellectual engaged in a genuinely
curious and open discussion on the subjects of gender fluidity
and the "trans experience," and that the variously outraged students, parents, journalists, and alumni were as interested in
thoughtful, unemotional debate as she herself was. This was
a folly of one, of course, but so far it had disarmed everyone from the various students to the *New York Times* writer
(whose name, as a lifelong reader of the *Times*, she'd read-
ily recognized), and the serious (i.e., not-political, not-satirical)
coverage had been, as a result, rather encouragingly dignified.
The issues Radclyffe Hall raised were valid and even essential
topics for scrutiny at a place like Webster, she liked to remind
people, and as pertinent and pressing as politics, class, religion,
race, or any time-honored -ism. "Universities are not static environments as a rule," Naomi had insisted to the *New York
Times* reporter, who, gratifyingly, reproduced her words exactly
and in the right order to boot. "Stasis is the last thing we want.
Webster is a place where discourse happens. This is a place
where ideas come to meet one another." And then, as if she

hadn't been reading this man's byline for decades, she asked him what his feelings were on the subject.

That line in particular—*a place where ideas come to meet one another*—where had it sprung from? It sounded like something she'd been fed years earlier, when she and her ex-husband had trained for their VISTA year at a campus in the Appalachian Mountains. (Though VISTA, in its wisdom, hadn't sent them to the Appalachian Mountains or any place like the Appalachian Mountains, but instead to a picture-perfect village in northern New England, complete with steeple and general store. She and Daniel had separated a decade later.) Still, when it emerged, unbidden from her own mouth, it had sent a little trill of rightness through her. *The old good fight. Still there, after all.*

"But this particular dormitory, as I understand it," said the reporter, "is meant to be women only. Why would you choose to live in such a place if you wanted to be male?"

"That's not a question I can answer," Naomi said. "I'm sure you wouldn't want me to speculate about how a given student might feel."

"Do you think," the reporter continued, "that a self-identified male in a female-only space has a right to complain of discrimination?"

Naomi frowned. She was just formulating her response when the reporter upped the ante.

"I mean, say you were a white transfer student at Morehouse or Spelman? Or...an atheist at Brigham Young. Are you entitled to complain of discrimination?"

DANGER, NAOMI ROTH, Naomi thought. For a heady instant, she envisioned her own personal robot with wildly oscillating arms.

"What I can tell you," she finally said, "is that Webster is exactly the place where we would like these questions to be raised and considered, if not answered. They may not be answerable. But these are important issues for intelligent, thoughtful, and globally attuned young people to work through, and this university—like most, I would hope—is a safe place to work through them."

And then, that very week, President Coulson announced that he would retire the following year.

And then, Naomi Roth had found her participation on the search committee requested by parties unknown.

"Well, I suppose . . ." she told the dean, pausing for a moment, as if he still might be inclined to give her an out, "I can do that. Do you have a sense of the time commitment?"

"Until we've chosen a president," he said, with a chill that made it all the way across the campus from his office on Billings's second floor.

They would begin the following Monday, with a preliminary meeting in the conference room at the Webster Inn.

But by the following Monday, the Radclyffe Hall story had overflown the levees, with a dedicated tirade about lesbian separatists "getting a taste of their own medicine" on Rush Limbaugh and a crass comment on David Letterman (which seemed especially upsetting to the dormitory's envoys, who were waiting for her at her office the morning after it aired). Naomi would miss that first meeting in order to hold a conference call with parents of the Radclyffe Hall women (the ones who were still women), and she would miss the second due to an emergency session with Neil Jones-Givens's counselor from Webster Health Services, who was twisting herself into knots in an effort to communicate that the situation was *bad* without breaching confidentiality. Their conversation—a study in creative nondisclosure—would have been comical had it not also been so weighted. Neil, by then, had fled Radclyffe Hall, and two days earlier he had turned up at the health center, where he was "resting" and "comfortable." The staff there were in contact with his parents back home in Illinois, and various options were under discussion. There was—and this was of course always the case, the counselor reminded Naomi, with any student at any time—the possibility of self-harm, which must always be kept at the forefront of one's thoughts. "I'm...moderately...erring on the side of caution...*concerned*," the counselor managed to say, which Naomi interpreted as *This student is in real trouble and if we don't handle the situation in exactly the right way, a way I am expressly not authorized to describe, then you and I and this college are potentially in deep, deep shit, so do not fail to take this seriously and do not fuck things up.*

Naomi did make it to the next meeting, a few Mondays after that. This time she arrived only fifteen minutes late and left only fifteen minutes early, in order to be at the crisis gathering in the Radclyffe Hall common room, an event that (she'd been informed only hours earlier) was also to be attended by a camera crew from 20/20, which was news to the college press office. President Coulson, who had chosen this moment to go on a house hunting trip to San Mateo (he was joining an "education/technology think tank," whatever that was), had expressed his full confidence in his dean of women's affairs (a comment that gave rise to a small explosion of its own, with its condescending whiff of patriarchy, as if the trouble at Radclyffe Hall were no different from any other problem that might arise when a bunch of out-of-control gals moved into a house together). Naomi received nothing in the way of guidance from the president or the trustees. The press office (one crusty alum who'd edited a local paper in Tennessee, and his student intern) offered no crash course in media readiness, nor even a tepid suggestion of talking points relaying the college's official position. There was no official position, she understood. There was only herself, and she would not know whether she'd handled it well or not until they either fired her ass or didn't. All she could think to do (and this came from a *Ms.* magazine article about women in the brave new battlefield of corporate America, which she'd read many years earlier) was to inform every single person in a more senior administrative position than her own every time she did anything at all, and invite the college's attorney (thankfully, a woman) to accompany her to each press interview. It would not occur to her until later that she had already begun to act like a college president, but it did occur to someone else.

That someone else was a food entrepreneur, less than a decade out of Webster and already at the white-hot epicenter of the culinary zeitgeist. He was named (fittingly) Will Rennet and he had endowed a professorship in the Department of History, a biannual college conference on food and culture, and the Webster Farm Co-Op five miles from the Stump in West Webster, tended by students with output (milk, vegetables, eggs) used to supply the dining hall and various food outlets on campus. Will Rennet was one of four Webster trustees on the search committee, and while he hadn't said much in the inaugural meeting, nor in the one that followed, he happened to be speaking when Naomi blustered in late to the third, trailing press releases and not quite off the phone with Rosa in the college attorney's office. This won her some entirely understandable glares from her fellow committee members, but Will Rennet—who, as the interrupted party, might have had the most reason to be irritated— was not one of them. He looked thoughtful as Naomi ended her call, apologized, gave a succinct, two-sentence appraisal of the Radclyffe Hall situation (incorporating both an aura of "everything's under control" and an eye roll at the absurdity of it all), sat down and appeared to focus in on the matter at hand. Ninety minutes later, with almost two dozen names on a long list compiled by the committee secretary (notable alumni, notable members of the business community, a former Massachusetts

senator, and the current deans of the faculty and students),
Naomi rose, apologized again, suggested that they all acquire
and read an obscure work of educational philosophy, long out
of print, that had influenced her own transition to academia
after earlier stints as an entrepreneur and VISTA volunteer, mentioned that her ten-year-old daughter had strongly suggested that
the new president, whomever he or she happened to be, should
"be chill" because (in Naomi's daughter's opinion, she reiterated)
"chill" was something Webster had not enjoyed in its president
for a good long while, apologized one final time and headed
out to the crisis meeting and the cameras of *20/20*. The fringe
of Naomi's Tibetan scarves fluttered from beneath her ancient
Russian army coat as she exited the room.

And then, in the general deflation that followed her departure,
as the others shuffled their papers and a few actually wrote down
the title of the book Naomi had mentioned, Will Rennet sat forward in his chair, tapped his pen against the table, and said, in
the tone of a person used to being listened to: "I want *her*."

CHAPTER TWO

THE TENANT OF RADCLYFFE HALL

When Naomi Roth became Webster College's seventeenth president, first female president, and first Jewish president (that is, if one accepted the gentleman-protests-too-much assertions of a certain Charles Myer Stone, who was Webster's president from 1921 to 1935 and a man of self-described "solid German stock"), her daughter and only child Hannah Rosalind Roth was eleven and an effective gadfly in the making. Named for two of Naomi's heroines—the brave Senesh and the inexcusably passed-over Franklin—young Hannah had seldom failed to make known her dissatisfactions with the world. Why did the nursery school cafeteria place upon her tray each day a sandwich of salty pink meat, when each day she refused to eat it? Why did the boys at recess start kicking a ball to one another even before they were out the door, while the girls went to the other end of the playground with the bucket of chalk? Of her grandparents—especially Naomi's mother, who'd outlived her father by more than a decade—Hannah was bluntly vocal in her grasp of the circumstances ("They don't like me, do they? Do they like you? I can't tell.") And when it came to the world beyond their American lives (first in Amherst, where Naomi did her PhD at

UMass, and then in Webster), Hannah Roth flatly refused to accept that everyone else was apparently okay with the terrible endemic injustices of the world. A child lived off a garbage pile in an unpronounceable city in a country Hannah had never set foot in—and yet everyone just went about their business as if this were not the case? It was an outrage. It was a bafflement. And there was hunger. There was suffering. There were kids caught in the crossfire. There were men who threw shrouds over women to hide and imprison them. There were embryos from their mothers untimely ripped, only because they lacked a Y chromosome. There were women forced to bear children of rape. There was rape.

Hannah had made her first march on Washington while still in utero. She'd been pushed along in a stroller for her second. By her third, she claimed to know the way from the train station to the Mall (MapQuest, admittedly, had been a big help in this) and where the porta-potties should be. Naomi's own fundamental beliefs and political positions had not shifted a millimeter since she was Hannah's age, and her life still orbited the principle of speaking truth to power, but...it was also true that at this particular point of her life...she was tired. And she was busy, with a child and a teaching career, and the deaths of first her father and then her mother to get through and manage. And look, the world was *still* full of terrible things! Some of the same terrible things there had always been, and even— who would have guessed?—a whole raft of *new* terrible things. No matter how many marches she'd gone on, how many petitions she'd signed (or, indeed, written), the meetings, the rallies, the online campaigns, Fair Trade symbols and recycling receptacles, no matter how clearly people were shown how the chickens and pigs were raised and who was stitching together the clothing in Bangladesh, people just kept eating the same things and buying the same things and throwing their plastic bags out with the garbage, to swirl forever in the Pacific Ocean. The melting ice caps could reach their knees before conservatives in Congress admitted all that annoying science wasn't some lefty hoax, and classrooms of shrieking kids mown down in bloody heaps would fail to persuade them that any other rights trumped the right to bear arms.

For Naomi there had come a moment, a few years before she became president, when she had quietly set down the burden of her own outrage. *There will be poor always, pathetically suffering. Look at the good things you've got,* she might have said in explanation, were she not just plain embarrassed to be quoting *Jesus Christ Superstar.* But the fact was that not many people did ask, or even notice, that Naomi Roth had retired from the ramparts. The people in question—her compadres, her kammerades, her fellow travelers—were just as tired as she was, it appeared.

Hannah had been raised in the only way that Naomi, who never precisely planned on becoming a mother, could imagine raising a child: every opinion applauded, every argument celebrated, every position given the serious debate it deserved. Of course it helped that the two of them, despite Hannah's clear taste for debate, were on balance in agreement, but this was not always the case. When Hannah declared eternal resistance to the consumption of animal flesh at the age of four, Naomi wasted precious time, energy, and money trying to move her, not because she thought it was healthier to consume meat than not, but because she had previously tried and failed at vegetarianism herself, and was totally uninterested in going through that again. Consuming a steak in front of her four-year-old daughter would never be a peaceful, stress-free experience, and preparing two meals for one dinner table was also going to be a major pain in the ass. She offered Hannah, therefore, adaptations: ground turkey burgers, lovingly raised and humanely euthanized fish. She bargained six vegetarian nights for a regular Sunday chicken. She proposed a guest exception for when company came to supper. All negotiations fell at her daughter's small, Velcro-strapped feet. And the baleful expression, the reek of daughterly disapproval that met the hamburger Naomi might order in a restaurant, the scoop of osso buco over barley at her friend Francine's house— the truth was, no meat tasted good enough to make up for that. She soldiered on for a couple of years, bringing home the bacon because it was her right to do so, serving up various cuts and steaks and ground-up bits for her own consumption alongside Hannah's wok-tossed broccoli and mashed potatoes, and then, one day, exhausted by yet another frosty meal over chicken Marbella, she just gave up and stopped. Now, when Naomi ate meat at all, it was on the sly, and in fear of discovery, like a high schooler holding her cigarette out the bathroom window. Only in the guise of her presidential self, going about her official duties on campus and especially on the road—cajoling (and soothing) alumni, courting donors, convening with other presidents of other universities—did Naomi get to actually enjoy meat when it was unapologetically served. (Sometimes, in the South, she even got barbecue.)

But there would be no barbecue, no flesh nor fowl nor creature that swam on the first Sunday evening in October, on this, the ninth autumn of Naomi's Webster presidency, which happened also to be the autumn of Hannah's sophomore year at the college.

To anyone who did not happen to be her mother, Hannah Roth probably looked like any other Webster student, scuttling to class across the Billings Lawn with her head down, pulling closed with one hand a down jacket over a green Webster hoodie, her heavy rubber boots avoiding the icy patches on the packed-snow path. Hannah Roth was only a sophomore from Webster, Massachusetts, a probable history major, an active member of Webster's activist community (which was, this being Webster

College, essentially the entire student body) and resident of—*O, Irony*—Radclyffe Hall. She had that typical-for-Webster hair in a semi-intentional ponytail and a mildly underslept presentation, and her sharp edge and considerable intellect buried beneath a few layers of upspeak and *I was, likes*—the patois of her American generation, by which they might know one another where'er they roamed. Naomi herself had occasionally failed to pick Hannah out on the campus walkways and, once on Webster's Main Street, when she was submerged in groups of other students, only reaching out for her—that was involuntary, she could not be faulted for that—when mother and daughter physically passed each other by, close enough to touch. The only thing that practically distinguished Hannah Roth from her fellow sophomores, history majors, or tenants of Radclyffe Hall were the weekly Sunday dinners she ate at the president's mansion—aka home. Sunday was the night of the week Naomi most enjoyed, and the only dinner she still cooked herself. And even if it meant eternal ratatouille and tofu she was loath to allow any other commitment to impose itself on this night of nights. And so, barring the seriously ill student or incensed parent, or any of the other fires that could, and did, flare up on any college campus, Sunday afternoons would find her in the comically oversized kitchen of her official residence, chopping, grating, sautéing, and generally stirring the pot, as NPR delivered the bad news, with musical interludes, from a shelf over the spice rack.

The president's mansion was formally named the Stone House, after that same solidly German (and not Jewish *at all*) president Charles Myer Stone, but it was indeed built of good, substantial post-glacial Massachusetts stone. When Naomi first toured the place in the immediate aftermath of her surprising nomination by the search committee, she had been overwhelmed by its scale, its baronial pretensions, and, quite frankly, by its physical chill, but the dwelling, like the job itself, was a cup she could not decline. Downstairs were meeting rooms, rooms for mingling with a cocktail in hand, and a central hallway ringed by the portraits of Webster presidents past. There was a thoroughly masculine den (dark paneling, massive leather chairs), and a long dining room with a stone floor and a timbered hearth straight out of *Tom Jones*, as well as the kitchen, which had been equipped with industrial-strength appliances for the college caterers. Upstairs: four bedrooms, another den (this one a bit more user-friendly, with a television), and at opposite ends of the corridors (as if Stone House were only another Webster dormitory), two identical bathrooms, unreconstructed in their Colonial Revival splendor, with dark wainscoting and wondrously original fixtures. It was mainly while using the bathrooms that Naomi found the wherewithal to think kindly of her predecessor, or at least of his taste.

That first Sunday in October, walking downtown in the morning to buy the *New York Times* at Jerry's and read it over eggs at the Webster Diner, Naomi had felt the first discernible chill of the autumn, and she'd decided to make something thick and hot, something Hannah could be counted upon to eat. She settled on a borscht recipe from one of the cookbooks she'd brought from their old house (now rented to a Latin professor and his family), and a last-of-the-summer-tomatoes and red onion salad. On her return she began the contemplative task of making a vegetable stock from the carrots and onions in the fridge, which was kept modestly stocked with staples by the catering staff—a distinct privilege of the presidential lifestyle. There was sacred music on the radio (there always seemed to be sacred music on NPR) and the act of cutting and peeling began to seem also, vaguely, sacred. Out of these roots of the earth she was making dinner for her daughter, the root of her own life, and all, or at any rate most, seemed basically well with the world. There were, on this particular day, at least in her

immediate presence, no crises. The new freshman class was set-
tling in nicely. The "Webster at 250" capital campaign had been
launched months earlier without even the anticipated alumni
grumbling, and she had begun to discuss her own pet project, a
reunion and celebration of Native American graduates of Webster, with Douglas Sidgwick, the college's unofficial guardian of
institutional memory. Even the little group of protesters who'd
begun, several weeks earlier, to gather at the Stump were bothering no one and carrying on a great tradition of nonviolent student
protest. Not that anyone had said anything to her about why this
particular group was taking its stand. But Naomi felt calm. And
she felt, well...*happy.*

Her daughter, Hannah Rosalind Roth, was coming to dinner.

She left the tomatoes on the sideboard, ready to slice. She put
the borscht on to simmer. She fed the cat, who, truth be told, did
not look as if he needed to eat ever again. And then she went upstairs to run a bath and finish reading the highly overpraised novel
of one of the college's best-known graduates (and donors), a man
she was due to host at a laudatory dinner a few weeks hence. She
climbed into the deep 1920s tub, and the rising heat made it ever
more difficult to follow the novel's story: a missing briefcase full of
something. A formula? A code? The paper-thin female character,
described with a leering male eye, insufferably perky. She hoped
that the author did not go around crediting the creative writing
teachers he'd studied with at Webster, not for this. A car chase, cin-
ematically described. The hero's name was Chance. Of course it
was. She set down the book and sank under the water and her hair,
long and almost uniformly gray now, rose to the surface. It was so
quiet under there. It was so warm, and still. It was—she would not
see this for a long time—the very last moment of "before."

When Hannah arrived, a bit after six, she found her mother in
the kitchen, taking a call from the dean of students, who had just
taken a call from the superintendent of buildings. The students

at the Stump were greeting the first autumnal chill not by abandoning their blankets and groundcloths and retreating to their warm dormitory beds, but by sinking tent poles into the dense Massachusetts soil of the Billings Lawn. This was . . . well, it was a couple of things. Certainly an eyesore. Somehow, surely, a fire hazard. And a crossing of the line, according to the dean, though Naomi wasn't sure she understood whose line, exactly, or where the line had been located. But none of that mattered, because the problem, whoever it might have belonged to before, now belonged to her. "I will," she said as she heard the door of the president's mansion squeak open and slap closed. "I'm going to. I'm going to do just that."

"Hi," she heard Hannah call from the foyer. "Mom?"

"Yes," said Naomi, hoping it served both interlocutors.

"Where are you?"

"Bob," she said, gripping the phone with one hand, waving at Hannah from the kitchen doorway with the other. "Yes, I can see that. Yes, I will call him."

She reached for her daughter, hating that she had to share this moment with the dean of students.

"Hiya," said Hannah, who at least seemed intrigued. She mimed: *Who is it?*

In response, Naomi made a face.

"Where is he now?" she asked the phone.

The superintendent, apparently, had gone home. Well, that was all right. And where was the harm, if some kids were camping out on the Billings Lawn? At least they were doing it with proper tents. Actually, she did know what the harm was, but she wanted her evening with Hannah more than she wanted to confront a gaggle of committed twenty-year-olds on the very first night of their serious entrenchment. Everyone would just have to chill till morning, and speaking of chilling, it would not be a disaster if the drop in temperature proved persuasive.

They would meet on Wednesday and talk it over—that is, if the students hadn't (literally) folded their tents and departed by then. "But, Bob, let's not overreact."

"I just don't want it to escalate," he said, with a clear emphasis on the *I*, as if *she* wanted exactly that.

"Can I have some wine?" said Hannah, and Naomi pointed at the fridge.

"See you then," Naomi said. "Good night."

She returned the phone to its cradle on the wall and shook her head in distaste. "Oy."

"Oy." Hannah laughed. "Should I guess?"

"It would be unseemly," Naomi said, taking two glasses from the cupboard above the sink, "for you, an undergraduate student of this college, to guess which of your august deans, scholars deserving your respect and esteem, is behaving like a whiny toddler, so no you should not."

"Bob Stacek," Hannah said simply. "Obvi."

Naomi sighed. "Well, with a rare and unique name like Bob. *Obvi*. But I'm invoking the Sunday Night Rule now."

Hannah looked disappointed, but the Sunday Night Rule had kept them sane, and the Sunday Night Rule went both ways: Pot-smoking friends, classmates who did not seem capable of producing their perfect test scores or eloquently argued papers, these were not to attract the attention of the president's office, while faculty and administrators who, in the opinion of the president, behaved poorly or might not entirely deserve their cushy tenured berths, these were not to be paraded before the tenants of Radclyffe Hall.

"Are those new earrings?" Naomi said. But what she actually meant was: *Are those new holes in your ears?* Because she suddenly could not remember whether her daughter had been thus punctured four times on the left (including into the wince-to-think-about cartilage) and five times on the right, or vice versa.

"Yes. Willow and I did a trade. I loved these. I mean, I coveted these. I know it's bad."

"But human," said Naomi, touching it. It was green and round and cold. Jade? Fake jade? "Human to covet. What did you trade for it?"

"Nothing important. Silver thingy. Like a teardrop."

"The Elsa Peretti?" Naomi asked with a sinking feeling.

"I don't know. Maybe. I only had one. I lost the other one somewhere."

"Okay," Naomi said, trying to sound cheery. The Elsa Peretti earrings had been a gift from Francine Rigor when Hannah turned thirteen, the exhaustively negotiated age at which she would be permitted to pierce her ears. Francine, unlike Naomi herself, had pierced ears and a sizable collection of items to put in them: silver and gold, pearls and gems. She was partial to Elsa Peretti. The silver earrings had doubtless been expensive, not to mention sentimental. Well, they ought to have been sentimental.

"They're very pretty," said Naomi, who knew when a battle was worth picking.

"Yes, more my style," Hannah said, fingering the little green stone. She handed her mother a glass of wine. Red. Left over from a trustee dinner two nights earlier. "I read somewhere you're supposed to drink an inch of this every day. Then you don't die young."

"An inch," Naomi said, considering. "And it protects you from plane crashes and having a piano fall on your head?"

Hannah pulled back her chair from the long table. "Well, it must," she said dryly. "Because I read it in the science section of the *New York Times*. And they never lie."

Naomi went to the stove. She had left the borscht simmering for most of the afternoon, not because the recipe had said to do so but because she liked the idea of it there, making the sterile kitchen feel more like a kitchen was supposed to feel. Now it occurred to her that she had sacrificed the actual taste of the actual soup for some idea of soup, handmade by mother for child, and she delayed tasting it until she had sliced the tomatoes and the red onions, poured a bit of olive oil over the fanned-out slices.

"Smells good," Hannah said, rolling the stem of her wineglass between her palms. "I didn't know you like beets."

"Every Ashkenazi Jew loves beets. We crossed the steppes, powered by beets." Naomi dipped the ladle down into the stainless steel pot. The dark magenta solids fell obligingly in. And Hannah was right. It smelled divine.

"I thought that was potatoes," her daughter said.

"Cucumbers. Potatoes. Beets. My father loved beets," she remembered out loud.

"Oh yeah?" Hannah sat up straight. She was interested in anything to do with her grandparents. She hadn't been while they were alive, but now she viewed them as withheld pieces of the puzzle, kept back to make things tougher to solve. "So, like, what did he like to eat? Borscht? Is this a family recipe?"

Naomi couldn't stop herself from laughing. There had never been anything like a "family recipe" in her memory. Her mother had loathed cooking; she had been a stranger in the strange land of her own kitchen, struggling to extract basic sustenance from its alien food-making apparatus—stovetop and oven. As soon as the brave new world of frozen and "instant" meals materialized in her local D'Agostino's she resigned any feelings of guilt over the matter, and their mealtimes became a cycle of aluminum trays with peel-back covers, punctuated by dinners out (Naomi's parents were partial to two diners in their Upper West Side neighborhood) and, naturally, it being Manhattan, takeout and delivery. When Naomi remembered that her father loved beets she was only remembering the descriptions on restaurant menus: sliced beets, beet salad, and, yes, borscht.

"This is a Silver Palate recipe. But yes, he did like borscht, I remember. Do you want a little sour cream on yours?"

Hannah inhaled the bowl Naomi passed her, and then nodded.

"Where'd you find those tomatoes? It's late for good tomatoes."

From the Webster Farm Co-Op, Naomi told her. "We had some great stuff for the trustees' dinner the other night, and Will Rennet was here. It's nice to be able to feed him the vegetables he endowed."

"That is an abuse of privilege," said Hannah. "The vegetables are supposed to be for everyone. Not just the trustees."

"They're not just for the trustees," said Naomi, sitting opposite her daughter and taking a very deliberate bite of a yellow and red tomato. "The farm grows food for the community. The trustees are a part of the community. Ergo, Will Rennet gets a nice tomato when he comes to supper."

"A tomato he personally endowed."

"Sure," she conceded. "But I believe I have made my point."

Hannah drummed her fingers on the tabletop, an old habit that, in her case, did not seem to signal boredom or impatience. Her fingers were long and bony, ending in narrow fingertips with short and never polished nails. Much of her, indeed, was long and bony, so unlike Naomi herself. Naomi had once pretended, at least inwardly, that she had made Hannah all alone, that there was no other half of her daughter's composition meriting acknowledgment, but the conceit had not been maintainable after Hannah reached the age of four. At four her child had suddenly elongated into a shape that neither Naomi nor any woman related to her had ever assumed; even then it was clear that she would be tall and straight, her only curves concave. Hannah's hair grew lighter with time, and bones emerged at the collar, hip, wrist. Naomi, who had produced, in her lifetime, yards of waves of Ashkenazi tresses, fanning behind her in a nimbus of ethnic glory, who was broad of torso, thick with muscle, and gifted with the general physical density of a shtetl woman who'd had to pick her own potatoes (and beets, and cucumbers), looked undeniably like her mother, Rachelle. Rachelle had looked like her own mother, Judith. There was only one photograph of Judith's mother, Gerda (born in Kiev in the last years of the nineteenth century; died at Babi Yar at the official end of civilization), but she had looked very much like Judith, who had looked like Rachelle, who had looked like Naomi. Hannah looked like none of them. Hannah was, Naomi thought, watching her daughter lift the soup spoon to her lips, the first of her line ever to have produced a visible collarbone.

They talked about Radclyffe Hall and the mood therein, which was peaceful (thank goodness), the only issues currently up for debate having to do with matters menstrual. ("Whether to menstruate?" Naomi suggested. No. Whether to allow disposable sanitary products. It was not a subject Naomi especially wanted to consider, really, at least over such a deeply crimson bowl of soup.) One girl was moving out—it wasn't conducive, she had explained, for her music, which had come as a surprising statement to the others, given that not one of them had ever heard a note—even a recorded note—emerge from her third-floor chamber. But: whatever. There was a waiting list to get into Radclyffe Hall. There was always a list. And at least two of the current residents had friends hoping for the vacancy.

"Still like your room?"

Hannah liked her room fine, having hauled over the quilts she had slept beneath since childhood (the quilts had been made by a New Hampshire sewing collective that Naomi had established in her long-ago VISTA days), and the oversized and scarily close-up portraits she had made of Naomi during her edgy photography phase in eleventh grade, and the flute she no longer played (not—in truth—a great loss to the world of flutes and flautists). She liked the window seat that overlooked what had once been the back garden (it was now a thoroughly ignored brick patio, complete with unused grill). She liked the food, which was reliably vegetarian if not always exactly tasty. And Radclyffe Hall, which really did feel like a home with its kitchen and wood-burning hearth, was still close enough to the Billings Lawn and hence the center of campus that she could roll out of bed a few minutes before the bell in its classic tower chimed the start of the class period, and still stroll in on time. The house could, in years when the inhabitants were especially in sync, offer a highly creative communal environment (Naomi was thinking of the annual one-act play competition, open to dormitories, fraternities, sororities, and college-owned living co-operatives, which Radclyffe Hall had dominated over the past few years) and tended to rank high on surveys of student housing satisfaction. She hadn't been surprised when Hannah, who like her infamous predecessor, Neil Jones-Givens, scored a highly advantageous lottery number, had similarly selected a cozy bedroom under the eaves in Radclyffe Hall.

In fact, Naomi happened to know that her daughter lived in the very chamber once briefly occupied by Neil Jones-Givens, though Neil had never actually returned to it after decamping to Health Services in the early days of the crisis. His parents had arrived to pack up the little room in Radclyffe Hall, and everything in it, including Neil himself, went back to the Midwest. Naomi, for her own part, had hoped it would not end there, and it didn't; when fall rolled around again, Neil returned, looking broader and more muscled, infinitely more hirsute. He had an apartment off campus and a decidedly fierce attitude about what he wanted from his remaining time at Webster, which included a senior independent study in queer studies (Webster's first, fittingly), and a summa cum laude. The last Naomi had heard, Neil Jones-Givens was a law student at the University of Illinois.

Hannah had never said anything to her mother about the Radclyffe Hall affair, and probably had no idea that she was sleeping in the same bed, under the same sloping ceiling, as that now-forgotten campus martyr, Neil Jones-Givens. But that was less surprising than it sounded. If the events that had so tortured Radclyffe Hall and the college in general (and Naomi's life in particular) were taking place today, while Hannah herself was a Webster undergraduate, the subject would be dominating their Sunday dinners and, Naomi knew, the lion's share of her daughter's intellectual bandwidth, but the autumn Radclyffe Hall exploded her daughter had been ten years old and oblivious to any part of Webster except, perhaps, its swimming pool, art gallery, or the annual Persephone Festival (which celebrated the arrival of post–mud season spring with bands and outdoor parties), and possibly Naomi's own little office in Crump-Eustis Hall, where Hannah sometimes spent days coloring or reading if there was no school. Of course the controversy had come up once or twice. How could it not? Not even the most narcissistically distracted child can fail to miss a perpetually ringing kitchen phone, with ABC or *People* magazine or the booker for Greta Van Susteren or someone equally barky and terse on the other end of the line, or the town car forever in the driveway, waiting to ferry Mom to a morning interview at the affiliate studios in Springfield or Boston.

But that was all of ten years ago. That was the misty past. And within the magical prism that was time on a college campus, only the great and wondrous *now* ever seemed real.

Life at Webster, for the students at least, existed in this eternal present, as the college endlessly regenerated itself with eighteen-year-olds and regularly discharged its own collective memory into the ether. And so, for those young people engrossed in their own college adventures, it followed thus: There was no longer a Neil Jones-Givens at Webster, and therefore there might never have been one at all, unless, of course, you cared enough to actually go looking for him in the archives, where he might certainly be, alongside every other sepia-toned rugby player and Latin scholar who'd ever smashed a pipe against the Stump. Even the most historically minded of Websterites, those with a vague or even informed idea that the college had preexisted them by a couple of centuries, still experienced each hallway and walkway, each portrait of a past Webster president, even the old Stump itself, as belonging not to some former Webster student, not to the historic continuum of Webster students, but to themselves, alone, and to their own exclusive experience of *right this minute*.

Neil Jones-Givens and his difficulties, Radclyffe Hall's struggle (For...what? Sovereignty? Identity?)—they felt as distant from the glorious now as the town's colonial skirmishes of two centuries earlier, when the Billings Lawn itself was only an indistinguishable patch of woodland around a settler's log house, and the Stump was...well, Naomi supposed, only another tree in the forest of New England elms. Such paroxysms in the life of the institution! Such obsessions for the students and the faculty and for Naomi herself as their spokesperson and figurehead! Such critical bullet points in the great Webster story. And then? And then the entire cast of undergraduate characters had marched across a platform, flipped a bit of tassel from one corner of a funny hat to the other, and scattered off from the little Massachusetts town and out into the wide, wide world.

After which: poof! The whole damn thing evaporated. The lawns were reseeded. The dormitory boilers serviced. The tenure decisions made. And another crowd of stressed-out high school juniors trudged across the Billings Lawn, moms and dads and bored younger siblings in tow, trying to keep up with a backward-walking undergraduate.

Bright college days, indeed, thought Naomi, who could barely remember her own through its haze of pot and constant sex with Daniel, her future husband.

"How're classes, honey?" she asked now.

"Well," Hannah said archly, "if you mean, how am I doing. Like, grade-wise? Fine. I'm doing just fine. But if you want to know are my classes scintillating, am I having that awesome educational experience we hear so much about, I have to be honest."

"Oh, be honest." Naomi had to fight the urge to roll her eyes.

"Like, no. I mean, I get out of bed, I read the *Times*, I get up to speed with every fucked-up thing that's happening in the world, and then I trot off to my Shakespeare and His World seminar, to talk about the curriculum at young Will's school in Stratford, and there's a disconnect, you know?"

Naomi set down her spoon. "No. I don't know."

They were facing each other across the table. It was a narrow table at that.

"Just…why do I care about this again? Why do I care what class Shakespeare had on Wednesdays when there's rampant shit all over the planet?"

Naomi shrugged. "Well, you must care a little bit. You signed up for the class."

"I needed a European history seminar cross-listed with English, that met in the afternoons."

"Ah."

"Because I'm still not sure if I'm declaring English or history, and I had to make room this semester for a science distribution, because, as we all know, a broad understanding of arts, humanities, and science is the foundation of a liberal arts education, and the intention of Webster College is to graduate young scholars who are connected to knowledge across the spectrum of disciplines, the better to enable them to thrive in and positively impact this very complex and connected world of ours. Because isn't that exactly why I'm here?"

Naomi smiled. She knew better than to take this particular bait.

That her daughter had landed, of all the colleges in all the towns in all the world, right here at Webster had of course been an issue widely discussed by many people, whether it was any of their business or not, but it had never been a topic between by the president and her daughter, nor between Naomi and Francine Rigor, Webster's dean of admissions and Naomi's closest friend. For the two women, who usually walked together in the wooded hills just west of the campus at least once a week, the topic had been radioactive in its neglect, and from the early decision deadline to the notification day one month later, and even afterward as Hannah attended the Welcome Webster weekend for admitted applicants and Naomi wrote a check to the bursar, and mother and daughter hoisted a massive duffel across campus to the freshman dorms down near the lake—the subject of Hannah Roth's Webster application and college choice had remained utterly lockboxed between all involved. Not only was it never discussed, but the fact of its having never been discussed was similarly never discussed.

Even now, even at moments when they were technically speaking of Webster, and Hannah's experience as a student thereof, or Naomi's experience as an administrator thereof, there was a kind of no-fly zone in the middle of the subject, which neither of them had ever breached, despite provocations like the one her daughter had just offered, and this was the actual fact that, out of the thousands of American colleges and universities Hannah Roth might have applied to, the vast majority of which would have been delighted to admit her (Hannah had been her class valedictorian and, over three attempts, had clawed her way up to a 2250 on the SAT), she had selected exactly one: the one on her literal doorstep, the one her mother was president of. The process by which she had made this decision had not been shared with Naomi, who in truth had been dreading the whole kid-applying-to-college ordeal for years. Not a word. Not when

Hannah was in fifth grade and they had moved into the Stone House and her daughter, for the first time, was seeing Webster students every day, their lives in her face (for better or worse), and another mother might have said something innocuous like "Maybe *you'd* like to go to Webster one day." Not when Hannah was in tenth, and the first tendrils of college-related anxiety began to percolate through her high school friends, a few of whom were more than happy to tell Naomi that *they* would love to go to Webster one day...if only they could get in. Not in eleventh, as the general stress began to intensify, frog-in-boiling-water style, and most reasonable parents would at least have broached the subject, and not in twelfth, when each of her daughter's classmates seemed to be in full possession of everyone else's SAT scores and class ranking. Between them, Naomi and Hannah had avoided any conversation about this whole thing, by silent, enthusiastic, and mutual agreement.

Except for once—one time, during their only joint meeting with the college counselor at Webster Regional. This was a very stressed-out guy doing his best to serve nearly two hundred students (a quarter of whom, to be fair, weren't pursuing college, and half of whom, also to be fair, were going straight into the UMass system, and perfectly happy to be doing so).

"She's a legacy at Cornell," Naomi had said in the middle of their session.

He'd been talking about the legacy thing, the counselor had, and Naomi, now that she was thinking about it, suddenly remembered that she herself had actually gone to Cornell, which was, the last time she'd checked, an Ivy League school. She had even graduated from Cornell, once certain matters of disagreement with the institution (mainly involving whether ROTC had the right to operate on campus, and whether undergraduates had the right to occupy administrative offices) were expunged from her official record. So wasn't Hannah in line for a leg up there? And didn't she deserve it? (Here, Naomi conveniently spaced on the fact that she had tithed not a single penny to her alma mater.) It was the whiplash in perspective, she would later think, this through-the-looking-glass disorientation, so unsettling, so dangerous, that had come to her as she listened to the counselor. But then she had always thought of Hannah as, well, as *Hannah*. And Hannah was bright and tough and generally wonderful, the kind of person who'd go out there and make things better, or at least less bad. And yet, until that very moment, Naomi had never once thought about how Hannah would likely appear to a college admissions officer reading her application (yes, even in spite of the fact that her closest friend was—wait for it!—the dean of admissions at a highly competitive college!). Hannah Rosalind Roth—another smart, decent, busy, and likable girl from an exurban school in a state crammed with brilliant college applicants. But not a STEM female, not a recruited athlete, not a legacy, not first in her family to attend college. Not a lot of things, when you broke it down according to the maddening algorithm of competitive college admissions in America, circa 2014. And suddenly, there in that cluttered and claustrophobic office, the desperate situation had broken through at last.

And so Naomi said it: "She's a legacy at Cornell. What about applying to Cornell?"

"What about no way?" Hannah had said.

And that, at least, took care of Cornell, but it didn't quite explain the fact that Hannah, when all was said and done, chose Webster and only Webster.

Naomi had been bracing herself, of course. She had said nothing about keeping her daughter close, and saw every reason to assume that Hannah, having spent nearly every day of her life in New England, might wish to sample another setting (with another *climate*) for four years, or indeed the rest of her life. When the topic moved into range, she confined herself to cheery, supportive questions, unburdened (she hoped) by innuendo. Had Hannah considered the Midwest? So many great colleges out there. Should they plan a trip down south to look at a few places? Any interest in a city school? New York or Chicago, even Boston? (So close, Boston. Naomi regretted even suggesting it. Would Hannah think her mother was afraid to let her go?)

But Hannah only nodded and said she was handling it, she was on top of it, and then she went back to her Common App essay about how even a kid growing up in a rural Massachusetts town has a responsibility to be aware of global issues. She went in for regular meetings with the college advisor. She did not want to visit the Midwest. She did not want to visit the South. She didn't even want to tramp through lovely Harvard Yard alongside the freaked-out debaters and math prodigies and their frantic parents. Whatever she did want, she kept it to herself.

Webster Regional's college counselor was actually pretty capable, according to Francine, who had taken any number of those students over the years—faculty kids and not a few unaffiliated locals. (*Academic noblesse oblige*, Francine had explained. *It's important to look after our own backyard.*) Naomi, after her little flare of inspiration had been shot down, decided that what she really wanted to do was stay out of the whole thing and let the guy in the claustrophobic office handle it. And when, in due course, Hannah dispatched her one and only college application, Francine had done her the courtesy of never alluding to it, which made for a generally more intense atmosphere when they went for their walks, which they regularly did, that fall as every fall—swifter pace, steeper incline, more panting, less talking. In any case the whole thing was over in a couple of weeks; when Hannah clomped down the wide oak stairs one evening that December and announced that she'd been accepted early to Webster, her mother let out a long breath and thought, *Well, that wasn't so hard.*

Naomi never even told Francine thanks. She couldn't do it. It wouldn't be right.

Now she got up and went to the bread box on the counter. She had just remembered that there were a couple of baguettes there, also left over from the trustee dinner. They felt a bit stiff, but she took one anyway and ripped off the end.

"Want some?"

"No. Thanks."

"You know, Hannah, it's not just a question of what class Shakespeare took on Wednesdays. It's about how his early education gave him the foundation for what he wrote later. Little village school, right? Produced the world's greatest dramatist. That's something you can care about."

"Well, I don't accept that he's the world's greatest dramatist. And neither should you. I'm not saying he isn't, just that it's irresponsible to make a statement like that before you've acknowledged and studied the work of every single dramatist, from every culture, throughout history. But we don't bother to do that, not in my class, not in the world. Isn't this supposed to be about broadening the perspective? Citizens of the planet and all that shit?"

Naomi dropped a few pieces of stale bread onto her cooling soup and drowned them with the back of her spoon. It was a heavy spoon and bore the college crest: the leaning tree that would become the Webster Stump. She wasn't sure she felt up to this tonight.

"Just to be clear, are we actually arguing about Shakespeare's education? Or are you picking a more general fight with me?"

Hannah, for the briefest moment, looked as if she was trying not to smile. But then she located some inner ferocity. "It's a serious issue, though."

Naomi was unmoved. "Every issue's serious to somebody."

"Oh, really? And this is why you've bothered to go out and talk to the students at the Stump? You want to see what's on their minds?"

Naomi sat back in her chair. She had lost the trail of this conversation somewhere, obviously. But where? What were they talking about again?

"You mean the protest group? I don't have a problem with them. I think it's great when young people gather peacefully. I'm for it."

"You're for it," Hannah said. When she got frustrated her whole face flushed. It had always been that way. It was that way now. "That'll be a big relief to them."

"What would you like me to do? Give them each a medal?"

"Nothing so extreme," Hannah said. She had sat back in her chair, leaving more than half of her borscht to cool in its bowl. "Go listen to them. Hear what's on their minds. There's a grievance."

"Really," she said dryly. "I had no idea."

"It's not a little thing. It might be, to the *administration*," she said, pronouncing the word with extravagant archness. "But, you know, if we can't respond to injustice on our own campus, how are we supposed to address global issues?"

By doing a bit more than squatting on college property, Naomi thought.

"What is the grievance? Nobody's thought to tell me."

"Nobody should have to tell you," Hannah said, with perfect snark. "And nobody should have to issue you a formal invitation, either. You're supposedly our activist president. You give that speech to the freshmen every fall about the big sit-in at the administration building when you were in college. Should the protesters occupy your office?"

"Jesus, no," Naomi said, with whatever humor she could muster, though it was obvious that Hannah saw nothing funny about this...this...small and localized and not, truly, very significant gathering. A coming together of young, disgruntled people, buoyed by the very facts of their being young and their being disgruntled, did it matter so much about, you know, the *issue*? Animal, vegetable, mineral...it could be anything. From Webster's recycling program (not comprehensive enough!) to the bequest some class of '54 Texan had made to the football team, or something a political science prof had said, offhand, in a lecture, or the fact that the pad thai in the dining hall was inauthentic and hence culturally insensitive. It could be the trace elements of nuclear energy or mining or De Beers in the college portfolio (the exhaustively investigated and cleansed college portfolio), the fact that men outnumbered women on the faculty (still, but only just!), that wealthy students of all ethnic and cultural backgrounds were the still the norm in every admitted class (frankly unavoidable), or that dogs were not allowed in the classrooms or *Mein Kampf* was on the curriculum of at least three history courses or that *Birth of a Nation* was being taught in a film studies class on the rise of the art form, or that economics planned to offer a senior seminar on Ayn Rand. Or perhaps it was the old, old story of Josiah Webster himself, whose charitable educational mission of 1762, which culminated in the founding of Webster College, now looked a whole lot like plain old Native culture–suppressing, murderously insensitive, ethnically monomaniacal colonialism. Really, the possibilities were so numerous; who, when you got right down to it, even had the time?

The fact was that until Dean Stacek's phone call, less than an hour earlier, Naomi had barely thought about the group, except with a nostalgic, vaguely maternal kind of approval. They were there whenever she'd crossed the Billings Lawn, and had been since a couple weeks into the semester, reclining in the sweet afternoon sun, still warm into the first few days of October, at least until the air had taken on its current chill. They leaned against the Stump or against one another, textbooks and laptops unfurled, a few of the women knitting. (Knitting! When had that happened?) The scene they made was not an unusual one. Webster students were protesters. Since the 1970s students had selfselected for Webster—and not Williams, and not Amherst, and not Hamilton or Colgate or, increasingly, the Ivy League— because they viewed their own intelligence and fire as already in service to some more general human good. Pro-choice. Divestment in South Africa (later, divestment in Dow, Exxon, BP, anything related to oil). ACT-UP. Pro-choice (again). The day of fasting for solidarity with Darfur. Factory-farmed proteins out of the college dining facilities. Amnesty for the undocumented. Pro-choice (again, again, again).

All good reasons to gather in protest, and for the record, most of the local requests had been responded to and honored by the administration, because if Webster wasn't producing young people who cared to and believed they could change the world, what was it for? Naomi loved that kids were still with it enough to notice all was not well in the universe, and that mattered, somehow, even if it didn't seem to affect them personally, what with their senior projects and LSATs, and the recruiters who still came—yes, even to Webster—from Procter & Gamble and Citibank. This fierce little college, which had once declined membership in the then-forming Ivy League (that had been a question of funding for the athletics program, if truth were told), which waited till the last possible moment to accept women (but then went to male-female parity in three short years), which abandoned its commitment to Native American education within a few decades of the school's formation (only to come roaring back two hundred years later with one of the best Native American studies programs in the country), turned out captivating, committed, brilliant, and fired-up young citizens. And Naomi loved them, if not exactly like a mother (she was the mother of only one of them, she cautioned herself), then in loco parentis, which was, it could be argued, one possible interpretation of her job.

It made her feel a little guilty, sometimes, especially on Sundays, when she got to see Hannah like this, but also on other days, ordinary days, when she simply happened to cross paths with her daughter, on the Quad or one of Webster's few streets. Once, purely by chance, the two of them had met at a late-night film department screening—the only two people on campus to turn out for *Sunday Bloody Sunday*—and they'd had the theater to themselves and shared a big bag of cheese popcorn. It meant that she was one of the very few Webster moms who could see firsthand that their child appeared happy, seemed to be eating enough, was hanging out with kids who gave every impression of being nice. All of those other students had left home. They had packed up their clothes and loaded their family cars. They had flown across the country and taken a Peter Pan bus from Logan or the Hartford-Springfield airport. They had set off on their own, or sent their traumatized parents away with a hug or a wave, and then they had either kept in touch with the place they'd come from and the people they'd come from or they hadn't. But Naomi...she got to feel the presence of her daughter at Webster College. The Sunday dinners, the chance hugs in front of the Webster Inn, even the glimpses when they didn't technically interact. She knew how fortunate she was. She knew not to abuse her privilege. She didn't ask for more than was offered. And if, somewhere in that no-fly zone of conversation, there was an actual reason Hannah had chosen Webster, and if Naomi didn't know what that reason was, so what? Because Hannah was still here. She was a college student, in a dorm, on her own, living her life and doing her thing, of course, of course. But she was still here, and their separation hadn't happened, not really. And because it hadn't happened, Naomi never had to admit to herself how much she'd dreaded it.

Hannah declined coffee. She had an assignment for her Shakespeare class, and wanted a few things from her room upstairs. "You know it's cold in here, right?" she asked as Naomi followed her out into the foyer.

"Yes. At least, I know it empirically because I get told that a lot. But I don't feel cold. Maybe I'm like that Kathleen Turner character in *Body Heat*, whose temperature runs a bit high."

"Maybe you're a menopausal woman," Hannah responded. "Ever think of that?"

"No," Naomi said, truthfully enough. She had powered through menopause a decade earlier, symptom-free, and had been so distracted by the other, outward changes in her life that she'd noted this one—this Change with a capital C—only in retrospect. Not even a whiff of trauma! "What do you need?" She turned on the light and her daughter walked past her into the oversized bedroom that had been hers for seven years. "There isn't much left here."

Their move into the president's residence had coincided with a moment of some acceleration of character on Hannah's part. Certain childish things had been put away that summer, and certain people (two girlfriends, who had never been especially nice to her) abruptly left behind. Hannah, in the preparations for their move, had chosen to pack and store many of her belongings in the attic of their home, soon to be rented, furnished, to the Latin professor and his family. To her new and much bigger room in the Stone House she had brought a largely new wardrobe, two Hudson River school reproductions, a rather disturbing Henry Darger poster from their visit to the American Folk Art Museum in New York, and four boxes of books. Some of that was still there, but most of her belongings had moved on with her to the little room at Radclyffe Hall.

"I need my down jacket. And my sleeping bag."

Naomi looked at her. Hannah had gone to the closet and was reaching up, grabbing at the shiny blue bag, its drawstring knotted.

"Why do you need a sleeping bag?" Naomi asked, but as soon as she said it she realized that she already knew.

"I'm going to start sleeping out with the others," Hannah said mildly. "You can't possibly be surprised."

Naomi said nothing. Her daughter was now feeling around on the shelf. "Didn't we have another one? I need one for Omar. He doesn't have anything."

"Oh. Well, there's mine." They'd had matching blue sleeping bags, supposedly capable of keeping you warm and toasty down to some Jack London–esque temperature. But they'd only used them a couple of times. The Presidentials in Maine one summer. The back porch of a friend's summer house in Pennsylvania, where they'd had been, of course, up all night, unbearably hot. Not for years, though. "I can have it cleaned," she said.

"That's okay. He'll be grateful to have it."

"Who will?" Naomi said. She had lost the thread somewhere.

"Omar. Jesus," Hannah said, with an expression of such spectacular superiority that Naomi, on principle, declined to react. "You really have not been paying attention, have you?"

No, she really had not been paying attention, and after Hannah left she did the strangest thing. Without thinking about it, without realizing what she was doing, not really, she closed the door behind her clever and lovely and breathtakingly decent daughter and went right back up the stairs to the room that was not—not really—the room Hannah had grown up in, pulled back the covers of the seldom-used bed, climbed in, shoes and all, and went sadly and instantly to sleep.

CHAPTER THREE

INTO THE WOODS

Francine and her husband, Sumner, lived in a heavily forested valley eight miles north of Webster, in a development of larger homes, each out of sight of the others, called The Woods. The first time Naomi had driven out there, years before, she had become so lost that she'd had to drive all the way into West Webster just to find a public phone to call for directions, and even later, the GPS unit stuck to the inside of her windshield, its little screen would stubbornly refuse to admit that there was anything at all branching off the main road and penetrating the trees, let alone an exclusive settlement known as The Woods. If she was determined to go up there, in other words, she'd be on her own.

Now, of course, she knew every inch of the journey, but after years of making her way here—by car, by bike, once, during a 2004 blizzard, on cross-country skis (which had ruined cross-country skiing for her, hopefully forever)—she didn't need it. On a wet November Saturday she drove out over familiar roads with an apple pie from one of the roadside stands and a bottle of Merlot, listening to *A Prairie Home Companion* along the way. Garrison Keillor's voice had a narcotic vocal element that always made her feel sleepy, each word a nepenthe puff, each sentence a lullaby mantra of its own. Speaking for herself, Naomi had long had a thing for Keillor, and there had been Saturday nights during the years in Goddard—after her husband had decamped for a more reassuringly counterculture place to live and a more reassuringly counterculture woman to live with—when the only thing that got her through a weekend was the news from Lake Wobegon. The notion that there were silent listeners everywhere in the country, leaning toward their radios in homes (and cars) from sea to shining sea, and they were connected to one another...something about that had sustained her. It was a time she thought of now as the very lowest point in her life, not even because of the lousy marriage and the baffling reality of her continued tenure in such a strange place, or even her myopic stubbornness in remaining so many years past the time she ought to have left, but because things had not yet fallen into place for her intellectually, and she hadn't yet admitted to herself that she was not a humble volunteer and aid worker, giving selflessly to the needy of Goddard, New Hampshire, with no hunger for personal advancement, but actually an entrepreneur with skills and that shameful character flaw: personal ambition. Before academia, students, the company of other feminist scholars. Before publication and a job title that she still could not quite believe. Before Hannah.

Garrison Keillor was just completing a long and evocative description of an untended parking lot when Naomi swung into the Rigors' drive, a curving little lane marked by a stone column with the 62 affixed to it in large brass numbers. The style of the marker was identical to every other stone column in the development, but inside the house itself there was only one aesthetic opinion that registered, and it was not Francine's. Once, on a long-ago walk, Naomi had asked her friend about this, and

Francine had offered the opinion that an ideal marital household included one partner who cared passionately about making things beautiful and another partner who did not care at all. Naomi couldn't really argue with that. Francine might have come home to a hovel or a mansion, and as long as the kitchen functioned and the bathrooms were scrupulously clean, she spared not a synapse's worth of thought for the way her home looked or how, for that matter, it was perceived by others. More likely than not, she would not have been able to tell you what color the walls were painted in the various rooms of her house or what pictures were hanging on them. She'd given Sumner carte blanche with the furniture, asking only that the bed be extra long (for her extra-long body) and the couch be upholstered in a dark color, because their dog at the time was also a dark color, and that seemed only practical.

Sumner, in almost comical contrast, was a guy who obsessed over the details. He tried four shades of green in the foyer (they all looked the same to Naomi) before picking the one he vastly preferred. He went to Brimfield at least twice a year, usually coming away with nothing, because there was nothing—in field after field stretching along Route 20, each of them crammed with dealers—that he liked enough to bring to his home. Curtains were made only after a trip to Boston for the fabric, and custom sewn by a woman whose name he'd gotten from the director of Old Sturbridge Village. He had selected the most baronial of the available house styles from the plans for The Woods, and then filled the large new rooms with objects supporting that illusion. The chandelier you circled when you went upstairs was from Waterford. The dining room was long, with a long table and a long sideboard. The masculine den was painted dark red and had a wall of hunting prints.

The library, adjacent to the living room, was, at least, a real library, with real books, and Naomi did not doubt that every one of the volumes on the dark and glossy wooden shelves had been read by Sumner, possibly more than once. Sumner adored history, and he had taught it at a Connecticut boarding school with a reputation for bad behavior. (He and Francine had met eighteen years earlier, when she had come through as a Vassar admissions officer.) But he wasn't teaching history anymore. For the past sixteen years he had been the headmaster of a private K through 8 school in Southborough called Hawthorne Academy. Naomi, who had visited the school only once, to speak at the annual Founder's Day celebration, had had to remind herself that the large campus and stunning facilities were in use by students aged thirteen and under. Hawthorne Academy, founded in 1922, appeared to have an endowment that many prep schools would envy, and not a few colleges to boot. And Sumner loved it. He loved the somber responsibility of serving as a school head and the perpetual high spirits of young schoolchildren. He even appeared to love the parents, and Naomi supposed it was possible that even wealthy and ambitious mothers and fathers might not have ventured too far down the rabbit hole of Ivy League madness by eighth grade, and were still, more or less, a pleasure to be around.

She descended the steeply pitched drive to the house and turned her car around before parking next to Francine's Subaru. There was an unfamiliar car there already, a red BMW, and Naomi tried to remember if Francine had mentioned another guest, but her email, a few days earlier, had merely said "Come Saturday for dinner? 7 pm?" She reached in for the Merlot and entered the house through the open garage, calling "Hi!" from the mudroom.

"Hello!" Sumner called back. He was in the kitchen, basting something that smelled truly spectacular on the stovetop.

"Oh my God," Naomi said. She kissed him on the cheek and set down the Merlot on the countertop. "What is that?"

"That," said Sumner, "is a saddle of venison. And no, I did not shoot it myself. Not that I wouldn't have loved to shoot the ones who decimated my roses this summer." He settled the copper pan back onto the oven shelf and closed the door. "A proper hello!" he said, giving Naomi a squeeze. He picked up the bottle. "Oh, this looks fantastic." .

"The woman at Webster Wines recommended it. You know I don't know anything about wine. I didn't know we were eating Bambi, though."

"This will pair beautifully with Bambi."

"And...we'll agree never to mention Bambi to Hannah, okay?"

"We will never mention it to Hannah." He laughed. "I value my life too much."

He reset the timer on the stove. Sumner was practiced at a certain kind of social interplay, the down-to-earth schoolteacher mingling with the parents of his students in a paneled room, beneath the portraits of men in academic robes. He shared with these men and women an origin story of New England winters and old schools, a common root of observed traditions and somber expectations. They knew one another, accordingly, when they met, and fell into the old rituals and means of communication, and the sight of this had always riveted her, but then again, she too had always been able to recognize a member of her tribe. (Years before, she had come upon a Jewish woman, clearly a misplaced New Yorker, standing in mute and horrified judgment of the lettuce selections in her New Hampshire supermarket, and all but embraced her on the spot.) And besides, he was a good egg. Or a good enough egg. And besides, it didn't really matter what kind of egg he was, because he was Francine's egg, and Francine was her friend.

"Come along," said Sumner, taking the wine. Naomi walked behind him into the living room, eyes on the back of his yellow cashmere sweater. He was a tall man, taller by an inch or two than his wife, which could only have appealed to her enormously. He had, moreover, a wondrous head of white hair (prematurely white hair, Francine had once informed her: white since the age of twenty-five) that his face had only gradually, and quite gracefully, caught up with. Sumner, at the time of Francine's fateful Vassar visit to his boarding school, was the divorced father of two college-aged sons. They had no children together.

"Frannie," he said, "Naomi's bought us a lovely Sonoma Merlot."

"Hi!" Francine popped to her feet. She was a woman who had never accepted and would never accept the reality of her substantial height, whose every decision of posture (slouched) and clothing (disappear-into-the-background colors, usually black) and hairstyle (severely parted in the center, bluntly cropped at the chin) seemed motivated by the wish to minimize. Sometimes Naomi watched Francine move among other people, ducking and bobbing, trying to get down to their level. So much wasted effort. It made no difference at all.

"Welcome home," said Naomi, because her friend was only just back from a two-week admissions swing along the West Coast, the Southwest, and Texas. She was eyeing the person on the opposite couch. Unknown person, classification: male of a certain age. Her heart sank.

"Naomi, this is William Grosvenor."

He reached out with a long arm, also cashmere clad, but barn red. Nantucket red. *Another of the tribe,* she thought.

"A pleasure," he said. "Billy, please."

"Billy chairs my board," said Sumner. "His daughter Caroline was with us from . . . was it first grade?"

"Kindergarten," said Billy. "All the way through."

"She's at Groton now. A senior. Lovely girl and a super tennis player."

Why are you telling me? Naomi thought crossly. *The dean of admissions is right over there.*

"Want some of this Chardonnay?" Francine said. "Or shall we open up the Merlot?"

"No, this looks great," said Naomi. She took a glass from Sumner, resisting the urge to ask for an ice cube. Putting ice in her white wine was a mild vice, as vices went. But it still wasn't something she wanted to admit to.

"How was the trip?" she asked, taking a seat beside Francine.

"Oh, fine. Intense. Somebody left a package at my hotel in La Jolla. That was creepy."

"What kind of package?" Naomi said. "Not...a bribe?"

"Better a bribe than a threat!" said Billy Grosvenor, which didn't make Naomi warm to him any more.

"Well...brownies. From a girl who said she was applying early. With a CD of her playing a violin concerto. The note said I was supposed to relax in my hotel room, eating the brownies and listening to the concerto."

"Ick," Naomi said.

"I threw it all out. I'm giving her the benefit of the doubt, but I'm not crazy. Besides, somebody probably put her up to it. Otherwise, though, it was a great trip. The college counselors kept taking me aside and telling me their students are coming in with Webster in their top three. Which is anecdotal, obviously, but I'm very pleased."

Naomi nodded. The college's flourishing appeal to current high school students could not be attributed to any one thing; it built upon itself, and undoubtedly contained a hefty dose of whimsy, but they were still entitled to enjoy the moment. Little Webster College!

"More popular than Harvard!" Sumner quipped.

"Well, not quite. But over half the Ivy League, yes. Depending on how you juggle the numbers."

"It boggles the mind," said Billy Grosvenor, not very kindly. "I mean, when I was applying, this was the safety school."

Francine and Naomi, instinctively, looked at each other, reached an instantaneous meeting of the minds, and looked away.

"I don't doubt that," said Naomi, as diplomatically as she could manage. "A celebrity makes a college selection and suddenly the whole deck is reshuffled. Or a popular professor. Or someone uses a beautiful campus to film a movie or a TV show, and then it's on everyone's radar. Remember when John Kennedy Jr. decided to go to Brown instead of Harvard?"

Grosvenor nodded. "I remember that. My father wouldn't stop talking about it. But he was a Harvard man, so he took it personally."

"Well, after that Brown really came into its own. It was always a great school. But in the shadow of some of the others."

"Like," said Sumner brightly, *"Wait, the football star wants to date her?"*

"How are you holding up?" Francine said sharply, turning to Naomi. This had the immediate effect of terminating the former subject. "I have to say, the first time I walked across the Quad after I got back, I was shocked."

Naomi frowned into her iceless glass. "I don't think it's a major issue. It's only a small group."

"Not really," Francine said. "There were five people there when I left on my trip. Just a few hours a day. Now there are thirty or forty out there, in sleeping bags. And they've got plastic sheeting up. What's this about?"

"What is 'this'?" said Sumner, looking intrigued.

"This is about young people expressing their discontents in a creative and nonviolent way. This is our students saying they care about more than just themselves. Even if I wanted to confront them, which I don't, I have nothing to confront them with.

I mean, trespassing? It's their college. And by the way, they're the neatest protesters in the world. They recycle everything. I'm proud of them."

"It's starting to be an issue in the office," said Francine. "We have people coming in for their interviews after the campus tour, and they're all talking about it."

"Good!" Naomi smiled. "We want students who notice a protest and are curious about it. I mean," she said, remembering whom she was talking to, "I would imagine we want those students."

"That's the criteria now?" Billy said. "I'm not sure they know that at Groton."

"No," Francine said. "They wouldn't. It's part of the secret position paper we admissions officers generate every fall at our undisclosed summit. Every year it's a new thing. Specific hip-to-waist ratio. Ability to rap in Latin. Kids from towns beginning with the letter Z. We can't let it get out to the general public or everyone would be moving and going for lipo."

"But how do you learn to rap in Latin?" Sumner said. "I did Latin all through my school years, and at Colgate. I couldn't rap in Latin to save my life."

"Well,"—Naomi shrugged—"it's a good thing you're not applying to college today."

He got up. He went back to the kitchen and a moment later they heard him call that dinner was ready.

"I bought the venison from my contractor," Billy told Naomi and Francine as he walked behind them into the dining room. "Hunts with a bow and arrow. Seriously. He freezes most of what he hunts, for his family, but he offered me the saddle."

"Oh," said Francine. She seemed uneasy with only two degrees of separation between the forest and her dining room. "Well, that's great."

"I can't wait to see what Sumner's done with it," he said happily. "Ladies?"

He pulled out Naomi's chair. Then Francine's.

What Sumner had done with it was to braise it with mushrooms and onions, and serve it over spaetzle. Naomi was not unhappy to see meat come her way, but she, too, was having a moment of difficulty in pairing the gamey smell of her plate with the memory of mothers and foals, frolicking in the forest. *Bambi*, all joking aside, had been one of the first films she had ever watched with her daughter, and she could not help recalling its unambiguous indictment:

What happened, Mother? Why did we all run?
Man was in the forest.

But now Sumner was looking at her in confident anticipation. She took a deep breath and ate.

"Oh, Sumner," said Francine. "So good."

"Delicious," Naomi said. "You know, I think I'll take that Merlot now. Or anything red."

He got up to fetch it for her, and when he returned Billy was talking about the company he'd started the year before, which was "not a hedge fund, exactly."

"What is a hedge fund exactly?" Naomi asked. "I mean, I know what it is. Well, not technically, but generally. But what makes a hedge fund a hedge fund?"

"Volume," Sumner joked.

"Small groups investing their own or others' funds," said Billy, who did not appear to joke, or at least not about this. "Often using high-risk methodology, like leverage. Usually by invitation. You can't just walk in the door and hand them your money. Well, I suppose with some you can, but most of us like to have that control."

"But you said," Naomi pointed out, "you're not a hedge fund."

"No. I'm not looking for investors at all. Sometimes they come to me through someone I know and trust, and sometimes we open a door to that person, but it's rare. Mainly I invest funds for my family members and longtime friends."

"How nice," Naomi said.

"Billy has been so extraordinarily generous to Hawthorne," Francine said, and Naomi instantly caught the note of warning. "He's just made a gift of some acreage adjacent to the campus."

"Beautiful acreage," Sumner said. Naomi, who was not unclear about the price of acreage in Southborough, Massachusetts, was reluctantly impressed.

"And full of deer!"

The two men laughed. Francine speared a cube of venison, observed it for a second, and put it in her mouth.

"I wanted Peter and his friends to be able to walk in the woods," said Billy humbly.

"Peter is Billy's fourth grader."

"My second marriage," said Billy, disconcertingly.

So did that mean, thought Naomi, that this was not a fix-up? She certainly hoped that was the case. Billy was not, she was chagrined to note, entirely unattractive. He shared with her exhusband, Daniel, a certain lankiness that she had always been drawn to. The cashmere sweater, Nantucket red though it was, hung with a pleasing drape over an obviously slender frame. He had hair, too. Brown hair, only a little gray. Hair was important. She didn't care what they said about baldness and masculinity. She would take hair and femininity every time. But she didn't like him, so none of that mattered.

"How many children do you have?" Naomi asked politely.

"Three," he said. "Matilda's at Harvard. Caroline's a senior at Groton. My ex-wife and I have Peter, who's nine."

"Our fourth grader," Sumner clarified unnecessarily.

"Do you have children?" asked Billy.

"My daughter, Hannah, is a sophomore at Webster."

"Well, that's . . ." He paused to laugh. "Unsurprising."

"Actually,"—Naomi glanced at Francine—"I was very surprised. I kept out of it completely. I mean I kept out of her college application process in general, apart from one or two general conversations. When she decided on Webster, naturally I was delighted."

"Why naturally?" Billy asked. He was refilling his own wineglass with the Merlot Naomi had brought. "I hope you're not trying to keep her close to you."

She stared at him. She was trying to come up with some scenario that would make this statement not extraordinarily rude. Who was this man? He'd only just met her!

But "Of course not" was all Naomi could manage.

Francine, who did not cook much but had made a cake, served it with coffee back in the living room. Sumner had reanimated the fire from its own embers, and Naomi looked into it, feeling the warmth all the way out to her place on the sofa. Billy had excused himself to the bathroom. Sumner had gone for milk.

"I am so sorry," said Francine, taking the opportunity.

"No, don't be silly. Unless . . . it's not a fix-up, is it?"

"Well, it's not my idea of a fix-up, let's put it that way."

"Oh lord." Naomi shook her head. "Really?"

"He wanted to meet you. He asked to meet you."

"I can't imagine why."

"He's interested in Webster. For the daughter."

"Well," she said, "you know better than anyone else, that has nothing to do with me. Unless, are you saying this is a development issue?"

"Actually,"—she glanced over her shoulder, toward the kitchen—"I don't think it is, no."

She couldn't immediately grasp this. "But . . . acreage? In Southborough?"

"Family property. It couldn't be sold. Some tax thing. But it could be sold. Very lucky for Hawthorne that it happened to border the campus."

"And the hedge fund that isn't really a hedge fund?"

"Family money, again. Look, he's wealthy, obviously. But not development wealthy. He's important, though. To Sumner. Very, very important to Sumner. I'm sorry."

Naomi frowned. "Why are you sorry? It's been a lovely evening." But that wasn't exactly what she meant, and she really did want to know why Billy was important to Sumner.

"Let's talk about it another time," said Francine. The men were coming back. Billy sat beside Naomi on the sofa and, instinctively, she leaned away. Sumner, unnecessarily, stoked the fire.

"The two of you," Francine said. "Between the bow and arrow and the fire building. I feel like I'm in the eighteenth century."

"Next time," Sumner said, "I'm going to roast the venison in the fireplace. Like they used to do at that place in Connecticut. What was that place?"

"Randall's Ordinary," said his wife, filling in the spousal synapses. Naomi had once done something similar for Daniel when he forgot the streets they'd lived on, or the names of their friends' pets. Oddly, it never seemed to work in the other direction. Did husbands ever carry these tiny mosaic pieces of memory for their wives, slotting them instantly and adeptly into place when needed? Naomi could still recall the name of a cat who'd lived upstairs from the first apartment she and Daniel had shared in Collegetown. She knew which brand of milk had been preferred by his mother—now long deceased—because his mother had told her once, just once, nearly thirty years before. She remembered the barbecue restaurant down the road from the VISTA training center in Berea, Kentucky, where she and Daniel had spent six weeks the summer after their marriage, preparing themselves for, as it would turn out, Goddard, New Hampshire. That barbecue restaurant, more of a shack, really, was a one-man show and the man himself was called James. He was a Korean War vet, a native of Tennessee, and a genius with beef ribs. It had been while eating one of his beef ribs, in fact, that Naomi had truly and permanently understood she would never be a vegetarian, not really. And yet, were Daniel here at this moment, in this baronial living room with its over-sized couches and faux-timbered ceiling, Naomi did not doubt that he'd be unable to remember not only the beef ribs, but James, his shack, the town where they had once prepared for their twelve-month (ha!) VISTA stint, or the fact that he had ever spent any significant time in Kentucky, at all. What was that about?

"Can I just say how exciting this is?" said Billy Grosvenor. "Dinner with not only the president of Webster, but the admissions dean!"

"Well, you got the right emphasis there. Francine is way more important than I am," Naomi said.

"Please." Francine rolled her eyes.

"I'll tell you one thing," he said. "For my daughter's class at Groton? Webster's more popular than Harvard. Could have knocked me over when she told me that. I mean, back when I applied? People didn't talk about Webster like that. Of course it was always a good school," he said apologetically. "But you know, this is a big change."

"We have an extraordinary faculty and a gorgeous setting," Naomi said. She was trying, hard, not to sound as defensive as he'd made her feel. Or as annoyed. "We also have a reputation for creativity and entrepreneurship. It's hard to find all of those things in the same place. And we have our secret weapon: a dean of admissions who consistently assembles brilliant classes for us. Long may she wave," Naomi said, raising her coffee cup.

"Cheers!" Billy raised his wineglass.

"Yes, well," said Francine. "Not hard to do when you've got ten overqualified candidates for every place in the class."

"*Especially* hard to do when you've got ten overqualified candidates for every place in the class," Naomi said. "Sumner! Your wife is selling herself short. Why don't you stop her?"

But even as she said it she was thinking: *Why should I have to ask him?*

CHAPTER FOUR

A Long History of Capitulation

Naomi had inherited her assistant, Mrs. Bradford, from the previous president, Logan Coulson. Mrs. Bradford (her first name was Susan, but very few people knew that) had worked devotedly for Coulson since the end of the penultimate decade of the previous century, and far be it for Naomi to upset this particular apple cart, though there were days—many, many days—when the severe and plainly mirthless smile of Mrs. Bradford, the first thing she saw when she climbed the top flight of Billings Hall's broad mahogany steps each morning, would set the tone for the entire day. It was a smile that said, in arctic essence: *You? Again?* It was a smile that made the soul wither.

Mrs. Bradford had passed the suggested retirement age in the last millennium, but the HR office's initial attempt to bring this to her attention had met with a freighted silence, and no one brought it up again. Over the years, also, Mrs. Bradford seemed to have arranged matters in the office in such a way that no one but herself could really fulfill her duties, not without shredding all the systems and starting over, an undertaking that might take months, or be impossible. There was never a good time to try that, and never a reason Naomi could feel justified in pointing to: The office ran beautifully, its business quietly dispatched, and most callers made to feel known and valued (which was no small thing, especially each April when the admissions decisions went out and Naomi's phone commenced to thrum with vitriol), and she brought nothing of her personal life into the office, apart from a line of well-tended plants on the window ledge, which were hardly objectionable. If Mrs. Bradford didn't want to retire, why should she? And no, the fact that there existed no great affection nor even detectable goodwill between them was not a good enough reason to make her go.

"Good morning!" Naomi said, cheerily enough. She was pushing open the heavy outer door with her shoulder, her arms full of tenure folders. The president's offices were not substantially changed since Billings Hall had gone up in the 1880s, its edifice composed of the same gray stone that would later be used for the Stone House. Titus Billings, a Presbyterian minister, had been the president then, and though his tenure would be abbreviated by tuberculosis, he still cast a long shadow in the form of his namesake administration building and of course the Billings Lawn, which stretched from its door to the library on the left, classroom buildings on the right, and the chapel on the far side. Naomi occupied the same chamber every one of her predecessors had, since Billings himself, though she'd also requisitioned the seminar room next door for meetings, and broken through to it from her own room the year before (an innovation that also allowed her to put a bit more distance between herself and her assistant when the urge arose). To the basic decor of manly nineteenth-century dominion she had added very little in the way of an individual touch, only a single quilt from her VISTA days (a favorite pattern called Drunkard's Path in blues and greens, which happened to be Webster's colors) tacked to a frame and hung on the wall behind her desk, and a discreet eight-by-ten of Hannah holding her flute to her lips, long hair flying evocatively behind her in some well-timed puff of wind.

She set down her files and walked around the great oak desk, and by the time she reached her chair on the other side Mrs. Bradford was in the doorway. Naomi, to her annoyance (but also to her shame), recognized her assistant's efficient summing up and customary expression of disapproval, which translated to: "You're wearing *that*?"

It was, indeed, a truth universally acknowledged—and not least by herself—that Naomi Roth had no idea how to dress herself for the grown-up world. It hadn't mattered in her own student life. It hadn't mattered during her VISTA years, when mostly the standard was how much of the New Hampshire cold you kept out. It *had* mattered, but in an inverse way, when she'd stood in front of a classroom of hatchling feminists, trying to explain why Erica Jong mattered every bit as much as Philip Roth did (more! more!); for such an occasion one's army boots meant that you were prepared to march, one's forswearing of logos meant that you declined to pay Ralph Lauren for the privilege of advertising his brand, and the deliberate choice of hand-made garments, created by collectives of women and brought to market with micro loans to women entrepreneurs in the Third World, meant that you cared to express more in your sartorial choices than what your favorite color was, or what made you appear the thinnest, or that you took your cues from the ultimately patriarchal gaze that was *Vogue* et al. And yet, with the news that she was being seriously considered for the job of Webster's seventeenth president, Naomi understood that her luck in this matter had run out. The idea of leading Webster College, making policy, overseeing thousands of students, and getting people to give the institution their money didn't faze her in the least. Dressing for it, however, did. A lot.

College presidents did not wear army boots to meet with

alumni about a scholarship fund or a naming opportunity in the new gym. They did not wear sweatpants and flowing embroidered Indian shirts to oversee convocation or speak at commencement. They represented their institutions in outfits that were planned out in advance, in clothing that came from stores, not collectives: normal but well-constructed items like dresses and jackets and skirts, with carefully edited accessories. None of these were to be found in Naomi's pre-presidential wardrobe, which filled not even one of the small closets of her pre-presidential home. Indian skirts with elasticized waists. Leggings (so useful, leggings, not to speak of their comfort!). Oversized men's shirts from the excellent thrift stores of the Pioneer Valley. The very same Frye boots she had brought with her to Cornell, at the height of their original chicness, though many times resoled. A black Diane von Furstenberg wrap dress that she had taken from her mother's closet to wear to her mother's funeral (her mother would have *wanted* this; she would have been *thrilled*— had she not been dead), which, nonetheless, Naomi had never found reason to wear again. Birkenstocks, of course. So sturdy, so *honest* in their intentions. Her collection of accessories included a white Swatch and a macaroni necklace from Hannah's kindergarten period, along with a canvas bag that read, no longer so wittily, A WOMAN WITHOUT A MAN IS LIKE A FISH WITHOUT A BICYCLE. She did own a Ghanaian garment, immense and voluminous, of some very pretty but very *loud* purple and yellow and sky-blue cotton fabric. It had been a gift from one of the other women in the women's studies program at UMass, brought back from a Semester at Sea expedition, and Naomi had never even put it on (though she did, occasionally think about making it into pillows—it really was a very pretty fabric.

Obviously, all but a few of these items of clothing were going to be useless; even Naomi could see that. Perhaps there would be a use for one black turtleneck sweater (it itched horribly), a pair of brown tweed pants that gave her ten highly unnecessary extra pounds at the waist, and three pairs of leather boots in various shades of brown, but bags and bags of those oversized men's shirts, loose fitting jeans and khakis, and It's-a-Small-World ethnic outfits would have to go into storage or be deported to the Springfield Red White and Blue. And what would be left? Not a single jacket, dress, skirt, heel, or purse—meaning, a proper handbag. When that whole *You-Might-Get-to-Be-a College-President!* thing became so real even she could not ignore it, she'd picked up the phone and called one of the trustees, a Webster grad about her own age whose clothing had always struck her as understated, non-restricting—this woman was no stick figure herself!—and yet entirely grown-up, and she asked for some guidance. A week later Naomi was in New York, trawling the stores with a personal shopper named Margie. (In due course, the well-dressed trustee would confide that it was this very phone call, and Naomi's willingness to admit to a gap in her own expertise and ask for help, that persuaded her to support her candidacy.) A new job, and the clothes to go with it.

Now Naomi's wardrobe filled a walk-in closet (actually a small room) in the Stone House's master bedroom suite. Much of the new inventory had come from Eileen Fisher, but there were a few Eskandar shirts that Naomi thought she could have loved even in her prior circumstances: clean but flowy, white and black and slate gray. ("You should never wear earth tones," Margie the personal shopper had said. "I mean, under no circumstances.") She now wore a chunky silver necklace, shockingly inexpensive, from a store near Penn Station, and a proper-looking watch that was supposedly a copy of some other, iconic watch. The canvas bag was gone, replaced by a leather bag that fit easily over her shoulder and could usually accommodate whatever she needed to carry. Her surviving leather boots were now in constant rotation during the school year, though Naomi did, over the summer, allow herself to return to Birkenstocks. (She maintained a stubborn loyalty to Birkenstocks. Who didn't love Birkenstocks?)

Today, in black pants and an Eskandar shirt, over which she wore a long gray sweater, she had felt invulnerable enough, but Mrs. Bradford looked as if Naomi had taken a unilateral casual Monday, and moreover chosen the wrong Monday on which to do it.

"You know the honorary degrees committee of the Alumni Council is coming for lunch, right?"

Naomi nodded. Of course she knew. Her schedule, daily and weekly, was beamed into her brain each morning via each and every screen in her life. Naomi generally enjoyed dealing with the Alumni Council. These were Websterites who'd chosen to view their graduations as merely a transition in their lifelong relationship with the college. While undergraduates they had tended to run student organizations and chair fraternities and sororities; now they served on committees like alumni relations and development, athletics, and undergraduate affairs, remaining involved members of Webster's eternal community even as they pursued their careers and carefully raised the next generation of Webster students. And while it was true that Naomi herself felt none of this passion and loyalty for her own alma mater, she found their ardor for Webster quite touching, and actually envied it a tiny bit. When the class of 1997, at their tenth reunion, voted to make her an honorary member of that class, she took it as a legitimization of her own affection for the college, and thereafter appeared, in all official print, as Naomi Roth, '97 Hon.

The honorary degree committee would be here at noon, and college catering would serve them turkey sandwiches in the conference room next door, but before that she had a meeting with Douglas Sidgwick, whose department of one had the arcane mission of research and assessment for the college. Naomi, who liked Douglas very much (and privately believed

him to be squarely in the Asperger's zone of the autism spectrum), considered him a human repository of institutional memory, which was a matter of knowing not only the history of the
college but every link in the various chains of Webster folklore, statistics, trends, and transitions. She had been entirely
unaware of Douglas, his "department," or indeed his physical
office in Billings's basement (which had, incidentally, its own
walkout egress—no wonder she'd never run into him on the
stairs) until she'd become president, and then his presence had
been revealed to her, like a secret room for which she was now
the guardian of the key.

She used the moments before his arrival to call the department chairs of math and biology and officially confirm their
tenure rulings. There would be a celebration tonight, she knew,
in the household of a young and brilliant math professor, lured
from Yale as a postdoc, who'd already done a cataclysmically popular TED Talk on number theory, and the woman in biology was,
according to her department head, on the threshold of some life-
altering discovery. This, she thought, as she made the calls, was
the way things were supposed to unfold in tenure decisions (no
surprises, happy candidates, delighted departments), and today's
news would be a relief all around.

If only they were all so orderly.

For months, by contrast, the anthropology department had
been fording dangerous waters with a very different tenure decision. The candidate in question was a teacher named Nicholas
Gall, and he was creative and charismatic and extremely popular
among the students, but the publication side of his skill set was
a bit more problematic. After years of creative inactivity and several extensions from the department, Gall had finally published
only a monograph on "The Mountain Whippoorwill" as folkloric
source material, and this, horrifyingly, had been found to contain
plagiarized passages. He'd been warned the previous winter that

a tenure offer was highly unlikely, advised in April that the decision would go against him. The official verdict, handed down at the beginning of the fall term, had been merely a formality: a dotting of *i*'s and crossing of *t*'s to close out his unfortunate employment at Webster. Gall, whose contract would continue through the current academic year, might wish to appeal, and he was entitled to do so, but why take the chance of having it all come out? Naomi hoped he'd go quietly. As far as she was concerned, the situation's only saving grace was its containment within the department, the tenure committee, and her own office. It was all a great shame, since as a teacher Gall had been well liked, but well liked wasn't enough, not at a college like Webster and not today.

She looked up to see Douglas Sidgwick stepping into the room. He hadn't knocked. He probably didn't understand that knocking was customary. It wasn't the kind of thing you could hold against him.

Douglas Sidgwick had attended business school at Harvard, but quickly discovered that he did not enjoy working alongside other human beings. He'd been a Webster student during the 1980s and he had loved and felt included at Webster. And so, because all he wanted after a four-year stint at Paine Webber was to return to that feeling, Douglas Sidgwick had essentially conceived and proposed his own position to the newly inaugurated President Coulson, proving his worth by constructing a plan to raze two of the college's least loved dormitories and build in their place an "Arts Neighborhood" of studios, editing suites, and theaters. (This had the one-stone-three-birds effect of eliminating a campus eyesore, bumping up the college's profile for arts-minded applicants, and creating no fewer than eight significant naming opportunities.) Even so, Coulson had never been more than a grudging fan of Douglas's abilities. Naomi, by contrast, considered him something of a secret weapon.

Their meeting, like all of their interactions, began with one of Douglas's obviously rehearsed jokes, and Naomi did her part by laughing heartily. She asked Mrs. Bradford to bring a mug of the herbal tea her strange colleague liked, and coffee for herself. She had actually called this meeting, and she was eager to get it under way, but before she could get to her own matter of interest she had to strap in for the usual tour.

The "holistic evaluation" that ensued took them each through their respective mugs and halfway through a second, and comprised everything from Douglas's assessment of their place in the US News college rankings to their stature within the "Little Five," the mainly whimsical grouping of New England colleges Webster had been attached to years earlier. (That the Little Five had, at certain moments in recent history, been to a tiny degree harder to get into than Harvard was merely an example of how malleable statistics could be, and moved Naomi not at all, but the news had been unexpectedly exciting to Webster grads, and had resulted in a surge of new giving, not to mention an instant classic T-shirt at the Webster Co-Op: *Webster College— The Harvard of Massachusetts*.) At the moment, Naomi learned, sipping her second mug of coffee, Webster was being regarded as highly attractive by young artists, activists, entrepreneurs, history of science students (they had hired, two years before, one of the country's most visible defenders of Darwin, a well-mannered but determined firebrand with shoulder-length black hair, constantly in demand to debate Young Earth proponents), and more and more associated with, Douglas Sidgwick said dryly, reality television.

"What?" she asked, looking up. She'd been, surreptitiously, checking email.

It was one thing to have her own passing familiarity with reality television, but the notion of Douglas Sidgwick keeping up with *Project Runway* and *Survivor* really was beyond. He nodded, referring back to his perfectly organized notes. Webster graduates had, of late, won or come close to winning *The Amazing Race*, *Project Runway*, *America's Next Top Model*, *American Idol*, and *Top Chef*, with a current Webster junior now loping toward victory in the *Jeopardy!* College Tournament. Naomi, who watched none of these programs (currently watched none of them—she and Hannah had gone through a *Jeopardy!* phase during a particularly bleak period in their mother-daughter journey), was amazed.

"Wait, so people are thinking Webster's a good college to attend if they want to win *Project Runway*?"

Sidgwick frowned. "It's more that we're associated with a general sense of producing very driven young people. Spunky, creative kids who go for what they want, and prevail."

"Well, I hope that's what it is," she said, still perplexed. "What else?"

What else was a survey, currently out to alumni, on the question of adding a graduate program in public health, a not insignificant move for a college that had been rigorously focused on the undergraduate for more than two hundred years. Even with a pledge to retain the moniker Webster College, the issue was proving heated. Very heated.

"We should pick a date to stop coding the responses." Naomi sighed. "It doesn't sound like the patterns are going to skew massively."

"No. Remind me, when would you need to break ground, if you're going ahead?"

"Two years from September. There's still time."

"And you think it's worth it?"

Naomi shrugged. But Sidgwick didn't really do gestures, not even the obvious ones. He was waiting for words.

"I really don't know. I really don't."

"All right." He made a note. "And I have two budget call issues for you. I don't know how involved you want to be at this point?"

"Not very," said Naomi. What she did want was to move things along now. "So, can we talk about the Native American conference?"

"Yes, fine," he said. "I have a whole dossier for you."

She smiled. She was sure he did.

"But how much do you know in the way of background?" asked Sidgwick, for whom everything that was not happening right this second should be considered background.

"Oh...the usual amount, I guess. Josiah Webster graduates Columbia, sets up an outpost near Albany to tell Native Americans all about Jesus, gets sent packing by the Iroquois, then another tribe invites him to start a school here."

"Well," said Sedgwick, entirely without humor, "more or less."

Naomi, who preferred to remain in the present day, hoped it would be less, but suspected it would be more.

"Josiah Webster did graduate from Columbia in 1750 and by 1755 he'd set up a few miles south of Lake George, just in time for the French and Indian Wars. So he was lucky it didn't end right there. But even without the hostilities he wasn't having a lot of luck with the Iroquois. They weren't feeling the need for conversion, which is what Webster was selling, though he did offer Greek and Latin, too. That was kind of his bait and switch, I guess you could say."

"Right," Naomi said. She was noting the time on the wall clock over her doorway.

"But he had managed to attract one student, or more of an acolyte. He'd come to the Webster Indian school from one of the Praying Towns in Massachusetts."

"Praying Towns," Naomi said. "What's that?"

"Well, you can think of them as kind of prototype reservations. They were an experiment to encourage the Indians to give up whatever the English considered savagery, which was basically the entirety of their culture. You know how King Philip's War turned on the death of a 'Praying Indian'? A convert, in other words."

Naomi, who really, really did not want to linger in the eighteenth century, said, "Yes, I know."

"So these were whole communities of 'Praying Indians.' And one of them was a settlement in Connecticut, called Maanexit, a few miles from where we are now, though eventually we wound up on the other side of the Massachusetts/Connecticut line. And he invited Josiah Webster to come home with him and rebuild the school here. We don't know his original name, but his baptismal name was Josiah. Also Josiah."

"No ego there," Naomi observed.

"And that was kind of the official beginning of Webster. The Webster Indian Academy."

"And two and a half centuries later, here we are!" she said brightly, optimistically.

"Yes. Well, but no. Because within twenty years or so there was no more Indian Academy. Or there was still an academy but there weren't any more Indians. Native Americans. Josiah was dead. Both Josiahs were dead, and Josiah Webster's son—that was his successor, Nathaniel Webster—was just keeping afloat by taking in the sons of Massachusetts farmers. The ones who weren't going to Harvard and Yale. But their families didn't have much money to spend on education. Most of the money, in general, was in Boston and Philadelphia and the South, and to be frank there wasn't much incentive to keep things congenial with the Indians anymore, because by then things were pretty much settled on that front—we'd won, they were no longer a threat. If they didn't want to be Christian, that was okay. And meanwhile nobody was going to send their son to study with Indians when they could go to Yale or Harvard and be with their own kind. So Nathaniel found this whaler named Samuel Fairweather, and Fairweather pitched in the money for the establishment of Webster as a new college, distinct from the Indian Academy. And because he didn't want to lose this donor, he kind of had to give in to Fairweather's primary demand, which was that there wouldn't be any more 'Indian' in the name; from now on Webster would offer theology and Latin, and whatever else they were teaching at Harvard and Yale, or Nathaniel could go somewhere else for the funds. And that was that. Not a single Native American for two centuries. Not till Sarafian in sixty-six."

From the next room—*the next room*—Naomi heard Mrs. Bradford clear her throat. Without ever having verbally established this fact, the clearing of Mrs. Bradford's throat had come to mean that Naomi's next appointment was growing nigh.

"Douglas? I am so sorry. I am finding this fascinating, but I have the Alumni Council coming in soon and I want to get to the conference."

And Douglas was nodding. Douglas understood. Probably. But his brain had to connect every dot before he could go forward. He was like the tribal historian that Alex Haley encountered when he finally made it back to his ancestor's African village. Why yes, this man could tell the visiting American author about his great-great-great-grandfather, but only if he started back at the commencement of time. It would take a day or two, or several, but what was time, really, when today was just another day in the life of an African tribe or a 250-year-old American college, every moment of which was as compelling and intricate as this moment, right now? At one of their very first meetings, which had unwisely taken the form of a casual lunch in the pub at the Webster Inn—"unwisely" because Douglas, it would be immediately clear, did not function well in social settings of any kind—he had mentioned that his life-long project was a history of the college. An exhaustive history, which he intended to call *The Devil and Webster*.

But why? Naomi had asked. "I don't believe we have a history of Satanism. Do we?"

"No, no. Well, not unless you went back to colonial times, when the Europeans considered every surrounding forest to be home to Lucifer and his minions. But if you think about it, Webster College has enjoyed a long history of capitulation. First, there was a mission; then we went for the money. Then two centuries later, we went for a different kind of currency, and gave the first money back. But both times there was a mouth at our ear, and we listened."

She nodded, but really she found the metaphor a mite dramatic. Naturally, over the years, the college had cut its conscience to fit the fashions of the time, but didn't any institution do that, more or less? And for that matter, weren't they each, on a personal level, finally products of the only times they knew?

"Sarafian understood that we needed to do something, to shift something," Douglas said. "He was a shock to the system in a lot of ways. Foreign born. Not a native speaker. A serious academic, not a businessman. Not an alum—believe it or not there'd only been a few presidents before him who weren't Webster alums, and most of those were way back at the beginning. And he looked different. He had long hair. He wore the same kinds of clothes the students were starting to wear. He listened to the same music. And he was single, which meant there was a chance he might be a homosexual, which a lot of people couldn't get past, even after he started living with a woman in the Stone House. Which was another thing, but the point is, he had none of that gimlet eye stuff when it came to Webster. He saw things really clearly, like that we were the safety school. We were stuck in this orbit around the Ivies, and that was unacceptable. And because he saw where all of us were going—the culture and the colleges—he decided we were going to go there first. We were going to coeducation. We were throwing out the quotas for blacks and Jews. And most of all we were going to bring back the Indians. He put that front and center, in his inaugural speech.

He said: 'Webster will recommit itself to its original purpose. We will welcome to this college Native American and First Nations students from all over the Americas.' It was a scandal."

"Oh yes," Naomi said, defeated.

"But when they got here, that first group in the late sixties, they were shocked. First football game and there are white boys prancing around in Indian costumes on the field yelping these Hollywood war whoops. A delegation of them went to Sarafian and said, 'You can have us or you can have the Indian symbol. You don't get to have both.'"

There came the distinctive rap that Mrs. Bradford's knuckles made against the mahogany door. The door opened up enough for her large, pale head to come through. "Alumni Council is here. They arrived a few minutes ago."

"Wonderful," said Naomi. "We're nearly finished here. Why don't you put them in the conference room and...is lunch here?"

"In the conference room."

"Good. Well, they can start and I'll be in in a couple of minutes. Unless, Douglas, would you like to join us for lunch?"

He gave her a look of real horror. She might have asked him to walk over coals.

"A few minutes," Naomi said, and Mrs. Bradford's head was withdrawn.

"I'm glad you have so much perspective on why this matters," said Naomi. "I'm only surprised that it's never been done. Fifty years since Sarafian's inauguration. More than eight hundred Native American students. And we've never had a dedicated conference. Why is that?"

Douglas looked as if he was about to answer. At length and in detail.

"So I want you to know," she cut him off, "that this is a priority for me. And I want the conference to be as much a part of our institutional story as Sarafian's rededication was. I want their perspective, warts and all, and I want our entire community—alumni, students, faculty, everybody—to be looking ahead to this as a major event. Now"—Naomi got to her feet; she had no more time spend on this right now—"I want you to do one thing before we meet again next week. I want ten alumni of Native American or First Nations descent we can approach as an advisory committee, and one of them to chair the committee. Send me bios, and contact information. I'll ask them personally. But I want to move on this." She stopped. He was still seated. He was making notes in his spidery handwriting. "All right, Douglas?"

"Mm-hmm," he murmured, not looking up.

She left him there, with the door to the outer office wide open so that Mrs. Bradford could keep an eye on him, because who knew how long he would continue to write, still there in his wooden Hitchcock chair with the college crest, before he realized or at least fully understood that he was now supposed to get up and leave?

CHAPTER FIVE

THE VERY SOUL OF WEBSTER

After that, the rest of the day was nearly a pleasure. Chewing over the merits of a dozen highly meritorious individuals (even while chewing far less meritorious turkey sandwiches) proved a satisfying way to spend an hour, and by the time it was over she and the committee had a dozen potential honorees, including two scientists on the current faculty, a recently retired professor of Spanish and Portuguese, a historian whose biography of Aaron Burr had won the National Book Award the previous year, a young alumna who'd founded an orphanage in the Central African Republic, three older alumni who'd given so generously to Webster that they'd all get honorary degrees eventually, the longtime head of the college housekeeping service, two current Massachusetts congressmen, and a folksinging icon of Naomi's youth whose daughter was due to graduate the following June. Within the next month the committee and Naomi would vote on this list, reducing the number to eight. With luck, letters would go out before the winter break.

When Mrs. Bradford brought in a plate of cookies and a tray of Webster mugs filled with decaf, the generally understood signal was that it was now permissible to address more personal concerns, and these were accordingly forthcoming. Admissions, naturally, ranked at the top of everyone's list, and given that nearly all the honorary degree committee members were between thirty-five and fifty years old, each and every one of them seemed to have a child in the zone, or know a child in the zone, or know a child unfairly rejected in (direct?) favor of another child unfairly admitted. It was extraordinary how they all seemed to carry around the academic and extracurricular data of so many young people. Their own children, understandably, but their children's classmates, rivals, romantic partners? Naomi tried to listen sympathetically. She'd placed her faith in Francine and had no problem singing her praises (read: passing the buck) to these or any other interested parties. (And when it came to college admissions, she had learned, every single parent on the planet was an interested party.) Francine was not, as a rule, an approachable kind of person, but that was probably no bad thing given the unique challenge of being a dean of admissions at a highly competitive college.

"I personally phoned her office last spring," a man from suburban Washington, DC, was saying. "My business partner's son applied early to Webster and was deferred. Seven hundreds on his SATs, and he played varsity football all four years. Of course his father knew my son wasn't nearly as qualified, but Connor got in the year before, and my partner's son, they didn't even waitlist him. It's crazy."

Naomi, sipping her Diet Coke, was half-heartedly rummaging through her well-worn collection of platitudes, wondering which to select. Perhaps: *It certainly is crazy. Applications were up another eight percent last year!* Or: *They have to make such tough decisions. Aren't you glad you don't have that job?* Or possibly: *Oh, I know, you should see our applicants. They're all like that! Smart and involved and ambitious. If we were applying to college today, I don't even like to think about it!* And, naturally, by no means:

You're absolutely right. We should never have taken your son Connor. This kid was obviously a stronger applicant. But in the end she didn't have to say anything. They just wanted to vent, really.

"And you know, Samantha's roommate freshman year? She didn't even really want to be here. She stopped studying, stopped going to class. Finally she wasn't getting out of bed. One day Sammy came back to the dorm and the girl was loading up her parents' car. Not even a goodbye."

"How awful," Naomi said, trying to remember if this girl had been brought to her attention. Last year's freshman class? There were about four, she thought, who'd left before the year was through.

"But I mean, what is this girl doing taking up a place? There were two girls in Sammy's class who were dying to come to Webster. And one of them got into Yale. But she wanted to come here!"

Naomi tried to concentrate on this non sequitur. Or was it two non sequiturs, in sequence?

"I just don't know what they're doing over there," the woman said. And there were nods and sighs around the table.

"We're only as strong as our admissions," said the man whose business partner's son had been rejected.

Naomi, looking around at them, was suddenly concerned. Was this . . . had this become . . . a thing? And if it had, when had it? And how had she missed it?

"I have every confidence in Dean Rigor," she said. But she had taken note.

After they'd gone, she walked to the Arts Neighborhood to meet with the head of theater and dance, who wanted to show her exactly how the new dance studios were deficient (it boiled down to the fact that they had been designed by the former head of theater and dance, and not by him), and then she went downtown, ostensibly to pick up a book at the Webster Bookstore but mainly to stretch her legs. She had not been for a walk with Francine for weeks, partly due to her own speaking schedule (September was a popular time of year for alumni groups) and partly because her friend was away on that trip to California and the Southwest. Apart from the dubious brownies delivered to her hotel room in La Jolla, the other highlight of that trip had been a boy at a public school in Houston who'd come up after the Q&A for a chat about Webster's philosophy faculty. "Then he told me he'd read your book," said Francine.

"Oh?" Naomi said. They were on the phone together the morning after that odd dinner party, each drinking coffee from a Webster College mug at her own desk, in their side-by-side buildings on the Billings Lawn.

But she was not as impressed by this as Francine seemed to be. If a potential applicant was ambitious enough to approach a visiting dean of admissions on his own behalf, he was also ambitious enough to have read (or claimed to have read) a book by the college's president. Besides, a lot of people had read her book. After she'd become Webster's president, in fact, her publisher had reissued *Divide and Conquer*, and it had done rather decently. Not, of course, *New York Times* best-seller decently, but name recognition and reliably-present-in-your-better-bookstores decently.

Francine, though, had laughed. "No, the other book. Your first book."

And then Naomi *had* been surprised, because this *was* newsworthy. The book that had begun life as her doctoral thesis at UMass had barely made it into print as *No Boys Allowed: The Battle for Shulamith Records 1972–1986*, and was now well and truly out of print. Not even the surprise ascension of its author to the presidency of one of the country's most selective colleges had been enough to bring *that* title back.

Shulamith Records had been a "women only" recording

collective, steered by a core group of lesbian/feminist separatists in Ann Arbor, Michigan. Shulamith caught some of the updraft from the Michigan Womyn's Music Festival, held each summer on the other side of the state, and operated out of a communal house a few blocks from the UM campus. Even in its pre-internet lifespan the collective had managed to tap into a truly subterranean vein of feminist, lesbian, and feminist/lesbian cultures, a feat that could only be explained by the true hunger of the women in those cultures for anything that reflected back their realities and concerns. But Shulamith had also managed to bring genuinely powerful voices into the open, especially those of Louise Kamen, a folksinger from Georgia, and Rosanna Powers, a stunning Cherokee with a silken alto, who posed bare breasted on a rusted-out car on her album cover (an image that instantly became the lesbian equivalent of the famous Farrah Fawcett poster, published the same year). The collective grew and grew, nurturing its two stars and touring them to intensely grateful audiences around the country, while taking chances on even more experimental artists, as well as comedians and poets. Every Shulamith job, from artist to publicist to childcare provider for the offspring of collective members, was held by a woman. It was their manifesto. It was also, as things unwound, their downfall.

"Women only" meant...*only women*. But what was a woman, anyway? This was a question no one was bothering to ask in 1975, because, after all, feminism back then was about acquiring male privilege, taking the night and the jobs and the control of the physical body back from the patriarchy. Women were on the move, but the going was tough; who'd want this struggle if they weren't female by birth, de facto controlled and disenfranchised? Who, in other words, would choose to be women if they weren't actually born that way, if they'd been born, in other words, into male privilege, automatically endowed with everything feminism was toiling to acquire? (And by the way, could you even do that back then?)

You could do that, though just barely, even in the mid-'70s. And indeed, someone at Shulamith actually *had* done it before turning up in Ann Arbor and taking on the position of mastering engineer (a job that had not existed for the collective's earliest albums, which was why the first thing this person did on arrival was to remaster them).

She had come from Alabama, where her early life had been, frankly, hellish. Born Joseph Ignatius Owen to a family of former sharecroppers, she hadn't even bothered to come out to her family. (Come out as what? She didn't even have a name for what she was.) Instead she'd joined the navy, and at the other end of the Vietnam War she found herself in San Diego, where a miraculous being, an actual postoperative transsexual, brought Joseph to her own gifted and compassionate surgeon. The woman who emerged would be named Josie Owen, and she would never see her family again. She picked up a degree in sound engineering at a San Diego community college and headed to Michigan, to the thrilling collective she had heard of (like every other lesbian in the country, she owned the debut albums of Louise Kamen and the stunning Rosanna Powers), where her singular ear and skills put Shulamith's sound quality on a par with the major labels in New York and LA.

She didn't keep it a secret. She was structurally female, but she couldn't quite pass, and she knew it. Even if that weren't the case, though, she would have told the truth; she was that kind of person, and she was tired of living a falsehood. But was Josie Owen a woman because her anatomy approximated that of a woman? Or was she a woman because she had chosen to be a woman and declared it to be so? Or was she not really a woman, and if not, why not? Because the state of Alabama still knew her as Joseph? Because her honorable discharge from the navy, which had paid for her education, still knew her as Joseph? Because her family in Alabama had no idea what had become of Joseph? Or how about because each and every one of the 37 trillion cells in her body was home to a Y chromosome?

This question would tear the Shulamith Collective apart. Even after Owen herself withdrew, citing her pain at the pain she was causing, moving with her partner to Maine, where she founded her own recording studio in Portland, the women who remained in Ann Arbor could find no peace. Had they expelled their mastering engineer unfairly? Had Josie Owen come into their midst with some evil, disruptive subversion already in mind? What did sisterhood mean when it preached the ether of womanhood but could not untie itself from cold, earthbound biology? The group disbanded for good in 1986, with one small faction drifting to Northampton, Massachusetts, and the rest dispersing.

Naomi had first heard of Shulamith as a college student during the collective's heyday, when she'd traveled to Michigan with Daniel and a couple of their friends to experience the Womyn's Festival. Poor Daniel had not truly believed that he—evolved and feminist as he considered himself to be—would not actually be allowed onto the festival's woodland site, and when a towering woman in a reflective vest and the police hat of a made-up jurisdiction stopped their car and would not permit them to pass, he had thrown the kind of fit that your basic male chauvinist will throw when prevented from accessing his traditional privileges. The two couples argued with the guard and then with the festival organizers. Daniel and the other man attempted to present their progressive credentials, and then commenced a general debate on feminism, and when neither of those worked, they threatened legal action to expose the festival's blatant discrimination (which did much to lighten the mood), and when this, too, failed to work the foursome turned their car around and went to the nearest town and had a two-hour screaming argument over chicken sandwiches and iced tea at a diner. The upshot of all this was that Naomi and her friend, Kimberley, dropped the men off at a nearby lake, set them up in a rental cabin, and drove back to the Michigan Womyn's Music Festival, where they put up a tent like everyone else and settled in for two days of bare-breasted music and sisterhood. They did not specifically tell anyone that they were a couple, but they didn't specifically say they weren't, either. And the music was beautiful. And the sisterhood was powerful. And they were glad they'd done what they'd done.

Shulamith had a big presence at the festival, naturally, and Naomi brought some of the albums back to Cornell, where she listened to them whenever Daniel was out. Eventually the albums moved with her to New Hampshire and then to Amherst, and when she discovered, in a chance conversation in a vegetarian café in Northampton (Rosanna Powers was playing over the sound system) that the collective had broken apart over a transgender engineer, Naomi had known instantly that she'd found her thesis topic. *No Boys Allowed* might not have made much of a splash in the wider world (its great moment was an essay of grudging praise by Mary Daly in *off our backs*), but it had proven crucial to her hiring at Webster, where the faculty then boasted not a single feminist scholar. Right place, right time. And if the book passed quietly out of print a few years later, Naomi's far more mainstream and accessible *Divide and Conquer* came quickly on its heels, and was still often read, even by certain boys attending high school in Texas.

"Well, I hope you got his name," she had told Francine on the phone. "Because if he ends up at Webster I'm definitely taking him to lunch."

By the time Naomi returned to the office that afternoon, the dean of students was waiting, hunched over his phone and tapping away furiously. Mrs. Bradford was out (she preferred an afternoon break to lunch), but Bob Stacek—the selfsame Bob Stacek who'd long ago passed her the buck of the Radclyffe Hall mess—had made himself at home. From his briefcase, open on the glass-topped coffee table in the waiting area, folders and papers unfurled, and a takeout coffee cup sat on the glass in a crusting ring of light brown goo. "Hi, Bob," said Naomi, with a sinking heart.

"Oh. Hi," he said. He looked for a moment at a loss, as if he had forgotten her name, and couldn't quite recall what she was doing here in the president's office.

"I think I told Dean Martell three thirty?"

"Oh?" He shot a look over her head, at the wall clock. Ten past three.

"Just let me make a quick call," she lied, noting that she was not required to make a power play here, only that there was something about Bob Stacek that made her want to do just that. He did not like her. He had never liked her in a personal way. For the past five years, however, he had also not liked her in a professional way.

Was it because Bob Stacek, Webster's dean of students for nearly eighteen years, understood that Radclyffe Hall, the disturbance he hadn't wanted to handle himself, had led directly to Naomi Roth's presidency? Did he imagine that a similar transformation might have come to him if he'd dealt with the matter of Neil Jones-Givens himself? Naomi did not know and could not bring herself to care. She went into her office and closed the door, and spent the next few minutes answering the email of a sophomore's mother who had taken issue with her son's midterm grade in an introductory government course, the professor's teaching style, the course's reading list, and the entire department's scholarly emphasis on what she called "left-wing socialisms." It was not an entirely unpleasant way to spend a quarter of an hour.

She heard Mrs. Bradford return. She could just make out the disapproval in her assistant's voice, undoubtedly at the sight of that coffee cup on the tabletop. And then, a moment later, the genial greeting of John Martell, the dean of residential life. Naomi sat for a moment, listening to the murmur of their conversation through the thick door, delaying the getting up, the opening, the falsely hearty tone of her own welcome. It shouldn't be an adversarial meeting. There was no reason for it to be an adversarial meeting. She wasn't sure why she was dreading it this much.

"Hiya, John," she said when she finally made her move. "Bob? You want to come in?"

Bob Stacek started to gather up his papers. Even in this he had an air of being put upon, as if someone had encouraged him to spread out in her waiting area, to make himself at home. She offered them tea but both declined, and she decided not to ask Mrs. Bradford for any, herself. Then she closed the office door again and went back around the desk to face them in their Webster College chairs.

"I take it you two spoke on Monday, so I'm hoping you can bring me up to speed. What is going on out there? It looks bigger every time I walk across the Quad."

"It looks bigger because it *is* bigger," said Stacek, as if she were a preschooler.

"Also it got down to the twenties over the weekend," said Dean Martell. He was a big man with a gut that overhung his brown tweed pants. He had been the dean of residential life since the previous year, having taken a leave from the art history faculty, probably because he'd thought the position wouldn't be terribly time-consuming and he could do some work of his own. (Not an unreasonable assumption. After all, once you sorted out the annual strife surrounding the housing lottery, what could happen? Mechanical issues went to Buildings and Grounds; disciplinary issues went to the dean of students. And there was hardly going to be another Radclyffe Hall scenario.) But somehow the protest at the Stump had crossed a borderline the moment the students had unfurled their sleeping bags and driven their stakes into the well-tended grass of the Quad. Now this was a housing issue, according to the dean of students. Naomi did not know that she agreed with him, but she had no problem roping in Martell. She appreciated having another body in the room. It took a bit of the sting out of Stacek, having him there.

"I saw a lot of down sleeping bags," he was saying. "But, you know, those can be very warm."

They certainly can, Naomi thought.

"I wonder how many of them are going to class and keeping up with their work," Stacek said.

"Well, but...what's it about?" she asked, with impatience. There'd been a shantytown once, on the Quad, years earlier, when the trustees were talking about divesting from South Africa. She'd brought Hannah, then seven or eight, to the Quad, to hear the speeches one day, and naturally she had signed the petition for divestiture. But Webster had been out of South Africa for years. The college burned clean fuel and recycled every substance known to man, and Webster Food Services had even weeded out factory-farmed animals and genetically modified produce. What was getting them sufficiently worked up to forswear their beds and showers and sleep out?

"You don't know?" said Bob Stacek shortly.

"I do not."

"Well," said Dean Stacek with rich disapproval, "I'm shocked that you don't know this already, but the issue is apparently Nicholas Gall's tenure decision."

Naomi felt the impact of this work its way through her.

"A tenure decision?" said Dean Martell. "You mean that he got tenure?"

Stacek turned his attention from Naomi to the man seated beside him. "That he didn't," he said. He was making a meal of this.

"But...how'd they find out about a negative tenure decision?"

This was an excellent question, Naomi thought. Tenure decisions, after all, were not made public, so Gall must have said something himself. But why? Who'd want to call attention to the worst news an academic could receive? She herself had been terrified of being denied tenure when her number had come up twelve years earlier: Where could she go with that cloud over her head and a small daughter in tow? The life of a professor cast adrift from the tenure track was a vista of adjunct positions, itinerancy, and bitterness. Or it would have been, she knew, for her. But maybe this Nicholas Gall had a different way of looking at such a catastrophic event, or maybe he was close to his students in a way that Naomi, who loved teaching, never had been. She couldn't imagine sharing any kind of personal information, let alone a setback of that dimension, around a seminar table or, worse, with a lecture hall full of Webster undergraduates—that just wasn't in her DNA as a professor. But Nicholas Gall was popular with the students. Very popular. She remembered that from the file.

"So you've been out to speak with them?" Martell was asking Dean Stacek, but this time Stacek was the one to demur.

"It wasn't necessary. Two of them came in to see me. A girl named Chava Friedberg and a boy. She wanted me to know that this group considers the denial of tenure to a professor of color to be an outrage. Her group represents Webster's conscience, she was kind enough to let me know."

"*Terrific,*" Naomi said, though she hated to agree with him.

"Because we've apparently become estranged from our dearest principles. And it's a betrayal of everything we stand for, et cetera, et cetera. And I almost said, *You know he's a plagiarist, right?*"

"Wait," Martell said, glaring at him, "you didn't say that really."

"I'm not an idiot," Stacek snapped. "I'd rather not be the reason Gall sues us for violating the privacy of his tenure proceedings."

Naomi exhaled. There was that, at least.

"Anyway, according to Chava Friedberg, Nicholas Gall's tenure decision indicates that the very soul of Webster has become tainted, and we've lost our activist roots and other general nonsense. Apparently the college pays lip service to difficult ideas like diversity and engagement, but we're not really diverse because there's so much wealth in the student body, no matter what the ethnicity is, and we're not really engaging because fewer and fewer of the students are going abroad, and the ones who are going are avoiding the hard places. They're going to Florence, in other words," Dean Stacek said pointedly, naming the annual art history program Dean Martell had established and for which he frequently served as the on-site faculty member.

"Florence is the best place on earth to study art history," Martell said defensively. "Always has been, always will be."

"But we canceled Kenya, and Vietnam. This was mentioned."

"Vietnam, three people signed up for the last two years we offered it," Naomi jumped in. "And Kenya, two years ago a girl came home with malaria. I had her father threatening to sue us. And after the bombing at the stadium in Nairobi, everyone pulled their kids out for the following year. Look, nobody would love it more than myself if we had a thriving study abroad program. It doesn't seem to be what our students want right now."

Dean Stacek put up his hands. "Hey, this is what she told me. Don't shoot the messenger."

"I'm not shooting anyone," Naomi said irritably. "And I'm not upset that there's a protest in the Quad. I like to hear dissent and I really like debate. And this Chava Friedberg most likely has a warm sleeping bag, so if she wants to sleep out under the beautiful Massachusetts stars, she can go right ahead. And if she doesn't, she knows the way to her dorm, just like the rest of them do."

"We should clear the site," Stacek said. "If they don't want to live in their dorms and go to class they can withdraw for the term. That's what I think."

Great idea, thought Naomi sourly. *Worked out so well at People's Park, too.*

"I don't think it'll come to that," she said with care. "I'll try to get out there and talk to them. Chava, right? Was that her name? The leader?"

"Yes. Chava." said Stacek. "But the leader, I'm not sure. I mean, she did the talking, but if I had to guess I'd say the other one. The boy. I didn't get his name, exactly—*Ali, Muhammed.* Maybe *Hassan?* Something of that ilk," he said with obvious distaste. She winced. Stacek was such an embarrassment, really. "But he mentioned he was Palestinian. He definitely told me that."

Naomi, who hadn't known that Webster had any current students from Palestine, took a brief moment to feel some pride at this news. And the fact that a Palestinian student and a student named Chava Friedberg could be united in a peaceful action at one of the country's oldest colleges, in protest of its theoretical loss of purpose, made her quite happy. Webster College. You just had to love it.

"The arrogance," Stacek fumed. "The two of them, in my office, deigning to let me know why they've been forced to object to one of the most liberal college environments in history. They seem to think they've invented student activism."

They have, Naomi wanted to say. Because it had to be invented every time. That was the point of it. That was why it meant something.

"I'll go talk to them," she said. She said it as if this tiny outreach was all that was required, all the protesters had been waiting for, after which the crowd of them would congratulate themselves at having been heard, because that was what it had always been about: being listened to, being heard. The two men looked relieved. Perhaps they believed this, too. Perhaps she even believed it herself.

After they'd left, she got up and went to the window and looked out over the Billings Lawn. The light was failing already and the sky had that rosy glow she loved, and it reminded her that her chosen home was not merely a place she had ended up due to the roulette of academic openings but a place she actually found lovely. Webster, the place, which was gifted with pine and birch, her favorite trees, and wondrously polychromatic in fall, and lush in summer, and grueling but glorious in winter and just about tolerable in the mud season sometimes referred to as spring, was home now. It had welcomed her in a way that Goddard, New Hampshire, her VISTA posting and place of residence for more than a decade, and which was also a beautiful New England town, emphatically had not. And now, looking down on the student encampment around the Stump, trying pointlessly to locate her daughter underneath the bivouac of tarp and plastic sheeting, she couldn't help indulging in a tiny bit of nostalgia. She'd been just like that in college, willing to sacrifice time and personal comfort for a principle that was more important than her student self, privileged and entitled as she was. These young people had stepped away from their own lives and needs in order to align themselves with a principle, and that was a beautiful thing. It was. Even if, in this particular case, it was so totally and pathetically misplaced.

PART II

—∞∞∞—

DISSEMBLE

CHAPTER SIX

HE LOST A FEW YEARS

A few days later, news that a small delegation from Yale had joined the regulars at the Stump reached Dean Stacek, who seemed to take great pleasure in passing this nugget upstairs to Naomi's office. Mrs. Bradford presented his communiqué toward the end of the day, along with the message (actually, messages) from a *Boston Globe* reporter who wanted a comment on "the unrest at Webster" for a report she was preparing, but Naomi was already on the phone getting an earful from the father of Chava Friedberg. He'd begun phoning almost daily from San Francisco, threatening and irate, wanting to know why nothing was being done about his daughter and the others, "sleeping rough" in the mud. (There was significant mud, it was true; November had been mild, and rainy.) It was now more than two months into the "action" and no one from the protest seemed interested in actually communicating with her. Hannah, too, no longer seemed to be interested in communicating with her. Hannah had canceled their Sunday night dinner, first once, then again.

And this, to be brutally honest, was what finally got her out there, despite her selfless offer to Deans Martell and Stacek.

Naomi went to the Stump on the second Sunday night,

breaking—at a single blow—every one of their agreed-upon bar-
riers, looking for her daughter, whom she did not find. What she
did find were twenty or so kids around a battery-powered heater,
a couple drinking beers, others blowing on cups of coffee. They
all looked relatively clean, at least from the boots up. (From the
boots down they were uniformly filthy.) They were huddling—
perhaps for warmth, perhaps for the reasons young people have
always huddled—some with blankets thrown over their shoulders, some with sleeping bags unfurled around them, but it
was all highly civilized. She heard murmuring and soft laughter.
There was a spirit of accord. It might have been a tailgate party
that continued on after the big game, winding down to a camp-
fire, everyone reluctant to go home.

"Hello," said Naomi.

No one appeared overly surprised.

"Oh, hi," said a girl with a knotted red scarf. Naomi squinted
but did not recognize her. "It's President Roth," she announced,
not without a detectable edge of sarcasm.

"Hi, President Roth," said a boy who shared the red-scarf-girl's
unzipped sleeping bag. Naomi squinted at that, too. Was that
Naomi's own unzipped sleeping bag? It certainly looked like it.

"Oh. Yeah," someone else said. "I thought I recognized you."

Naomi had her winter hat on. It had flaps down the sides. But
she hadn't been trying to hide.

A few others looked up with interest.

"Everyone warm enough?" Naomi asked, helplessly maternal.

"We're okay," said the girl who'd recognized her. "The last
couple of nights have been the worst, but we're sticking close
together."

Naomi nodded, even as her internal alarm began to rise. "Anyone seen Hannah? Hannah Roth?"

No one spoke right away, but then the boy in the sleeping bag
said, "She had a paper, I think. She went back to her room to

work on it." He had a slight accent. Very slight, very not obvious as to its origin, but definitely there. He was wearing a brown hoodie, heavy dark boots, no coat at all. He'd have to be freezing, sleeping bag or no. Why didn't he have a coat? He was skinny, too. "She might stay over there, she said," said the boy. "Of course, this is fine."

Well, thank you, Naomi thought. *And you are?*

"Hi, Professor Roth!" said a girl. "It's Elise?"

Elise. Basketball player from somewhere in the South. Georgia? She had been in Naomi's freshman seminar last spring. Naomi still taught one freshman seminar a year, usually some variation on second-wave feminism. Last year it had been mainly Friedan and de Beauvoir. "Hey, Elise. C'mere."

And Elise came and was hugged. She smelled . . . not bad, but just a tiny bit *sharp*.

"How long have you been camping out?" she asked Elise.

"Um . . . ? Couple weeks? I'm going to classes, though."

Naomi frowned at this. *I should hope so*, she wanted to say. But didn't.

"What about food?"

"Thatcher," the girl beside the boy in (probably) Naomi's sleeping bag said, meaning the dining hall, with a shrug. It was close enough to the Billings Lawn that students often took their food outside to eat on the grass. Though not in November.

"Sometimes people bring us pizzas," Elise added.

"Sometimes we get pizzas delivered!" someone said, and there were a few sputters of laughter.

Naomi, at this, reached some kind of internal barrier. Yes, there was camaraderie in foxholes. Yes, there was humor (usually black) on the barricades, but only in proportion to the deadly serious matter at hand. Civil rights. Free speech. Women's liberation. Vietnam. Reproductive rights. Gay liberation. Animal rights. Let the refuseniks go. Euthanasia. Gun control. And this was supposedly about one guy not getting tenure? What was going on here?

"What is going on here?" she heard herself say, but so softly that almost immediately she said it again, and louder, to hear it more clearly. "Can someone explain to me what is going on here?"

"This is a peaceful protest," said a girl in a Sojourner Truth House sweatshirt.

"I don't doubt it," Naomi said tersely. "And I commend you for that. And I respect your right to protest, believe me. But what I don't understand is, why haven't you come in to talk to me?"

No one, immediately, spoke. And then, there was something: not so much a noise as a sudden vacuum of noise, and all of the non-noise came from one place, or, more accurately, one person, and that one person was the boy, of course, who was so slight that she had not yet really managed to have any sense of him at all. Light? Dark? Not just on the short side but, actually, almost...well, *stunted* was the word that came to her. He was stunted, and yet the power that came from him, that thing that made her look at him and not anyone else, though the others were, almost uniformly, taller and broader, more physically imposing in every way that someone can be. She took an involuntary step in his direction and asked his name.

"My name is Omar," he said. He didn't hold out his hand. He was holding the sleeping bag at his shoulder and had his other arm around the girl, with the sleeping bag draped over them both. The girl was a foot taller than he was, and had a mass of rippled hair. Hair like Naomi's hair—the sort of hair she had always thought of as "Ashkenazi deluxe." It was a private joke with herself; who else would find it amusing?

"I'm Chava," she said.

"Hello," Naomi said, registering the daughter of her highly displeased caller from San Francisco. But she didn't take her eyes off the boy. Omar. "I take it that's my sleeping bag," she said, feeling instantly ashamed, though she hadn't meant it unkindly. She'd been glad to lend it. She'd have lent it to any of them, let alone a friend of Hannah's.

"It is. And thank you," he said. "I don't have a sleeping bag."

She could not even see his face, really. The brown hoodie he wore came down over his forehead. Dark hair over his cheeks. Very dark eyebrows. Not African-American, she was sure. But not Caucasian either.

"Where are you from?" she asked him, without even thinking. She felt like the two of them were weirdly alone amid all these extraneous bodies, like that dance at the gym scene from *West Side Story*, where the edges are blurred and the only a shaft of clarity links the characters, Tony and Maria. But that was love. This was something else.

"It would depend," said Omar, "on how far back you wanted to go."

Then a small group was walking across the Quad, laughing loudly together, bundled into their down jackets. They were indeed carrying a couple of pizza boxes from Jerry's on Webster Street. Somebody said, "Oh yeah."

"I got one veggie, one pepperoni," a girl said, opening the top box and sending it around. The smell hit Naomi (whose own dinner plans, after all, had been canceled) with a stab of hunger. It was all she could do not to grab a steaming slice as it passed by. It was deeply cold now, and they were all standing close to one another. They seemed to have entirely forgotten that she was there, or perhaps it was more accurate to say that her being there hadn't made much of an impact in the first place. For the first time since the first protester had unrolled the first sleeping bag on this ground—this, well, not hallowed, maybe, but this *important, symbolic, meaningful* (at least, to many) Webster ground—she was furious at them. And they had gotten her own daughter caught up in this, whatever this was. And Hannah had better things to do. Naomi caught herself. They all. They all had better things to do than this. Whatever this was.

The conversations were muffled by pizza and the cold. She made out only snatches: *Why not?... Sorbonne... I said to him, I said... just devastated by that.*

"You know who he is, right?" a voice said, very close to her. It was Elise, her former student.

"Who is?"

She nodded in his direction. Already Naomi knew whom she meant.

"Actually, no. I assume he's a Webster student." (*He'd better at least be that*, she thought.)

"He's a sophomore, but he's a few years older. He lost a few years."

Naomi braced herself. Webster students usually came straight from high school. Sometimes, increasingly of late, they took gap years, but seldom more than one. When a Webster student "lost a few years" that usually meant hospitalization. And hospitalization usually meant depression. But sometimes it meant other things—worse things. Worse than depression? Cancer. Psychosis. *Oh crap*, she thought, remembering the father who called every day. Please do not, not, let it be psychosis. She took a breath. "Oh? How so?"

But Elise shook her head. "Not for me to tell you. It's his story. If he wants to be public about his life, he'll do it. He always says this isn't about him. It's about what happened to Professor Gall. And Webster, of course."

"What happened to Professor Gall?" Naomi said, entirely aware of the irritation in her voice. *You mean the part about how he committed plagiarism, or the part about how he was caught?* But that was off-limits. The whole process was cloaked in privacy, padlocked by institutional secrecy. She couldn't tell them, even if she wanted to. She was pretty sure she didn't want to. "You know," she said instead, "if there is an issue to be discussed, let's discuss it."

But Elise looked away—evasive, certainly, but not, somehow, in a hostile or even particularly self-conscious way. It was as if she simply had run out of things to say.

"Look!" Naomi thundered. She felt as surprised to hear herself as everyone else clearly was, but they all stopped talking. "I would like to be of help to you. I would like to hear what you have to say, but you need to start talking to us, and by us I mean the college administration." She made a point of looking at all of them, taking her time to turn her head so that everyone had her dedicated gaze, albeit briefly, but really she was speaking to this one, this Omar. He had said nothing to imply it, but it was his response that mattered, and they all listened for it. Naomi willed herself to sound rational, but her thoughts were reeling. "I happen to believe in peaceful protest. I happen to have taken part in many peaceful protests." (And a few that tipped into the less-than-peaceful, she thought, before pressing on.) "But in every single instance we made sure that our message was well defined and clearly articulated. That is not so much to ask of you, and I don't think it's fair of you to expect the college to tolerate your continued occupation of this communal space if you aren't prepared to engage in dialogue."

No one responded. She made herself wait. She let him know she was waiting for him, and he looked back at her from inside the brown hoodie—so small, and so powerful. Finally, she had to give in.

"I understand that you may be disappointed by a tenure decision. Tenure, as I'm sure you know, is a very complex process, with many factors. It's also a process that protects the privacy of the applicant. I'm sure you can understand that."

They did not appear to understand that at all.

"But obviously I would like you to be able to express your opinions and your feelings about this, or any other issues that are troubling you. So you are all, cordially, invited to my office tomorrow afternoon. I am clearing my schedule. I am holding office hours for *this group*, though you can come individually if you prefer. My only interest is in learning more about your concerns and your intentions. We share this community, and I'm sure we all want the best for it. If there are problems to be identified, issues to be discussed, changes to be made ... *whatever*. It won't happen if you won't ..." *Talk*, she wanted to say. *Open your fucking mouths* with their years of orthodontia and use those expensively educated voices to articulate your pathetic complaints about this ... this halcyon, evolved, rarified, creative, and intellectual college campus, where you are free to learn and nap and make things and have sex and get high and change your fucking gender even, and clean water comes out of the tap and you wave your school ID under a scanner to help yourself to smorgasbords of food (meat! meat alternative! vegan! lactose-sensitive! nut-free! gluten-free!) and all we expect of you is that you pass your classes and don't hurt anyone else. But she didn't say these things. Of course she didn't say them.

"Please," Naomi said. "I'd like to hear from you."

And she left them all, in the unnecessary cold, and went home.

CHAPTER SEVEN

PSEUD'S CORNER OFFICE

Omar Khayal, his name was. This was not difficult to discover. There were only three Omars in the system, and the other two were a professor of poetry whom Naomi knew slightly and an assistant swim coach, six-foot-two and bald as a stone. Omar Khayal was a sophomore with a room in one of the newer dorms, the tall, graceless, and frankly Soviet-style Eagle Road buildings, generally the default selection of students with bad lottery numbers. His hometown was listed as Arkoma, Oklahoma, a place Naomi had never heard of. When she looked it up, she found that it straddled a state line with a place called Fort Smith, Arkansas, which she had likewise never heard of. There was no listed high school, which was unusual but not unique. Webster, with its penchant for quirky and self-driven students, had looked favorably upon the homeschooled for years, often taking kids who were well beyond their conventionally educated peers in subjects that interested them. And these kids, in turn, loved Webster.

Omar Khayal. She sat for a long moment trying to figure out why the name sounded so familiar, and when she could not she Googled it, and when her computer auto-corrected to Omar

Khayyam she understood. Of course. How much of the strange thing he emitted came from that—the little chiming charge from a name that wasn't even his? *The prophet.* The way they looked at him. The way *she'd* looked at him.

The father from San Francisco called again the next morning, and when Naomi spoke to him (listened to him) she received the apparently calamitous news that Chava had gotten a C on her last paper in European history, this girl who had never received anything below an A *in her entire life*. And that Chava's roommate had been calling Chava's father to say that Chava had not been in the room for more than a week, not even to use the shower or wash her clothes, let alone to sleep in her own bed. Also that Chava had an organic chemistry exam in a few days that she had not begun to prepare for.

"I saw Chava last night," Naomi said as soon as he paused for breath. "She seems really okay. Of course it's concerning that her schoolwork is taking a hit, but you know, it's the kids who never stop driving themselves academically that we really worry about, in a way. She's having a different kind of educational experience right now. But it's temporary, I'm sure."

"How can you possibly be sure of that?" the man asked. He sounded irate.

Because I'm a mother, she almost said, but that wasn't it. The fact was, she had no business thinking anything at all about Chava, whom she'd only met once, in the dark. And it was actually quite possible that there was a great deal that was wrong, not just with Chava but with all of them.

"Do you even know why they're doing this?"

"A popular professor has been turned down for tenure," she informed him, as if she herself had been in constructive negotiation with them for some time.

"That's it?" he asked, the outrage bounding down the line. "A professor?"

"Apparently. But it's often the case that general or individual discontents can coalesce around an issue like this. The bottom line is that they're upset. They're coming in later today, to talk to me," she said.

"In other words," he said darkly, "these kids have got you over their collective knee."

She declined, to the best of her ability, this distasteful image.

"We are opening a dialogue," she told him, trying to keep her cool. "Dialogue is the foundation of everything. Figuring out what you think, learning to articulate that and learning to listen." *It's what we in the business call "education."* She didn't say that aloud.

When he finally let her go, she sat back in her chair. She was exhausted. She had not slept much the night before, and what little sleep she'd managed had been broken. Hannah, after a cruel hour or two, had returned a text at one in the morning with a terse *Mom. I am fine.*

Was she? *I wouldn't know,* Naomi thought. Hannah might have been, at this moment, a sophomore on the opposite side of the country from her concerned parent, but instead she was only a short hop down Fairweather Road to Radclyffe Hall—what was the difference? *I caught him with an unseen hook and an invisible line which is long enough to let him wander to the ends of the world and still to bring him back with a twitch upon the thread.* Evelyn Waugh had written that about Catholicism, but it was just as true for parenthood, wasn't it? More true, thought Naomi, who had no authority in asserting this, even to herself, given that she had never believed in a Catholic god nor any other kind of god. Had Evelyn Waugh been a father when he wrote that? She had no idea.

This Nicholas Gall—she'd had to catch up, and quickly. What she'd known of him came only from the tenure file with its light-weight CV, and the general scuttlebutt that his classes were always oversubscribed. The previous evening she'd emailed the acting chair of anthropology, and he'd come in first thing that morning to fill in the gaps: Francis Kinikini, an ex-Mormon of Tongan descent who'd once played football for Brigham Young and whose own fieldwork had been done, not surprisingly, in Polynesia. He was filling in for the long-term chair, whose sabbatical year in Burkina Faso could not have come at a less convenient moment, and he sat Naomi's office Hitchcock chair looking supremely uncomfortable, as if he feared that any question he might be asked was a question he didn't quite have the authority to answer. But Kinikini had been around for most of Nicholas Gall's Webster career, and while it was true that he hadn't specifically been paying attention to his popular colleague, he'd seen enough.

Nicholas Gall had arrived at the college as an adjunct, one of three teachers imported at the last minute when a tenured professor decamped to Yale and, almost simultaneously, two faculty members failed to return from fieldwork sabbaticals—one because he insisted on remaining in Yemen for an additional six-month period and the other because he had dropped dead on the island of Lesbos. Gall had been teaching at a community college in Georgia that offered anthropology courses through its social sciences department, and though he'd been there only two years, that had been long enough to win—twice—its student-selected distinguished professor award. Before Georgia he'd been at a four-year school in the Ozarks, teaching the anthropology foundation course for future majors, as well as Ozark history and culture. There, again, Gall had received a number of student-generated accolades, including the distinguished teacher award, three times in a row. Before the Ozarks, Naomi was stunned to discover, Gall had spent a decade on his doctoral thesis at UMass, Amherst, meaning that he had almost certainly been there while she was working on her own degree. He had been a

UMass undergrad before that. He had actually grown up down the road in Springfield.

A hometown boy. A prodigal son, returning.

Well, *prodigal*. Not so much. After all, when you looked at Gall's journey in chronological order it looked like a success story; obviously, he had not had a privileged start, but he had still earned a doctorate and was teaching college, with a few very pleasant laurel wreaths to boot—not so shabby. It was only if you considered Gall's story in reverse that it all began to sour, beginning with the worst of academic crimes and reaching back through two employers who'd declined to hold on to him, despite the fact that he was popular with students. Something had gone wrong here, but what?

"Life can only be understood backwards, but it must be lived forwards." Kierkegaard said that, and Naomi had always admired the eerie perfection of this simple insight. Considered in reverse, from her presidential office in Billings, her own life certainly seemed as if it must have been intentional. Her rise at Webster, and before that the later-in-life return to academia, and before that the in-the-trenches experience of grassroots organizing in Goddard, New Hampshire, and before that her pure, youthful political activism...when you looked at everything from that perspective, where else could she have ended up but here, in the corner office on the third floor of Billings?

But while it was happening, while every single step of that was happening—from the early activism to the decade-long detour of "volunteer" work in a town that truly did not comprehend why she'd come, to the husband she'd stopped loving but had stuck to long enough for him to leave her, to the unexpected child who'd become the most important presence in her universe—nothing had actually *felt* intentional. Nothing had even felt *rational*. The truth was that it had all been one extended stumble, a meander during which she had trailed a few ethnic identities and picked up a few political notions: no narrative, and certainly no plan, she thought, only half-listening to Kinikini elaborate upon Nicholas Gall's more recent misdemeanors. But *I myself am a fraud and a dissembler*, it suddenly came to her.

She had done some things in her life that even she had to categorize as successful, but they had never quite registered as accomplishments while they were actually happening. Moving to back-of-beyond New Hampshire as an irredeemable (Jewish, feminist) outsider and starting a little company that somehow earned national (pre-internet) attention and supported a dozen women? Accomplishment. Getting a PhD and a tenured position at Webster? Accomplishment. Singlehandedly raising the extraordinary Hannah Rosalind Roth to near-adulthood? Massive accomplishment.

And yet she had never quite believed she could accomplish *this*.

She remembered surreal approbation of her Webster inauguration, held a few weeks into a glorious fall term; the students had made a cheering corridor across the quad from Webster Hall to the athletic arena (it was threatening rain), and that unmistakable sense of a wedding procession was echoed in the academic bridesmaids who preceded her to the ceremony. These were female college presidents from all over the country, most of whom she'd never met or even spoken to. "Welcome to the ultimate sorority" was a phrase used more than once in their congratulatory calls after the college made the announcement. Barnard, Princeton, Brown, Harvard, Dickinson...she would pick up the phone in her poky little office and a clipped little voice would say: *Please hold for President So-and-So.* (Naomi doubted they even knew she was answering her own phone.) She'd wanted to ask them everything, these amazing women, these college presidents, but the whole thing dazzled her out of her senses. "We have to stick together," said the brilliant president of the University of Pennsylvania. Only a few months earlier Naomi had heard this same brilliant president of the University of Pennsylvania speak to a major conference on higher education. *Brilliantly.* For an hour. Without notes. "Seriously, no one else can even imagine the insanity of this job," she said on the phone, as if she and Naomi were actual friends, or had even met. "Do you have kids?"

A daughter. A teenager, Naomi had sputtered.

"Yeah. Like that's not a full-time job in itself. But you know the best way to get something done is to give the job to someone who already has too much to do. That's usually a woman, right?"

"Right." That was true. That was *crazy!* Why had she herself never recognized such a simple truth?

Five of them had even shown up at the inauguration: the astonishing presidents of Swarthmore and Smith and Oberlin and Trinity and Connecticut College. The luminous president of Smith had given a speech just before Naomi's swearing in and had thousands of Webster students, parents, faculty, alumni, and staff laughing, and then getting choked up. Hilarious, powerful. Afterward there'd been a quick hug, and then the luminous president of Smith was gone, back to Northampton in a car driven by her administrative assistant. The only contact she and Naomi had had since then had been a hug before a panel at the annual conference of the American Association of University Women and a gracious, proper exchange of letters the previous year, when the husband of the luminous president of Smith died suddenly of an aneurysm.

The luminous president of Smith was substantial, lovely, calm—even, Naomi supposed, in grief. The astonishing women who had walked her down the aisle to this unexpected bridegroom, this Webster College, any one of them could have stepped in at the last moment, and no one, once they'd fanned themselves and roared in shock, would have sent her away, because these were the very women that women like Naomi had dreamed of seeing in the presidents' offices of colleges and

businesses and governments. These were the exceptional crea-
tures, credits to feminism who would begin the great redress
of all that patriarchy had wrought, forever and everywhere. And
yet, "President Roth"—it was as unreal today as it had been on
that day, the day of her inauguration, and now she began to think
she understood why. President Roth was a pseudonym, and her
office was Pseud's Corner. *Pseud's Corner office*, she thought, not
really amused. *And I am in it. For why?*

Nicholas Gall, Kinikini was saying, for maybe the fourth or
fifth time, was one of the most popular teachers in the department, and had been since he'd come to Webster. If Webster had
a student choice award (*naming opportunity*, the pseudonymous
President Roth automatically thought) Gall would certainly have
won it, judging by his scores on RateMyProfessors.com and the
Webster-specific site some imp had set up for students to vent
anonymously. He had crab-stepped from his initial adjunct status onto the tenure track, in itself a highly unusual—well, all
but unheard of—maneuver. *How had he managed that?* Naomi
wondered aloud, but Kinikini only shrugged and said something
about the department's need for a dedicated folklorist. The man
who'd died in Lesbos had been their only folklorist, and apparently they weren't all that easy to find. Folklorists, often—not
always—were the country cousins of anthropology and sociology
departments, but sometimes they came out of English, sociology, linguistics, religious studies, music, and ethnic studies, and
hiring one was not as straightforward as interviewing a dozen
candidates at the MLA or the AHA, and picking your favorite.
But here one was, on the spot as it were, popular with the students and working hard on his first book, an adaptation of his
doctoral thesis on "The Mountain Whippoorwill."

Professor Kinikini himself had arrived at Webster shortly after
these events, and found his new colleague, Nicholas Gall, already in situ, an avoidant guy with oversubscribed classes and

not much to say in those few department meetings he attended. In the years since then, various administrative positions had rotated through the department, but Gall declined to act beyond his compulsory responsibilities. He didn't offer himself for any committee work, either specific to his department or for the college as a whole. He didn't attend any department social events, not even the locally famous Christmas party of his anthropology colleague Michel Louviere, who prepared a mind-blowing gumbo from a closely guarded family recipe each year. But shirking work and avoiding social contact—while hardly strategic in terms of achieving tenure—were not criminal, and they were not particularly unusual. If Gall chose to isolate himself from his colleagues and concentrate, instead, on his own scholarly work and the challenges of being an inspirational teacher to his students, then this was not to be vilified. Webster's reputation as an academic center, its attractiveness to the nation's best students, and its own institutional pride—all were built upon these very things.

But. Nicholas Gall did not seem to be concentrating on his scholarly work. He made no evident headway on a publishable version of his doctoral thesis (which was what he had told Professor Kinikini and Kinikini's predecessor he was doing), and he seemed not to have begun another project. He declined an opportunity to write a chapter for a textbook another anthropology professor was editing, though this would have netted him an easy publication credit and required no extraordinary effort (the chapter was to cover basic fieldwork principles and techniques, which any anthropologist could easily discuss). He attended no conferences and gave no lectures at other colleges. Each autumn he requested, and received, department funding to travel to Georgia, where he spent the winter break in the mountains near Rabun Gap. Each June he added to his dossier of professional credits: nothing.

And as for being a superior, inspirational teacher to his

students…well, those websites could be somewhat problematic. Looking beyond the numerical ratings to the actual commentary unveiled a theme that went something like this:

"Professor Gall is a smooth dude. I totes played World of Warcraft all semester and I still passed the final."

"I don't know why, but I got an A in his course."

"Need a mid-morning place to snooze? Check email? Gall's your guy."

In brief: Nicholas Gall graded high and his classes demanded little. Very high and very little. Doorways and Crossroads (Anthro 113) and Loki, Coyote, and Br'er Rabbit (Anthro 115) had been like secret performance drugs passed between Webster students for the past eight years. No wonder he was a popular guy.

At a formal review the previous year, Gall had been told that a tenure offer was unlikely, and unless he had publications the department wasn't aware of, or were shortly forthcoming, he ought to be thinking about his next move. Webster's academic protocols called for a final year of teaching once tenure had been formally denied, and this was a courtesy to allow teachers an opportunity to plan, but in fact very few took up the offer. Typically, given a year's warning, those who knew which way the wind was blowing were already making arrangements to leave.

Gall wanted to stay at Webster, that much was clear. Since his warning he had moved quickly to publish an academic monograph, adapted from a portion of his UMass thesis, with a private press located in the North Georgia mountains. A copy of this slender book, which had a plain green cover with only the title *"The Mountain Whippoorwill" and Lowe Stokes* and the author's name, Nicholas Gall, in white letters, was not much more substantial than a pamphlet. It had been allocated its own official folder from which Kinikini extracted it now and he handed it over, apparently assuming that Naomi would want to examine such a critical piece of evidence herself. "The Mountain Whippoorwill" was a poem Naomi had never heard of, and Lowe Stokes was a fiddler she had likewise never heard of (honestly, what fiddlers had she heard of?) who had won some fiddle contest in Tennessee, had his hand blown off, and played for the rest of his long life with a metal contraption attached to his forearm. Sitting in her high-backed leather chair, in her corner office and reading the century-old poem as the afternoon began to choke all the light out of the room, she felt increasingly disoriented. Kinikini sat on the other side of the broad desk, waiting as she read, and she let him wait, and she let it take her far from where they were both sitting:

> Hell's broke loose,
> Fire on the mountains—snakes in the grass.
> Satan's here a-bilin'—oh, Lordy, let him pass!

She had never read much poetry. She really had no idea what to think about it.

Folklore might have been an archipelagic discipline, but it wasn't vast. Folklorists read widely in the field, even beyond their own specific areas of interest. Still, it wasn't a folklorist who first realized what Nicholas Gall had done.

The monograph, *"The Mountain Whippoorwill" and Lowe Stokes,* had been tucked away in the very folder Professor Kinikini now held, and that folder had been resting on the granite countertop of his colleague Diana Arditi's kitchen in West Webster. Arditi's teenaged daughter Sabrina had just settled in on one of the bar stools to drink her morning smoothie when she began to amuse herself with the contents of the folder, and by the time her mother got downstairs, ready to drive her to Webster Regional, Sabrina was already shaking her head. "Really?" the girl said, in a caustic tone that—without even knowing what her daughter was talking about—her mother was already taking personally.

"The Mountain Whippoorwill" was obscure, arguably, but its author was a little bit less so, and Sabrina had in fact prepared an oral report for tenth-grade English (Twentieth-Century American Poets) on this very person. She recognized language from the Poetry Foundation website that she had herself cut and pasted into her report, then laboriously rewritten, fulfilling at least the intention of original work. Gall hadn't even done that much.

Plagiarism, plagiarism, Naomi thought, scanning the printout from the website, which Kinikini had brought for her. It was an ugly word, ugly to anyone who'd ever attempted the delicate but gut-wrenching task of setting words onto paper (or its techno-logical equivalents). Words might feel universal, but they were not, because when they were put together they made patterns, and those patterns were as personally composed as any line of music or labored-over pigment on a canvas. The theft of words, however, stalked every university, no matter its prestige, and fighting it felt, at times, like whacking away at the Angel of Death from Cecil B. DeMille's *Ten Commandments*: thick green smoke winding its way down every hallway and into every classroom.

Once, a few years earlier, Francine had told her about some website that sold academic papers and custom-made application essays, and Naomi had spent an hour examining it, clicking around with a sick fascination. There were actual testimonials on the site, praise from its satisfied customers: "Plagiarism is completely off bounds for my professors!" a boy from Memphis, Tennessee, had written. "So whenever I order a paper at EssayHelp.com, I always check the Plagiarism Secure option, so I can be completely sure my essay is not copied from anywhere." A girl in New York City had said: "The most embarrassing thing is to get caught trying to pass off some already published work as yours! I don't want that to happen, so I always check the Plagiarism Secure option. It's worth the extra money to be sure."

Hilarious. Also appalling. Also tragic.

Not to mention epically pervasive. Never had this been more clear to Naomi than in a class she'd once TA'd back at UMass, when she was a doctoral student. The course was a big survey of twentieth-century political activism and social movements, and Naomi's assigned seminar group had had the usual mix of the clever and the dense. Naomi's favorite student was a young woman from Holyoke, Massachusetts, whose family had emigrated from El Salvador a few years earlier. The girl was sweet, serious, hardworking, and genuinely interested in the subject matter—everything one could desire in a student—but her relationship to the English language was not a peaceful one, and while she could communicate well enough aloud, the written assignments she turned in were usually broken and illogical. When the girl submitted her final paper, Naomi knew right away that they were both on thin ice. The paper began with her typical choppy and mangled prose, then suddenly morphed into a beautifully argued overview of patterns in American activism. On and on, with nary a comma out of place for eight delightful and thought-provoking pages, only to conclude, on the ninth page, with another paragraph of tortured sentences, signifying nothing.

What to do about it? Naomi liked her student personally, thought of her as diligent and serious, and knew perfectly well that she was the first person in her newly American family to attain the heights of a college education. The dilemma kept her up for a few nights (well, two-year-old-Hannah was also keeping her up, so that wasn't much of a stretch), and then, all at once, she arrived at a perfect solution.

At the next class meeting she announced that a serious matter had come up. A person in the seminar group had plagiarized his or her paper, she informed them. This person would not be named, but if he or she phoned Naomi at home that evening to discuss the matter, Naomi promised that they would not fail the course or be reported to the disciplinary committee. The student would, naturally, be required to submit a new paper, and could expect a lower grade, but that was of course far preferable to failing the class and facing the serious penalties of plagiarism.

That evening, as she was feeding Hannah, the calls began, and by the time she had put her daughter down for the night, fully half of the class had checked in. Every time she picked up the phone, Naomi had had to suppress her shock and pretend that the caller was the very student of whom she'd spoken. The tenth and final call was from the plagiarist. The original plagiarist.

That was bad. But it was also, in a way, understandable. College students were young (almost always). They were dumb (often). They were figuring things out (one hoped). If a person were going to make a mistake in life, and making a mistake could be a powerfully formative experience, then making it as a college student would be the best of all possible times for that to happen. For Mr. Gall, on the other hand, the window on forgivable plagiarism, to the extent that it had ever been open, was now long closed.

Things had moved quietly but quickly after the alarm raised by Diana Arditi. The committee was summoned to a special meeting and the matter was revealed, discussed, and made official. Within days a formal charge of plagiarism was levied against Professor Nicholas Gall and Gall was invited to respond, as was only fair. He did not. He simply continued to teach his course, even as the wheels of his fate made their inevitable rotations. Perhaps he was simply lazy. Perhaps he had his head in the sand. Perhaps he was panic-stricken, and understandably so. It occurred to Naomi now, for the first time, that perhaps he simply handed over the matter, in its entirety, to his students—inadvertently, in a moment of weakness? or willfully, venally?—deputizing them to rail against the system. However it happened, whatever the order of events, there were tent poles in the Billings Lawn only days after Gall held the official tenure ruling in his hand.

Still, as soon as Kinikini had wrapped up his sorry account and taken the file and the monograph away, she started picking the story apart. Academia, like any other world, was full of the lazy and uninspired, but most confined these tendencies to the post-tenure portion of the run, when they could settle in for a nice long stretch of lowest common denominator teaching and research. Gall, who'd never had trouble filling his courses, and who was still the only dedicated folklorist in the anthropology department, looked very much like a faculty member the department might like to hold on to, however lukewarm he was about participating socially or bureaucratically. The only thing standing between him and that attractive life was publication, and Gall had a completed doctoral thesis that was fully adaptable and ready to go out to publishers. He had elected not to pursue this obvious avenue, but why? Writer's block? Depression? Had his interests wandered into some other area, and he couldn't bring himself to start over? Or perhaps the thesis itself was problematic in its academic integrity. It might have gotten past the auditors of his own graduate program, but academic publishers typically sent books under consideration to independent reviewers in their field. It had to have been either laziness or deceit—two roads in a yellow wood: both well traveled, both utterly unacceptable. And a person like that? Well, the sooner Webster got shot of him, the better.

The irony was that, apart from Gall, Webster's current tenure class was actually phenomenal: the brilliant young mathematician, two historians with major books already published, the biologist on the verge of greatness, a film studies professor who wrote frequently for *Rolling Stone* and *Esquire*, and a poet whose second collection had won a Pulitzer. They were superstars any great university would be thrilled to employ, but they had chosen to make their academic homes at Webster. And there were half a dozen other newly tenured faculty members who might not be destined for the cover of the *Webster Alumni Monthly* but were still solid scholars who'd done the work and, more important, followed the rules. Each of these men and women had earned their tenure confirmations, and the security and respect that went with them. And unless Naomi found a way of bringing this Nicholas Gall problem to some reasonable conclusion, every one of their positive tenure rulings would be, in some way, devalued.

They had certainly grown spoiled, these last years, when it came to getting, and keeping, the people they wanted. It hadn't always been like this. In the bad old days, for two hundred years at least, Webster College had orbited what would become the Ivies, taking those students who might or might not make it through, academically speaking (which was saying something, as the Ivies themselves were concurrently admitting large contingencies of the less than intellectually distinguished). The graduates of Webster might not have been the brightest lights in their high school classes, but they ascended—en masse, so it seemed—to long and lucrative post-college careers, usually in business. And they were very loyal to Webster, especially when, in due course, they sent their sons to the school to have the same great time they'd had themselves: drinking in the sticky basements of their fraternity houses, cramming for finals, road tripping to Smith and Holyoke, cheering the tough little football team with their war-painted faces and yelping their made-up war whoops. That had been good enough for a very long time, but it hadn't been good enough for Oksen Sarafian.

How on earth had Webster managed to find Oksen Sarafian? As in her own case, the college hadn't had to look far. Sarafian was a professor of education, a theorist on childhood learning whose ideas made Rudolf Steiner schools seem Old Etonian by comparison. He'd come to Webster from Harvard, but really he'd come from France, and long before that his family had come from Armenia, and it was hard to say which of those multiple origins made him most difficult for Webster's Old Guard to accept. With his long black hair, European tastes (in fashion and food), and distinctive accent (French flattened by Boston), Sarafian attracted attention from the moment his custom-made loafers first set foot on the Billings Lawn. The students loved him. He held an open house in his home every Sunday night, and Webster undergraduates began gathering, in greater and greater numbers, to talk about everything—what was happening in the wider world, how things were changing. Naturally they also talked about Webster, and how it worked, and how it was broken.

There had never been much of a counterculture at Webster. Partly due to the uniform wealth and social stature of the students and partly because, for most of them, college was an interlude of recreation, interrupted by a few sadly necessary academic obstacles to be negotiated. But Sarafian, somehow, made even the heartiest partier set down his beer for a moment, and consider. *Why not?* There was something about him that seemed to make the earth tremble, just a tiny bit, and that wasn't as bad as it sounded. The tiny frisson of a new idea, well, it had an unnerving effect on people, even people who weren't prone to thinking about much. And one February night, only a few years after Sarafian arrived at Webster, as the trustees gathered for their usual midwinter conclave, a truly stunning percentage of the student body assembled at the Stump and walked calmly to the steps of the Webster Inn, shutting down traffic on Webster Avenue and backing up to cover half the Quad. Their purpose was to politely ask that Oksen Sarafian replace the college's longtime (too longtime) president, Thomas MacDiarmid, class of '28 and protégé, himself, of that product of good German stock, Charles Myer Stone. And because the unstated agenda of that very gathering was to oust MacDiarmid (who showed not the slightest intention of retiring, ever, though he'd been asleep at the wheel for years), the trustees listened. Perhaps *their* earth, too, had trembled. Perhaps they understood that Webster's best future lay in a direction they themselves had not yet considered. Only six months later the new president was speaking from the steps of Billings Hall to a sea of wooden chairs stretching across the Quad, conjuring a Webster of women and minorities, art and scholarship, an intellectual utopia for every student, including— especially—those students the school had turned its back on, centuries before: men and women of Native American descent.

It was the very first moment of the new Webster, the curtain rising on their own present multicultural utopia, with its international stature and crazy competitive admissions profile. And yet, even with his great bravery and ambition, how amazed Sarafian would be today if he could see how far his vision had extended. That same Webster of the fraternity basement and the road trip, that enclave of the white, the male, the Protestant, and the academically complacent . . . now it was a place of rigorous intellectual discourse, profound diversity, thrilling social conscience—a place where young and engaged people took injustice so personally that they were willing to sleep out in the cold and the mud to register their dismay. This was the Webster Naomi herself had come to love, and the one she was honored to lead. She wished that Oksen Sarafian were still here to be walked around the campus, introduced to what he'd made, and to the Jewish female (feminist!) scholar who now sat at his old desk. She wondered how he'd be handling the kids out at the Stump. She wished she could ask him.

The afternoon began. Naomi took her lunch at her desk, in case some of them—in case *he*—decided to come early, but no one came. She had downgraded her meeting with Douglas Sidgwick to a phone call, and after they hung up she went over the

list of Native American alums he'd compiled for her. A novelist
in Seattle. Two attorneys, one in Memphis and one in New York.
Four for whom no profession was listed, but whose children had
also attended, or were attending, Webster. A professor of American history at Amherst and two physicians, one in Minnesota
and one in Arizona. She had heard of the novelist. One of his
books had been made into a film. She hadn't known that he was
a Webster grad, and indulged in her typical moment of Websterian pride in his achievement.

Douglas had done a good job. There was a geographical balance, a generational balance, a balance of men and women. It was
exactly what she had been looking for, and before she even rose
from her desk she had drafted an email, inviting them to participate in the advisory committee for a conference on the long and
conjoined history of Native American students and Webster College. "That this complex and meaningful relationship has been, till
now, unexplored by the college is something I don't fully understand, but I do mean to rectify. To me, the story that began with
Webster's Indian Academy and progressed to our current Native
American studies program, one of the finest in the country, is both
fascinating and important, and I believe that our graduates and our
current undergraduates will all benefit from a clear-eyed perspective on it. I would like to invite you to help plan this event, so that
we can share your experiences with the Webster community, and
help us all to understand our common journey." To the Amherst
professor she wrote a slightly different email, asking him to chair
the committee and proposing that they meet soon if he was interested, either at Amherst or at Webster, or somewhere in the
middle, to talk about it. She forwarded these documents to Mrs.
Bradford, to have them proofread and sent on. Then she glared at
the clock over the office door. Four thirty. Still, no one from the
protest had come.

Suddenly, Naomi was furious. Why was she obligated to sit

here, just waiting for them to meander over so they could deign to reveal what it was they wanted? Why should her own day be reduced to this pathetic act of attending, this debasement before somebody else's self-perceived grievance? She felt like a teenaged girl, wallowing at home, waiting for a boy to call— something she had not done even when she actually *was* a teenaged girl.

"I'm going out," Naomi said to Mrs. Bradford, charging through the outer office.

"I thought you were having dedicated office hours for the protesters."

"I was. But they haven't favored me with their attendance, as you see."

Mrs. Bradford looked past Naomi, into the office, as if the students might have slipped past her somehow. They weren't there.

"Well, what if they come?"

Tell them to go fuck themselves, she thought.

"Tell them to wait," she said.

"All right." Mrs. Bradford looked amused.

"And get their names. Everyone signs in. If they don't sign in, I don't see them."

"All right."

She went outside. It was late in November now, and in two days everyone would leave for Thanksgiving. At least, she hoped they would leave. She hoped that the protesters, in particular, would leave, rediscover the delights of warm beds and hot showers, and return to campus content that they had fulfilled their obligation to Professor Gall's honor. *Then we can all return to that fusty old business of getting educated,* she thought as she stomped over the mildly slippery ground. She was halfway across the Quad before she fully realized that she had no destination, and Naomi stopped for a moment, looking around at the options. To her left, the Stump itself, now ringed by a network of tents and tarps. If there were students in there, right now, they were under cover, keeping warm, discussing, at least (she hoped, she truly hoped) something vaguely edifying.

Well, she was hardly going there.

To the right: town. But she had no real reason to go to town. What college president aimlessly wanders the few streets of her own little college town on a weekday afternoon, popping into stores, peeking into windows? Shopping? Did the male presidents of Princeton and Yale go shopping when they were fed up with the grind of running a first-rate university? She had a brief and unpleasant reverie in which she was chatting with Christopher Eisgruber and Peter Salovey at an NAICU reception, when one of them (which? did it matter?) said, with an accompanying sneer: *You were seen shopping on a Monday afternoon. What do you have to say for yourself?*

It was so cold out. She stuck her hands in her pockets and, as she did, the gift of an idea, a reasonable, compelling idea, slid neatly into her head. Of course. An actual errand requiring timeliness and the privacy of a face-to-face conversation. With a little sigh of relief, she turned sharply around and went back in the direction she'd come, but not to Billings Hall. The building next to Billings had been built in the '20s by the same architect and builder who'd created the Stone House, and the similarities were obvious. Service Hall was named not in reference to an imagined tradition of selfless acts on the part of Webster graduates but in honor of Lawrence Service III, class of '14, who did not return from the fields of France to assume his rightful place in the Lawrence family's brokerage dynasty. Lawrence Service II, Webster class of 1886, had given the new building in his son's memory, and there remained in its gray stone entryway a bas relief of Lawrence III's handsome profile. Service Hall, for its first half century, had administrative offices on the ground floor and classrooms at the top of the wide stone staircase, but

when college admissions became far more than a matter of automatically enrolling the sons of graduates (and select others),
the administrators and classes were shown the door and the entire building turned over to this strange new enterprise. From the
mid-1980s Webster Admissions had been the sole occupant of
Service Hall, with Francine's comfortable office on the ground
floor, financial aid and a warren of administrative rooms on the
second floor, and assistant and associate deans of admission on
the third floor. The year after Francine's arrival, a large and bright
lounge area had been created, opposite her own office, and it
was there that crowds of prospective applicants, and their parents, awaited the departure of their student-led tours and took
part in Q&A sessions with the admissions officers. Outside in
the stone entryway, teams of students directed the visitors into
the waiting area, and if those nervous applicants and their parents realized how close they were sitting to the seat of power
itself, Francine's own assistant was stationed just outside the
heavy doors of the dean's office at a very long, very solid, and
slightly elevated oak desk, and everything about her trumpeted
the message *Don't even think about it.*

This assistant was a woman in her thirties, black, broad
shouldered, and wearing a headdress of some bright African
cloth: black and green. It was an arresting sight, this headdress,
which had been roped and folded and tucked in around the
woman's head, and Naomi could not stop herself from looking at
it, rather than into the eyes of the woman herself, a small action
that would come back to haunt her.

"Excuse me," the assistant said.

Naomi now met her stony gaze.

"This is a no-access area."

Is it? she thought. It was one of those things that must be
intuited, she supposed, though there was no physical boundary
separating this holy of admissions holies from the ostensibly

public lounge a few feet beyond. It occurred to her now that she had not visited Francine's office in years; always, Francine came to her when there was something to discuss. Something Webster-related to discuss.

"I'd like to see Francine," she told the woman. Whatever she was feeling, she tried to keep it out of her voice.

"And you are?"

"Hello," she said, extending her hand. "I'm President Roth."

After a moment, the woman raised her own hand, and they shook. Cold and dry. Now it was she who would not meet Naomi's gaze. She did not give her name. "Do you have an appointment?"

"No," Naomi said. She declined to make an excuse for herself.

"Well, she's in with someone."

"Fine." Naomi crossed to the waiting area and sat heavily on one of the banquettes, dumping her coat on the cushion beside her.

And for the next ten minutes they sat, no more than ten feet apart, in complete silence, except when the woman took a call.

Dean Rigor's office. No, I'm afraid not. No, she can't speak directly with parents, I'm sorry. It's our policy. Yes, I do understand.

Dean Rigor's office. Well, I can put a note in his file to double check that the DVD arrived. We're very good at keeping track of submissions. You don't have to be concerned.

Dean Rigor's office. Certainly. Yes, she can move it to four. Next Monday. Yes. Goodbye.

The time passed so slowly. She could hear Francine from beyond the office door. Francine and a man. Two men. Naomi was too irritated to ask who they were. Instead, she stewed on her banquette. At one point she even picked up one of the thick Webster brochures from the table and opened the page. There she was, President Naomi Roth, resplendent in one of her Eileen Fisher ensembles, teaching a freshman seminar in Webster Hall.

And was that Elise, the protester, to her right? She peered, but the photographer had artfully blurred the students into the background. The photograph was all about her: *Naomi Roth! The president! Who still taught freshmen!* Because Webster was that kind of place, where students and faculty and administrators all drew from the well of scholarship, and gave of their intellectual and creative gifts, back to the community, and the old trees dropped their Kodachrome leaves onto the Billings Lawn every fall, and protesters got an open door to air their grievances, whatever they happened to be.

The office door opened and out came two of the associate deans, both men in their twenties, and then the basketball coach, Lester McFadden, and his assistant coach, smiling and already shoving their arms into their coats. Behind them, Naomi saw Francine. She was walking them out.

"Naomi?" She stopped in the doorway. Naomi got to her feet. The young admissions officers nodded but went past, up to their own offices.

"Oh, President Roth," said the basketball coach. He introduced the assistant coach, and there followed a brief but vaguely surreal conversation about the team's prospects for the year. One of the more difficult hurdles of Naomi's ascension to the presidency had had to do with sports. Learning about them. Acquiring the ability to discuss them. Appearing to care about them.

"Just beat Amherst," she told Lester McFadden jovially. "You know that's all I ever care about."

Unfortunately, he took this request very seriously, and began a monologue about the current Amherst lineup, which happened to include two players he'd requested for Webster two years earlier.

"And we admitted them," said Francine, reminding him. "They chose to go to Amherst."

"No accounting for taste," Naomi said with false cheer.

"Anyway, Dean Rigor's going to make it up to me this year. Right?" he said pointedly.

"We will do what we can." She sighed. And the men departed.

"Leanne," Francine said, turning to her assistant with clear annoyance. "You should have buzzed me."

Leanne seemed nonplussed. "You were in a meeting. She didn't have an appointment."

"It's okay," Naomi said, though a part of her would have liked to see what happened next. "I just wanted a few minutes, and she's right, I just dropped in. Very unorthodox."

Francine paused. She seemed to be making up her mind.

"Really," said Naomi. "It's okay. Can we talk for a few minutes?"

Her friend nodded. "Of course. Come in. Do you want something?"

"No, no," said Naomi, who did not want to see any more of Leanne than she had to.

They went into Francine's office and Francine closed the door behind them. It was a large office, actually larger than Naomi's, and looked out on the Quad from a wide window, the black-and-white Webster Hall just opposite, and the Davis Chapel with its gray stone turrets. She sat in the armchair opposite Francine, and they disappeared from view.

"What's up with your assistant?" she couldn't help asking. "It's cold enough outside without the arctic blast of her personality."

"Oh, I know, and I'm sorry," said Francine. "Usually she's much nicer to be around, but she's in a bad way right now."

"Oh? Why?" asked Naomi, but almost immediately she wished she hadn't. It was going to be something horrible: an illness, a death. And then she would feel terrible for this woman in the elaborate African headdress. And then she would feel terrible about herself.

"Well, actually"—Francine looked away from her—"it's her

husband who's just been denied tenure. She's kind of going back and forth between being heartbroken and raging at everyone. I just need to cut her a lot of slack right now, especially since, A, she's always been a great assistant, and B, obviously they'll be heading off to another college soon."

Not necessarily, thought Naomi. There would not be many open doors for a plagiarist who'd been denied tenure, since who else could Leanne's husband be? A plagiarist who'd been denied tenure really ought to be looking for another profession, and it was entirely possible that Nicholas Gall would end up staying right here in Webster, where at least his wife was gainfully employed. Francine might well have her disagreeable assistant for many years to come.

"That's a very difficult situation to be in" is what she said. "Very difficult. Very unfortunate for all concerned."

Francine put her hands up. "I don't know the details," she said, which Naomi quickly and correctly interpreted as *I don't want to know the details.*

"Have you met the husband?"

"Yes, of course. Nick Gall. He comes to pick her up sometimes. He writes about music and folklore."

Well, or someone else writes about music and folklore, and he signs his name to it, she had to stop herself from saying.

"And how long has his wife been your assistant?"

"For five years," Francine said. "I'll be sorry to lose her."

Naomi nodded. "I'm sure. Well. Can you help me out with something? I don't want to take up too much time."

Francine smiled. "Of course. And don't be silly."

"I'd like to look at a few application folders, of current undergrads. You keep those, right?"

"As long as they're enrolled, yes. After that they go to storage. What are the names?"

Of course, in the painful instant that followed, she could only think of Omar's name. The others, who were only there to obscure her interest in Omar, she suddenly could not remember. And Chava's father had been on the phone with her only a few hours before. She closed her eyes. Friedberg. Yes. It wasn't gone, after all. "Chava Friedberg."

"Can you spell it?"

Naomi began: F-R-I...

"No, the first name."

She spelled that, too.

"And Elise...oh no, I can't think of her surname. She was in my freshman seminar last year. So, a sophomore now. And from Georgia, I think?"

Francine was typing the name into her keyboard. "Wait..." She stared into the screen. "I have an Elise Gibson? Athens, Georgia. African-American?"

"Yes," Naomi said. "That's her. And also...Omar Khayal. That's K-H-A-Y..."

"Oh, I know Omar," Francine said, looking up. "Omar isn't easy to forget."

She sat back in her uncomfortable chair. "Yes? Why so?"

"Magical application. One of the ones you pull out of the pile, the first time it comes across your desk. Like so," she said, gesturing to a shelf behind her. It had, as far as Naomi could make out, four or five Webster-green folders stacked on it. The folders had hot pink Post-Its affixed to them, each with a surname.

"I don't understand," said Naomi. "What does it mean?"

Francine stopped typing. She sat forward in her chair, elbows braced against her desk. "So, they're all one hundred shades of wonderful, right? Nearly all. Wonderful in all the ways a seventeen-year-old can be wonderful. Wonderful at this, wonderful at that, wonderful at everything at the same time. Mostly I'm making piles of wonderful, to build the class. And that's great. That's an embarrassment of riches. But then you read an application like Omar's, and you just start to shake. Like...a kid who's at the top of her class at Bronx Science going home to a homeless shelter every night. Or someone from the middle of nowhere who's never met an intellectual, let alone an academic, but who's already doing serious scholarship. Like that."

"And that was Omar's application?" Naomi said, remembering that he was from the middle of nowhere in Oklahoma, bordering the middle of nowhere in Arkansas. Had he already been doing serious scholarship? And if so, about what?

"No, not exactly. Even in that category he was a one-off. Well, you'll see when you read the file. But why do you want to read it? Is he up for an award or something?"

He's up for something, Naomi thought. But what she said was, "I'm trying to understand our activists. Omar and Chava and Elise. And the rest." Like Hannah, she thought.

"Omar's out there?" Francine frowned, looking toward the window.

"Well, yes. I'm not singling him out," she said, a tiny bit defensively. "The others seem to defer to him. He may not be self-identifying as a leader but he's clearly influential in the group. I just thought, maybe...if I knew a bit more about him. I mean, them. The leaders. It might help. I'm only trying to understand."

"But you wouldn't expel him," Francine said. It wasn't a question. It almost sounded, not that this made any sense, like an injunction.

"No, of course not. For activism? I just..."

"Want to understand," Francine said tersely. And her long fingers returned to the keyboard and began to move. Naomi stood watching, wondering what had just passed between them: something not pleasant and not innocuous. And because she truly did not understand, and because the very idea of it frightened her, she chose not to think about it more deeply, or indeed at all.

Instead, she distracted herself by thinking about Francine, and how strange it was that her friend could even ask that question. Naomi, with her own activist past, expel a student for engaging in a peaceful protest?

But Francine had never truly understood the dynamic of this kind of commitment—not deeply, not personally; this had always been clear to Naomi. Francine could evaluate activism as a desirable, even a *competitively desirable* quality (Webster applicant who organized a local charity fun run versus Webster applicant who organized march on Washington), but she herself had never been sufficiently moved by an issue to do more than sign a petition or cast a vote. It was something that separated the two women, certainly, but no more than their other differences, like background and physical appearance. Watching her friend at the keyboard, Naomi understood that Francine probably understood the motivation of those kids out on the Quad as superficially as she understood Naomi's own political actions in college, or the years she had given to an idea of rural community work as a VISTA volunteer. Obviously, she'd heard Naomi's stories, but it was clear that Francine considered an anti-ROTC occupation of a president's office a roughly comparable college activity to the Barnard Glee Club, her own extracurricular interest.

They were exactly the same age, the two of them; in fact they'd been born only weeks apart. But Francine had managed to navigate the '60s and '70s without once being touched by the counterculture and its discontents. From Barnard student to Barnard fund-raiser to Barnard admissions officer, and from there to associate dean at Vassar, and finally to Webster—all without a major change in either hairstyle or fashion preferences. Socially liberal but fiscally conservative. Open to hearing what people had to say, but somehow wishing everyone would hold back, just a little bit, instead of sharing every tiny thing. Francine, who preferred "humanist" to "feminist," who considered certain right-wing radio blowhards "buffoonish" rather than "evil," was a witty and strong and accomplished woman, full of ideas and opinions, with a ramrod sense of institutional fidelity and a work ethic to match. They were made of different stuff, but their variations were finally superficial and mattered so little, given the thing they finally did share: They were both women who hadn't had many close friends, and they were close friends.

"I'm having Leanne pull the files," Francine said when she was finished. "You know that Nick and Omar are close."

Naomi had the reaction before she understood the reaction: a chill. Something physical, untethered to anything she could have named. "Nick. Leanne's husband, Nick?"

"Sure. I hear about Omar all the time, from her. He practically lives in their house."

Naomi shook her head. "I don't understand."

"Well, he's probably going to be an anthropology major. Omar is. Given his background I would have guessed politics, maybe history. But Nick Gall taught his freshman seminar and the two just connected, I guess. And of course he doesn't have anywhere to go during the breaks, so he stays with the Galls."

"But, what about...Oklahoma, right?"

"Oklahoma?"

"I thought...well, his records list his hometown as somewhere in Oklahoma."

"Oh. Yes. But it's not as if he grew up there. Or has family there. He doesn't have family anywhere."

She had no idea what to say to this. All at once she wanted to leave. She wanted to go somewhere and read the file, herself. But this wasn't just any colleague. This was her ally, and the woman she walked with. This was the person who had given Hannah her first pair of earrings.

"How are you doing?" Naomi said abruptly. "I've been feeling a little sheepish about that night at your house. I mean, with the guy you set me up with. Of course I appreciate it, but it was such a colossal miss."

Francine, unfortunately, did not rush in with an instant denial.

"Oh," Naomi sat up in her chair, horribly embarrassed. "It was a setup, right?"

"Not really. I mean, as far as I was concerned, no. He just asked to meet you."

"That guy asked to meet *me*?"

"Yes. But you, president of Webster, not you, Naomi. I'm sorry. It's a tough situation."

"Wait." She wondered if she had missed something. Were they still talking about her single-ness? Or had they ever been? "Wait," she said again. "What is?"

But Francine seemed to have entered a different space. Her face had changed. "You know," she said, after a moment, "I'm not sure I'm ready to talk about this."

Naomi caught her breath. "Of course. I didn't mean..." But what didn't she mean? She'd had no idea that there was a "this" at all. "Whenever you're ready. Or never."

"Never's good!" Francine said lightly. It was from a *New Yorker* cartoon they'd laughed over once. *No, Thursday's out. How about never—is never good for you?*

"Yes, never's perfectly fine for me." She got to her feet. "I'll be off then. Are you going to Timothy's for Thanksgiving?"

Timothy was Sumner's son. He was married with a four-year-old and a newborn, and lived in Darien, Connecticut.

"Yes. Just a day trip. If eighty-four is clear, it shouldn't be bad." But 84 wouldn't be clear on Thanksgiving Day. Francine looked resigned. "And you?"

"Me and Hannah at the Stone House," she said happily. Hannah would have to come home for Thanksgiving. "And next week, I'll bet you anything the students will all have returned to their dorms." There was a sharp knock at the office door, and Leanne, not waiting, opened it and stepped inside, carrying three files and looking balefully at Naomi. Too late for anything to be done about that. Naomi took the files with as gracious a thank-you as she could muster.

"I'm not a betting man," Francine said.

CHAPTER EIGHT

PERMISSION TO ENTER

Sometimes people ask me what it was like to grow up in
the middle of a war, and they are surprised when I tell them
that most of my earliest memories were of very peaceful,
happy things. My mother was a nurse who worked with babies and small children, and my father was a mechanic.
I also had a brother, five years older. Of course, even in
periods when there was no fighting, we were constantly
in conflict with our neighboring country, but as a child
somehow that just becomes the way things are in the background, and my life was about my family. We were Muslim
(in Bureij, everyone was), but looking back I don't remember religion being a big part of our lives. Even when the
first Intifada began our lives seemed to go on as before. My
brother began school at a UN (UNRWA) school. Later I
would join him at the same school.

Naomi, who was reading this in bed, set down the pages of
Omar's application essay to take a sip of her tea. The past tense
references to his family members did not, of course, bode well.

But she could already see what Francine had meant. From its first sentence, it was about as different from the typical Webster admissions essay as it could be. *Stage fright at the piano recital? Tutoring the autistic girl down the street?* She set down her mug and braced herself.

It is very difficult to talk about what happened, and I do not feel it to be appropriate in this application context. I am a result of what happened to me, but I am not only what happened to me. One day, that was in every other respect a normal day, my brother and father died, and my mother could never recover from this. After she died, I was very lucky to meet a man with the American NGO working for schools in Bureij. He asked me, would I be willing to leave Palestine to go to the US, if it meant I could never return. I had to think about this a long time, but finally I decided: yes. If I could really go, I would do that. I don't know if that is what my father and mother would have wanted, so I struggle with that. But I made the decision to go.

I came to the US through PRM (Bureau of Population Refugees Migration). I was placed in Milwaukee to undergo resettlement counseling. After this I was sent to Houston to live with a foster family, and try going to an American school, but my English was not strong enough to support this. Finally I met through my foster mother a woman in Oklahoma who knew a Lebanese family willing to host me, and for the year I lived in Oklahoma I spent days at the town library trying to learn and think about what had happened already in my life and what I wanted to do in my future. Only then do I feel ready for attending an American university like Webster College.

In Gaza I had hoped to go to University of Palestine to study law and judicial practice. I still would like to pursue international law as my career, but I also want to learn American history and art and culture.

I have made my decision to apply to Webster College from reading its brochure and researching about the college on the computer at the library in Arkoma. I have a big mind that wants to learn everything and hopes to meet many people from different parts of the world who have all different ideas, because I think that talking about ideas, even if you disagree with others, is the best way for every one of us to share the planet we all live on. I hope to be lucky enough to attend the school if you will grant me the permission to enter.

Naomi put the pages down and lay there, feeling the cold in her feet and hands, even under the quilt. The temperature, on the eve of Thanksgiving, had dropped once again, and she was reassured beyond words that the encampment around the Stump appeared to have been abandoned as the students dispersed to hearth and home. Hannah was home, too, down the hall and still asleep at eleven a.m., which (after her nights under the stars) was just as Naomi wanted it. For herself, she was looking forward to a quiet holiday, marked only by leisurely sessions with the *New Yorker* (the backlog stack was now nearly a foot tall) and real time with her daughter.

She set the essay back into the green folder, extracted the reader's card from the inside cover, and read the summary notes at the bottom. Like every Webster application, Omar's had had two readers—one who signed his comments JG (this was Joseph Gill, one of the lifers in the admissions office and Francine's stand-in when she had to be away from campus) and FR, Francine herself. Both had filled their comment boxes with raves—*the intelligence, the spirit, the humanity*. It was as if the magic of this boy, his pure yearning for education and life itself, had risen off the page and embraced his unworthy evaluators. "Incredible kid," Francine had written. JG had ended his notes with: "I cannot remember ever having been so moved by an application. My top priority for the year."

Naomi herself had not looked at a student's application folder since Neil Jones-Givens's, back in 2006, and she couldn't help thinking about that essay now. Neil—or Nell, as she still was at the time of her Webster application—had vividly described her breast binding and attempts to make the men's cross-country team, in beautiful prose, so very different from Omar's careful wielding of what was obviously a second language. Trauma and trauma, as different as traumas could be, and yet both still were traumas for young and sensitive human beings. Omar had lost his family to a war that no one could really understand, whether they were on one side of the world making free with their opinions or on the other, just trying to live. Nell—Neil—had only wanted to make a place for himself. Both had wanted a safe space in which to think and learn. Neither had meant harm to anyone else.

But even Naomi recognized that there were serious discrepancies between the two cases, and they were going to be a problem. In either gender Neil had been a fine student, only losing his footing briefly at the height of his crisis. Omar, though—Omar had not been faring well academically. Not well at all. Ascertaining this had required no personal visit to a dean, nor to anyone else; as president she had access to every student's transcript, though she'd only made use of that access twice (once, indeed, for Neil Jones-Givens, and once to see whether Hannah had managed to pull out an A from her very challenging Political Thought seminar last spring—she had). This time the result was not so reassuring.

Omar was running a C– average, but that in itself was not the worst of it. He was only a sophomore but he had already failed two courses (European History and, surprisingly, The Politics of the Middle East), and he had barely scraped through another four with D's. In fact, the only marks above a C he'd earned (and these were what had pulled his average up to C−) were the two A's from courses in the Anthropology Department: Music and Folklore in American Culture (that had been his freshman seminar the previous fall) and Magic, Myth, and Religion in the spring. Currently he was enrolled in a third: Folklore and the Supernatural. The professor in all three, it shocked her not at all to discover, was their troublesome plagiarist, Nicholas Gall.

She and Hannah had a quiet Thanksgiving dinner: tofu vegetable loaf, but everything else defiantly traditional, down to the marshmallow-studded sweet potato casserole, and concluding with a pecan pie they made together. Hannah, despite her virtue in matters of animal flesh, was downright hedonistic when it came to desserts, and Naomi made sure to lay in a supply of her daughter's favorite ice-cream flavors, complete with various syrups and sauces. Back from the barricades, Hannah seemed grateful for the warmth, and she was happy to spend whole evenings on the sofa in the upstairs den with a bowl of ice cream in her lap and a blanket over her shoulders, clicking happily away at the remote control. When she could stand it, Naomi joined her, though not even Webster's domination of reality TV competitions could make those shows watchable. "You're kidding," she said, when Hannah embarked upon an *America's Next Top Model* marathon.

"My brain is on vacation," her daughter informed her. "It is *vacating*."

About the protest, Hannah tolerated very little discussion, in spite of—or more likely because of—her mother's extremely keen interest. She volunteered nothing and parried most of Naomi's questions, dispensing only a few shards of useful information. Yes, the conditions at the Stump were challenging, but nothing compared to the way most people on the planet lived. No, she did not find it morally problematic to attend her classes, work in the library, eat dinner at Radclyffe Hall, and then join the others at the encampment on the Quad; the point was not to debase oneself before an ideal, but to physically embrace a principle, to bring one's energy and strengths to an achievable goal. Everyone at the Stump had reached an individual decision to make the stand they'd made—Naomi, of all people, should understand and respect that. And surely she could see how the denial of tenure to a prominent and beloved African-American professor was a grave symbol of the state of affairs on their campus, the poisoned fruit of the poisoned tree that was Webster today. What the tenure decision implied about the institution as a whole was heartbreaking but accurate: What was happening to Professor Gall was the thin edge of a wedge that was comprehensive institutional racism and intolerance. The students at the Stump were prepared to stand their ground until the college lived up to its own stated principles, Hannah assured her mother.

Naomi, of course, refrained from saying that the college already had lived up to its own stated principles, the ones regarding academic integrity. As for the tenure decision itself, the matter had been resolved, and wasn't going to be unresolved, ever. She might not have spent her years in academia preparing herself to be a college president (unlike some she might have named), but the job, she had quickly learned, was basically a game of Whac-a-Mole. You didn't have the luxury of going back to contemplate the wisdom of having swung your mallet, because the next crisis was already exploding somewhere else, and you had no time to spare. Comprehend the problem, hear the grievances, get advice, and then decide. End of story. She could just keep doing that, she supposed, unless she managed to fuck something up so badly that her critics (and she had always had them: too soft, too weird, too Jewish, too incompetent about finance, too female, too "intellectual," too not-a-graduate-of-Webster) would seize the mallet right out of her hands, and whack her instead. But that hadn't happened so far. And if she was lucky, really very lucky, and very, very careful, it wouldn't happen now.

"And Professor Gall is on board with all of this?" she asked instead.

Hannah had looked at her mother with scorn: It had insulted her, this question. Each and every one of them at the Stump was a sentient, principled, and committed young person, acting at the behest of his or her own conscience. Was this Naomi-mom speaking? Or Naomi-apologist-for-a-profoundly-compromised-institution?

Wisely understanding that neither of these was the right answer, she backpedaled.

"I respect your integrity, Hannah. I always have. I'm very proud of you."

"And yet, you refuse to do more than give the impression of hearing me."

She wanted to argue with that, but her daughter was right, and she herself was a dreadful actress. What fascinated her most, she decided, was not that Gall had done what he'd done but that so many people seemed to care so much about his tenure status. Rare indeed was the professor who attracted the kind of passionate support this one was now enjoying, on the Webster campus and beyond, and crowded as his courses were, she doubted that more than a fraction of Webster's student protesters had actually enrolled in them. And what about the students from other colleges, near and now far? What did a barely published folklorist from Webster represent to a Yale student or a Hampshire student, or a delegation from Bard, all of whom were now apparently in situ around the Stump?

What had he told these people to make them leave their lives and come here?

Naomi knew what he hadn't told them. He hadn't told a single one of them that he was being removed from Webster because he'd broken the college's brief and succinct Honor Pledge in its entirety: *I affirm that I have neither given nor received unauthorized assistance on this work.* And she, of course, could not tell a single one of them, either. Not even this one.

"I'm sorry," she said to Hannah. "I'll try harder. I will."

And then, sensing that it was the best she could hope for, she joined her formidable daughter on the couch for as many episodes of *America's Next Top Model* as she could stand.

With virtually no students on campus, Naomi's own days were gloriously empty of tasks, weighty or mundane, and she luxuriated in her *New Yorker*s and the nearness of Hannah, despite her daughter's preferred entertainments. Her only act of presidential business was to fix on a date for lunch with Robbins Petavit, the Webster alumnus who taught at Amherst. Petavit had sounded distinctly unenthusiastic about the notion of a dedicated reunion for Webster graduates of Native American ethnicity, and even less enthusiastic at the prospect of heading an advisory committee thereto, but in the end he had said yes.

On Saturday night they hosted Francine and Sumner for dinner and an evening that culminated in a series of increasingly cutthroat Scrabble games. On Sunday, as if to drain the last possible drop of their togetherness, they drove to a multiplex south of Worcester and saw two movies in a row.

And then it was time to take Hannah back. She walked her daughter across the Quad, and they picked their way silently around the deflated tents and the snowed-on tarps, neither of them saying anything about it. At Radclyffe Hall the lights were on, and housemates who'd already returned were in the kitchen mulling cider, which smelled wonderful, but Naomi gave Hannah a hug at the door and made herself leave. She walked back alone, feeling both sweet and sad, relieved that the holiday had passed without too much conflict, about the protest or anything else, and yet already wondering whether she'd been wrong not to force a more air-clearing dialogue on the subject while they were together.

The next morning Naomi rose in her once again empty house, dressed, drank her coffee and read the *Times*, then stepped outside to find that the Stump protest had, by some breathtaking alchemy, thoroughly reconstituted itself. The students, who beat their own arms for warmth, or hugged, or blew on coffee, were greeting one another like any other Websterites returning from vacation. The tents and tarps were resecured, and new covers had been stretched over the frozen ground, delineating the separation between occupied and unoccupied territory. And there was more—more of everything: tents and people, tarps and plastic sheeting. Overnight, all of this had happened. It had happened between her walk home last night and her waking this morning. And, if the encampment itself wasn't enough to be processing on a frigid winter morning, the very first news van could now be sighted on the far edge of the Billings Lawn. It was as if the volume on the entire undertaking had suddenly been turned up, and Naomi, stunned and utterly livid, couldn't stop herself from wondering whether Hannah was in there, too.

CHAPTER NINE

THE UR-RULE

After Thanksgiving, the Quad was never free of them again. The ring of protesters around the Stump grew, spreading outward like a nautilus. The press office began taking calls from Hartford and Springfield, then from Boston and New York. In Naomi's own office the callers were parents and alumni, first curious, then concerned, and then irate, demanding to know her intentions and requesting an explanation as to why she hadn't personally bulldozed the Billings Lawn—*Because I'm not a fascist dictator,* she'd wanted to yell at them—sending the kids back to their overheated dorms and the classes they'd competed so hard to attend in the first place. It was maddening. But it was also— now that people well beyond Webster were beginning to watch—very, very delicate.

The three-week period between Thanksgiving and Christmas break was a widening gyre. She canceled most of her nonessential appointments (including, annoyingly, the lunch with Robbins Petavit that she had just scheduled), and arranged for a conference call with the trustees, just to keep everyone up to speed and everything out in the open, and by now she was speaking regularly to the college attorney about the evolving situation.

This was no longer Rosa, her comrade-at-arms during the Rad-clyffe Hall affair; Rosa had gone west, following her husband to UC Irvine, where he'd been offered an endowed chair in the economics department. Her replacement was a straight arrow named Chaim Wachsberger, who made what she already knew officially plain: She could make no reference to or statement about the reason for Gall's denial of tenure. The privacy of the tenure process was absolute, and any implication that the professor had committed plagiarism would be a violation of that—a violation that opened them up to a very winnable lawsuit. She could say that the process was complex, careful, responsible, and rigorous. She could say that decisions were reached with a broad range of factors in mind. She could say that the tenure was a longstanding and intrinsic part of academia, and its principles were understood by those who submitted to the process. But she could not say that Nicholas Gall had broken a rule. He had broken, in fact, the ur-rule, the one that tolerated no mitigation. And he had done it knowingly, and with full awareness of what might—what *should*—happen as a result.

She accepted only one media request to discuss the Stump protest, from the college's own student daily; everyone else got the boilerplate statement, curtly emailed by Mrs. Bradford:

> Webster College is an educational institution at which we attempt to learn from one another as much as we learn in the classroom. This is an opportunity for our students, indeed for all of us at Webster, to do just that, and we will continue to support this nonviolent student action, in hopes that the exchange of ideas will benefit the entire Webster community.

It satisfied none of them, of course. It satisfied her least of all, but the parameters were clear, and terrifying. And she would not be the college president who opened her institution up to *a very winnable lawsuit.*

"You know," said Douglas Sidgwick one morning in the middle of December, "this has actually happened before."

He'd come upstairs, unnecessarily, to present her with a hard copy of the formal proposal for the Native American Gathering—the term *reunion* had been jettisoned in favor of this warmer alternative—now scheduled for the first weekend in April: a gathering at the First Nations Center, dinners at the Webster Inn and the Alumni House, panels on the history and the individual stories and the current state of the Native American studies program. April was far, far in the future, Naomi told herself. All of this would be long concluded by then.

"Has it?" she asked. She was surprised, and sort of relieved. *Good.*

"Well, not exactly this...configuration, of course. But we did have a protest encampment around the Stump in the 1950s, and I believe it lasted for several days."

"Really?" Naomi sat back in her chair. She hated the note of childish hopefulness in her voice. "What was it about?"

"Well, there was a student the college admitted in 1956, named Luther Merrion. From...I want to say Indiana. Arrived here to register for classes with the rest of his class and everybody was surprised to see that Mr. Merrion was not white. The registrar refused to let him register, and there was a protest. The students started gathering around the Stump and they stayed out all night, and for a few days after that, till it was resolved."

Naomi nodded in satisfaction. It made her happy to think that Webster had made such a gesture, so out of character, so distinctly ahead of its time. "You know," she told Douglas, "it's great to hear that. There were very few college students who would have protested like that in the 1950s."

"Well, I don't know about that," Douglas said.

"You kidding? Defending a black student's right to register before the civil rights movement was even under way? It's amazing. Yay, us."

"Oh." Douglas seemed lost for a moment. "Well, yes, but that wasn't why they were out there. They were making sure the college turned him away, is what was actually going on. And I mean, the boy was staying at a faculty member's house while it was decided, which took a few days. But if he'd been on campus things might have gotten really..."

She stared at him. It all took a moment to work out. "I see," she finally said.

"Yes. So. Definitely a precedent for camping out around the Stump! But very different circumstances, obviously."

Sometimes, often, she forgot what Webster had been like. Before Sarafian. Before blacks, Jews, women, LGBT people, anyone who was not a white male. And then someone told her a story like this.

Webster was an institution that combined the strength of centuries with an almost diametrically opposed kind of strength— the strength (and courage) to change itself. The Ebenezer Scrooge of colleges, she had once said in a (holiday season) speech to the Boston alumni association, and it was only the obvious confusion and dismay on the faces of her audience that made her retire the allusion. Scrooge had always been her favorite Dickens character, an affection undimmed by the sheer weight of all the *Christmas Carol* adaptations she had seen (and mainly loved). Yes, Scrooge was odious, reactionary, rude, cruel, and most probably malodorous...but he was also brave. It was for a reason larger and deeper than his personal salvation that he broke open before his own grave in the dead of a Victorian night and forced himself to feel the pain and wonder of human connection. He changed himself because he had connected to some deeper and truer understanding of life.

Webster College might have remained a precious and rigid institution, educating the wealthy sons (and, perhaps in due course, daughters) of the East Coast middle class. It might still be producing conservative politicians and guardians of the banking and manufacturing industries, who settled in the suburbs, sent their children to private schools, and, in due course, dropped them off at the very dormitories they had once occupied. But the college, like that miserable old man, had broken open to a deeper and truer understanding of what education was, and what it meant.

The Omars, the Chavas...even the Hannahs were here because of such institutional courage, and Naomi considered it her responsibility never to lose sight of that. Webster students might rush on ahead into the *right now* of their personal college experiences, but that was to be expected. If, as they flew down the corridors and stairways of Webster Hall, they even noted the sepia photographs of dour young Webster men (posed with footballs, baseball bats, snowshoes, or fabulously antique typewriters), those images only lent the burnish of history to their own accomplishment of having been accepted to Webster. The self-involvement of this was neither awful nor particularly surprising, because the students were young and occupied the centers of their individual universes, same as students ever were and ever had. Each of these purposeful young people was the hero or heroine of their personal bildungsroman, every single one of which was art directed by a Hollywood master with a comfortable budget (towering trees with falling leaves, ivy-covered buildings, white marble, and—until the advent of Webster Dissent—an irreproachably green and pleasant quadrangle). They were enraptured by their own illusory success, but no more, in the end, than Naomi was by her own.

"What happened to him?" she asked the repository of Webster's institutional memory. "Do you know?"

Of course he knew.

"Luther Merrion attended Morehouse College and Howard University Law School. He became an appellate court judge in Indiana."

She sat with this for a moment. It felt good to have an idea to sit with, something she might actually be able to act on. "We should be doing something for him," she told Douglas. "An honorary degree."

"It was talked about," he said, looking distracted. "Sarafian wanted to do it, but he died first."

"Sarafian died?"

"Luther Merrion died. Then Sarafian died. Same year, but in that order. So it never happened. Goodbye," he said in his typically abrupt way, already turning to go.

"Well, thanks for that," Naomi told him. More accurately, she told the door after it had closed behind him.

With the winter vacation now only a few days away, she'd have been forgiven for hoping the same Thanksgiving magic would descend again. Three weeks without the encampment, the freezing students who refused to speak with her, the weight of responsibility that never seemed to leave her, no matter what she was doing. For three weeks these students would be their families' problem, and maybe a few of them, when they returned in an even bleaker, even more frigid January, with the prospect of months until the glorious mud of a New England spring, would decide that they'd made their point, and pack it in. Because she was getting very tired of defending their right to be outraged and committed, even as she simultaneously had to defend what she herself had done about it.

What Naomi had done was erect a warming tent at the edge of the encampment, equipped with heaters, blankets, food, drink, and a ten-stall toilet trailer—the kind of toilet-trailer you found at your swankier outdoor wedding: porcelain sinks, hand soap, and premium paper products. This not inconsiderable structure (which was costing the college just shy of $1,500 per day) had been positioned far enough from the Stump not to intrude on the protest, but within a week or two the trailer was completely swallowed up by shelters and bivouacs as new participants arrived, unfurled their ground cloths, and staked their claims to the action. Now, standing at her own office window, Naomi actually had to look for its flat roof among the shambles.

What else had she done? She had maintained her open door, making sure that every parent, student, and trustee she spoke to knew that she was still hoping for a dialogue with protest leaders and participants, and was eager to hear their concerns and respond to their suggestions. She had returned to the Stump herself, on several occasions, initiating conversation with whomever seemed amenable, hoping that the ripple of her presence would somehow make its way to the person at the epicenter of the movement, but she never saw Omar. "How can we help?" she would ask the students, if they seemed even remotely open to speaking with her. But when they said that she could help by reversing the unconscionable denial of tenure to Professor Nicholas Gall, she told them that the tenure process was complex and rigorous, but above all private, and she could not discuss what might have contributed to the committee's decision. Also, the decision would not be reversed. And there the conversation, such as it was, would end.

She gave another interview to the *Webster Daily*, this time about her own experiences as a campus activist at Cornell in the '70s (which unlike Webster in 2016 had actual, serious, worthy-of-action issues, even above and beyond the ROTC presence, like calling attention to the literacy rates for Tompkins County—outside of wealthy Ithaca, of course—and picketing one of the bio labs where scores of unfortunate dogs were being injected with fatal toxins. She gave the paper a highly unflattering photograph of herself and Daniel occupying the president's office with their fists in the air (she did not identify Daniel to the paper, and was secretly pleased when they used the caption "President Roth and an un-known male"). She spoke passionately about the honor of protest, her personal imperative to speak truth to power, and how without justice there would be no peace, et cetera, et cetera.

She canceled classes on a snowy Tuesday just before the break began, convening a "Day of Campus Discourse" on the "issues we face as a college, as Americans, and as human beings," arriving early at Webster Hall herself to set up chairs and start the coffeemaker. But the only people who came were students who'd never joined the protest in the first place, and their major issue was *when was all this going to be over?* And outside Webster Hall, across the street on the Billings Lawn, under the snow and under the tents and bundled into their warmest clothing, her army of adversaries huddled and grew strong.

The ones she knew, or knew of, were getting personal emails from her, naturally. Hannah, Elise, Chava, and Omar—she rotated them so daily so as not to seem pathetic.

Elise, I would love to speak with you about what you're doing. I'm very impressed by the stand you've taken. Would you come by my office for a few minutes this afternoon?

Hi, Chava. Oy, I need to tell you that I'm hearing from your father a lot. Would you call him please? I keep telling him you're fine, you're doing something important. But he's worried. While I have you, would you come in and talk with me for a few minutes? I'd like your thoughts on how to respond to the parents who are calling in.

Dear Omar, I'm very concerned about your academic work. Please make an appointment to come in at your soonest convenience. I'd like to help you avoid automatic penalties. What you are involved in now is a legitimate and important project, but we need to make sure that you are on firm footing with the college.

Hannah, would you please call me, for fuck's sake?

Hannah was the only one who responded, though she didn't call. Her texts were brief, communicating only that she was alive and that her opposable thumbs were fully functional.

But what Naomi could not do was make them stop. And that was where things stood when—at last, at last—the holiday break arrived and, like a rising flock, they all departed.

CHAPTER TEN

JUST ANNOYING BUREAUCRATIC SHIT

This time there would be no vacating for Hannah's vacation. This time she stayed only as long as it took to clean up and complete a history paper for which she'd secured an extension, and then she was gone, off to New York to spend the break with another Radclyffe Hall resident whose family apparently owned a massive loft on a cobblestoned street in SoHo. It happened without discussion, and so quickly that Naomi did not at first comprehend how unhappy she was about this turn of events. But then, driving out from the train station in Springfield, waiting at the light, all of this came to her in a great rush of self-indulgent misery. And there was something else—something equally troubling. It had, at that very moment, occurred to Naomi that she could turn left at this particular intersection, instead of turning right, and that if she were, indeed, to turn left instead of turning right, then the path of least resistance would bring her smoothly to 91. And then the same path of least resistance would merge her onto 91 and point her north, and for the first time in years she could actually drive . . . not only as far as Northampton, which she sometimes still visited, or Amherst, which she also occasionally still visited, but farther up, all the way up past Greenfield and

Brattleboro and Hanover...all the way back to Goddard. And no one would know, because she was alone in her car and would be equally alone in her house if she went home.

She had told Hannah's father once that she would never go back, and she never had. Not even for his funeral.

It had long been Naomi's habit not to correct people who believed that her long-ago marriage and her long-ago-conceived daughter were somehow related, and it was no great leap to assume that her ex-husband was Hannah's other parent. If directly questioned, and if it were not possible to avoid directly answering, Naomi tended to say that Hannah's father was someone she had known during her VISTA work in New Hampshire, and this was perfectly true. It was not a matter of being coy, and there was no drama—or if there was, it wasn't drama she wished to indulge in herself, let alone convey to anyone else. What had happened in Goddard belonged to another Naomi, one who was not a feminist scholar or a college president, or a woman who guarded her emotions and was almost cryptically cautious in the offering of friendship. Most of all, it was a Naomi who was not Hannah Rosalind Roth's mother. Even now, two decades since she had driven away from there, she couldn't face the notion of going back. Back to what? A place that had never understood her, or wanted her there. Back to whom? Those people, even the ones whose lives she'd changed, whose lives she might actually have saved, hadn't lifted a finger to prevent her leaving. And the one friend she'd made there, or thought she'd made, had turned out to be...not. Just, not. Even now, thinking about her filled Naomi with horror.

When the light changed she gripped the wheel so tightly that her fingers throbbed, turned right (of course), and drove back home. Five days until Christmas Eve. Another twenty-four days until the college opened up again. And not a single plan except to resist the incessant pull of her own sadness.

Francine, at least, was around, and when it warmed up unexpectedly on the day after Christmas the two women attempted a hike over one of their favorite trails, but the going was rough—slippery and filthy—and walking in single file did not make conversation easy. And something was not right with Francine, Naomi had decided, and having decided it she backdated this decision to the beginning of the fall, and perhaps even earlier. Surely the protest and Francine's travel schedule and the cold weather weren't the only reasons they hadn't managed to get out on the trails till now. And yet, even summoning her full paranoiac abilities, she could not identify any friction or issue that had arisen in their friendship. Nothing, despite the simmering resentment of the honorary degree committee back in the fall, had changed in her own private support of Francine's work, let alone in the way Webster's president supported its dean of admissions. Watching her friend's broad back ascend a muddy bank ahead of her, Naomi persuaded herself that whatever was happening with Francine was something else—something not about her and perhaps not about Webster at all. The marriage? There had never been a whiff of anything, as far as she was aware. Francine—mystifying as this had sometimes seemed to Naomi—loved Sumner Rigor. Their formal courtship and soberly conceived marriage, a marriage that would, by mutual wish, add no children to those produced by Sumner's first union, was as genial and pleasant as any Naomi had ever observed. The two of them were like perfectly suited roommates, or good neighbors straight out of a Robert Frost poem in which everyone understood what was expected of them and the property lines were reassuringly drawn. They lived in harmony, traveled together, worked separately, visited Sumner's children on the appropriate occasions, and entertained in a relaxed and welcoming manner. They appeared to value each other every bit as much as a happy couple should.

She wanted to ask. She couldn't ask. It was another thing,

another boundary that been settled early on, within a year of her having arrived at Webster and found herself one stationary bicycle away from the also newly arrived (and newly wed) Francine at the college sports center. They both, it turned out, hated stationary bicycles, and treadmills, too. (The on-site childcare at the sports center was what got Naomi to the gym, but as soon as four-year-old Hannah was settled in the playroom she would remember how much she despised those machines.) Soon the two women had begun to meet for walks outside, and talk. And after that, Naomi supposed, they were friends. Francine loved Hannah, that was for sure, and Hannah had actually stayed with the Rigors more than a few times, when her mother was away at conferences or, later, speaking to alumni groups as Webster's president. And over the years Naomi had met the important people from Francine's pre-Webster life: her mother (who'd moved to Florida) and her sister (an antiques dealer in Michigan who came east for Brimfield every September), and a Vassar colleague she had kept up with. Naomi had met Sumner's son Timothy, and Sumner's son John, both (like their father) respectable and boring, and also Sumner's twin sister, who lived in Seattle and did something tech-related. It was all very congenial, if not precisely intimate.

They made their way back to their cars without having slipped, and Naomi, just as Francine was about to unlock her door, and without planning to do so, suddenly heard herself ask whether everything was all right. Francine stopped. "What? What do you mean?"

"Oh no," Naomi said. She had alarmed herself almost as much. "I just...I wondered. If there's anything I can do."

"Do about what, Naomi?"

"Well,"—she was backpedaling frantically now—"I don't know. I don't know what I'm talking about, I'm just...I was wondering if everything's okay with you. I mean, a few weeks ago you said you weren't ready to talk about it. And I don't know what 'it' is, but I wanted to say that if you ever did want to talk, you can talk to me."

Francine appeared to soften slightly. Her broad shoulders fell forward, and she looked down. "I appreciate that, but I don't..." She shrugged. "It's not me, really. It's just...Sumner and work. Just annoying bureaucratic shit. And you know he works so hard, and he's so devoted to Hawthorne. It just appalls me how under-appreciated he is."

"That's hard," Naomi said, carefully, neutrally.

"People love to hurl crap," she said bitterly.

Who was hurling crap at Sumner? Naomi thought. But if Francine wanted to tell her, she would.

"It's going to work out, I'm confident. But it's not pleasant."

Naomi surprised herself, again, by asking, "What about that guy at your house?" And again, she could not fail to note Francine's physical reaction. "You know. The Grosvenor who doesn't actually have any money."

"That's not to be repeated," she said, alarmed and tense.

"Of course not."

"Well, no. Not really. He's Sumner's closest advocate on the board, actually. He's been a great support."

"Okay. Good," said Naomi, feeling more confused than before. "As I said, the last thing I want to do is pry. But please, if you need to...vent. Or whatever. Anytime."

Briefly, Francine looked as if she might actually be considering this offer, but then she seemed to get hold of herself. She opened up her car door. "When's Hannah back?" she asked.

"The day before classes start. Think she's trying to tell me something?" Naomi asked with deep sarcasm.

"Maybe," Francine said seriously.

This required a full five seconds to land.

Oh, she wanted to say. *No, no, we're fine. Everything's fine!* But it occurred to her that she did not want to hear Francine's opinion on this subject, so they hugged awkwardly, got into their cars, and drove away in opposite directions.

A week later she was back at Francine's for New Year's Eve, a small dinner to which the problematic Billy Grosvenor had also been invited. This time he came with a woman, but the woman turned out to be another trustee of the Hawthorne School, and very married to someone whose plane had been grounded at O'Hare. Joanne Lattimer was tall—nearly Francine's height— with a default facial expression of such severe displeasure that her obvious plastic surgery struck Naomi as having been pointlessly undertaken. "Oh, good," she said tightly, shaking Naomi's hand. "I was told you'd be here."

And here I am, Naomi refrained from saying.

"This is extraordinary, this transformation at Webster."

Was this about the protest again? Naomi wondered. Had the news penetrated even the old guard of Southborough? "Oh?" she said noncommittally.

"Well, certainly. You never used to hear about Webster. If you weren't going to the Ivies or the Seven Sisters, it was state school. Nothing wrong with state school."

Never said there was, thought Naomi.

"And now, all the private school kids know about it. They're choosing it over Harvard and Yale. Half of Groton applied last year. I can tell you, the parents are really playing catch-up with this. Webster College!"

"Well," Naomi said dryly, "we've always been here. We've been hiding in plain sight. Ooh," she said, eyeing the small but distinctive mounds of caviar on toast, wafting by on a platter in Francine's hands. "Is that caviar?"

"Yes, but really, what can you offer them that the Ivies can't?"

It was worth a try, Naomi thought.

"Those are eight fantastic schools. Major differences among

them, of course, but all great schools. But just because this particular eight decided to form an athletic league in the fifties, that has never meant there was something magical about them. And the term itself is only sixty years old, you know."

She could see from Joanne Lattimer's frozen and unhappy face that she hadn't known. And also that she didn't care.

"But these are ancient schools," the woman objected. Only an American would refer to the seventeenth and eighteenth centuries as "ancient." "And Webster..."

"Founded in 1762," Naomi said shortly. Now, her Irish was up. And she wasn't Irish.

Lattimer looked as if she wished she could widen her eyes at this, but sadly wasn't able to do so.

"Really?"

"Really."

So why wasn't Webster an Ivy? she probably wanted to ask.

Because we probably had a lousy football team in the 1950s. Okay?

"Well, then, why did we never hear about Webster until now?"

It was, of course, a circular argument, and hence not winnable.

"Just one of those mysteries." Naomi sighed. "And you work with Sumner, I understand?"

Joanne Lattimer looked, again, flatly irritated by the question. Or maybe amused? It was so hard to tell.

"I'm on the board of the Hawthorne School. I have been on the board since 1995. All three of my children attended Hawthorne."

Naomi nodded. This time, the tray with the caviar, carried by Francine herself, was coming too close for her to miss it. "They must have had a wonderful experience for you to have given so much of your life to the school."

"Hawthorne, I believe, is one of the finest private elementary schools in the state. Perhaps the country."

"Mm," said Naomi. She was taking one of the little toasts from Francine's tray. "I love this!" she told her friend. "And so far it's one of the few proteins Hannah doesn't object to. Not that I get to eat it often."

"Who is Hannah?" said Joanne Lattimer.

"Naomi's daughter," Francine said. "She's phenomenal."

"Where does she go to school?" Joanne said, cutting to the chase.

"She's a sophomore at Webster," Francine said, because Naomi's mouth was full. But if Naomi was expecting the usual *Naturally* or *Of course she is*, it didn't come. In Joanne Lattimer's world it passed without comment that connections were everything. Undoubtedly her own children had progressed from the hallowed gates of Hawthorne to the hallowed gates of Groton to the hallowed gates of Harvard, and that was as it always had been and always would be, forever, and ever, and ever...amen.

"Joanne has done wonderful things for Hawthorne," said Francine, extending her tray to give both women a second stab at the caviar. Only Naomi availed herself of this.

"Tell me more!" Naomi said. She smiled at her friend.

The woman, not remotely interested in deflecting praise, but not, apparently, enjoying it either, said, "I designed our capital campaign in the 1990s. We raised over fifteen million for the school and built a new gymnasium and a new media center for the children. We also have our own stables, thanks to a donor. The children ride twice a week."

"That's..." but Naomi felt lost for words. What that was was many things. She wasn't sure she should say most of them out loud. "Wow."

"Yes. Wow," Francine said helpfully. "And of course Joanne

headed the search committee that brought Sumner to Hawthorne. So we are endlessly grateful for that!"

She said it jauntily, lightly, but it was anything but light. Naomi saw that right away, and it hit with a fitting blow. *Holy cow*, she thought. But she was flying blind.

"Oh...well...then I have reason to be grateful to you as well!" Naomi managed. "If Sumner hadn't come to Hawthorne, I don't think our present dean of admissions would have applied for an opening at Webster. And since this woman"—she linked her arm through Francine's, the one that was not holding the tray—"is my very good friend, I personally owe you a debt."

But even this physical gesture of female solidarity failed to impress the chilly woman before them. She drained her Champagne as her gaze drifted up, past the shoulders of the two women to the far end of the room, where someone more interesting might or might not soon appear. Her snowed-in husband? The president and dean of admissions for Harvard or Yale? Elijah's ghost? "Well, I don't know about that," she said simply. "One never knows how these things are going to work out, ultimately."

Naomi merely stared at her, but Francine flinched. Actually flinched. It passed through them both like a current of rasping electricity, and Naomi, involuntarily, turned to look at her friend. But Francine would not look back. Impervious to this (or was she? it was so hard to tell with that petrified face), Joanne Lattimer thanked her hostess and announced that she would now head home to await her husband, though at this point he would certainly arrive in the new year, and her escort, the by comparison warm and delightful Billy Grosvenor, could plainly be seen laughing and enjoying himself with Sumner over by the fireplace. Then she set her empty glass among the caviar toast points on Francine's silver tray, and walked away, giving both women the back of her narrow, cashmere-encased shoulders. She tapped

Billy Grosvenor on his wrist, and with remarkable swiftness he, too, had put down his drink (on the mantelpiece, at least) and left his clearly affected host to accompany her from the room. It was all over in less than a moment. And on that note, soon after, the year itself came jolting to an unhappy end.

PART III

SYMBOL

CHAPTER ELEVEN

THE BASEMENT OF SOJOURNER TRUTH

Then, with the new term, they were back. Some of them looked notably tan, others red-cheeked in the distinct manner of winter sports enthusiasts, but once within reach of the Stump they magically regained their shared posture of flinty and united resistance, securing their tents (again!) and making their sordid nests. Naomi, watching them (surreptitiously from the guest room window of the Stone House), felt a dull mood begin to settle over her neck and shoulders. She didn't call anyone. She couldn't bring herself to do it, and not merely because she wasn't sure whom she'd be calling or what she'd expect them to do. By now, her primary feeling about the students around the Stump—the ones from Webster, at any rate (because she'd learned from the media she wasn't speaking to that there were now student contingents from Wesleyan, Yale, Brown, Mount Holyoke, and, incredibly, MIT—though were they not, as in an Arthur Miller play, *all her students?*)—was a persistent undertow of shame. She was ashamed of what was happening now. Because she had not solved it. Or stopped it. Or—worst of all—truly understood why it hadn't ended already. And as the last days of the break passed in thin January sunlight, more and more and more of them arrived: landing, fluttering, unfurling, expanding the encampment out to the edge of the Billings Lawn and impinging upon even the broad avenues on the east and west perimeters.

Hannah returned from New York and departed almost at once for a crisis meeting at the Sojourner Truth House, dropping bags of books she'd hauled home from the Strand (postcolonialism in Africa, biographies of—bizarrely—both Herzl and Göring, slender volumes of poetry from the 1950s), suitable for period set decoration. Was that what they were for? Naomi wondered, guiltily looking through the shopping bags right where Hannah had dumped them on the floor of the entry hall, spreading out the books on the stone slabs and groping for meaning, as if they were a broken rune language. That night, the Saturday before winter term began, was especially bleak, especially cold. The administrative and classroom buildings around the encampment were all dark, except for the first and third floors of Service Hall, where Francine and her staff were barricaded in their offices, reading applications. (She had not seen Francine since New Year's Eve, and to be honest she had a pretty bad feeling about that, too.)

Hannah, naturally, had not been forthcoming about what constituted the "crisis" of the crisis meeting, and so when the house phone rang several hours later, catching Naomi horizontal on the couch in the TV room, where she had accidentally fallen asleep, it took a few minutes before she understood who was calling her and what they were trying to communicate.

The caller was Peter Rudolph of the campus police, a sweet man, soft-spoken, who had a part-time carpentry business in town and took eager advantage of the staff auditing program. And what he was trying to communicate was that something had happened at Sojourner Truth House that she'd better come over and see herself, and could she come right away?

The pieces of this—Sojourner Truth, and Hannah, the crisis meeting, and "something happened"—went jolting through her, making her rattle with fear. "My daughter's there," she managed. And after a moment Peter Rudolph, who had three daughters of his own, said, without condescension, "Oh no, nobody's hurt. There's nobody hurt. Just damage. So just come."

"I'm coming!" she'd said, as if her speed was some logical way to repay him for not telling her an awful thing had happened to Hannah. And she dressed and raced through the now freezing darkness, wondering what could be so bad if it was not the so bad of actual harm to her daughter. Or, naturally, another Webster student. (Or, of course, anyone else!)

Down the stone walkway that ran behind the old classroom buildings and the chapel and the Stone House. Down the little hill to the athletic center and its complex of courts and fields, and then the right turn on Fairweather, counting her way along the row of them: the Co-Op House, the French House, the German House (they were going to have to close the German House, she thought as she reached it, or else adjust its mission; no one seemed to be studying German anymore), and finally, just before the First Nations Center (a massive faux Tudor that dwarfed everything else on the street): the Sojourner Truth House. This was a stately redbrick Colonial Revival, gifted to the college by its last owner, an alum who'd hoped (but sadly failed to specify, in writing, in his will) that his home would be occupied in perpetuity by his own Webster fraternity. It really was so important to put everything in writing, Naomi thought, hurrying up the walkway.

The door was ajar, and the rooms full of people, the hallway full of people, bodies displaced behind the door as she pushed her way in. Automatically, she looked for Hannah, but there were too many heads, too much din. A girl just inside the threshold was weeping, inconsolable, though not for the lack of consolers: Two skinny, bearded boys had their arms around her waist, their hairy cheeks on her shoulders. "What?" Naomi said.

"I told her not to go down there," said someone. Naomi turned. It was Chava, but she was moving. She had elbowed past Naomi without stopping and continued on, into the living room (or what had once, at some more domestic moment in the house's life, been a living room), where she was swallowed up.

"Are you okay?" Naomi asked the girl. There was no response from her, but both of the bearded boys lifted their heads to look at her. Not a flicker of recognition.

"Are you media?" said one.

"You shouldn't be here," said the other. "This is a safe space."

Safe from whom? she nearly said.

"I'm President Roth," Naomi said.

"President of what?" the first one said, with mild curiosity.

"President of Webster," she said, trying—but failing—to summon some authority.

"Oh, sorry." He didn't seem remotely sorry. "I don't go here. But you got a bad thing down there, man. I mean, you know, that shouldn't happen anywhere. It's a very hurtful thing."

"I ..." Naomi took a hard shove from her left, but it was only someone backing up, violently, not personal. It knocked right out of her whatever it was she'd been about to say, which she now, helpfully, couldn't even remember. Was it outrage? Denial? A defense of some kind? Who were all of these people who "don't go here"? And where was her daughter?

"Hey! President Roth!" Naomi looked around. Peter Rudolph was at the far end of the hallway, under the staircase. He had his back to the cellar door, and his arms crossed. Beside him was one of the others. New to the security staff? Newish? He'd been at the Day of Campus Discourse, so called. Before she could censor herself, she thought, *Oh good. At least one of them is black.*

Excuse me, she told the students, moving very slowly. Hand on a shoulder here. Gentle nudge there. *Pardon me. Hi?*

Sorry... They parted and closed around her, pressing her off balance and righting her, conveying her down the once-dignified hallway. Now the walls were institutional beige with old flyers (campus speakers, themed events) in never-cleaned frames randomly affixed, and a bulletin board of "ding letters" posted by the residents. "Dear Mr. Jonas," she read while wedging past a cluster of agitated young men, "I thank you for your interest in our trainee program. As you know, Goldman Sachs receives many hundreds of applications for each of our limited places in the program..." The word "limited" had been encircled by thick red pen, and an arrow pointed, from this, to the commentary: "Limited in what way, exactly?" Farther down, at the start of the final paragraph, the hapless writer had blandly offered "We wish you all success with your job search," but his merciless copy editor had underlined the phrase "We wish you" and added the words "a merry fucking Christmas, cracker!" Beside this, a letter from Yale Law, dark blue ink on heavy cream-colored stock, informed a Ms. Townsend that it was simply impossible to say yes to every one of the impeccably credentialed applicants who had sought admission to the class of 2020. "Et tu, Eli?" someone had written over the Yale crest at the top of the page. "Already too many black people in New Haven!" was written in another hand in one of the bottom corners. Naomi, briefly released from the baffling present, felt a spike of entirely unrelated depression. Then, beneath that, she read: "Nigger, what?" And the involuntary gut punch came immediately. It was as if she had found her quarantined city breached by the feared microbe, a riddled body inside the wall, burrowed under the wall, catapulted over the wall, wormed through the stones: all lost within. All lost. *Et tu, Sojourner Truth?*

On the hallway floor, three young women were seated, backs to the wall. Two were crying silently. The other one appeared to be asleep. Or—Naomi peered at her—drunk? Stoned? She was black and a tiny thing, and she wore a very oversized Webster sweatshirt marked VARSITY CREW. Naomi, without thinking, bent over her. "Are you okay?" she asked, but her voice didn't register over the noise, even to herself.

"We gave her something," the girl next to her said. "She just kind of lost it."

"What kind of something?" Naomi said, eyeing the girl.

"Only a Xanax. She lives upstairs. She was the one who found it. She went down for toilet paper or something, and she found it."

Naomi, who figured she'd know soon enough what "it" was, didn't ask, and the truth was that she didn't want to know just yet. "She lives here?"

"Yeah, but I don't think we could get her upstairs. There's too many people."

"Who are all these people?" she asked, but the girl looked at her as if she didn't understand the question and didn't especially care whether she understood it or not. Naomi looked up. She was nearly within reach of Peter Rudolph now. He was waiting for her.

"Peter? Can you call health services? I want her to taken over to the infirmary."

He reached, so slowly, for his phone. What was the matter with these people?

"I think she's probably okay," said Peter Rudolph. "She was just upset."

And you're a doctor too? Naomi thought unkindly.

"Nevertheless." She got to her feet. "I'm President Roth," she told the man beside him.

"Trevor." They shook hands.

"You'll take her outside," she told him, and as she did, some part of her was watching, commentating: *Well, aren't you the bossy one?* "Out to the sidewalk."

He appeared unpersuaded, and this infuriated Naomi, who

was still outside herself, narrating the occasion. "Shouldn't I go downstairs with you?"

"No. Take her outside. You," she said, grabbing the nearest male shoulder. "And you. The three of you, please help take this young woman outside and wait for health services. They're on their way," she said, looking at Peter. "They are, right?"

"Yes, of course." He appeared, finally, to have grasped her sense of the occasion.

She stepped back as the three men—Trevor and the two students (she hoped and assumed that they were students)—reached down for the girl, who groaned but did not resume consciousness as she was lifted, first up and then overhead, like a bride. She was so light. Up she rose.

"And one of you," Naomi said, eyeing other two girls, who had watched all of this as if it had nothing to do with them. "Who's going to the infirmary with her?"

They looked at each other. "But we don't really know her. She lives here."

"So what?" Naomi shouted.

"Well..." one of the girls said, "what I mean is, she isn't really a part of this, she just lives here. She lives upstairs. She was just..." She looked at her friend for clarification. "Wasn't she going down to get toilet paper or something?"

"Yeah. Maybe paper towels. Something for the bathroom. But, like, we never saw her before tonight."

"Oh, no," her friend said. "I was in a class with her. Chem, freshman year. When I still thought I was going to medical school." They both laughed, bizarrely. Naomi glared at them.

Naomi reached down for the one on the right and pulled her arm up so hard that the girl was standing in a flash. And taller than Naomi, she noted, defensively. "You gave her a pill. You are going with her to the infirmary. And I want your name."

"I got her name," Peter Rudolph said. At least he had done something.

"So go now. Please." Naomi said, and the girls both went, picking a meandering route through the hallway.

Naomi shook her head. In the former living room, a drone of voices seemed to be rising, punctuated by staccato shouts. Anger. Someone was very angry. A lot of people were angry. "Peter," Naomi said, taking a breath, "why haven't we cleared the house? What are we waiting for?"

"I didn't want to make that decision for the police." He shrugged. "Far as I'm concerned, this is a crime scene," he added.

"What's down there?" She nodded at the cellar door. "Just tell me. Is someone hurt? Is someone...has someone been...harmed?" It was all she could manage.

"Not exactly. But it's a mess." She pushed past him, catching the tail end of sweat and a recent cigarette. The step, wooden and a tiny bit warped, gave a loud creak at her weight, and the string descending from a single lightbulb grazed her forehead, making her jump. There was no sound from the space below. Nothing, nothing. She stood for a moment, letting herself pretend that the unconscious girl, the campus police, the teary faces, the angry voices, were somehow unattached to anything—seeable, touchable, real. "Nothing is happening," she spoke, aloud, sending the whisper of it down the stairs to whatever there was, whatever the reason for all this was. And then she went down after it.

First, the wetness, not underfoot but everywhere else: wet walls, wet ceiling. Wet with something brown and matted. What was it? Naomi frowned, consciously instructing herself to smell the wet thing. It was dull, but it was unmistakable. *On the blanket*, she thought, retrieving a term she'd heard often enough in the '80s but seldom since, for the hunger strikers in the Irish prisons who'd painted the walls with excrement—their signature protest. Amazing how the exact words can lurk, waiting for us to need them. *I need them now*, she thought, taking it all in. On the ceiling and the walls, but not all of the walls. One of the four walls looked utterly undisturbed: cheap prefab shelves stacked with paper products, garbage bags, batteries, cleaning supplies, items of peaceful communal living. Had the person responsible for this left the Pine-Sol and paper towels in place as a way of saying, *You're gonna need these, pal*? She stood, stuck in place on one of the lower steps, one forefinger and thumb pinching her nose. She had not set foot on the basement floor, which was glittery with broken glass, bottles from the upended recycling bin, most likely, green and clear and brown, the residue of cola and beer mixing freely with the fecal matter in a ferment of odor. She had not touched a thing, *because it is a crime scene*, she told herself, but the truth was more elemental, more visceral: disgust and horror and shock. It took a long, pulled-apart moment before she understood that there was order to the brown smears, and a message, so clear and so horrible that it exploded in her head. The words spelled: NIGGERS OUT.

Naomi stood, holding her nose, swaying a bit. She discovered, after a moment, that she had closed her eyes without quite noticing it. It was so peaceful with her eyes shut, but then she opened them to test this theory. NIGGERS OUT. Shit on the walls and glass underfoot.

Eyes open: *the shit, the word.*

Eyes closed: *the darkness, the peace.*

She released her nostrils and peered through her own fingers, and the reek assailed her, and then the nausea, and then the horror, because the world was going to see this, there was no way of stopping that. Frat boys chanting racist slogans. Confederate flags allowed to flutter over Southern campuses. Alcohol poisonings. Acquaintance rape. Drug overdoses. Cheating scandals.

Everything that Webster had been above since Sarafian's time. And then his successor's time. And then his successor's successor's time. And, until now, her time. But she had broken the chain, all right. This—she regarded the walls and the floor balefully—had broken the chain. This would make another chain, linking Webster back through the years of evolution and revolution and all of the many gains and the comfort of their present position in the academic landscape of early twenty-first-century American liberal arts. Back to the 1950s, to Luther Merrion, the freshman who'd neglected to inform the admissions committee that he was not white. Luther Merrion, sent home to Indiana because he wasn't welcome at Webster College. *Niggers out.* It was a tradition.

Behind her, the cellar door creaked open, and the light and the noise came shuddering down the steps. "You okay down there?" said Peter.

"Oh, sure," she said with heavy sarcasm. "Peachy."

"It's a mess," he suggested.

It was a mess, no doubt.

"You called the police," she said. It wasn't a question.

"I was waiting for you."

Her first impulse was to be enraged. He was waiting for her? But then she was grateful; whether or not he had understood this himself, Naomi knew that she should be the one to call the police. She would report this herself. It was something. "I don't want anyone to leave," she told Peter. "I want everyone to be available to the police. And I want to speak to everyone in the living room."

He considered this. He seemed to be trying to remember how this was supposed to work, but there had never been a "this" before, thankfully.

"I don't think we're allowed to force anyone. They can, but we can't."

Naomi was getting out her phone. "Do you have a contact, or do I use 911?"

He read her the number for his liaison officer, whose name was Werner.

"Werner what?" Naomi said, pressing the numbers.

"Bill. Bill Werner."

"Oh." The phone rang twice, and then a man with a high, quavering voice answered. "Werner?" he asked, as if it were up to the caller to say whether he was or wasn't. From the corner of her eye, Naomi saw the front door open. People were starting to leave. No one should be leaving, she thought, in a panic.

"Stop them," she told Peter. "Go to the door and make them stop."

"Hello?" said Werner, or Bill.

"Hey, sorry," Naomi said. "I'm Naomi Roth, at Webster. President Roth," she confirmed, though he had not asked for confirmation.

"Yes," he said. "What is it?"

Naomi opened her mouth, but found that the words had fled. What was it? What, indeed, was it? An act of brutal stupidity? An orchestrated statement? Whatever it was, in a moment it would be out—it would have escaped the artificial containment of the college, of its bright college days and auld lang syne, this Elysium lily pad between childhood and adulthood. *What happens at Webster stays at Webster*, or at least had, once. Not anymore. It was quite possible that Naomi herself was the only human being in the Sojourner Truth House tonight without a Facebook page or a Snapchat account, or an avid Instagram following. This...atrocity, this indictment, had already been seen by human eyes, and by young and early-adopting human eyes, which meant that it might already be on the web, or attached to a text, dividing and copying in the dark and endless incubator of cyberspace. Soon, the press would be dispensing this latest proof that the world was sliding back to the civil rights era and taking up residence on the other side, which was bad enough when it was other places, other colleges. How had it been allowed to happen here? How had she, personally, made it possible? She felt as if she might wail.

"We've had," at last, she managed, "an incident. I would imagine that an investigation is warranted." Even as she said it she was shaking her head at her own formality. So many words to say so little. So many police procedurals. So much *Masterpiece Theatre*.

"Incident," he said, almost gently.

"I...don't want to describe it on the phone. The basement of the Sojourner Truth House on Fairweather. Could you come right away, please? And there are a lot of people here. You'll want to..."

"Is it an assault? Vandalism? What?"

"Vandalism," she said quickly—too quickly. She was grateful for the word, and seized upon it as soon as it was spoken. It was so...innocuous. *Vandalism!* Like throwing toilet paper at a tree on Halloween! Nobody got in real trouble for vandalism. No college would earn fatal notoriety because of vandalism. Well, she would hold on to that for as long as she possibly could.

"Oh. All right." He sounded almost disappointed. "Well, I'll send someone over."

"More than one," she said sharply. "And quickly. I mean, technically vandalism, but...well, you'll see. There's...language. Involved."

Suddenly, there were raised voices in the next room. "I need to go," she told him, but it was so loud, suddenly, that she was pretty sure he hadn't heard her. "Stay here," she told Peter. "Nobody goes down there. Not one person. Understand?"

"Oh, absolutely." He nodded, as if he had just figured this out for himself.

She turned and pushed her way back through the hallway. "Do you mind?" she asked one girl, no fewer than three times, when gentle pressure on her shoulder and then her hip did not shift her at all. The girl turned to her with a face full of bland resentment and slowly pivoted her body, which was thin and made a thin space that Naomi, who was not thin, nevertheless pressed through. The room was hot, she noticed now, and there was the faintest smell of ash. From the fireplace, it occurred to her. The notion of all of these kids in one building with a fire made her feel faint. "Excuse me," she told a tall boy with a Chinese symbol etched in red behind his ear. "Excuse me, I'm trying to..." She reached out for the doorframe, honey oak and grimy with handprints, and actually pulled herself closer to it, and the doorway, and the living room itself, which was tight with people: on the floor, mashed against the walls, sitting on one another's laps on—Naomi assumed—couches and chairs, so overladen that they could not be seen beneath the bodies. "Fuck that," someone said, directly behind her. "I can't hear a thing."

"Well, shut the fuck up," somebody else said. "Try that, why don't you?"

She tried to turn to see them, but at just that moment she felt herself hoisted up, actually off her feet, and pressed forward into the already packed room. An entirely different scenario of horror and mayhem rushed through her, banishing the fire, and she thought of all of these students crushed to death, together, in the contracting living room of the Sojourner Truth House, their president along with them (going down with the ship), which would be comforting to exactly no one, Naomi gasped. "Wait," she said, to nobody, but the sound disappeared in another surge of protest.

"Let him speak," said a woman. "Everybody? Could we all...?"

Just get along, thought Naomi, automatically, amid her coursing panic.

"All right," said a single voice, which, suddenly, strangely, now became the only voice she could hear. It was like a voice on another frequency, to which her brain had tuned itself in desperation, a last resort, and the blur it made seemed to descend from the ceiling, down over them all. "All right," it said again. "Can everyone sit where they are? We will wait. We will wait."

And then she felt first one and then both of her feet meet the blessed levelness, solidness, of the floor. The relief of that tumbled through her. Then she felt the bodies beside her begin to move apart, relinquishing her. She could breathe. Her lungs could take in breath. That was glorious. That was euphoric.

"Okay," said the voice, which was male but not, somehow, overtly masculine. It was a high voice, a sweet voice, musical. "We're almost there."

The body in front of her suddenly went down. The body beside her—short, round, how had it held her up off the floor?—also went down. She suddenly felt conspicuous. She was standing. She was one of only a dozen or so in the room who were still on their feet. Then she was one of only a handful.

"Come on," the short person said, looking up at her without recognition, but with familiarity, as if they had been introduced but jointly forgotten each other's names. "There's room here." And she patted a miracle of open carpeting with her hand. It wasn't big. But it was big enough.

Naomi sat, her legs folding into some position of temporary comfort. So great was her relief at returning to the earth that she had completely lost any sense of urgency about what was happening here, because as long as that person was speaking her only job was to listen, and how simple, blessedly simple was that?

"I just needed to say this before we leave," said Omar, because of course it was Omar. He had stepped up onto a chair exactly in front of the fireplace, and his slender form now stood directly before the abstract portrait of Sojourner Truth herself, which was large, unframed, and distinctly student-made. Sojourner's eyes hovered, peering over his right shoulder, an endorsement across the ages.

"Louder, please?" said someone behind Naomi. But she said it hopefully. She truly wanted to miss nothing.

"I needed to say, before we all leave here," said Omar, and this time the sound went out on phantom waves of amplification, "whatever has brought each of us here, it's unimportant now, because now we are here together. We speak from our shared humanity, and we speak a shared truth."

And what is that, pray tell? Naomi thought. She had to stop herself from saying it out loud, because it had now occurred to her that if she kept quiet and called absolutely no attention to herself, she might actually get them to talk to her, or at least in her presence. Months of open doors and appointments that weren't kept, "Days of Campus Discourse"—what a joke that had been—and pleading emails, asking, in so many ways, something that had begun as *What can I help you, my much-respected and admired Webster students, to accomplish?* decompressed into *What's going on here?* and finally collapsed beneath the weight of *Will somebody fucking talk to me, please?* Keeping quiet was not the same as uttering a falsehood—not at all! She wasn't hiding; she was absolutely, utterly, honestly present and ready to be accounted for. That the Webster students surrounding her had failed to recognize her from the cover of their Webster Welcome packets or her frequent photographs in the campus papers or any of her innumerable and conscientious outreaches to them (convocation, presidential office hours, teas, seminars, midnight ghost story readings at the freshman bonfire, for goodness' sake!), then that could not be considered her fault. Naomi had extended herself; they had withdrawn. And now she was here, and they didn't realize. *Well, tough.*

Her right leg already was howling, but she grabbed it to shut it up because the room was quiet, because Omar was speaking. He spoke like the spirit-orator girl in that Henry James novel: still and small—a still, small voice in a crush of listeners. For a moment she merely heard the musical notes of it, and not the words at all. He had such an interesting face, Naomi noted: sharp features, very black hair that came down over his forehead and stopped where it landed. His eyes were large and extremely dark and he was narrow and undersized: *stunted* was the word she thought of again. Well, of course: stunted. With that childhood, that deprivation, how could it be otherwise? And did they know? These American kids, with their fluoridated water and vaccine schedule, what the life of two-year-old Omar and eight-year-old Omar and fourteen-year-old Omar had been? How, as they'd drilled for their travel soccer teams, he and his friends must have kicked a battered, pockmarked sphere around some battered, pockmarked lot. How, as they'd conferred with their tutors and typed notes into their laptops, he and his schoolmates had hoped Israeli bombs would not fall on their school, such as it was. And where were those friends and schoolmates now? Dead under exploded buildings? Dead in delusional "martyrdom"? Dead of preventable illnesses or ordinary poverty? She had no idea, but she highly doubted that even one of them was standing in a once-grand Colonial Revival on the campus of a lauded American university, holding the children of immense privilege and wealth in the palm of his slender hand.

But listen to the words, she remembered. Naomi dug a fist into her calf, which only spread the pain around.

"I understand that, in normal times, we are defined by our differences, and differences are fine and beautiful things. But these are not normal times. What happened here, tonight, or whenever it happened, should not be normal at any time, or anywhere in the world. We may not be able to fix all the problems in the world—"

"Why not?" said a woman to Naomi's right.

Omar sighed, deeply, contemplatively. "I can't tell you how much I respect that...optimism," he said, speaking directly to whomever had spoken, a person he, presumably, could see more clearly than Naomi. "I can't help but feel that the magnitude of unfairness, injustice in the world, is too much even for the commitment and intention in this room. But I grew up in a very different place from this room. And this ability you have, as Americans, to see a good future, I never met anyone who could do that, until I came to this country. I don't know how to explain it to you except to talk about my life and my family, and that is hard for me to do."

A ripple of anticipation passed through the room. Naomi was not the only one, she saw, who had been waiting for some window into this contained, eloquent boy.

"My father wasn't educated. He was a car mechanic. But he was intelligent. He could have been a physician or an engineer. My mother was a nurse, but she could have been a physician, too. And my brother..." Omar choked a little, but rallied. "He was the cleverest one in our family."

Omar closed his eyes and swayed a little. Naomi could hear the broken breathing of the woman beside her.

"Wait," said a voice behind her—male, low but soft—"what happened to his family?"

And quick as a cat, the woman beside Naomi twisted back to glare at him, and hissed: "Don't you know?"

He went red, almost comically. He was a big kid and very pale, with already receding brown hair.

He shook his head. "I...no, I'm sorry."

"All dead," Naomi's neighbor said, as if that were the kid's fault. "You remember that little boy and his father, who were caught in crossfire in Gaza? The father tried to protect him, but they were both murdered by the Israelis. There were thousands of pictures on the web. It went viral. Don't you remember?"

"I think so," he whispered. Naomi, who did not need to think that she remembered, who knew that she remembered, who had never forgotten that little boy, terrified in his father's arms as they huddled against a building, praying for it to be over, was already numb. What did it mean?

"Wait, that was him?" said the kid.

"Of course not," said the woman, harshly, but not without a certain satisfaction. "I just told you, that little boy died. And the father. They were Omar's brother and father."

Holy shit, said the poor guy, but maybe he didn't. Maybe it was Naomi who said that, or maybe she didn't, but she was thinking it. It was on a loop in her head, at screaming volume: *holy shit, holy shit*. How was she supposed to have known that? Did Francine know? Had it been in the essay? No, no, it hadn't; Naomi was forcing herself to remember the essay. She had read the essay, the same essay Francine would have read. But, maybe, somewhere else in the application? Something Admissions would have had access to? Like…an official report of some kind? A letter from the refugee agency or one of the foster parents?

Then Naomi thought: *Does Hannah know this?*

Of course Hannah did. Of course she did. No wonder she'd regarded her mother with such superior disapproval that day in her room, reaching up into the closet for that extra sleeping bag. For Omar. Sweet, sad Omar would not have had a sleeping bag of his own, of course. Omar would not have done much sleeping out in Yukon temperatures, not in the Gaza Strip. And besides, she supposed, Omar would not have owned much of anything. What had he brought with him to Webster from Oklahoma, Texas, Wisconsin, Bureij? She imagined him climbing up onto a Greyhound bus in some dust bowl town with just a back-pack, and shaking someone's hand, solemnly, goodbye. Alone in the world, and yet bound for glory. Or at least, for this. It all felt utterly inevitable now.

A Palestinian boy, with a backpack, climbing onto a bus. It made her shudder, first with fear, then with guilt for the fear.

"Oh wow," said the poor boy behind her. "That sucks."

And with a look of glorious disdain, the woman beside Naomi wrenched herself around again and assumed her mask of pained solidarity as she waited for Omar to resume.

"I want you to know that I'm not envious when you tell me about your childhoods, and your families. I love to hear about your parents and the houses and neighborhoods you grew up in. My feeling has never been 'Why did you get to have that, and I did not?' Of course, I wish I'd had it. The safety alone, you can't imagine what it would have meant to me and my brother and really everyone we knew. Just that relief of thinking, 'Yes, I can walk to school'—the school will be there. 'Yes, I can play outside. My house—no one is going to blow it up. I can have good health and a good education and I can choose what to do when I'm a man.' I should have had that not because I was such a special and unique boy but because every child should have that, every-where. And we don't. And we won't, not anytime soon. But I also believe that if every person begins in their own place and makes it his or her business to remove violence and harm and injustice, then one day we are going to look around and see that there are no more problems in the world to fix." He stopped. He looked at them. After a moment, he shook his head. "I'm sorry. I shouldn't talk about this. I hate to talk about this."

"It's all right!" someone said, from up front, apparently at his feet.

"Oh, I know." He smiled wearily. "Only . . . I want to go forward in my life, not back. There is nothing good that comes from going back. But in my home, my family's home, there was always only back, because we never talked about the future, only our grievance. The American mind is almost, nearly, the opposite way—no past at all, just the now and what we look ahead to: our careers and goals in life. Maybe because you are such a young country and my country is so ancient."

Naomi, like, she supposed, many others in the room, found herself considering this point for the very first time.

"The short way to tell this story is to say that my family died and I came to America by myself. But there is another chapter in between that I am very ashamed of. Some of you, if you have lost a parent, you will understand what I am going to say. You have felt what I felt—the need to replace that person is so powerful. And you understand: My mother and father, they were as human and as imperfect as I am. And I think, you know, it's because I never got to have that experience of disappointment with my mother and father, there wasn't time, that I have had the weakness of letting certain people come into my life and take that role of a parent." He shook his head, and the dark locks moved over his eyes. Naomi now was trying to remember something from that application essay—some detail that might illuminate this dark, decidedly dark, allusion. Did he mean the American, working for the NGO in the schools, who'd pointed him in the direction of emigration to America? Was there some accusation here that hadn't been in the essay? What exactly was he saying? She nearly raised her hand to ask, but in the next instant she no longer needed to ask. Because Omar, who wanted so badly to go forward in his life, was being borne back ceaselessly into the past again. He trembled, fought with himself, and broke anew.

"You might be sitting at your breakfast table, or in a Starbucks somewhere, reading the newspaper or looking at the news on your phone, and there is a story," he gasped, "about someone walking into a market or a restaurant and setting off a bomb. And you might think: Why would anyone do this? And I am glad this is such a mystery to you, because to a healthy mind, yes, it has to be a mystery why a person, especially a young person, would even consider doing such a thing. But in my world, this was an entirely ordinary event, and to a person like me, who wanted more than anything to have back the family that was taken, I would have done far more to feel that I was still in a family. And I will tell you that the day came when I was ready to do this, and even more, for people I'd persuaded myself were my family, my new family."

He seemed to have run out of breath. He stood, feet slightly apart, head hung. Naomi could see Chava, suddenly, moving toward him. She was undeterred by the bodies in the way, by the impossibility of making room for her long legs and long arms as she picked her way. She took the room she needed. She went to him and reached up to him atop his chair and encircled his small waist in her arms.

"I am so..." Omar resumed, one hand on Chava's shoulder, "so amazed at what I would have done. What I fully intended to do. I am humbled by it. I am appalled." He nodded, apparently to himself. "I would have been a murderer of children. I would have been a murderer of mothers and grandmothers. I would have been a self-murderer. I hate the person I nearly was. And after that I ran away from those people, and I found someone else I thought I could trust, and this time I chose wisely."

The American, Naomi thought. The NGO, yes? Wait, did that mean they were back in the story now? Was this the original story, or an addition to the original story, or some parallel story, meant to coexist, enhancing what was already known? Omar, the suddenly orphaned. Omar, the lost scholar. Omar, the wandering Palestinian. Omar, the nearly suicide bomber? No wonder he'd left that part out of his Webster application; it was hard to imagine Francine, or any other admissions officer, letting that particular extracurricular activity go. She'd heard of child soldiers finding again, after years of violent acts, the rafts of their own humanity. She'd heard of it, but how could it be true? If this was true, and if she was interpreting it correctly, Omar Khayal been ready to reduce babies to pulp in a crowd. He'd been ready to show children the scattered limbs of their parents. He'd been ready to be made use of, for someone else's brutal notion of justice.

"So yes, I am ashamed of myself. But I am also ashamed of Webster," said Omar, and now he had located some inner flint. The penitent on a chair, self-shaming before his comrades, had shifted into a disappointed teacher. "When Chava brought me downstairs this afternoon, I was very angry, and very shocked. Now, I find that I am still angry, but no longer shocked. And why is that?"

There was silence. If they knew, they didn't want to say.

The woman beside her drew the back of her hand across her face, and Naomi saw that it was wet. She had been weeping, silently, for how long? The woman on the other side of her was weeping, too. Was everybody weeping? Was she weeping, herself? She touched the back of her hand to her cheek. She was not weeping. *Why not?* Naomi thought. She knew enough of Omar's story to know how awful a story it was. Why wasn't she moved by this, by him?

"When I came here two years ago, I was so amazed. I saw the beauty of this place. I felt safety. I felt the willingness of my fellow students to be connected to me. I felt forgiveness, though I told no one about myself or what I'd done, what I needed to be forgiven for. Every day there was something that shocked me, astounded me—a safe room, as much food as I needed. If I was sick I just walked over to the health center and they took care of me. I could study what I wanted. If I needed clothes someone gave them to me. If I needed books they were handed to me, usually to keep. The only fighting was with words, and when it was over we all just went home and no one hurt anyone else. How can you understand what that felt like to someone who grew up as I did? I used to imagine—"

But he stopped himself. He seemed to be considering something, very carefully. "I know it will sound crazy, but I used to imagine I could bring my family here to live with me in my dorm room on Eagle Road."

There was a reaction: brief, uncomfortable mirth. The Eagle Road dorms were notoriously unlovely. And small.

"I had this daydream that the four of us were living in my room, going to the dining hall for our meals. And going to classes. So in my private paradise, which is what Webster was to me, all four of us are here. And much of that paradise was because of Professor Gall. Professor Gall is a great scholar and a great teacher and a great spirit. And does Webster College recognize his effort and his value?"

Naomi saw that many heads were shaking, gravely, bitterly. Either Nick Gall had been deeply influential to many of his students, a large contingent of whom happened to be in this very room at this very moment, or Omar's passion had already affected them deeply. His cause, now, was theirs, or had become the thin pointed end of their shared cornucopia of yearnings and complaints. A better Webster, she understood, was to begin with righting the perceived wrong done to one professor. But where would it end?

"When I arrived here a year and a half ago," Omar said, and his voice had taken on a dreaminess, as if he had slipped into a fugue, "I knew no one. I knew nothing. When people asked me what school I'd gone to I said—Webster. I didn't know you were supposed to bring your before with you to a place like this. I thought everyone was supposed to start over, like I was doing. And then it began to get cold and I didn't do very well in the cold. I wasn't prepared for my classes. I didn't understand what

I was supposed to be doing. And I didn't know how to ask for help."

Well, so much for our safety net, thought Naomi sourly. All that Welcome Week counseling, the special receptions for foreign students and homeschooled students. So much for the big brothers and big sisters assigned to freshmen, with their ice-cream socials in the new students' dormitory common rooms and their great big college-catered picnic down at the boathouse. So much for the RAs, four to a floor in the freshman dorms, and their late-night pizza parties, also underwritten by the college. And the writing resource centers and the tutoring network, both devised to make at-risk freshmen feel supported and inspired. And the academic advisors who met with every single student at least twice a year, but at least every other month for the freshmen. Good to know the checks and balances were working nicely. Good to know all of that effort and care had been worth it.

"Professor Gall saw me struggling. He singled me out. He asked me: What's wrong? He wanted to know who I was and what had brought me to Webster. He encouraged me to connect with the material in his course, to see myself not as a person at the mercy of war and politics and ethnic or religious discrimination but as a human being connected to other human beings. He made me realize that I had choices, I did not have to be controlled or penalized or discriminated against. I did not have to be somebody else's instrument of violence. He made me a part of his family. And this man," he said, eyeing the crowd with a sternness Naomi had not seen from him before, "this man, this teacher, and scholar, this inspiration to students like me, but who just happened to also be a black man—was denied tenure."

The room seethed. Naomi, looking around at them, as best she could, felt the darkness of real anger. They weren't merely echoing back the powerful emotions coming from the boy on the chair; they were involved, individually. They were enraged. For the very first time, she felt real fear—from them, and for them. Then, from outside the room, and the house itself, away down the street, came the first low drone of a siren. Finally: the police. But right away, she thought: *not yet.*

"Usually, when tenure is denied, the applicant is allowed to remain in his position for a period of up to two years, in order to secure a teaching position elsewhere. It's a common courtesy." *It is?* thought Naomi, who'd never heard of such a policy, at Webster or anywhere else. "But was Professor Gall offered this option?"

Omar shook his head gravely.

"Summarily dismissed. Informed that his services would no longer be required from the end of the spring semester. No extension on the lease of his home. No means of redress or opportunity to challenge the decision. Just appalling."

Just untrue, Naomi smoldered. She was thinking of all the warnings Gall had received, all the extensions he'd used. Her calf was howling. She wanted to get up. She couldn't listen to this anymore, but it wouldn't move, and so neither could the rest of her, and it was shooting numbness and pain up and down the length of her leg. She thought of her own long-ago sit-in at Cornell's administration building: three days of action in protest of ROTC's continued presence on campus, three days cross-legged on the red carpeting of Day Hall. She'd been wedged between her then-roommate Margo and her then-boyfriend Oskar, happy as a clam with only a bit of stiffness upon rising, at last, and making her way outside with the others, arms linked, singing "We Shall Overcome." For this infraction she had received only the promise of a demerit of some sort, to be incorporated into her academic record, but when she happened to see the record itself, a few years later, in the office of her VISTA training supervisor, there was nothing in there about her activism at all. Policy? Or clerical oversight? She wasn't sure whether she'd felt relief over this or mild disappointment, but she never said anything about it either way, because, by then, the personal fallout from the sit-in far outweighed the political; she and Daniel had become close in the course of that very action, and within weeks of its completion (its unsuccessful completion—ROTC would never retreat from the shores of Old Cayuga) she had told Oskar to go his own way as she went hers (hers being directly to Daniel's bed). You could argue that the harm, the hurt, would come much further down the line, but as for physical impact, there was nothing. She'd been twenty years old, and slim, and flexible, and strong. Her legs had come through it all without a chirp of protest.

Not so this evening. Barely a half an hour into this . . . whatever it was—action? teach-in?—and she'd had to grab her calves and knead away at them to make them shut up, but that only seemed to have the opposite effect. "Sorry," she whispered to the boy in front of her, who looked around as she nudged him with her foot.

"The college, of course, refuses to say anything about this. We have asked repeatedly for an explanation, but they will not respond."

Naomi looked at him in amazement. She was not aware of any student delegation making inquiries into Gall's tenure status. Why had no one told her the students from the protest wanted to see her? Mrs. Bradford—had she taken it upon herself to keep this from her? Naomi was seething. How could Mrs. Bradford possibly not understand how important it was, communicating with the students from the protest? Or . . . wait, maybe they hadn't come to her at all. Maybe they'd gone to somebody else. Maybe they'd gone to Bob Stacek—that was possible. But why had she heard nothing about it? She had spent months entreating the Stump contingent to talk to her, inviting them to her office, personally setting up the chairs for the town hall meeting that never materialized, using both carrots and sticks to draw them into actual civilized debate, and Bob hadn't seen fit to tell her that Omar and his gang were downstairs in his office?

Repeatedly? But then she remembered that Bob Stacek would rather have walked over coals than sat down with student radicals intent on challenging a faculty matter. That couldn't have happened. It couldn't have. And then she thought of something else, something even stranger. What if none of what Omar was saying was actually true?

But then...how could *that* be true?

"Are these the actions of an open institution devoted to scholarship and creativity?"

"No!" said someone. More than one person, actually. There was a cluster down in front, all in agreement. Someone actually raised a hand, a fist. The fist was pale, the wrist bony. Naomi recognized the flannel from which it protruded, but the actual connection didn't quite get made. *I know that arm* was as far as she could go.

"Fucking way," someone else said helpfully.

"Our college is racist!" Omar cried. "It hurts me to say it. The truth is, I can hardly bring myself to say it. Or I couldn't, until tonight. But then I was taken down to the basement of this house..." He shook his head vigorously, as if to dislodge the image. "The disgusting thing I saw. The desecration, of this building in particular. *This building!* Not the science building or the art enter! Not the alumni center!"

Which would have been...better? Naomi thought bitterly. She took the chance of wiggling a toe, and was rewarded only with streaks of quivery pain.

From outside, the siren again, but now growing neither louder nor fainter. The car was in front of the house, and not moving. The pigs had arrived.

"You might think," Omar said, his voice solemn, "that this is an overreaction. Webster College isn't some...superpower bombing its neighbors, or shooting a child in the street as his father desperately tries to shield him. It's not some death-obsessed fanatic sending a kid to blow up a bus. But in my heart, I know it's not different at all. And I'll tell you something else. If we don't stand up, if we don't say, 'This is wrong,' if we don't say, 'Stop,' then not one of us is any safer than that little child in the street, or the innocent person riding that bus. So this is what I'm doing today. It's a very simple thing, but it goes beyond just standing on the sidelines and grumbling because you feel that something isn't right. This is about stepping forward and raising your voice and showing that you see the problem and you're not walking away from it. I am saying this for myself. I don't speak for anyone else. I say, 'This is wrong.' I say, 'This is unjust.'"

They clapped and cheered all around her, and it was so loud that Naomi let the deep and howling *Ow* that she had been pushing so hard against slip past her effort and out. *Ow, Ow,* her leg throbbed and raged, and *Ow* she said, in observation of that, but it turned out that actually saying it out loud didn't help very much. The leg still throbbed and raged. There was no room to stretch, but she stretched anyway. The boy in front of her shifted; she could see his annoyance even in the posture of his back.

"Disgrace," said someone behind her . . . or off to the side.

"Could you . . . excuse me?" said someone else. But it wasn't someone else, it was her.

She had placed each hand on the shoulder of a neighbor and pushed herself up, but now neither of her two wonky feet seemed capable of bearing her weight.

"They're asleep," she observed, to no one in particular. The two people on either side looked up at her with curiosity, but did not seem particularly exercised about the situation, which was a grace note. "Sorry, I'm just, I couldn't keep sitting like that. Old legs," she said, illogically.

She put one down and tested it again. Her entire body shivered.

"President Roth?" somebody said.

Call me Naomi, she almost replied. It was her usual response to a Webster student. But they were all looking at her now. Omar was looking at her, and Chava. And, yes, clad in that all too familiar brown flannel shirt, her own Hannah Rosalind Roth. *I know that arm*. She knew that face as well—disapproving, determined.

"No," Omar was saying, calmly, in response to something she had obviously missed. "No, it's good. It's right. She needs to know."

"Well, thank you," said Naomi, finding her voice as both feet found—finally and at the same time—the ground. "I appreciate the welcome, but I didn't realize I was coming to hear you speak. I'm here because of what happened in the basement of this house."

"Webster is a racist environment," said a voice. Male, low. Naomi looked in its direction, but no one seemed to be owning the statement. A room full of bowed heads, avoiding contact. Omar was looking at her, but he listened with his head cocked slightly to one side and a half smile on his face, as if she were some precocious child about to say something adorable. It made her crazy.

"I'm offended by that," she said. "Webster is many things, and I'd be the first to tell you that we have our challenges. No community is perfect. But inherently racist? Endemically racist? Absolutely not. And frankly, I'm also offended by the fact that whoever said that..." She paused to give him another chance, but whoever he was he didn't take it. "Has chosen not to identify himself. No community can grow without honest debate, and no debate can be honest if people don't own their positions. I hope you'll think about that."

"And I hope you"—Omar nodded, with maddening condescension, at Naomi—"will think about what you heard here tonight—without having made your presence known." There was a deep rumble of assent.

"That's right," said a girl with a high voice.

Yeah, so much for honesty.

"I didn't come here to attend a rally," Naomi shouted. "I'm not here to infiltrate a meeting. I was summoned by campus security because a morally repulsive and criminal act took place in this house, and this house is the property of the college. What happened downstairs is a crime against Webster, and that means every one of us, myself included. And I'm expecting all of you to cooperate with the police as we attempt to identify the responsible party or parties. This community will not tolerate what I saw down there." She stopped herself. She was alarmed at her own shrillness, which carried an unmistakable edge of something no feminist cared to be associated with, and that was hysteria. She was not hysterical, if only because there was no such thing as hysteria. It was a made-up thing, made up, moreover, by a man. She would not be pushed this far.

"I'm leaving," said Naomi. "But first, I'm going to talk to the police outside, and offer them the assistance of our entire community. Then I'm going to tell the rest of the Webster community what's happened here, and that includes the other students and the faculty, not to mention our alumni and parent communities. Because we don't hide things like this, not if we're serious about fixing *all the problems in the world*," she said, somewhat archly, looking at Omar. "And when we figure out who did this, we won't be hiding that either. So whoever's responsible had better get ready to be publicly identified, prosecuted by the police, and, if they're a Webster student, expelled. Everyone clear on that?"

It sounded authoritative. It sounded...well, presidential. The very opposite, she noted with satisfaction, of hysteria. But it only lasted a moment and then it was gone, and she was only herself again—wobbly on her legs and quite unsure of anything at all, especially the truth of what she'd just said.

CHAPTER TWELVE

THIS IS THE PLACE

Mud season (known in some other parts of the world as "spring") would almost entirely preempt winter that year. The same cold that had settled in so early the previous fall, bringing the leaves down fast and hard on the Webster lawns and quads and bestowing extra discomfort (and nobility!) upon the Stump protest, would leave sheets of dense Massachusetts mud in its wake. The physical encampment—those tents and shanties and the no longer quite so luxe toilet trailer—remained in situ, but now the student movement on the Billings Lawn no longer seemed tied to the Stump. After the Sojourner Truth House incident the Webster protest expanded to consume the entire campus—dormitories and classrooms and naturally the administration buildings. Some critical algorithm had been reached with the joining of feces and hate language in the basement on Fairweather Road, some epidemiological tipping point attained, and by the time Webster College arose from its innocent slumber the next morning the entire campus was locked in a paralysis of outrage.

Overnight, too, every one of the movement's missing elements had been located. The action that so recently lacked a name and a

public leader now possessed both of these, as if someone had made
a late-night run to the activist superstore and loaded up the van.
The students, unlike the college's own press office (which had
barely progressed since the days of the Radclyffe Hall debacle),
were fully capable of interfacing with the world, and by late morning, position papers were being distributed, and the new entity,
Webster Dissent, had a Twitter account, a Facebook page, and a
website, loaded with photos: the campus, circa 1955, in all of its
pre-Sarafian maleness and Caucasian-ness, and the stalwart encampment (minus toilet trailer), and the grievously wronged professor, Nicholas Gall, and (she was shocked to see) the smeared
abuse on the Sojourner Truth wall (well-lit images, and perfectly
composed) and also, of course, the college president, Naomi Roth,
whose highly unflattering image was accompanied by her office
phone number and email address. Media inquiries were directed
to websterdissent@gmail.com and interview requests for Professor
Gall and the young, charismatic Webster student Omar Khayal
(sophomore, anthropology major, hometown: Burcij, Palestine)
were directed to an 800 number that, when Naomi tried it, went
straight to a recording, instructing her to leave her name, number,
and email address. The voice delivering that instruction? One she
knew very, very well.

By Monday afternoon, poor Mrs. Bradford had been bedeviled
by every news outlet she could personally have named, and
many she'd never heard of. Naomi, sensing that to leave this
tsunami of intense type-A personalities to her elderly assistant
was hazardous—both to the college and to Mrs. Bradford
herself—phoned Bob Stacek, the surliest person she knew, and
deputized him to deal with these requests, an opportunity she
figured he'd enjoy. From then on, Mrs. Bradford would forward
the calls to Stacek's office downstairs, and Stacek would inform
one and all that the president would be unavailable until the
trustees had met to confer about the situation.

Getting that very thing to happen was now Naomi's primary concern. The board had not been due to meet until its annual gathering in March, when the usual priorities were Webster's endowment and admissions profile, and the group seemed less than compelled to schedule an emergency session. Not every trustee shared Naomi's sense of urgency about Webster Dissent, and one who did—the retired history professor Milton Russell—had been loudly encouraging a response best summarized by the words *National* and *Guard*. Webster, even without the college's cooperation, was on the news and in the news. It *was* the news, part of any number of larger stories about race and intolerance, and the whole situation was boiling down to this: a 250-year-old college, a college still well remembered for its boorish, dim, and drunken male students, was refusing to come to terms with a changing educational and social landscape. Horrified, Naomi watched the Webster College of an earlier era reconstitute itself in descriptions by commentators and journalists, its homogeneity and conservatism untempered by the intervening years, as if the entire generation of post-Sarafian students had never set foot on campus. The college's new critics—*her* new critics—were legion, riled up, and getting louder with each passing day. She felt trapped beneath the collective boot of a thousand angry people, all misinformed, all with intractable opinions, all out for blood.

And now, into the furor, with the deliberate step of a long offstage leading player, came martyred professor Nicholas Gall: "reluctant" figurehead. He was slight with a short but uncurbed afro, a narrow nose, and a mouth so small that it actually looked uncomfortable to speak through. Naomi, who had never laid eyes on the man she'd now thought of for a solid year as the anthropology plagiarist, couldn't help but consider him disappointing.

She had taken to making a mental check mark each time she'd wished she could say what she wanted to say about Gall. No, Professor Nicholas Gall had not been denied tenure because he was a black man (check). That was absurd. No, it was not because his field of research concerned African and African-American material (check). No, the members of his department were not envious of his obvious rapport with students (double check—tenured faculty did not pine for students' good opinion; dream on, students!). No, there was no resistance to the professor's use of blues, hip-hop, Negro spirituals, and rap in his lectures—these things were part of folklore, part of anthropology (check). No, it wasn't because some anthropologists perceive folklore to be a lightweight cousin to their own vein of study. (That had been news to Naomi when the whole mess began. *Academics!*) No, there wasn't an evil Webster quota system for faculty of color. (She was all too familiar with the parallel accusation of racial/ethnic quotas in admissions, but this was a new one on her.)

You are totally, completely, utterly, categorically wrong, she had wanted to say, over and over and over again. But Naomi knew, and the college's attorney took every opportunity to remind her, that revealing Gall's plagiarism would expose Webster to very costly—very winnable—litigation. The trustees knew about Gall. It was necessary that they know, and it relieved her to be able to reassure them that she wasn't out of her mind, but she worried every hour that one of the more impetuous types on the board would, while puffed up with righteous indignation, leak it to a civilian or—worse—directly to the press.

The matter was confidential: That was all. And as the days passed and the claims grew more inflamed, more paranoid, more batshit crazy, all she could do was make her mental check marks: check and check and check. No. (*He's a liar.*) No. (*He's a cheat.*) No. (*He is not what he says he is. Not at all.*)

But if Nicholas Gall was not what he said he was, who

was he? Watching him on television, where he was often in-terviewed alongside the ardent, sweet-faced Omar, there was a flatness to his affect that riveted Naomi. The two men, both short, both slight, both similarly hunched, sat with hands iden-tically gripping their knees, and arms identically braced. But Omar, for the most part, did the talking. He focused not on his own journeys across ideologies and the world but on his ex-perience at Webster: the isolation he'd felt—academically and emotionally—until Professor Gall, the most brilliant and pas-sionate educator he had ever encountered, reached out to him. To have that gift as a teacher and a human being, to be able to make contact across the professor/student divide, not to speak of the African-American/Arab-Palestinian divide, to impart ideas, offer comfort, forge such a critical link between human beings, it was a precious thing, sorely lacking in the world. Professor Gall was one of the most popular teachers at Webster College. His classes were routinely filled, and students often gathered at his home a few blocks from campus for meals and the kind of profoundly enriching out-of-the-classroom interaction that was both truly indicative of a great educational experience and sadly hard to come by. Professor Gall was also a noted authority on an area of folkloric study that intersected fields as disparate as religion, literature, music, history, and African-American stud-ies, making it a rare and perfect example of that much lauded interdisciplinary multi-genric thing to which colleges (Webster among them) claimed such devotion. And all Webster Dissent wanted from the college, all anyone could want from the college, the administration, and President Naomi Roth, was an answer to their simple, honest question: *Why?*

Her heart went out to them. She couldn't stop it. She couldn't help it, they were so bereft, so divinely outraged. How many times had she herself taken the harm done to another person and made it her own harm, her personal harm, and pushed back against it with all her strength and will? The world would never work if people refused to perform this exact alchemy, to recognize that any injustice paid to one of them was paid to every one of them, and it was the duty of those who had a voice to speak for the voiceless. She had spent those days on the floor of the president's office at Cornell not because she was an impoverished and endangered village child in Vietnam but because she was not. She had marched for women's rights not because she had experienced rape or lack of access to abortion but because it might have been her, it might one day be her, or her child, or her friend, or the woman behind her at the checkout counter, who had as much right as Naomi did not to be raped or denied crucial healthcare and who was also, therefore, her responsibility.

Watching one of these nominally joint interviews, Naomi was struck by the silent understanding between Omar and Gall, the rhythm of their partnership. Side by side on the couch, in a room that could have belonged to any college-town hotel in New England (but this time was, she recognized, the conference suite lounge at the Webster Inn), she analyzed their spoken participation at 75 percent Omar and 25 percent Gall, with Omar contributing fully rounded narratives of gratitude and admiration and Gall answering direct questions with marked pause of consideration and an air of allowing himself only a few carefully chosen words. As if, Naomi realized, with a spike of outrage, he were afraid of saying the wrong thing, of what *they* might do to him if he misspoke or inadvertently angered the gods of Webster. *They*. Meaning *her*. Meaning *me*, she saw.

"Webster believes that it is an evolved place," said young Omar Khayal of Bureij, Palestine. "For so long it was, you know, entirely white and male and heterosexual and conservative, and this was the Webster that so many remember. And then, when it finally experienced an evolution in the 1970s, I think, the college persuaded itself that it had become a city on a hill, a community that repudiated its earlier self, you see?"

The interviewer—Naomi knew her face, but not her name— nodded.

"But this is not true," said Omar, and Naomi could hear now, as she sometimes could not, the lilt of his mother tongue, there beneath his English. "Webster is not a city on a hill. Webster is still the reactionary place it was before. It is a place where we who are 'other' are made to feel, constantly, that we are not part of the real Webster. We are tolerated. And still, sometimes, the true feeling of the real Webster breaks through that very toler- ance. You may ask, how could the incident that happened here have happened at Webster College? At such a supposedly liberal and welcoming place, how could a member of our community have written this word, this disgusting, offensive word, in human waste, on the wall of the one student building on campus that is dedicated to the African-American experience at Webster? But that is not the same question we are asking, because we see this place as it really is. Our question is, why did it take so long?"

The interviewer nodded sadly. Her face was drawn with deep concern. "Professor Gall?" she said, turning to him as Omar sat back in deference. "Is that your question as well?"

One...two...three... Naomi counted off the beats as Gall ap- peared to think, deeply, carefully. He looked so very sad, so very disappointed, and when he finally spoke it was with an air of in- tegrity having gained the upper hand over loyalty, even heartfelt loyalty. It pained him, obviously. But truth must be paramount, and that was all.

"I have devoted many years of my life to Webster College," he said, his small voice crowded further by emotion. "I have be- lieved in Webster as an ideal. I can't bear to think that this is a place where such hatred and discrimination can flourish. But I can no longer pretend that it is not."

There. Done. Nicholas Gall sank back against the faux Williamsburg sofa with its pseudo-colonial pineapple print, and spoke no more. His honesty, his disappointment—they had exhausted him.

Naomi declined to sympathize. She was furious. And every week, as it passed, left her more furious still.

Francine, in one of her very few phone calls (mud season was also her season in what she called the admissions cave, in which her thousands of applications were winnowed down to the nascent class), expressed distracted support of the *hang in there* variety, and let her know that "everyone who knows what's going on" supported her unequivocally. (Given that so few people really knew "what's going on," this was not the comfort Francine probably intended it to be.) Could they have dinner? Naomi asked, feeling especially fragile at the sound of her friend's voice but already knowing the answer.

"Oh, sweetie, I wish. But I've got the entire Midwest before we start meetings in two weeks. I can barely take a shower."

"Of course, of course. Carry on!" Naomi said bravely. "Admissions is the umbilical cord of the college, and all that."

"A metaphor I always found ever so slightly nauseating," Francine said. Then she asked if Naomi had been keeping up with the *scandale* unfolding at a very large, very famous, and very respected university in a state adjoining their own.

Naomi's heart leaped. It was unkind, of course, but if ever there were a moment for academic schadenfreude, this had to be it. "Tell me. Please, tell me."

A certain international communications empire had been hacked by certain persons unknown, dispersing years of emails sent and received by executives from the lowliest low to the highest high all over the internet. Naomi had heard about the first delirious skim of this trove—five-thousand-dollar-a-night call girls, homophobic slurs about the CFO (a noted Democratic fund-raiser)—but that story had disappeared months earlier. Over time, however, the scrutiny, like an archaeological dig, had continued to descend through layers of stuff, uncovering as it went items both ordinary and precious. It was a vein of the latter that Francine now brought to her attention.

Several years earlier, the company's CEO had evidently contacted the university in question to discuss the possibility of a gift in honor of his distant cousin, a graduate of that fine institution. The cousin had died some ten years earlier, but there was apparently no time like the present for the CEO to memorialize him with a pledge of $5 million, which could be used as the university saw fit. The institution, naturally, responded with gratitude and pleasure, and asked if the CEO would accept an invitation to campus in order to be thanked personally. No need, the CEO replied, as he would be visiting in a month or so with his son, a high school senior. That very university, by pure coincidence, was his son's first choice college.

What followed was a series of emails that basically confirmed the deepest suspicions of every disgruntled parent of every rejected applicant, ever: a genteel dance around the bald fact of that money and the offer of acceptance it counterbalanced, in which a custom and private tour for the CEO and his son was led by the dean of admissions himself, and a civilized glass of Merlot was enjoyed on the back patio of the president's residence. And every single piece of it, the obsequious thank-you for the money and the detailed instructions for its transmission, the queries about father and son's visit to campus, the informational packets and student interest forms to be left at their hotel, the highlighted map showing the way to the president's residence, the follow-up reminders that the official early decision deadline was nearing, and the slightly more urgent query about whether the boy would be finishing and submitting his application before the official deadline (kids today! so laid-back!)...every last

smarmy piece of it was online for every last person on the planet
to peruse.

The money changed hands. The application was successful.
The young man in question was a current sophomore at that
very university. And admissions officers from sea to shining sea
were saying silent prayers to their higher powers that the institutions they served had not been the first choice of the son of
the CEO of this particular international corporation: *There but
for the grace of You go I.*

Naomi heard this. She tried just to let it sit with her, but it
wouldn't sit still.

"You mean, you too?"

"Me too what?"

"Well, could it have been us? Is that what we'd have done with
a gift of five million and a rising senior?"

Francine seemed to take a long time to consider this.

Webster alumni were generous. They loved their college. They
loved it, for the most part, even when it transformed before
their eyes: homogeneous to heterogeneous, conservative to beyond liberal, provincial to global. The older graduates were still
remembering the college in their wills, endowing chairs and un-
derwriting athletic facilities. The younger graduates were funding international programs and scholarships for students from
Third World countries. But if there had been a situation like this,
a specified or implied quid pro quo, Naomi had not been made
aware of it.

"That hasn't happened," Francine said finally, to Naomi's relief. "You know we work closely with Development, but five-
million-dollar gifts haven't come our way. I mean, in conjunction
with an applicant."

"But, if they had?"

Another silence. Naomi could picture her friend's expression: tired, cautious. Why cautious? If they were having this

conversation in the woods, on one of their walks, would it seem so charged? Francine was good at her job. Francine took the ever-growing crush of applicants (twenty-three thousand last year) and produced gloriously diverse classes of eighteen hundred. Somehow. Naomi hoped she was not conveying anything less than utter confidence. She was about to say as much when her friend spoke.

"My feeling is that I serve the institution. That's the bottom line, and it serves the institution to receive a gift of five million dollars, so if the applicant is qualified and likely to contribute, I have no moral issue. People bring many different gifts to Webster, and we appreciate them all. Personally, I enjoy having a good improv group on campus. I happen to know the dean of faculty is fond of John Philip Sousa marches. You need a glockenspiel for that. Every other year or so the marching band director says *Find us a glockenspiel!* Now if you're really lucky, your five-million-dollar applicant does improv or plays the glockenspiel. But even if he doesn't he still looks like a pretty compelling candidate, so long as he can do the work and isn't an axe murderer. Like I said, though: hasn't happened yet."

"But, just for the record, you'd run something like that by me, right?"

"You mean, by you personally? Not just Development?"

"Oh." Naomi sighed. "Right. Of course. Development." That was what Development was for. Sometimes it shocked her, how out of her depth she felt at this. After five years. "I'd want to know about a five-million-dollar gift. I'd want to write a thank-you note."

Francine laughed, but it wasn't a very happy-sounding laugh. "I can assure you that my colleagues in Development write elegant and heartfelt thank-you notes on your behalf, but I hear you. If it ever happens."

"If it ever happens," Naomi echoed. And she let Francine get back to her work. And Naomi went back to what she herself was doing: steadily, incrementally losing control.

Meanwhile, the term careened forward. In spite of the widening gyre, classes were happening, parties were happening. Some members of the community—most, actually—still seemed happy enough to do what they'd come to Webster intent on doing in the seminar rooms, lecture theaters, and labs. Vaguely, Naomi understood that plays were being performed and the basketball team was having a respectable season, and the reading series went on as scheduled in the poetry room of the Loring Library each Sunday night. And yet she left Stone House each morning already in a panic about some unfolding episode in the Webster Dissent saga—a new appearance on a national news program, a new think piece on a website everyone read—and all through the day she would be yanked back and forth between the hurtling train of this and the background (but still deafening!) noise of ordinary Webster and its students, faculty, staff, administration, physical plant, institutional challenges and aspirations...until she fell asleep with the light on and her reading glasses still on her face, the laptop slipping, slipping to the side.

And in between: the phone calls, the emails, the insistent voices, requesting, opining, complaining, haranguing, mocking, or actually praising her, which was weirdly the most distasteful of all. Every single person she had ever known—and every single person she had never known—was trying to get in touch.

And if that wasn't true, it still felt as if it were. Every single person.

Well, not every single person.

Naomi had not heard from Hannah since the night she'd left home at the end of winter break, and could not be sure where her daughter was spending her nights. At Radclyffe Hall? Down in the mud of the Billings Lawn? Perhaps, as the apparent media liaison of Webster Dissent, Hannah had been stashed (or had stashed herself) away somewhere off campus, the better to manage access to the movement's two certifiable household names—Nicholas Gall and Omar Khayal.

Or was that three new household names?

Doctor was a title Naomi had never done much with, and this turned out to be some small relief as that honorific was very much a part of her brand-new public persona, "Dr. Naomi Roth." Public, as in: belonging to the public, fulfilling the public role of, say, villain, like, say, Bull Connor upholding the God-given principle of segregation or Lieutenant William Calley bringing the war home to My Lai. All of those remote broadcasts from the edge of the quad, she could not help noting, made a meal of the mud, the now filthy tarps and tents, and the clearly fatigued young activists, but not one saw fit to include the very expensive toilet trailer, or the heating stations she'd insisted on, or the dedicated tent for health center staff, which always had a doctor or nurse in residence, even at night. These kids had to be the most coddled protesters in the history of nonviolent resistance, Naomi thought, taking her now customary place at the window to survey, again, her battered demesne: the muddy turf, the bodies, standing, lounging, chilling, most of them clad in once-brightly-colored parkas. Around this the media trucks, the reporters, the bloggers (for all she knew), the gawkers. (Perhaps *Gawker* itself.) And then the college buildings, the bare trees, the white winter sky. Even in its ugliest season and under its greatest assault for years, if not ever, Webster was beautiful. This spot in the woods, selected by Josiah Webster and his protégé, the other Josiah, the Native American Josiah, and cleared by the first students—it must have called out to them somehow. There must have been some prospect, some feature that had prompted the little party to stop exactly here and put down their packs and pick up their saws and shovels. Like Brigham Young on the ridge above the Salt Lake Valley, intoning, for the ages: *This is the place.* And it was still the place, two and a half centuries later. And it was her place, Naomi thought, allowing this whiff of sentimentality to briefly elbow aside her reportedly steely resolve. But for how long would she be able to hold off this narrative of Dr. Naomi Roth versus the noble young activists? It had first occurred to her a few weeks earlier, quietly, and truthfully without much pain, that Dr. Naomi Roth would likely end up hoisted on this particular petard. It was the way these things went, she knew better than most. Unless you were a Ronald Reagan, bulldozing an encampment of protesters and blithely loping on into the future until it was Morning in America for all! (Or at least for everyone who mattered!) But Naomi was no Ronald Reagan (thank all that was holy for that). One way or another, Webster Dissent was going to do her in. The only questions were, *When would it happen?* and *Was her own daughter going to lead the charge when it did?*

CHAPTER THIRTEEN

WHAT A LONG, STRANGE TRIP IT'S BEEN

The Webster cops had nothing. Weeks after the Sojourner Truth basement had been scrubbed to within an inch of its life by a crew of Webster Dissent activists (an event duly recorded by the Associated Press), they were still flummoxed by what had happened on Fairweather Road. That night, first in the house and after at the police station, she'd been frustrated to see that they did not immediately grasp the enormity of the event. The word "vandalism" kept coming out of various mouths: one belonging to the patrolmen who'd come to Sojourner Truth, one belonging to the clerk at the station, and even the one belonging to the chief, who'd arrived to confer with his men, and—reluctantly, and only because she was there and wouldn't leave—Naomi. It was not "a college prank," she insisted. It was not "frat boy behavior." It enraged her that she had to explain this to them. They did not know what, or who, *Sojourner Truth* signified. Perhaps, she thought unkindly, they did not know what *nigger* signified, either.

Every one of the Webster Dissent kids in the house that night had been interviewed, but only because she'd insisted. She hadn't hung around for that. She couldn't do that and also go to the police station, and it seemed more important to make sure they understood the college's position from the get-go: deadly serious, fully committed to identifying and prosecuting the person or persons responsible.

"Well, you know, it's kids messing around. It's, what, a frat basement, right?" the chief had said that first night, establishing the theme. He was a chief of recent vintage, and Naomi was just meeting him now. The previous chief had seen her and Webster through five years of raucous parties and minor assaults, and he had been brusque and unimaginative but basically sound, not that she'd been moved to forge a warm and fuzzy rapport with him. He had moved on to Florida or Louisiana or someplace without a mud season.

"No. Not a frat basement. This is a dormitory for students of color. Do you understand?"

It emerged a bit more harshly than she had intended, and he reacted with appropriate defensiveness. "Well, but still kids. Maybe there was drinking involved."

"It wouldn't change a thing, from our perspective."

"Sure, but I take it this is part of a bigger problem you've got right now. I don't know if isolating this one incident is going to make a lot of sense. Now if we can classify it as a vandalism we're on firmer ground, so to speak."

She wanted to rip his head off. She took one or two deep and ineffectual breaths. She wished she had the college attorney with her, but Chaim had felt that bringing counsel into a friendly meeting might set an adversarial tone—not wise. In this instance, the college and the police ought to be united on the side of the angels.

"Do what you need to do," she told the chief. "But as far as we're concerned, this is a hate crime, and as soon as you bring me the name or names of the perpetrators, and as soon as you charge them, I'll be initiating disciplinary procedures to separate them from the college. I won't have this at Webster. It won't be tolerated."

Wild applause, she thought, noting his blank expression. Wild imaginary applause.

She took his card. His name was Patrick Hogan.

But of the precisely ninety-three students Chief Hogan and his men had interviewed that night and all the next day, not one of them had any idea who'd smeared human excrement on the basement wall of the Sojourner Truth house to form the words *Niggers out*. Not one had observed a person descending the basement stairs en route (possibly) to doing this. Not one had heard or overheard any person speak of intending to do such a thing, or heard or overheard any person speak of having done such a thing. A house jammed with innocents, who saw, heard, and apparently spoke no evil. It was a wash.

What was there to do but reiterate her own outrage, the college's outrage, and her complete confidence (this was a lie, of course) in the investigative abilities of the Webster Police Department, which was working closely with their own security officers? What happened at Sojourner Truth, she would say again and again, to anyone who asked and more than a few who didn't, was not indicative of the culture at Webster. It flew in the face of the college's noted openness and principle of honoring all cultural backgrounds, ethnicities, gender positions (and non-positions!), and sexual orientations (and non-orientations!).

None of it mattered, of course. Out there, beyond the Quad, the town, the cozy grove of academe, Webster College had burst upon the American consciousness as an ivy-covered bastion of reactionary policies and racist personnel, where a beloved professor could be penalized for the color of his skin and a white supremacist could write *that word*, in shit, on the walls of the only building granted to students of color (admitted obviously for reasons of tokenism!), their one small solitary refuge among the

Aryan Nations extremists who made up the student body, faculty, and administration.

Currently, the only aspect of her job (or, to be brutally honest, her life) that was giving her any pleasure was the prospect of the Native American Gathering. On the day of her finally rescheduled meeting with Robbins Petavit, the Webster grad who tragically taught at Amherst, Naomi awoke to a barely remembered sense of energized purpose. This, she could do. This she wanted to do, and if the world was so intent on viewing Webster through a prism of distortion, then they were welcome to come and observe a few of the panels she'd planned for the Gathering. The advisory committee comprised six Webster alumni from across the country and two from Canada, and they were scheduled to meet in a week's time at a college-funded retreat in Tulsa (moved from Webster itself, in light of the growing encampment around the Stump, because why should the delegates have to step in this mess?) to discuss how things might proceed. A week after that, invitations would be sent to every living Native American or First Nations graduate the college could locate—about seven hundred in number.

That all sounded fine, very forthright and very productive, but Naomi knew that there was a subterranean current of resistance to the gathering, even within its advisory committee. She knew it because Douglas Sidgwick had related this news in his own special way, while perched on one foot in her doorway, his face a perfect Sidgwickian blank. "They don't want to do it, you know. I mean they're doing it. But they don't really want to do it."

"They . . ." Naomi said, exasperated.

"Advisory committee. More than half of them said they needed to think about it."

Well, that was okay, Naomi had told him. You want to think about anything that's going to take up your time.

"Yeah, no," he said. Oddly, he nodded as he said this. "But everyone who said he had to think about it decided not to do it. Professor Petavit ended up asking some of his friends, which is how we got to the eight."

Okay, so that hadn't gone smoothly, and it was news to Naomi. Still, she sort of appreciated not having heard about it till now. There just wasn't room in her head for any more resistance.

In the turbulent wake of Webster Dissent, Douglas Sidgwick had taken over the heavy lifting of the Gathering, though he—like the proposed advisory committee—had needed to think about it, since he was not (as he'd had no need to remind Naomi) very good at dealing with people. This was the reason Sidgwick would not be joining them at lunch at the Webster Inn, she suspected, though his stated excuse was a dental appointment.

Naomi, waylaid by yet another difficult phone conversation (this one with Chava's father, who had just learned from the registrar that his daughter intended to withdraw from the college, effective immediately), was late, of course. Ten minutes late, not terrible, but in light of the fact that she'd canceled their previous meeting, not really all right, either. She walked briskly along the sidewalk, her head down, dodging the bodies, and into the lobby of the Webster Inn, which was crowded with media types. This was when she realized that she had no idea what Professor Petavit looked like.

"President Roth?" A man had approached, with outstretched hand.

"Oh, hello!" said Naomi, relieved. He was younger than she'd imagined, his skin tone somewhere between dusky and dark. She hadn't looked up his tribal affiliation. She'd meant to do that, too. And his Webster class, and his major. Everything, really. Chava's father had driven it all from her head. "Naomi, please."

"It's a pleasure," the man said. "Do you have a few minutes to chat?"

Naomi frowned. They were having lunch, she'd thought. "I made a reservation," she said, gesturing toward the dining room.

"Just a couple of minutes. I'd love to hear your thoughts on the lawsuit."

"The . . . wait, are you Professor Petavit?"

The man considered. He looked as if he were seriously weighing the question. Would it help if he were, in fact, "Professor Petavit"?

"Sorry, no," he finally said. "Steven Bishop, MSNBC. I'm a producer for Kathy Solomon's show. You know Kathy," he informed her, so confidently that she actually wondered if she did know Kathy. Who was Kathy again? It knocked her so efficiently off balance that she just stood there, looking at him, trying to decide whether she was actually angry, embarrassed, or merely generally disappointed in the human animal. But before she could pick one somebody else had joined them, and then another somebody else. Cards were extended: ABC, NPR. Just a couple of minutes, one of them said. "Couple of minutes" seemed to be the preferred euphemism for this species. "I'd like to bring you outside on the porch, if you don't mind," said a woman about her own age, who had evidently taken her by the wrist. Somebody else had a hand on her shoulder and was talking to her about Diane Sawyer. They were like a zombie mass, newly alert to the presence of living flesh.

"I'm Professor Petavit," someone said, quietly, behind her. "I kind of want to say: *Come with me if you want to live*." He was laughing a little. Naomi looked at him. Unlike the other one, the one who had not been Professor Petavit, he was pale and, if not California blond, then at least very much blond. And pale. He was definitely pale. Did that make sense? But he did seem to know his own name.

"I was in the dining room, waiting for you. I saw what was happening."

He had leaned in to say this. She nodded.

"Great, let's go."

That hand was still on her wrist. "President Roth?"

"I've already stated our position on the protest and the tenure decision," she said tersely. "If there's something to add, I'll say so, but the privacy of our students and faculty members is my priority."

"Yes," said someone with clear impatience, "but—"

The hand on her wrist tightened. Naomi took hold of the fingers and peeled them off. "Don't do that," she told the woman. "Not nice." Then she followed Petavit to the dining room. To their credit, none of them came after her.

"Well, thanks for that," Naomi said, sinking into one of the inn's faux-Colonial chairs. "I might not have made it through the lobby. I'm Naomi." She extended her hand. "May I call you Robin?"

"No," he said mildly. "But you can call me Robbins. Don't worry," he added, noting her expression, "happens all the time. It's a family name," he explained. "Back to the 1840s."

"Oh. And Petavit?"

"Also family. Back even farther. Wayyyy back."

"Right," she said, remembering again that she knew far too little about him. "May I ask where your...what your affiliation is?"

Petavit was looking over the menu. "Like many of us, I'm a mix. But the Petavit is Nipmuc. And the Nipmuc, as I'm sure you're aware, are right here."

Naomi, who was shamefully not aware, said, "Right here?"

"Webster, Massachusetts, and across the border in Connecticut and a bit of Rhode Island."

"Oh, my God," she heard herself say. "I had no idea. I mean, I knew about the Praying Towns." She stopped. She had no idea how offensive any of this was.

"Yup, that was us. It was a Nipmuc who brought Josiah

Webster here from upstate New York when his first Indian school didn't work out. Do you know what you want?" he asked, and it took her a moment to realize he meant food.

She ordered the tuna sandwich. She always ordered the tuna sandwich at the Webster Inn. It was generally safe. Petavit asked about the soup of the day and then the fish of the day. Naomi, glad for an excuse to look at him, found herself newly perplexed. There wasn't a single thing about Robbins Petavit that called out "Native American," "indigenous," or any of the other currently approved verbiage to signify a category of people resident on the North American continent before the arrival of Columbus. At least not to her. What she saw, instead, was a collection of superficial observations, not one of which pointed her in the right direction. They included academic, Nordic, European, WASP, middle-aged. Also: attractive. He ordered a hamburger.

"I used to come here for the hamburgers when I was in college," he said, a little sheepishly. "When I couldn't hack the food in the dining hall for one more day. My roommate and I would go down to the pub." The pub was down in the cellar. It was technically off limits to Webster students, but maybe it hadn't been then.

"It's still on the menu," she told him. "Exact same burger, as long as I've been here."

"Which is how long?"

Naomi smiled. She was kind of glad he hadn't looked her up, either.

"Wow. Seventeen years. Seventeen years in the fall." *If I last that long*, she thought ruefully.

"And before that?"

"UMass, Amherst. I did my PhD there."

"Ah, did you love it? I've been very happy in Amherst, I must say."

Did I? she thought, already highly annoyed with herself.

"Well, it's a great town. I had a small child then, and I was a single mom, so my Amherst was mainly playgrounds and ice-cream parlors. I don't know that I really got the full Happy Valley version."

"The past-life-regression, gluten-free, my-baby-sleeps-with-me-till-he-can-drive version?"

She smiled. She hadn't thought about Amherst in a while. "No, I got that. You don't live there and not get that. I just mean, I didn't have much of a community life. I was in the library or teaching or writing or taking care of my daughter. I don't think I said goodbye to anyone outside my department when I left."

Their plates arrived. Petavit regarded his with satisfaction. "Exactly as I remember it. Same piece of kale for garnish."

"Well, but today you're supposed to eat the kale, not look at it."

He picked the hamburger up and took a bite. He looked happy.

"I hate to admit this," Naomi said, eyeing her own sandwich, "but I don't know anything about the Nipmuc . . ." Tribe? she almost said. Then she found a more dignified word: "Nation."

"Oh, well, not to worry. We've always been tiny. Only about a thousand today. But we're part of the Algonquin group, basically. Algonquin were all over the northeast. Pennacook, Mohawk, Massachusett, Pequot, Quinnipiac. All cousins. We're the ones who sold corn to the colonists in the 1630s. Kept them from starving. They gave us smallpox in return," he said lightly. "Not a fair trade."

She wasn't sure what to say. In the 1630s her own people had just reached the Russian steppes. It wasn't her crime.

"I'm sorry about last month," she told him. "I never cancel things. Well, almost never. But . . . I don't know how much of our present situation you're keeping up with."

"Oh"—he nodded—"only the part about how Webster is the

place to be if you want to re-establish the Hitler Youth or do a degree in advanced racist political tactics. And the kids are running the whole shit show," he said, cocking his head at the dining room window. They would be overlooking the Quad if they'd been seated closer to it.

"So, just the basics," she said grimly. "I don't know how it got past me the way it did. Obviously, I missed something. When they set up out there I tried to get them to talk to me. They wouldn't. And they still won't talk to me. They'll only talk to the media."

"Not your mama's political action, in other words."

"No, indeed."

She sat back in her seat. Two bites of her own sandwich and she didn't think she could eat any more.

"Can I ask," said Petavit, "and I apologize if I'm being blunt, but, is this conference—"

"Gathering," she corrected.

"Gathering, specifically for Native American graduates. Is it some kind of spin because of your little problem?"

Naomi stared at him. The fact that she had not anticipated this question was as arresting to her as the question itself.

"No. No, it isn't. I started thinking about doing this last spring, and talking it over with Douglas Sidgwick. We started planning early last fall. I'm sorry, I realize it looks..."

Desperate, she was thinking. Because now she saw that it did.

"Timely," he finished.

"But it's just coincidental. I have really wanted to do this, for a long time. In fact I can't understand why it hasn't been done until now."

"Well,"—he laughed uncomfortably—"I can. If you seriously want to know."

All of a sudden, Naomi felt it was the last thing she wanted, but of course she said yes, she seriously wanted to know.

"Native people at Webster." He sighed. "What a long, strange trip it's been."

"I'm sure." Naomi nodded. But she thought she'd better shut up.

"So, you know the background. Josiah Webster was a missionary, not really an 'educator' as we'd define that today. Not unusual for that time, of course, but the difference was that he had a specific population in mind. By which I mean: us. And we were halfway there because we were already a Praying Town. We'd been exposed to Christianity already. Oh, yeah, sure," he said to the waiter, who'd come to refill his iced tea.

When he was gone, Petavit started again.

"Webster only started becoming an educational institution when Josiah's son took the funds Samuel Fairweather was holding out. Fairweather made him an offer he couldn't refuse, because he needed the money, and maybe Nathaniel wasn't quite as committed to the missionary thing as his dad had been, and the other Josiah, the Nipmuc Josiah, had been. Fairweather wasn't interested in the Nipmuc or any other Native people. If he had been, Webster probably would have gone in a very different direction. Maybe by now we'd be an evangelical college with a focus on indigenous peoples. Or maybe we'd be a dedicated center for Native American studies. The guy with the money wanted something in return, and Nathaniel Webster did what he said, simple as that. And so here we are, two and a half centuries later. Two and a half centuries of white boys bound for Wall Street."

She didn't bother taking issue with this. With anyone else, she might have. Instead, she said: "Until Sarafian."

"Sarafian, right. I overlapped with him for a year, but I never talked to him. I wish I had, but it just never happened."

"But ... I thought he made a point of meeting with the Native American students. He was so involved with the recruitment."

"Well, that's just it." Petavit put down his burger. "I wasn't recruited. My Native heritage wasn't part of my application, and I came from a public school in Connecticut, not a reservation. I was very open about my affiliation at Webster because it was a non-issue for me, and everyone in my family. And I joined the Native community here and that was fantastic. But Webster didn't come to me; I came to Webster. Because it was a great college and not too far from home. And I didn't get into Yale," he added, grinning.

Naomi smiled. "Sorry."

"Ah." He put up his hands. "Easy come, easy go. But, if I'm really being honest, I was also curious. I grew up knowing about our relationship to Webster College, and that meant something to me. It meant something to my father, I can tell you. He'd always thought of it as this place that had once been ours, and it was taken away. When I got in, it was a powerful thing. And he was very proud, visiting me here. Sadly, he died before he could see me graduate."

"That is sad," Naomi said. She thought of her own parents, traveling to Ithaca for her graduation. She and Daniel had declined to take part, in protest over that ROTC chapter. She'd denied her mother and father the pride of watching her graduate, she realized now with a shudder of regret.

"He went out to the Turtle Mountain Chippewa reservation the summer before my senior year. He'd been Native American his whole life, but he only really got interested because of my studies at Webster. He was actually reading along in two of my Native American studies courses, trying to get two educations out of one tuition, I guess." Petavit smiled ruefully down at his hamburger. "So he decided he wanted to go to a powwow—the first he'd ever attended, isn't that rich? And on the second day there a drunk driver hit him. End of story."

"Oh, that's terrible," she told him.

"I was furious. I mean, I was furious because I preferred being furious to being sad. Which is the wrong move, by the way. It took me years to get back to the being sad part. Years and one of Amherst's legion of therapists."

"So very many to choose from." Naomi sighed.

"Why else would they call it the Happy Valley?" He smiled. "Anyway. At that time, Native American studies at Webster was already on its way to being one of the best in the country. I didn't know that when I came in, and I didn't know I'd end up gravitating to Native American history. History, yes, but not this, specifically. I credit the department with that—or I guess I should say the program, it wasn't a full department then. But I had excellent teachers and they helped me realize where my focus should be. I did my graduate degree at Berkeley and I came back to join the faculty at Amherst." He paused. He looked a bit sheepish. "You know, I just realized that you didn't actually ask for my life story."

"I'm glad I didn't have to. I'm always interested in how people end up where they do. I didn't have a clue that I'd be a college president one day, I can promise you that. I thought my life was going to be one long Peace Corps stint. And yet, here I am: Simon Legree in the corner office of Billings Hall."

"Oh"—he smiled—"that's only till they get to know you."

Naomi nodded. This was the problem, of course. They never did get to know you.

The waiter took their plates away. Petavit asked for coffee.

"Can I ask what you hope to accomplish with this... gathering?" he asked her. His hair, she noticed for the first time, was gently graying. It was so subtle she hadn't noticed at first. Her own once black hair was now aggressively silver, impossible not to see. It occurred to her that she didn't know his age. She only recalled that his graduation year had been in the '70s. Like hers. Older? Younger? At their age it seemed to matter less.

"What I hope... is to acknowledge the history of this

connection. And honor the experience you've had. I think it's a distinct experience."

"Oh, it is," he said carefully. "I'm just not sure that Webster wants to know how distinct it is."

She nodded. She wasn't sure either, but she decided to err on the side of principle.

"This is an intellectual community. We deal in truth here. Or at least, we strive to. Sarafian acted out of the ideals of his time, and I'm no different. I don't want to lose Webster's stories, good or bad. I'd like to hear them and preserve them. That's all."

He seemed to consider this as he stirred sugar into his black coffee. Then he looked at her. "Those first years after Sarafian started bringing us in. Very, very rough. You understand?"

"Sure. The Indian symbol."

"That was a big part of it. Getting here after two centuries and having to watch white boys cavort around the football fields, all done up in paint and feathers and acting like a war party from *The Searchers*? Not so good. One of the first things the students did as a group, after they get here, was take that on. Those guys got hit really hard."

"But Sarafian agreed with them," Naomi said, loyal to her predecessor. "He didn't have to hear it more than once. And to describe what he got from the alumni as 'resistance' doesn't begin to convey how ugly it was. It didn't die down for years." She had opted not to tell him that alumni still came up to her after speeches and at reunions to demand the return of the Indian symbol.

He nodded. He drank his coffee. "And what ground would you like to see covered?" he asked. He reached down into a leather satchel that leaned against his chair and retrieved a legal pad. He took a pen from his jacket pocket.

"It's entirely up to you," she said, but she couldn't help rattling off her own list even so. Programming from the Native American

THE DEVIL AND WEBSTER   227

studies program about Webster's Indian Academy years. A concurrent exhibition at the college museum. There was a Webster
grad, an Ojibwa from Ontario, who'd made an independent film
a year or two before—could they show that? Maybe something
about the position Webster occupied in Native American studies, on a national scale, and the position it occupied in the
general landscape of Native American higher education. But
mostly, she reassured him, she'd want to hear from the alumni
themselves. What had it been like here? How had it changed
them? "The story of Native Americans at Webster, generally," she
finished lamely.

"The story of Native Americans at Webster," Petavit repeated.
He read this sentence in his own handwriting, and frowned at it.
"I just don't know if it will be what you want it to be. I don't know
if it will help you"—he gestured at the window—"with that."

"It has nothing to do with that," Naomi told him, hoping it was
true.

PART IV

FUMBLE

CHAPTER FOURTEEN

NO ONE IS
BLAMING YOU

The lawsuit to which Steven Bishop of MSNBC had so casually referred turned out not to be a lawsuit at all but an intended lawsuit, which was a lot like a real lawsuit except for the fact that it did not actually exist. An intended lawsuit had indeed been announced by an attorney Naomi recognized all too well, given his habit of turning up whenever there was a perceived crime against a person of color, and when she got back to her office after lunch with Robbins Petavit (having survived, again, the scrum in the Webster Inn lobby) she had no difficulty at all in calling up the footage. The attorney, standing before the front door of Sojourner Truth House with a silent Nicholas Gall on his left side and a silent Omar Khayal on his right side, announced to the world that Professor Gall intended to file a suit against Webster College for wrongful termination, to the tune of $2.5 million, a figure that mystified Naomi.

Her first call was to the college attorney.

"It'll never happen," Chaim Wachsberger said. He sounded exhausted. "If it did, guess what would end up in the public record? Why would he want that?"

For the same baffling reason he'd wanted any of this, Naomi thought.

But the very notion of a lawsuit upped the ante. It would be out there in the world that Gall, the wronged scholar, was going to sue his employer. And Webster, with no actual charges to counter, would exist in a state of suspended indictment with nothing at all to say for itself.

Her next call was to Will Rennet, now the chairman of her board. He, unlike the college attorney, seemed to grasp the situation entirely. "Oh fuck," he said.

"I just heard about this. Chaim says it will never happen."

"It would be better if it did. Then the plagiarism would come out."

Naomi closed her eyes. Rennet had shown such devotion to Webster. He had always supported Naomi, and she felt that he'd always liked her personally. She wondered how much longer either of those things would be true.

From the beginning she had characterized the job of a college president as, first, doing no harm to the institution, second, improving the institution if at all possible, and third, getting out in one piece. There were bells and whistles, of course, myriad responsibilities, drudgery, absurdities, little challenges like speechifying and remembering names and riding the general rocket that was twenty-first-century selective admissions in a helicopter parent culture, but at the end of the day the job boiled down to these three.

So far it had all gone terribly well—too well, it seemed to Naomi now. The hardest thing had been Radclyffe Hall, and technically that hadn't fallen within the scope of her presidency. Her inauguration was—it embarrassed her a bit to remember—a love fest, with a general celebration of the fact that Webster at last had a Jewish president, a female president. Webster, whose mid-twentieth-century political demographic had been

93 percent Republican, now had a president who'd chaired the Women's Studies Department, who was faculty advisor to the Queer and Gender Discussion Group, and whose published academic work featured a lesbian separatist music collective. It didn't get cooler than that to your typical twenty-first-century Webster undergrad, and as for those older graduates who belonged to pre-Sarafian Webster—they'd shown real restraint, at least in her presence.

This, however. This was pushing her. She could feel the strain, in her muscles, in her breathing. She felt it at the witching hour of three in the morning, when she woke in her presidential bed in the Stone House, wondering where Hannah was, and how many were sleeping out tonight, and how it was all going to end. The fortitude she'd shown back at the beginning (or thought she'd shown) had been predicated on the notion that it wouldn't last long. It couldn't last long. These were Webster students, and however hardy they imagined themselves to be, they were also, overwhelmingly, the products of comfortable suburbia, family wealth, the kind of security that comes from knowing you're going to attend college in the first place. They, like generations of protesters before them, would make their point and then go back to class, because the ground was hard and holy cow, did people smell after a few days without a shower, and besides, they couldn't risk failing organic chem if they were going to med school.

But these kids, no.

She wasn't even impressed anymore. She was tired. And she was pissed.

And she was trapped, because whatever she did say about the movement and the tenure decision had to be true but could not be the truth, which was stressful beyond belief, and it promised only to go on, and on some more.

But then, at last, something fell into her hands.

The end of the fall/winter term brought its usual dispersal of official standings from the registrar, including those students who'd earned dean's list distinction (3.5 GPA and above) and those students who were circling academic probation or worse. The latter list was longer than usual and contained a number of names with which Naomi had recently become familiar. She was relieved beyond words to see that her daughter wasn't among this group of Webster dissenters. (That would have been impossibly awkward.) But Chava was. No wonder she'd withdrawn. And so was Elise, the basketball player from Naomi's freshman seminar. And so was Omar.

Naomi, scrolling down the line, gasped when she saw it, her hand frozen awkwardly above the keyboard. Omar's work for the semester had been... well, it hadn't been, that was the point. F in his history course on the Ottoman Empire. F in anthropology (Food Systems in the Pre-Columbian Americas). F in English (Outsider Voices in Contemporary Fiction). And an A in Anthropology (Advanced Supervised Independent Study, professor: N. Gall). GPA for the term? 1. The cutoff for academic probation was 1.5.

She put her hand down in her lap, and continued to sit, staring at the screen. Here, at last, was a thing, a definite thing, but did she dare to use it? The many, many ways it might make things worse, not better, weren't difficult to assess, and yet no one could take issue with the bald fact that Omar Khayal, whatever he might arguably have done for Webster, had done little or nothing in the way of his own schoolwork. Even the most cynical observer of those three F's (the college is trying to get rid of him!) would have to apply that same paranoia to Nicholas Gall's A—for "independent study" (a notoriously mercurial concept of academic work at the best of times). Omar, not a strong student to begin with, was flunking out.

Before she could talk herself out of it, she wrote him an email, summoning her best facsimile of institutional concern.

From: nroth@webster.edu

To: okhayal@webster.edu

CC: rstacek@webster.edu

Date: 2/3/16

Subject: Fall15/Winter16 Marking Period

Dear Omar,

I note with real concern the results of your most recent marking period. I'm sure it will not come as a surprise to you that these grades pose some difficulty for your academic standing. No one at Webster wants to lose you as a student, but it is critical that you come in to discuss the situation immediately. It may be possible to grant a retroactive leave for the past semester, which would enable you to go forward with these grades expunged from your record. Alternatives would include an agreed-upon period of leave, effective immediately, beginning Spring 16 on academic probation, or separation from the college.

Again, this will be a matter for us to discuss in a confidential setting. I have scheduled a meeting for you, myself, and Dean Robert Stacek for tomorrow, Wednesday, February 4, at 2 p.m. in the Office of the Dean of Students, Billings 205. Please call my office to confirm. If it is necessary to change this appointment we will make time to see you at your convenience over the next few days, but it's important that we do not leave it any longer.

Yours,

Naomi Roth, President

Billings 301

Webster College

The next day at one forty-five she descended the wide stair-case of Billings Hall, hand trailing the wooden banister like a self-conscious debutante, and entered the dean of students' of-fice, directly below hers, which Bob Stacek had now occupied for nearly fifteen years. On the wall behind his desk three crew oars were hung, each inscribed with the names of his crews in the English manner, and a framed silver medal from the Eastern Sprints below them. There were fraternity group shots (plastic cups of beer held aloft), an alarmingly young Bob Stacek on the Pont Neuf with a much younger version of Lois Stacek (Welles-ley, '77), and half a dozen formal portraits of the Stacek progeny: three stocky boys and—a good while later—an elfin girl. All of them had graduated from Webster, the daughter only a few years earlier.

"On the whole," said Stacek without preamble, "it works bet-ter if you schedule an appointment through my assistant, rather than by cc'ing me on an email to a student. I had to cancel something."

"I know. I'm sorry," she said briskly, taking one of his visitor's chairs. "I was impulsive. But we might have a break here. I mean, finally."

"We could have suspended him months ago," Stacek observed. "He hasn't been attending classes or responding to warnings. He's not living in his dorm. That's a violation."

Was it? Naomi frowned. Stacek might have mentioned that sooner.

"And he's agitating."

"Well, that is not a violation," Naomi said tersely. "Peaceful as-sembly and all that."

He said nothing. His scalp, through thinning hair, appeared moist in the overhead light. "What are you planning?" he asked finally.

"I'm not planning. Yet. I'm hoping."

He raised an eyebrow.

"I'm hoping he'll walk through that door in the next few minutes. I'm hoping he'll talk to us. I'm hoping he'll want to stay at Webster. But if he doesn't want to stay..." She took a breath. Even saying this much, in private, to someone far more pissed off than she was, felt like a betrayal. "Then I'm hoping he'll go away."

"Far, far away," Stacek agreed.

All the way back to where he came from, Naomi thought. For an awful second she wasn't sure whether she was attributing that nasty sentiment to the dean of students or to herself.

It was two p.m. now. The two of them sat in anticipatory silence. It was not pleasant, but given the germ of anticipation that popped to life as the bell in the Webster clock tower tolled the hour and swelled and strengthened with every passing minute of Omar's tardiness, it was not entirely unpleasant either. Five minutes—an entirely forgivable delay. Ten minutes—irritating, but students were not always attuned to the adult necessity of keeping exact time. Fifteen minutes. Twenty. Half an hour. Naomi, to her own mild disgust, was thrilled.

"I have a two thirty," Stacek said abruptly, as if he were interrupting an altogether different conversation, or any conversation.

"Yes. Well. I'm disappointed."

She wondered if he could tell how very untrue this was.

"From what I've seen of this kid, I don't think he'd cancel CNN for a meeting with the dean of students. Or even the president," Stacek added with a slightly smarmy deference.

"I'm afraid we have to suspend him," Naomi said. She thought, as she said this: *sound sad.*

"Well," he said unhelpfully, "that's up to you. It's entirely your call."

"Why so? You're the dean of students."

"And you're the president," Stacek said, as if she had ripped this very position from his own more deserving hands. *You wanted it? You got it, sweetheart.* "Even if I made a decision in this matter it would cross your desk before being implemented. But with this particular kid I'd clear it with you before doing anything. He may be one of a dozen looking at suspension after last term, but he's the only one with an MSNBC camera crew following him around."

"I'd like your input," Naomi said, channeling someone far wiser and more Zen than herself. Grace Paley, perhaps. Margaret Mead. Somebody. "I'd like to know what you'd be doing in my position."

He shot her a look of outright disgust and a message so crystal clear he might as well have said it aloud. *If I were in your "position," I would not have put myself in this position. Okay?*

"Suspension," he said, once he'd regained control of himself. "There's no alternative."

Merely to spite him, she declared an alternative. Another appointment: one more and one more only, to take place the following afternoon, again at two p.m. Again, Naomi wrote the email, and this time she gave it an unmistakable tone: "Failure to keep this appointment will indicate your unwillingness to work with the college in this matter, and leave us no alternative but to proceed with some form of suspension."

That night Naomi had the pleasure of hearing herself called "a despotic figurehead" live on CNN by Ms. Chava Friedberg, formerly an undergraduate of Webster College and part of Webster Dissent's "spokesperson collective," as an in-studio panel of experts on trends in higher education dissected Dr. Naomi Roth's apparently epic mishandling of the movement, from her cavalier dismissal of genuine student concerns to her arrogant assumption that no one would notice or object to the firing of a popular professor, who happened to be a person of color. According to Ms. Friedberg, Webster College—for all its posturing as a place of progressive education—had a shockingly low percentage of ethnically diverse faculty members. Naomi was just shooting off an email to Douglas Sidgwick for the actual statistics (she would make some *calm* and *dignified* use of them in the morning) when Chava said something else: something Naomi could not quite force through her own brain and out into the realm of understanding. "What?" she actually said to the television.

"This happened when?" said the panel's moderator. His name was Bill, or Phil. He wore a brown bowtie.

"This happened today. I'm sure that the college would love for this information not to be released, but that's not the kind of Webster we deserve. No just society is ever possible without transparency."

"You're saying Omar Khayal has been expelled, as of today."

"Technically he's been suspended," Chava said seriously, as if accuracy were very, very important. "Summarily suspended. Without warning and without recourse."

The panel seemed momentarily stunned.

"Well, that's . . ." said a woman from the *Chronicle of Higher Education*.

"I'm not surprised," said the other woman. She was much younger. She looked barely out of college herself. She wrote for *Slate*, according to the screen. "This president has a highly emotive and extremely impulsive leadership style."

"If you call that leadership," the older of the two men sneered. He was Naomi's age, more or less: gray, furry, dressed down in a denim shirt and jeans. He looked slightly familiar, and it crossed Naomi's mind that they might have worked together once, back in the day. "This is the kind of leadership we haven't seen since George Wallace in Alabama."

She was still too much in shock to respond to this. Her heart was tearing open her chest. Naomi's right hand, she now realized, was frozen above the keyboard of her laptop. She'd been in the middle of an email to Will Rennet about something else. What had it been? She couldn't remember. From the bedside table in the next room she heard her phone begin to rattle.

"It's hard to believe that a president whose own academic field is the history of feminism could have emerged as such a reactionary figure," said the moderator.

"Not really," said Naomi's gray contemporary. "Not if you'd made a study of her academic work, as I have. Always, there is this dismissive tone about earlier social movements. It's something that's come up frequently in my own research—a disparagement of events from which one has failed to emerge as a leader."

"Sour grapes, in other words," said the *Chronicle of Higher Education*.

"Well, I can't comment on this woman's inner life," he said with distaste. "But I can make the observation that this is not a person who is remembered for having been an activist at all, though it's touted as a big part of her biography, and I'm assuming it's something that made her attractive to a school like Webster. Having a former Weatherman in the president's office has a certain cachet, but Naomi Roth was no Weatherman," he concluded.

"Nor would she want to be!" Naomi shrieked at the screen. She had never entertained a single bombing fantasy. Now, though, she indulged in a brief reverie about blowing CNN's Boston studio sky high.

"What are Omar's plans?" asked the *Slate* girl.

"He is so passionately devoted to what we are trying to do at Webster," Chava said. "I . . . honestly? I don't think he's thinking about his own future at all. I think . . . growing up where he did, and how he did, the future was more of a luxury. He wasn't entitled that way, and he still isn't. Obviously," she said, with vigor. Her lower lip, in the wide, flat, HD screen that the college had installed when its predecessor died the previous spring, quivered in great detail. Naomi, mesmerized, stared at it. That lip—it had a worried plumpness, a bitten surface. It was not a thoughtless lower lip at all. That lower lip was being very deliberately presented to the international viewing public. In the bedroom, the phone gave a ping, conveying a voice mail. Then it began to rattle anew.

By morning she had endured difficult conversations with eight of the trustees, including Will Rennet, the closest thing she'd ever had to a champion (it killed her how much that meant, how grateful she still was). It wasn't, of course, the first time the two of them had spoken about what was happening. But it was the worst time.

In an ordinary calendar year, Webster's board met three times. On campus in June (reunions) and October (homecoming) and on a mid-March board retreat, somewhere rustic (yet elegant!) and usually adjacent to a golf course. The last retreat, nearly a year earlier, had been at a board member's Montana ranch, an hour north of Missoula. Morning trail rides that led to a tented breakfast spread in a stunning valley. Massive log rooms with wood stoves. Huckleberry soap and lotion in the bathrooms. Crazy good barbecue. The Native American Gathering, proposed at that retreat, had been met with a few interested questions and a round of generous approval, and the mood in sum had been elevated: *All was well.* Webster was holding its perch in the top ten of *US News and World Report*'s ridiculous rankings (one man's ridiculous was another's lifeblood, no one needed to point out). The endowment sat snugly between that of Williams and Amherst, and was even haler than those of certain Ivy League institutions, at least if you separated out their graduate schools' dedicated coffers. The quality of life reported by Webster's undergraduates was a stratospheric 94 percent positive, and (just as important) the degree of satisfaction expressed by their parents was a commendable 86 percent. In fact, it had occurred to Naomi then, and for the very first time in her tenure as Webster's president, that she was actually doing this. She was actually succeeding at this. Pulling it off. Fooling them with her impersonation of a college president, as if she were actually becoming one of those luminous, astonishing, extraordinary women, members of that wondrous little group that had accompanied her down the aisle at her Webster inauguration.

And this was the moment she realized that not one of these women had been in touch with her since the advent of Webster Dissent. No *Courage!* No *Hang in there!* No advice. She would not have turned down advice. Not a sorority after all, it appeared. Or maybe it was, but she had never truly been a member. Maybe they were all meeting up—right now, in a secret location—partaking of some exclusive sisterly ritual and deconstructing President Naomi Roth's mishandling of the situation at Webster. It was a sensation she had not experienced since middle school, but it came back fresh as a daisy. And hard as a wave.

What had become of that happy narrative—*The Tale of Webster College President Naomi Roth: Feminist Scholar, Shaggy-Haired Ethnic Single Mom, Standard-Bearer for These Latter Days*? She had been so refreshingly unconventional, so quirky but lovable—the kind of university figurehead any undergraduate might be super stoked to grab a beer with (or invite over for a vegan potluck and a life-altering chat about the Bloomsbury Group). That story—her story—was drifting. It was falling. It was getting hard to see the next chapter, let alone some soaring career crescendo she'd never actually conceived. (*Naomi Roth: Visionary Author and In-Demand Speaker? Naomi Roth: Secretary of Education?*) What would become of her own victory lap, the kind Logan Coulson had helped himself to in the final year of his Webster presidency? When would the final year itself begin? Maybe—it struck her now, and with an actual physical pang—

it was actually under way. Maybe this thing, this mess was already sinking her maiden (matron?) voyage, making her brilliant career, in Miles Franklin's indelible turn of phrase, *go bung*. For the very first time, Naomi let herself truly understand that she was no longer a success at this. Or more likely she had never been a success; the only thing that had changed was that she was no longer fooling anyone, herself included.

She was no longer fooling a goodly portion of her board—that much was plain. Those few who either weren't habitual MSNBC viewers or who had the self-control to wait for morning headed the list of names on her call sheet, which was handed over the following morning by a grim Mrs. Bradford as Naomi entered her office. The others had all called again, too: the retired Massachusetts governor, the television producer with the golden touch, the absurdly rich tech guy from Boston, the man whose impossibly luxurious Montana ranch had all that huckleberry soap in the bathrooms—each of them wanted her on the phone before she did anything else. The two mothers of current undergraduates (both, by strange coincidence, CEOs of Houston-based marketing firms) had checked in, each of them having called shortly after nine a.m. All three hedge funders (two Greenwich, one Atherton), hot on their heels, instructed Mrs. Bradford to have the president call them back immediately. Walter Hammer, a retired Navy engineer who'd graduated from Webster (like his father and grandfather, twin daughters, and, if Naomi remembered correctly, a grandson) had left a message of vague support and asked her to phone "when convenient"), and the novelist (poor, but respected!) had left word, wondering if she had a moment to speak. Even the recent graduate occupying Webster's largely symbolic board seat for young alumni (a position created by Naomi) had called in. And—hardest of all, that barely acknowledged Hope at the bottom of this Pandora's Box—Will Rennet, her once but maybe not future champion, was on the phone when Naomi arrived. For the first time in her experience, probably the first in any Webster president's experience, there had been two guards at the door to Webster Hall, and for a terrible moment, making her way up to the arched stone doorway through a scrum of media drones, she'd wondered if they intended to block her entrance.

"No." She waved at her stony assistant. She whispered: "I can't talk right now."

"I'll tell her," Mrs. Bradford said. She hadn't skipped a beat. "Yes, just as soon as she gets here. There's a crowd downstairs. I've asked security to stay at the door. It's probably taking her a bit longer to get in." She listened, one long finger tapping the faux leather corner of her desk blotter. "Yes, eleven thirty. Eastern. Yes. We have nearly everyone. Yes, I'll let her know."

She hung up the phone and turned her stony face to Naomi. "We're all set for a conference call at eleven thirty. I moved your meeting with the *Webster Daily* to four."

The *Daily*. The student papers were still the only publications she'd sat down with for on-record conversations about Webster Dissent, but that had been in the fall, before the group had deigned to name itself and when Naomi had still hoped to communicate with the kids on the Quad. It hadn't worked. She was pretty sure it wouldn't work any better now, but she'd said yes. It was her responsibility to be available to the student press; that hadn't changed.

A conference call with "nearly everyone"—they'd done that only a few times in five years. Once for a student suicide. Once for a batch of some party drug with the absurd name of Brown Betty that had sent a dozen Webster students to the hospital. Once after the Sojourner Truth House, and that had been only four weeks earlier. Everything was speeding up, it occurred to her. Faster and harder, just like labor. She'd read somewhere that women were programmed to forget the pain of labor, but Naomi hadn't forgotten.

"Professor Russell is coming in," Mrs. Bradford said. "The others will be on the phone. Wendy Lopez is the only one who can't phone in."

Wendy Lopez was the recent graduate in the young alumni seat. Her absence wouldn't have much impact. But Milton Russell was the trustee Naomi least wished to be physically in her presence while twelve other angry men and women remotely raked her over the coals. Russell had retired to West Webster after a long and undistinguished teaching career in Webster's history department. As an undergraduate he had won the Webster Key award for loyalty to the college (she had never discovered what he'd actually done to warrant that and wasn't sure she wanted to know), and as a professor he had overseen the *Heritage Review*, a conservative publication produced by an odious little club of his student admirers. Milton Russell was an unapologetic product and staunch defender of pre-Sarafian Webster College, and he had never attempted to temper his disapproval of Naomi.

"We'll need, I guess, coffee."

"Done," said Mrs. Bradford, with an unwarranted sharpness. "And cookies."

Milton Russell was partial to cookies. While he was still teaching he'd made a daily appearance at the Loring Library for its four p.m. tea ritual, when students briefly set aside the heavy burden of their scholarly pursuits and indulged in the traditional snacks. Trust Mrs. Bradford to know that. "Thank you," Naomi said. She went into her inner office and shut the door.

The calls had lasted until two a.m., and after that she'd lain in her bed, stiffly, on her side, as if she were suffering some acute pain. She was a bit of a coward when it came to pain, at least the deep internal variety (she would take a broken limb over a

stomachache every time, even factoring in the speedy resolution
of your average stomachache), and whenever she did get sick she
regressed utterly—a mewling, frozen lump, incapable of caring
for herself. It was a good thing Hannah hadn't been there to see
the sad thing she'd become last night, under the covers. That sad
thing, that weak thing—so repellently...well, the word she was
looking for was *feminine*, really—it was not something she'd have
wanted Hannah to see. It wasn't something she'd wanted to see,
herself.

It took no time at all to catch up on what the rest of the world
now believed: Webster College had expelled Omar Khayal, summarily and without affording him any opportunity to speak with
the college authorities, let alone to stay his execution. The young
foreign student's belongings had reportedly been packed up by
parties unknown and removed from his rooms in the Eagle Road
dormitories; he was not certain where they were, he told CNN
with admirable restraint, and yet the personal devastation—the
plain human hurt in the voice of this parentless young man so far
from home (not that he had a home) was plain to anyone with a
pulse.

"What reason did the college give for expelling you?" said the
woman holding the microphone.

Omar's narrow shoulders fell. "I wasn't given a reason," he
said.

Naomi was more furious than self-pitying. She was more self-
pitying than amazed. She was fully amazed. For another hour she
merely pushed back in her chair, feet up against the long desk,
staring at nothing. Her office chair was one of those old oak and
leather models that rocked back and forth at the base, like one of
the teetering toys Hannah used to play with—a Weeble, Naomi
thought, fishing the name (and the irritating jingle) out of the
murk in her head. Weebles wobble but they don't...something.
She couldn't remember what Weebles did not do. Weebles don't

feel defeat? Weebles don't get pissed off at idiots? *Wish I could be a Weeble*, she thought with—finally—a tiny breath of absurdity. She was wobbling all over the place.

Russell arrived a few minutes early, entering the conference room with his eyes averted. He already seemed furious, and barely produced the most basic of greetings. He sat himself in front of the ginger cookies and immediately inserted two into his mouth, fixing a baleful gaze upon the portrait of Josiah Webster over the mantel as he chewed. Naomi opted to focus on her notes, which she had finally begun an hour or two earlier and were now somewhat extensive.

Part one: how we got here. Part two: what our options are now. The crisis (and she was now forcing herself to name this a crisis, which meant admitting to herself that it was a crisis) was transforming itself into something almost orderly on the page before her, delineated in her always very good handwriting, bisected into column A and column B, with underlined headings and notes to herself in parentheses (toilet trailer, Day of Campus Discourse, open invitation, etc.). She was careful not to defend herself. She failed to see how Webster Dissent might have been more strategically, more compassionately handled. Naomi wouldn't go so far as to say that none of this was her fault (who else's fault could it have been?), but if someone on her board (and she briefly met the bitter glare of the former faculty advisor to the *Heritage Review*) had it in mind to request her self-sacrifice in this matter, Naomi Roth intended to aim for this individual's odious, wattled, and mole-covered neck.

That wasn't going to be necessary, was it?

Mrs. Bradford might have been of the old school, but she was oddly gifted with the particular technology of conference calls. Within a few minutes of the scheduled call, and after a minimum of adjustments and rebootings, she had everyone but young Wendy Lopez on the line, or online (Naomi wasn't sure which):

the board of trustees of Webster College, together in a part-actual, part-virtual conference room. She had to force herself not to entertain them all as they waited.

"Can I just ask everyone to identify themselves?" Naomi said. This was for the record.

One by one they did: Boston, California, New York, Walter Hammer on a hotel line in Paris. "Are you feeling better?" she asked Sally Roorbach in Houston. She and Sally had spoken at midnight, or thereabouts.

"I am," Sally croaked. "But bizarrely I sound worse. My daughter says I put her in mind of Lauren Bacall."

There was a bit of strange, disembodied laughing in the imaginary conference room. In the actual conference room, neither of the two physically present people laughed, or even smiled.

"And Wendy Lopez is unable to join us," Naomi noted.

"I'm sure we shall muddle through without her," Milton Russell said, though not precisely to her. He had embarked upon another pair of cookies, and chewed, disconcertingly, with his mouth partly open.

Naomi, in response, gave a nod, though not precisely back to him, and somehow, in that small gesture of diverted hostility, an unrelated but highly relevant bit of truth punched its way into her skull and exploded.

Mrs. Bradford might be efficiency itself, but she was not in a position to call and convene a meeting of the college's trustees. Only a couple of people were capable of doing so, Naomi, of course, among them. But Naomi had not called for this meeting. She had given no instruction, made no suggestion. She had not even raised the possibility in any of her phone calls the previous night, and yet here she was, seated opposite her least favorite trustee and waiting for the official unpleasantness to begin. *Wait a minute*, she thought as the final trustees checked in. Frantically, she tried to process her pathetic little revelation:

This meeting, the one that was happening right now—someone else had instigated it, and brought it about without her assistance. Also without her knowledge. And of course that meant something. And of course the something that it meant was not good. And all of this in a single wave as she sat, evading eye contact with Milton Russell and straining to differentiate the voices on the line.

Later, Naomi could begin to understand how she'd been capable of such a neat bit of self-delusion, and the essence of it was this: She was...not...herself. She had been under assault for months, even before she'd recognized what was taking place as both personal and intentional: the slow unfolding of Webster Dissent, the blunt horror of the Sojourner Truth basement, which was both emotional and frankly sensory (the smell, she couldn't seem to get rid of the memory of that), the knowledge that she was steadily running out of great ideas, not to mention the confidence they imbued. And then, more recently, had come the vertigo of rapidly unfolding events. The past hours, pockmarked with intense phone conversations and pallid sleep, and something that affected her even more deeply—a building sense that Hannah was present in everything Omar Khayal and Nicholas Gall were doing, even as she was increasingly *not* present in Naomi's day-to-day life. She had failed to notice this transition as it happened, and now that it obviously *had* happened she was failing to pinpoint its onset. She was also finding it harder and harder to imagine that it would pass, or to conjure any other outcome but the one in which she would assume culpability for everything and stagger off in shame: Naomi Roth's epic fail, from which she would be too tainted ever to recover, professionally or, yes, personally.

"No one is blaming you," said someone, and then someone else. Not in the room (of course not in the room; in the room Milton Russell absolutely was blaming her). It was from someone out there, in the virtual room. This did seem important, so she wrote it down ("No one is blaming you"), but even reading it on the page, in her own writing, didn't make it true.

"President Roth?" said Will Rennet. "If you could walk us through the situation with this student."

Naomi had her notes, but she didn't need her notes. She summarized Omar's failing marks and the suspicious A from Nicholas Gall, their email correspondence (if one-sided, unanswered emails could be considered "correspondence"), and cited the meeting he hadn't shown up for, and the second attempt to get him in the room with herself and the dean of students. Omar had spoken to the press before the rescheduled meeting could take place, not that Naomi imagined for a moment he'd have shown up for that one, either. Technically, she explained, Omar Khayal had been neither expelled nor even suspended. "I even raised the possibility of a retroactive leave, which would have enabled him to nullify the past term's GPA of one."

"Which is outrageous," said Professor Russell. "Academic standards should not be rolled up like a carpet every time a student falls short of them. If this student can't do his work he can give up his place or go away until he can appreciate a Webster education. Expectations are in the college handbook, and every single student receives the college handbook on matriculation. End of story."

If only it were, Naomi thought.

"I have to say, I do agree," said Lauren Bacall. "A one-point GPA is a pretty clear statement. Couldn't we...I don't know, pick the right media outlet and just explain that we had no choice?"

"Why should we explain?" growled Professor Russell. He was looking balefully at Naomi, as if she'd been the one to speak. "Just state the facts. Why should we apologize because a student did no work and failed his classes? He didn't meet our academic standards, and believe me, they are not difficult to meet if my final years on the faculty are any indication. I can tell you first-hand that Webster undergraduates have been squeaking by with negligible effort for decades. This kid is making a statement. He doesn't want to be here. Ergo, he shouldn't be here."

Never mind that, Naomi was thinking. She was still stuck on the very problematic phrase *the right media outlet*. What consti-tuted "right" in this context? "Right" as in right wing? Professor Russell, it occurred to her, probably had an entire Rolodex full of "right" media outlets.

"President Roth?" It was Will Rennet. "It's a reasonable sug-gestion. Would you like to respond?"

She took a breath. "Unfortunately, it's a moot suggestion. Right outlet or not, we are just not permitted to speak about this publicly, let alone to the media. The academic discipline process is armored in confidentiality, as delineated in the college hand-book. We can't comment on Omar's standing any more than we can make Nick Gall's plagiarism public. The only thing we can say on either subject is that the process is confidential and we can't discuss the committee's decision. Last month I gave an in-terview to the *Webster Daily* and I said something completely banal about how tenure decisions were not taken lightly, and one of the group leaders then gave an interview about how the col-lege was insinuating something nefarious or criminal, and how venal this was. That was a two-day story of its own, remember?"

She wasn't sure they remembered. She also hoped they weren't aware that the group leader in question had been Han-nah Roth.

"But look," a deep voice said, "I mean, how many journalists are circling this thing? And if just one of them had an under-standing of what we were dealing with, with the plagiarism and the academic circumstances, then they would have to investi-gate. I realize they're all in the kid's corner right now, but nobody turns up their nose at this kind of information. There must be some way to convey our circumstances without making a public statement."

Naomi gazed, with some irritation, at her computer screen. She wasn't sure who had spoken beyond its having been a male voice. The screen emitted silence. The man across the table was also, surprisingly, silent. *Who are these people?* she thought.

"We are not doing that," she said finally.

"No, of course," said a fully recognizable Will Rennet. Where had he been a few moments earlier? "No one is suggesting that we break confidentiality."

Not even the no one who'd just proposed exactly that? Naomi thought.

"But it's also true that we shouldn't be held hostage by our own principles. Especially not if we're being forced to respond to continual, intentional misinformation. There has to be a middle way."

"There isn't one," Naomi said curtly. She was feeling very martyr-y by now. She was marching off to prison with the Freedom Riders. She was lying down before the tanks in Tiananmen Square.

"With respect," she heard Lauren Bacall say, "however noble our individual principles on this subject may be, we're also dealing with institutional principles, which are arguably even more important than anything we may believe as individuals. And the institution can't speak for itself."

"I've spent the past twenty years persuading everyone I know that Webster has changed," Walter Hammer broke in. "I tell them we're not that right-wing, anti-intellectual Animal House they remember from Mom's Snow Carnival visit or Dad's away game on our campus. I'm so proud that my daughters' Webster was a completely different place than the one I attended. And this—you know, I'm actually hearing from people about this.

People are sending me news stories about the college and saying, basically, I thought you said things had changed. And I'm telling you, this is offensive to me."

"Well, what do you say to them?" said the other woman in Houston, the one who didn't sound like Lauren Bacall.

"I say, 'There's more that's going on here. There's a lot that isn't in the media.' And don't worry, I know that's as far as I can go. I'm not interested in getting sued or the college getting sued."

"We are getting sued," said Russell. "According to my son, this student"—he pronounced *student* like a lower life-form—"is suing us."

"Threatening to sue," said Naomi mildly.

"It's outrageous," he nodded, as if she were agreeing with him.

"If I may." Lauren Bacall was interrupting. "I'm sure we're all in agreement that President Roth has appropriately handled the situation. She's had an open door from the beginning. She's attempted to start a dialogue repeatedly. But we need to look at this with fresh eyes now. The Sojourner Truth House was a wake-up call that we're not in control, and we need to be in control."

Professor Russell was tapping his present cookie against the tabletop, building a stockpile of ginger crumbs. "Finally, someone brave enough to state the obvious."

Naomi looked helplessly at the computer screen. After a moment, Will Rennet rescued her.

"Professor Russell, forgive me, but I, for one, am failing to see the obvious. If you can enlighten us?"

This was said with commendable restraint. Rennet had told her, more than once, that Milton Russell was the most inept and yet condescending professor he'd had at Webster.

"Surely we all realize that Webster Dissent"—here he helpfully made quotation marks with his stubby fingers—"is responsible for the vandalism of that basement."

Naomi stared at him. For an odd moment she seemed to actually enter the virtual room. They were all there, the Webster College board of trustees, her collective employer, evenly spaced around a white round table, each person—curiously—with his or her hands splayed on the sleek tabletop. Every one of them looked stunned.

Again, Rennet's was the first voice she heard. "Speaking for myself, I certainly have not made that leap. In fact, I can't see any reason whatsoever to make that leap."

"No, you wouldn't," Russell said, with the precise condescension his former student had described.

"Professor Russell," Naomi said, "there is nothing in the stated positions of this student group that would tolerate, let alone sponsor, what was done in the Sojourner Truth basement. To the extent that I understand what they're doing, and I fully admit that I don't understand the entirety of what they're doing, we're talking about diametrically opposed positions. The group has said repeatedly that they're devastated about the incident. In fact, it's part of their invective against the college that this crime could even take place at Webster."

"Exactly," he huffed, maddeningly.

"Can I just ask, Professor Russell," said Lauren Bacall, "do you know something we don't know? I would imagine, living so close to the college, perhaps you're hearing things we're not hearing. If people in the community are talking about what's happening there, if there's anything you've got that you could share..."

"There is something I've got. It's called a brain, and thank God I have one. These people, these protesters, they are not interested in ideas. They are not interested in dialogue. Our president can set up consciousness-raising sessions and heart-to-heart chats in the dean's office till the cows come home, and they're going to stand her up every time. The only thing they care about is reaction, and we are obliging them by reacting. All we've said to these people is 'What can we do for you?' How did we reward them for turning the Billings Lawn into a mud pit reminiscent of Woodstock? We gave them a fancy toilet that's costing us a fortune! How can we make it up to them for not attending class or doing their academic work? Wipe the slate clean so their failing marks go away!" He was getting red as he spoke. Redder and tighter. He was a man well on his way to some kind of physical crisis. For a moment—a vile moment—it occurred to Naomi that she should just let him get on with it. "So here we're running around apologizing to the world instead of clearing up this situation."

"Clearing up." It was Will Rennet. Naomi didn't have to see him to know that he was shaking his head.

"Yes. Clearing the quad. If they want to passively resist, no problem. But they need to be removed. They're breaking the law."

"Which law would that be?" said Rennet.

"Trespassing, obviously. The Quad is Webster College property."

"And they are Webster students," Naomi said, locating her own voice from beneath layers of stupefaction.

"Not all of them. I think not most of them, at this point. And the ones who are aren't attending classes, if Mr. Khayal's grades are any indication. You may be apologizing to your friends about Webster, Mr. Hammer, but I am unwilling to apologize when I am in the right. Our only fault in this matter has been waiting for these highly unattractive young people to take responsibility for themselves, when they clearly have no interest in doing so. They are kicking up tantrums in our face and on our property, and we respond by handing over the reins to the entire university. Sure, go ahead and control how we're perceived by the world. Hold the trustees hostage. Discourage young people from applying here and scare their parents out of letting them attend, if they get in. Why should they care? They're out of here in four years with straight A's in...I don't know...Gender Queer Deconstruction, and they've got a job lined up making cupcakes. When my friends call up to ask me why the Webster grad they've hired in their office can't write a memo, or doesn't know what the Constitution says, and they want to know what the hell is going on up here, I'm not going to wring my hands because I'm not responsible for it. This...."—he gave himself a sputtery moment to locate the precise word—"*debacle* is the inevitable result of years of capitulation to liberal idiocy. It is patently not my fault."

Naomi, absurdly, looked at the computer screen, but no further rescue from that source seemed imminent. It would fall to her—and, she supposed, appropriately to her—to actually speak the inevitable response. Though her heart sank as she fed him his line: *So whose fault is it?*

"This president," he said, with who knew how many years of suppressed fury, "by her painfully misguided actions, is the prime mover of our present difficulties, and that this board apparently supports her, I cannot understand. If no one else is brave enough to put it into words, then I suppose I will have to do it. It wouldn't be the first time. I hereby propose that President Roth voluntarily rescind the presidency in light of her complete inability to handle a crisis she has largely created."

Then he sat back in his chair, still red, still puffing, as if he had undertaken some athletic feat or—gruesome as this was for Naomi to imagine—managed to complete an act of copulation.

No more cookies for you, she thought.

PART V

SHAMBLES

CHAPTER FIFTEEN

SPEAKING TRUTH TO POWER

A fterward nearly all of them phoned in again, individually, to reassure her. Russell had been way out of line. Russell was a token holdover, a reminder of how far Webster had come. Russell's sole purpose on the board was to keep the rest of them ever vigilant, to ensure that the college did not return to what it had once been. It wasn't that Naomi didn't appreciate the gesture (or gestures). She was appreciative. She thanked them and did what she could to laugh it all off, but she had never been much of an actress. Basically what she really wanted, at least in the aftermath of that appalling conference call, was to yank the phone cord from the wall, shut and bolt the door, and have a massive pre-feminist girls-in-the-workplace cry. It was only the sight of Professor Milton Russell's single uneaten cookie on its Webster crest china plate that stopped her.

Bastard.

Moron.

Chauvinist.

Mrs. Bradford brought in the mail, and Naomi did not miss her studious avoidance of eye contact. Had Russell been as loud as all that? Or had the entire meeting been monitored in the outer office? There'd been a call from the secretary of the alumni association, her assistant reported, and one from the *Times Higher Education Supplement*. Those were the important ones, anyway.

"Which means?" said Naomi.

"Oh, don't worry, I'm keeping track. There'll be a list when you're ready."

But when would she ever be ready?

She thanked Mrs. Bradford and went back to what she'd been doing, which was nothing, basically. Naomi sat, tipped back in her presidential chair, grinding her presidential ballpoint pen into the presidential leather blotter on her presidential desk as the afternoon hauled itself along. She was thinking, or trying to, but it wasn't getting her anywhere, and the hours passed with only the defacement of her blotter to show for them. The winter sun went dull and then out. The building was quiet. From across the room, a photograph of Hannah, dressed for Halloween as Rosie the Riveter, eyed her, making her ever more miserable. There were no more Sunday dinners with Hannah now. There hadn't been one since Christmas. And anyway, she was furious with Hannah.

But being furious at Hannah hurt so physically that it took her breath away, and immobilized her all over again.

At four the *Webster Daily* reporter arrived for their interview. This was the same young woman who'd interviewed her about the protest last fall and again, only a few weeks earlier, about Nicholas Gall. In the moments before her arrival Naomi roused herself to review the statement she and Chaim Wachsberger had settled on, and which she intended for the *Daily* to run, in full.

Webster College maintains the utmost privacy in matters of academic standing and academic discipline, just as it does with regard to our tenure process. We decline, now and in the future, to comment on a student's standing, and have every confidence in those faculty and administration members who make decisions on academic standing only after lengthy consideration and an effort to work with the student in question. The college will not participate in speculation about a student's action or actions that may lead to his or her separation from the college, whether temporary or permanent.

Deviation from this language would not be tolerated, she warned the reporter, a junior from St. Louis, not if the *Webster Daily* wanted the door kept open for future. And the *Daily* would indeed want the door kept open; the very fact that this small college newspaper (albeit the second oldest in Massachusetts, after the *Crimson*) now controlled a vital source for a national news story had given its staff a taste of the media vortex; they wouldn't want to risk that.

And no, she had no comment on the Sojourner Truth investigation, except to say that it was ongoing.

And no, she had no response to Nicholas Gall's latest laments. He was free to express his opinions, but she herself remained committed to protecting his privacy.

That should have been all there was to their meeting, but as the girl rose from her chair she declined to actually leave. Naomi, who had absolutely nothing else to do, could not stop herself from showing impatience, even so.

"Yes?"

"Well…" the girl said. "I take it, given this statement, that you're not going to comment on the *Clarion* piece."

"I…" Naomi frowned. *Clarion.* She knew that name. Which one was that? "Could you be more specific?"

The girl gave her an unmistakable look of superiority. Naomi did not like that at all.

"It's a news and commentary site attached to a conservative think tank in Washington. They ran an item about Webster today. We're already preparing our coverage."

She couldn't help feeling relief. "Well, I'm sure it's not the first time a conservative site has written about Webster."

"No, I mean, they have a source on the board. Well, 'close to the board of directors' is the citation. You haven't seen it, in other words."

Again, that very unpleasant superiority, accompanied by an equally unpleasant...oh my God, was it pity?

"I have not." There was no relief this time.

The reporter produced her cell phone from a back pocket, and her fingers moved over the screen. It took no time at all.

A source close to the Webster Board of Directors had informed the *Clarion*, and thus the world, that history professor Nicholas Gall was being denied tenure at Webster College due to a plagiarism charge that he had elected not to deny. Plagiarism was indefensible at any academic institution, and undergraduates were routinely expelled for such infractions. Webster College, like any other conscientious college or university, owed it to its faculty, undergraduate, and alumni constituents to identify and respond promptly to this kind of behavior. It should therefore be stressed that the responsibility for Professor Gall's current circumstances was his alone, and his decision to obfuscate those circumstances had only brought additional grief to himself and also, most unfairly, to Webster. The source could only add that he—or she—was personally appalled by the behavior of this faculty member, and by the equally reprehensible lack of leadership on the part of the college administration. The college deserved more. Higher education, which comprised the basis of a decent and informed society, deserved more.

Which made Naomi, apparently, personally responsible for

the decline of civilization. She couldn't help feeling amazed that Milton Russell thought her so powerful. Or that he had actually gone and done this. That little shit.

She barely managed to get the girl out the door before losing it completely, but soon she was alone again, the room nearly bereft of light, and it wasn't hard to fall apart the rest of the way. Mrs. Bradford, with a tap at the closed door, announced her departure, which was a relief. Now Naomi hadn't even the strength to hack away at the leather blotter with her pen, let alone form some intention of what to do. She was hurtling back and forth between outrage and exhaustion, with crushing embarrassment on either side.

People like Milton Russell, you never got to leave them behind, no matter how far you went or how well you moved things forward. They were put on earth to bellow that things were much better before, that every form of progress was a diminishment. It was a sleight of hand she had never understood, this magical wash that obscured the awfulness from the rearview mirror: backstreet abortions, unstigmatized drunk drivers, fatal diseases we couldn't even remember the names of today. For the Milton Russells of the world, no societal gain was worth what had been lost, and no possible benefit to Webster was worth the ongoing presence of those people he'd referred to as "highly unattractive."

This was a class of rhetoric that belonged on the playground, of course, but she hadn't been shocked to hear it from Milton Russell.

Many years earlier, at the time of her own student activism, an incendiary op-ed piece had appeared in one of the student newspapers at Cornell, decrying a national plague of "ugly protesters," young people opposing everything from apartheid to the visit of a *Playboy* photographer in search of subjects for its "Girls of the Ivy League" issue. The author hadn't troubled himself with ideologies; he didn't ask himself why anyone would take to the streets or occupy the administrative buildings of their campuses. He didn't wonder who they were or how they had come to care about the world beyond their own lives. The burning question that exercised him was: Why did they always have to be so...*unattractive?*

Naomi, when she'd read this, was outraged. And yet, whatever else she'd been at that time (agitator, feminist, crusader for the way things ought to be), she had also been...a girl. Whose mother's many injunctions—that she was too top-heavy not to wear a good bra, that she ought to be ashamed to leave the house with unshaven legs, that her waves and snarls of heavy black hair resembled nothing so much as a bird's nest left behind in a tree—still howled in her ears. An ugly protester was precisely what she knew herself to be. A protester. And an *ugly.*

How absolutely boring, she thought now. Not to speak of counterproductive. That even in this twenty-first century, even after two major waves (and how many wavelets?) of feminism, and ample examples, worldwide, of the utter competence of women to rule the planet (or at least their individual countries), your modern college president (subcategory: female) should still carry around her own inner middle schooler who wished only to be pretty. Inside Naomi Roth there surely resided...an *also* Naomi Roth: a once and forever kid with rolls of pudge around her midsection, a stubborn spattering of pimples on her shoulders, and hair that would not yield to any influence of any kind. Such a Naomi Roth was, and would always be, her constant companion.

She paused for a further pointless and self-punishing interlude to imagine how all this might have gone differently with a different version of herself, a Naomi Roth who was not now and never had been an ugly protester. This eugenically altered Naomi would not be named Naomi, any more than she'd be named Roth. She'd have a very American name, like Lisa, and her surname something Ayn Randian, like Rearden, and she'd have light hair and light skin and be long and sturdy of limb, and her field of study would be something like art history or classics. She'd have run her department and written her books (how many? more than Naomi's two, at least) and raised a family in one of the glorious Federal houses on the green in West Webster, her kids now scattered to the Ivy League and her husband nearing retirement from the bank in Boston to which he'd been selflessly commuting for decades. Lisa Rearden would not have needed to procure a wardrobe for her new life as a college president; to the contrary, her sensible, eternally appropriate dresses and suits would not have required so much as an alteration for years (she'd still be at her college squash-playing weight, thanks to the fact that she still played squash!), and in fact a few of her favorite pieces would have been handed down from her mother—true vintage, not that Lisa would consider them such.

What would Lisa Rearden have done with Webster's unruly board, or at least its most poisonous member? What, for that matter, would she have done about Webster Dissent? Or Omar? Or Nicholas Gall? Naomi imagined her *Mayflower* doppelgänger out on the Billings Lawn in an ancient Barbour jacket, thoughtlessly clomping through the mud in wellies she'd picked up in England on her junior year abroad. In the faux newsreel running through Naomi's head this president tipped her sturdy chin precisely as Margaret Thatcher had always done, listening (pretending to listen?) with pursed lips and an already formulating verbal clobber. *You are being ridiculous. If you wish to protest inequities, I can assure you the world is full of them. Must you really waste your efforts on an intellectual community devoted to academic freedom and discovery? Go feed yourself at the overstocked dining hall and return to your overheated dormitories and get on with your work. I am ashamed of you!*

It was shocking how easily this came, how clearly she could

hear Lisa castigating the students: Omar, Chava, Hannah. *Hannah*. And surely Lisa Rearden was just stating a truth she held to be self-evident: that a blow struck against a poorly identified enemy is a wasted blow, and by the way, if you were sitting around trying to drum up enemies where none existed, then you obviously had way too much time on your hands, you clueless and privileged pseudo-PC wannabe *losers*.

Naomi roused herself. She had no idea what time it was, but it was dark, and the dark carried with it a sudden and intractable sadness. Maybe she would just stay here tonight, she thought, with unexpected levity. Maybe she would become stuck to the old leather of the chair until they (who? the paramedics? the trustees?) came to cut her away, clearing the space for the eighteenth president. God help him. (And yes, obviously, he would be a him.)

Then something happened. Then there was sharp knock at the door of the outer office and a nearly forgotten voice. She sat up in her chair. She wasn't stuck at all, it turned out.

"Yes?" Naomi said, and it wasn't the voice of an autocratic Ayn Randian—far from it.

"Mom," someone said back. It wasn't a question.

"Hannah?" Suddenly Naomi was up. She was across the room, hand on the doorknob. "Hannah? Is that you?"

It was Hannah. It was Hannah, but nearly unrecognizable: gaunt and grim, wrapped in a heavy brown coat Naomi had never seen before. She threw her arms around her daughter, but Hannah pushed back. "No. I'm here to talk."

Naomi nodded. She was so pathetically happy to see her. It was a miracle. "Sure."

"Mom," Hannah said, "you need to do something about this. You need to retract it."

"The statement?" she asked, forcing her own head to clear. "I just gave that statement, to the *Daily*."

"No. No. About Gall. It's everywhere. You've got to say something. Look, I'm trying to help you."

She shook her head. "That wasn't me. The *Clarion*? You think I'd talk to a right-wing think tank?"

Hannah sat in one of the Hitchcock chairs. She was keeping her coat wrapped tight across her chest. Her hair, Naomi noticed, was short—above her shoulders. It hadn't been above her shoulders since . . . well, Naomi couldn't remember.

"You cut your hair."

"I'm not here to talk about my hair. Or my studies. Or anything but this, so let's try to stay on topic."

"Well, then, I'd better sit down."

And so she returned to her chair. The blotter on her desk was an outright desecration, she saw. She couldn't believe she'd done that.

"I just found out about the interview," she told her daughter. "The reporter from the *Daily* asked me for a response. Obviously I'm appalled."

"Then say so. It's unconscionable for Webster to slander Nicholas Gall this way."

"Are you sure it's a slander? The accusation might be unconscionable but also perfectly true. Have you considered that?"

"Of course it isn't true!" she said. "This man is inspirational to hundreds of students."

"Which is fascinating, but not relevant," Naomi said tersely. "If so many intelligent young people decide to support an individual they know so little about, that's not something I can control. I am *furious* with . . . with the person who made this statement, but my position is that the college will not comment on private matters like tenure. Or academic standing. And I won't. Would you want me to give interviews about your grades to the media? Don't you have a right to privacy?"

"Privacy is important," said Hannah, "but I hope you understand that even if you, personally, didn't say Nick Gall was a plagiarist, you're still responsible for the statement. It's on you."

"I don't see that at all, Hannah. I'm as shocked by it as you are. And if turns out to be someone on the board or someone with an official connection to the college, I'm going to come down on that person like a ton of bricks. But I don't think the *Clarion* is going to identify the source, even if I ask politely."

Hannah leaned forward. Her eyes were dark and angry. "I thought it would be a different equation with someone like you in charge. I was proud of you."

That hit her hard. The past tense of it. The unassailability of it.

"I'm sorry you're disappointed in me. My job is complicated. But this isn't complicated. This is very clear to me. I'd welcome the chance to explain it to you."

"No thanks, I'm good," her daughter said. "I've had a long education in how the strong take advantage of the weak. A black guy and a Palestinian kid. Very nice."

"Oh no," Naomi said, shaking her head. "No, that is not okay. That is not okay at all. For one thing, I can't see any way in which Nicholas Gall has been disadvantaged. He's had a light teaching load and a long run at tenure. He could have done a great deal in that time. For whatever reason, he chose to spend his time differently. How differently, I have no idea, since the guy doesn't leave much of a written trail. He had the usual warnings and extensions. Do you know about the extensions?"

"Jesus, listen to you!" Hannah shook her head. "You gave him an extension—can you hear how patronizing you are? You gave him an extension, and gee, he still fell short of your expectations. I'm just stunned. Stunned. How is this the same person I grew up with?"

"There was nothing untoward about Nicholas Gall's tenure process." Naomi could barely get the words out. "It's the same one everyone has. It's the same one I had. If I'd...If it were shown that I'd done what...what it's alleged he did, I wouldn't be sitting in this office. I wouldn't be employed by this university."

"There are other reasons to give someone tenure, apart from publications."

"There are other factors. But publications are the most important thing. I understand that he's a great teacher. He's a teacher students are passionate about. Obviously. And that's incredibly important, to have great teachers. But publications are paramount. The strength of our faculty is the most important thing we have. Without it we'd be a very different college."

"You mean," Hannah said, "differently *ranked*. That's what you mean. Ranked lower, meaning fewer applicants, meaning less competition to get in, meaning less prestige, meaning less alumni loyalty, meaning less money for Webster." She glared at her mother, waiting for her to disagree, but this in fact was a very succinct summary of how things stood in academia. Naomi couldn't help being impressed.

"I can't talk about this."

"Well, that's convenient. Should we talk about Omar? Do you know there's a rumor out there that Omar—*Omar*—was responsible for the Sojourner Truth basement? Who do you think's behind that?"

Naomi froze. Only hours earlier Milton Russell had made this very suggestion, but it was outrageous, of course. Surely even he hadn't said that in public. Oh my God, she was going to kill Milton Russell.

"I can't imagine who would say such a thing," she told Hannah. "It's an appalling accusation. For what it's worth, I don't think the police believe that. Well, I don't know what the police believe," she said, feeling, suddenly, very defeated. "If they believe anything, they're not sharing it with me."

But if this was a play for sympathy—intentional or otherwise—it hadn't worked. "Character assassination. Plain and simple. And I can promise you, even if you don't see that, the rest of the world is going to. I mean, holy shit, Mom. This kid's family is gunned down on the street in front of the entire world, isn't that enough? Dad, older brother. The mom dies of grief. The terrorists wanted to use him as a suicide bomber, did you know that? And he wouldn't do it. So instead he drags himself to this country, the country that underwrites his father's and brother's murderers, which means he can never go home. And all he wants is an education so he can get past all of this bloodshed. And this is the person being accused of writing racist statements in shit on the walls. Are you following this?"

"I am following it," Naomi said. "I don't know what I can do about it. I would never have said such a thing about Omar, but I can't possibly control every other person in the world. People have a way of speaking their minds, and if the *Clarion* is happy with an unsupported anonymous source, a source with an obvious agenda, then I'm not going to be able to prevent it. Much as I would like to," she added.

"'A source close to the board of trustees!' Are you telling me you couldn't have stopped that?" Hannah had gotten to her feet. She stood over her mother, looking grimly down. *You are too thin*, Naomi was thinking. In her head, she was screaming it. She couldn't see it under her daughter's heavy coat, but that collarbone, protruding at the best of times, must now be alarming. This was a new sensation, a new terror. Hannah had never had food issues, she was sure. The fever of body hatred, the fear of sustenance, Hannah had made it through her teens without any of that, due in part to her natural, unmissable height and slenderness, and in part (Naomi dared to hope) to her own constant maternal affirmations. Fat was a feminist issue; everyone knew that. But thinness was even more of one.

"I have no idea who gave the interview. I'm as appalled as you are, but I can't do anything about it now. It's done. And the college—"

"Oh, the *college*," Hannah sneered. "*The college, the college.* Webster is the great emancipator, isn't it? Webster sprinkles its liberal fairy dust over this downtrodden soul, and he's supposed to be so grateful he doesn't notice he's just being victimized by yet another constituency."

Now Naomi, too, was losing her cool. "Victimized by admitting him with a full scholarship? A first-class education and a valuable degree, free room and board and medical care, and limitless opportunity? That's rough. We never should have done it. We never would have, if he hadn't applied and asked us to."

"That," Hannah said, taking a step back, "is the worst kind of paternalism. I can't believe you don't see this. You've hurt him. You've hurt him just like the Israelis who killed his family or the terrorists who tried to make him blow himself up. And just like them, you don't even care that you've hurt him."

Naomi, at that blinding moment, actually did not care. She was that furious.

"I care," she managed finally, but she was barely convincing herself.

"Oh yes. That's obvious. Well, how about this? You've hurt me, too. And that's not so easy to dismiss, is it?"

It was not. Naomi wanted to hurl herself out of her chair and across the desk. She wanted to grab Hannah's shoulder and, like a fractious child, make her take it back. But Hannah was leaving; their conversation, their contretemps, was over with no resolution. "Wait!" Naomi said, but Hannah, her coat once again tightly wrapped, was crossing the room, opening the door.

And you've hurt me! she wanted to say, but she wasn't sure whether she was speaking for herself or merely parroting her daughter's words, and anyway she didn't get to it soon enough.

By the time she'd put the notion into language, Hannah was already gone, down the stairs and more than likely out on the stone steps of Billings Hall. Naomi sank back into her chair, the pain of this new awful thing mixing freely with all of the other bad feelings: the board, the blame, the lies, the drone of her own failure, the noxious Milton Russell. These things, they coiled around her in a winding sheet, until she was lashed to the mast of her own head, fully immobilized,

Another hour must have gone by—Naomi couldn't be sure and actually wasn't that interested, but finally, at some moment that seemed no different from the one before it, she found herself on her feet. She was up. She was leaving, after an absurdly long day of difficulty and pain, finally up out of her chair and into the hallway. She shrugged on her coat and pulled the door closed behind her till it made its heavy metallic *thunk. I arrived this morning,* she thought, descending the flights of stairs. *I worked all day. Now I am leaving.* It wasn't complicated. The air outside was crisp but lacked the brutal whack of the previous weeks, so when her hand went automatically to the zipper of her coat it changed its mind and left the parka flapping at her hips. Naomi looked around. The media types of the morning had moved on, or perhaps merely retreated to the four or five vans parked at the Quad's southern edge. It was past eight, she imagined, then confirmed with a glance at the library's clock tower; classes done, the students were mainly where they belonged, ensconced in their dorm rooms or in the library doing what they'd theoretically come to Webster to do. The Quad itself was dingy with old snow, pockmarked with new mud. Around the Stump, the encampment was at capacity, with hunching, stamping bodies filling the spaces between the tents and lean-tos. The dissenters were like the soldiers in that famous painting of Valley Forge, she thought, grateful that the temperature seemed, at least, to be on the rebound. The winter might just possibly end without their having lost a single Webster toe to frostbite. Which was, under the circumstances, a tiny victory.

The classroom and administrative buildings on the eastern and western sides were uniformly dark, and only the student center on the southern edge was alight. This vigorously modern structure, composed of New Hampshire granite, had been erected a year or two after Naomi's arrival at Webster, and had gradually been annexed to the older structures on either side, making all three into a kind of Frankenbuilding of cafés and meeting rooms, the film and media programs, and a basement cavern of pinball and arcade games. Apparently it was a widely disseminated anecdote that Webster's president could often be found at Josiah's, the student center coffee shop, hanging out and chatting with students (this had been reported to Naomi at freshmen parents' weekends; apparently the prospect of grabbing a latte with the president had proved the tipping point in many a decision to apply to Webster), but in fact Naomi never had held court at Josiah's or anywhere else in the building, and she had no idea how this particular rumor had begun. It was just another Webster myth, along with the happy Indians welcoming the Gospel or the good-natured shenanigans of Webster's pre-Sarafian bright college days.

But just at the moment she actually was, she realized, a little bit hungry. That was interesting. That was kind of encouraging, too. And obviously there was nowhere else she was supposed to be, and no one to miss her. Why shouldn't she get herself a coffee at Josiah's? Why shouldn't she buy herself an entire dinner?

Naomi set off, walking the perimeter of the Quad instead of cutting through the encampment. She felt unaccountably brave, as if procuring dinner for herself in some modestly public place were an outrageous and ballsy act, on par with those Victorian adventuresses trekking across the Kalahari. No one bothered her, or perhaps the darkness rendered her invisible, and even the two or three groups of men clustered, smoking, around the vans barely looked her way as she went by. She took her parka off as she swept through the revolving door and went straight into the café, smelling some kind of gumbo and some kind of baking chocolate and instantly wanting them both. Naomi lifted a tray from the pile and slid it across the ledge in the direction of food. She took a bowl of the gumbo (it was actually chicken stew) and a brownie and was just putting her wallet back into her pocket and turning to look for a seat when she saw, thrillingly, Francine, tucked into a corner, bent over a table with a telltale stack of folders.

"Why, hello!" Naomi said, rushing heedlessly to her friend and sitting without asking. Only then did it occur to her that she might not be welcome.

"Oh," Francine said. She looked up but a forefinger went instinctively to the place she'd left. "Oh, Naomi."

"I'm sorry!" she said pathetically. "I wasn't thinking. Of course you're working."

"'Tis the season." Francine nodded. "I mean..."

"I should have known. I'll leave. I was just..." Just? Naomi considered. Was this "grabbing a latte"? Did she sound as ridiculous as she felt?

"No, no, I'm glad to see you. If I can just finish this folder I can stop for a bit. You know, we don't like to stop in the middle. You lose the information. It isn't fair to an applicant."

"Yes!" Naomi was remembering. "*Applicatus interruptus.* Right?"

Francine smiled briefly. It was a term she'd made up, and too risqué to share with most people. But Naomi was not most people.

"Very much so. Just a sec."

She bowed her head over the folder, which like all Webster

application folders was green. She was reading intently, making notes at the bottom of the reader's card. She frowned through the two essays and the guidance counselor's letter, pursing her lips and nodding in a way that made Naomi think of a Hasidic Jew, davening. Naomi ate her chicken stew, which had a smoky overtone that she hoped was intentional and not the result of a scorching. She was trying not to look at the pages in front of her friend. She'd fought, for years, a fascination with these very pages, the invisible kids behind them, the invisible parents behind *them*. Here, before her eyes, was evidence of that devil's bargain between top-ranked colleges and the elements that kept them top ranked, because Webster and the others did indeed invite—*encourage*—every possible student to apply, and then denied entry to all but a sliver of them. There were many reasons for such a contradiction, and they'd been explained to her many times, and Naomi had in turn explained them to others, but when you got right down to it she couldn't fathom the specific horror of having to make these decisions. A basketball player from Georgia or a robotics whiz from northern New Jersey? An equestrian who'd bring her own horse (and a strongly hinted-at donation) to campus or a waif from Bangladesh who was being sponsored by a famous tech philanthropist? How could you weigh innovation against opportunity? How could you put a value on simple security—the experience of growing up in a stable society with guaranteed schooling—when others had no such thing? Francine had managed to pepper Webster's classes with the children of devoted and generous alumni, but she had also discovered Omar Khayal—for better or, as it was increasingly looking, for worse. Her method, whatever else it was, had no madness in it. Naomi knew that she wanted only the best for Webster.

"O...kay..." Francine finished, with an extravagant crossing of a final *t*. "I get to stop now. Not for long, but for a bit."

"I should have left you alone. I wasn't thinking."

"No, I'm glad. Human interaction is good for me. I'm in the cave. It isn't nice."

"A cave sounds nice to me," Naomi said, with extravagant sarcasm.

"Oh, God. Yes, I'm sorry, I heard that Omar Khayal's been expelled. I couldn't believe it."

Naomi sighed. "Well, that's good, given that it isn't true." She stirred her rapidly chilling stew with a spoon, just for the sake of it.

"It isn't true? You haven't expelled him?"

She studied her friend. Francine, she was now noticing, looked terrible. Her face was drawn and the circles beneath her eyes had deepened to aubergine. Her hair was long; Naomi wasn't sure she'd ever seen it this long. Usually, by the time it hit the shoulders Francine had taken herself in to have her chin-length bob restored. It was the cave, she supposed. Every admissions officer she'd ever known spent the winter in one, reading, reading.

"No, of course not. We don't expel students for academic failure. We put them on academic probation with the hope of their eventual return. You'd have to do something illegal or contra to the honor code to get expelled. But in Omar's case, we hadn't even gotten as far as probation. He didn't show up for a meeting, and then he made his own announcement before he could not show up for the rescheduled meeting. He didn't answer emails. I did what I could, though I suppose I could have done more."

"Well..." said Francine. But she declined to make the expected noises. *No! You tried so hard!*

"Really, what was I supposed to be doing? My door's been open for months. I've tried to get him to talk to me for months. What kind of protest declines dialogue with its opponent?"

"A modern one," Francine said dryly. "These kids are not like we were. You were," she corrected. "Interaction across the battle lines isn't what they're after. They want to build their own constituencies. They want to represent something to their peers more than they want to gain respect from their opponents."

"Or accomplish anything," Naomi said, rolling her eyes.

"Oh, they're accomplishing plenty. They're compiling influence. They're emerging from the crowd."

"Gaining 'likes.' Getting 'retweeted.'"

"That's part of it. No point denying it."

"Building their brands. Getting famous."

Francine shrugged. "Fame is power. Omar grew up powerless, remember. It's not like he's a Hollywood starlet. He has the entire Middle East to heal. Shouldn't we be helping him?"

Naomi had stopped stirring her stew, which had now congealed into a cold gray sludge. What she had already consumed was now hard and heavy in her belly. She couldn't imagine why she'd eaten it.

"You're not...defending him, I hope?"

"What has he done that needs defending? He got fired up about a perceived injustice. He established and led a nonviolent protest to call attention to it. Just as you would have done under the same circumstances. Unless I've missed something?"

"You have," Naomi told her. "But it's something I can't talk about publicly. A small matter of tenure denial due to a small case of plagiarism."

She couldn't believe she'd actually said it, even to Francine, even after the "source close to the board of trustees" had said much more. She watched the words land. *Plagiarism* first, then *tenure*.

"Oh. Well, fuck."

The word sounded utterly out of place in Francine's voice. Cave language, Naomi supposed. The Francine she knew did not curse. She said "witch" when she was annoyed with a female person, "jerk" when she disliked someone male.

"You mean Gall."

"I do. You're maybe too busy to have heard that a right-wing website made this public today. I am apparently responsible for that, as well, or I was supposed to prevent it from happening." She shook her head. "As to the plagiarism itself, I can neither confirm nor deny."

"No. Of course."

"But he's made himself very free to imply that his dismissal wasn't for cause, and everyone knows how popular a teacher he is. So that leaves race, at least according to these students. But it was always the plagiarism. We've protected him, and we've taken the heat for that, from his defenders. It's untenable."

Francine nodded. "For you, you mean."

"Yes. I guess from his perspective it would be nice if this lasted forever. Why should the matter of his academic dishonesty inter-fere with all of the teaching positions he's being offered? And the honorary degrees. And the lectures and appearances? You know, I had Hannah in my office an hour ago. She hasn't spoken to me for almost a month, and now I'm Roy Cohn. This whole thing, it's like a wildfire. It keeps whipping around and tearing off in a different direction."

Francine observed her. "Boy, you're pissed. I don't think I've ever seen you this pissed."

"You weren't around when Maddie Douglas invited everyone in the seventh grade except Hannah to her princess bowling party."

Francine laughed sharply. "Oh, yes I was. *That* was impres-sive. That was rock star trashing a hotel room pissed. But you know, this is something different. It's quieter, but it's worse."

"Well," Naomi conceded, "it's personal."

Her friend looked at her. "No, I don't think so. It's not

personal. Not like having your daughter ostracized really *is* personal. I understand that you feel disrespected, Naomi, I mean majorly disrespected. You're being accused of something and you can't respond to the charge. But it's also true that neither the plagiarism nor the tenure denial had anything to do with you."

Naomi looked over at the food line. She wanted something, it occurred to her. But what she wanted they didn't sell at Josiah's. And she was too exhausted and too embarrassed to go downstairs to the pub.

"No more than Omar not attending class all fall has to do with me. But I'm supposedly the author of his arbitrary expulsion, too."

"All fall?" Francine said, mystified.

"According to his professors. Nicholas Gall gave him an A, which is the only reason his GPA wasn't a zero last term. Still, it's well below the cutoff for academic probation. That's officially what he's on, by the way. And this fiction about his belongings being put out on the street? God, it's infuriating."

"Then why don't you just tell people that?"

"Oh...same old, same old. Privacy."

"Your privacy?"

Naomi looked at her, less than kindly. "No, of course not. Omar's privacy. We're as entitled to discuss his academic standing as we are to talk about Gall's plagiarism. Which is to say: not at all."

Francine was nodding. One hand, her right, was rhythmically tapping the pile of application folders. She wanted to get back, Naomi realized. She was ready to get back. She wanted to push this away, because she could, as Naomi could not.

"Like a quandary for Talmudic scholars to deconstruct."

Naomi shook her head. "No, there's no quandary. Not about this. I'm not allowed to do anything, say anything. It's kind of horrible, actually. My whole life has been organized around the principle of speaking truth to power. Now I can't speak."

"Oh, Naomi," said Francine, and just the way she said that, which was a way she had never said anything before, or at least never anything to Naomi before, made her flinch. "That isn't it. That isn't the problem at all."

"No?" said Naomi.

"The problem isn't that you can't speak truth to power. The problem is that you *are* the power. You see that, right? You're the establishment. You're the man."

"Well." She tried to laugh. Her head spun. "I don't think so."

"I think so. The students are the ones trying to speak truth to *you*. That's what they think, anyway. I can't believe this is a surprise."

But it was. It was more than a surprise. It was the kind of terrible shock you push back against with every bit of your strength, and then collapse beneath, because the pure, cold sense of it is so very heavy.

"I'm on their side," she said, without any conviction whatsoever. "I've been open from the beginning. I've been available."

"Irrelevant," Francine said. "Their job is to place themselves in opposition to authority. You are authority, whether you embrace it or not. That you opt not to resist them makes no difference at all. They've barely paid attention to you."

Well, that was certainly true, Naomi had to agree. The night at Sojourner Truth House, hadn't she waded into the crowd and settled herself, unacknowledged and unnoted? Their publicly identified adversary, utterly anonymous in their midst. She'd actually felt guilty about that, for hiding, but she'd also wanted to hear (at last!) what they had to say.

"Look, you're a good person. I'm sure you've followed your conscience in all of this," said Francine. Her tone had notably shifted, but somehow not persuasively. "I don't see you running a bulldozer through the encampment on the Quad. But sometimes that kind of move is probably kinder in the long run."

Naomi felt numb. She stared at her friend. "I thought you liked Omar," was, unaccountably, the first thing it occurred to her to say.

"Oh, Omar." She sighed. "Yes, Omar is very special. Of course I 'like' him, not that that matters. I like Nick Gall, too. Or...well, I like his wife, and she likes him. But again, not relevant. This should have been over months ago. I think..."

She seemed to trip over her own thought, and stop. Then, with intention, she continued.

"I have wondered, sometimes, whether you're not prolonging this intentionally. I've wondered if this is some nostalgia, some reaching back for you. I mean this with no disrespect, and I say it with affection."

And yet, the words strongly implied disrespect and the tone was fully lacking in affection.

"I know how important this was for you. When you were younger."

"This?" said Naomi, with an archness even she could hear.

"This position. This ritual of defiance. You do talk about your activist past, you know."

"Do I?" asked Naomi. *Did she?*

"The Cornell stuff. Vivisection? And the Peace Corps."

Naomi regarded her. "Not vivisection. ROTC. And not the Peace Corps. VISTA. I wanted to do the Peace Corps. I think my husband was terrified of the Third World. He'd never been out of the country. He thought he would die."

"So you ended up in New Hampshire."

It sounded, she had to admit, absurd. And it *had* been absurd, but also horrible. And she had managed to leave there only after years and the end of her marriage and the end, in some ways, of what she'd thought she might accomplish in the world. Away with a packed-up car and a future Hannah Rosalind Roth, the size of a walnut, deep inside her body. It was so long ago.

"Yes. Goddard, New Hampshire. But you know all this."

"And exactly how would I know all this?" Francine said. Her knuckles, Naomi saw, were tapping the pile of unread folders. "You're not exactly forthcoming. I asked you about it once, years ago, you pretty much held up a 'trespassers will be shot' sign. And I respect that, don't worry. And I know, I'm not such a big over-sharer, myself, but really, I hope you're not under the impression that you have actually *confided* in me about your life before you got to Webster. For all I know, 'Naomi Roth' used to be an underground radical, or came out of the witness protection program. You were radical on campus at Cornell, then you went to live in northern New Hampshire for fifteen years. Then you left. Why did you leave? For that matter, why did you stay fifteen years if VISTA's supposed to be the domestic Peace Corps and the Peace Corps is only for two years? You say you had a husband. I know you have a daughter. Are the two connected? Does Hannah even know her father?"

Naomi couldn't speak. Never, not once in all the years of their friendship, had she ever felt even a hint of this disrespect, this assault, and she withered beneath it. Francine had also seemed to run out of steam. She deflated, visibly, and Naomi suddenly saw anew how diminished her friend had become. Reading season? No. There had been many reading seasons in their friendship. Francine had never before appeared so depleted. Abruptly Naomi forgot how she had felt only seconds earlier. Before she knew what she was doing she reached her hand across the table and covered those tapping knuckles, that clamped fist.

"What is it?" she asked.

Right away, Naomi saw that Francine was crying. She sat with her head down, her too-long hair hanging forward over her face. Never had Naomi seen this, never. Not even at her mother's funeral the year they'd first met. It was as if someone had punched a hole in her.

"Francine, what?"

She only shook her miserable head. "I'm sorry."

"No, it's all right. Can I help?"

Francine didn't answer. Naomi watched her shoulders. They shook.

"Is it Sumner?" she asked. "Are you guys all right?"

Her friend looked up, her face streaked. "What do you mean, 'all right'?"

"I mean...is something going on? Do you want to talk about it?"

"I can't talk about it. I mean, I don't want to talk about it. I know you don't like him."

Naomi looked at her in shock. "That isn't true. I've always liked Sumner."

"Oh, please. Sumner offends you. He always has. But he's as much of his culture as you are of yours. His culture just happens to be everything you hate."

She saw that there was no point in denying this, and she didn't want to. "He's your husband. You love him and I love you. We might not have gotten beyond that, but I've always felt we were on good terms." She stopped, reluctant to inquire further. But she had to. "Are we not? On good terms?"

"Oh." Francine shook her head. "I don't know. Probably. It doesn't matter. None of this is about you. I'm sorry. I'm very sorry."

"What is it about, Francine? What's happened?"

Francine sat back in her chair. She pushed away the folders as if they were a meal she couldn't look at anymore. Then shook her head. "They're trying to get rid of him. The school. They've been trying for nearly a year."

Naomi stared. She hadn't been expecting that. A divorce,

an affair—in the last few moments the marriage had suddenly come into play: Sumner, that entitled shit, was carrying on with someone, Sumner was moving on, Sumner had no conception of how fortunate he was to have Francine in his life. But the school?

"Why?" she managed.

"Oh, it's all...it's nasty and horrible. The board, they haven't been behind him since four members were replaced a few years back. They think the school is stagnant, though Sumner's been great on their endowment. The board, and the faculty..."

Naomi's eyes widened. "The board *and* the faculty?"

"There was an incident. It wasn't Sumner's fault."

All at once, she didn't want to hear any more.

"That's...a tough place to be in."

"A few of the teachers left. It was in the middle of the school year. They just resigned and left."

"But that's outrageous!"

"I know," she agreed. "Outrageous."

Naomi was thinking, scrambling. Multiple teachers, resigning in the middle of the year? It was a drastic step, a clear gesture of protest. There must have been something extraordinary to precipitate it.

"Do you know why?" she heard herself ask.

Francine nodded. "I do. At least, I know what they've said. But it's a slander. I can't...I really can't talk about this. I don't want to."

"All right," said Naomi.

"And the board, just...they just jumped right on top of him. That woman you met at our New Year's party..."

"That nasty woman?" asked Naomi.

"She's been a nightmare. Some private drama about how she's been on the board for decades but never chair."

"Always a bridesmaid."

"Always a *bitch*."

Naomi started. *Bitch*.

"Okay," she said carefully.

"That woman has had it in for Sumner since the beginning."

"But...wait, I thought she said she'd headed the search committee."

"She did. But she didn't want him. She wanted someone else. If it weren't for Billy Grosvenor, he wouldn't have gotten the job. And now there's even less support. I don't know if he can hold on much longer. It's ugly. Really ugly."

She had stopped crying, at least. She looked miserably at her files, her hands, some vague place past Naomi's left shoulder.

"I'm just...it's been stressful. I apologize. None of this excuses the way I spoke to you."

"Please"—Naomi shook her head—"don't think of it. But...Francine, isn't Sumner going to retire soon? I mean, anyway?"

Francine bristled anew. "We've discussed it, of course. But it's immaterial. This is not the way his career should end, under a cloud like this. He doesn't deserve it. He's devoted himself to Hawthorne. He's devoted himself to the board. *And* the teachers, not that they appreciate it. I'm sure you can understand how unfair it would be to ask someone to step down for something entirely beyond their control. I'm sure you've been giving that some thought," she finished archly.

Well, yes, Naomi did understand. And yes, she had been giving that some thought.

"I wish you'd told me," she finally managed to say. "I could have..." What? Helped? "Supported you. Or tried."

Francine shrugged. "Appreciate that," she said simply. "Not much to be done, though. We'll just have to wait and see what they decide. I mean, they've set a dedicated board meeting in May, so we wait for that. And just...carry on."

She pressed her palms over her eyes and exhaled. When she took them away, she'd been restored to semi-normality. "Work," she announced. "Back to work. I have to get through this pile before I can go home. I am sorry, but I can't talk anymore."

So Naomi, dismissed, rose and left her there.

CHAPTER SIXTEEN

NOT THAT KIND OF A BOMB

Hannah had loved the Madeline books when she was a little girl. They hadn't been Naomi's choice. She had put her daughter on a steady diet of *Free to Be...You and Me* and Pippi Longstocking in a strictly Mattel-free zone, intent on raising a girl with no detritus of the patriarchy, and those privileged Parisian schoolgirls in their matching uniforms and neat straight lines, overseen by a Bride of Christ...they had definitely not been part of the plan. But once Hannah experienced Madeline and her crew at a sleepover in first grade, resistance had been futile, and soon the bedtime ritual chez Roth included one or more of the stories, and their frankly irresistible charms: the rabbit crack in the ceiling, the Spanish ambassador's naughty son, the stray dog hiding under the blankets. Naomi, after so many readings, was struck by the fact that Miss Clavel, who was not a mother herself, nonetheless possessed an inner maternal alarm when it came to the children; she rose from sleep when some imminent disaster called to her, and raced to the girls' bedroom *fast and faster* to discover the crisis at hand: puppies, a rumbling appendix, a room full of crying girls.

Naomi had never considered herself particularly maternal,

not even when she'd looked after a toddler for several months near the end of her time in Goddard. When Hannah was born, though, she had found, like most mothers, that the connection between herself and her baby long outlived the physical umbilical cord. One night, only hours after putting to bed a sparkling and chatty four-year-old, she'd woken to a physical seizure of panic and rushed to Hannah's room, where a small feverish body tossed beneath a patchwork quilt. That had turned out to be something Naomi had never heard of, called Kawasaki disease, which was frightening and dangerous but also gone inside of a week, leaving Hannah cheery as ever and her mother forever walloped by the omnipresent terror of parenthood. Mother and daughter had spent those days in the hospital in Northampton, waiting for Hannah's temperature to return to normal and hearing how fortunate they'd been to catch things early. Two weeks later, in a sour grapes gesture on the part of the illness, the skin of Hannah's hands and feet peeled off in sheets.

When Naomi sat up in bed, in the black hours later that night, she thought first of Hannah, and sat for a long moment in her bed, hand pressed to her heart, reviewing a lacerating array of possibilities. Only hours before, leaving Francine at the student center, she'd made an abrupt and unfortunate decision to go and look for her daughter again, to force some kind of a resolution. The day, already packed with so many lousy experiences, could not get any worse, she reasoned, by throwing one more uncomfortable encounter into the mix. At Sojourner Truth a truculent Chava Friedberg had met her with a deeply supercilious smile, holding the door open barely far enough to wedge a shoulder through. Hannah wasn't there, she'd announced, and no, she didn't know where Naomi could look. There had been a meeting in town, she didn't know where, and maybe everyone was out at the Stump, or maybe Hannah was in her room at Radclyffe Hall. "She's still a student, you know," said Chava viciously.

And you are not, Naomi had thought, remembering Chava's withdrawal from Webster. *So why are you still here?*

"Well, thanks," Naomi had said, but this had been delivered to the door itself as it closed behind the girl. *And fuck you*, she added silently.

At Radclyffe Hall a friendlier young woman delivered the same message, more or less. Hannah Roth wasn't in. She might be over at Sojourner Truth—she was there a lot—or out on the Quad, at the Webster Dissent encampment. Had Naomi tried there? She came in and out to sleep and study, the young woman said, but she was traveling, too. She'd just been to Boston to be interviewed on TV, and she'd said something about New York, too, in the next few days, or maybe she'd already left for that. Maybe ask her friend Chava something?

I'll do that, Naomi said, bereft, and she'd turned and trudged back up Fairweather, back to the Billings Lawn, where she'd treated herself to a desultory jaunt around the edge of the encampment, fruitlessly looking for a body that resembled Hannah's. Then she'd gone home, made herself tea, declined to check her email, and climbed into bed.

Where was Hannah and what had happened to her? Because something had happened, or was happening. Naomi's heart banged beneath her hand. *Something is not right*, Miss Clavel would have said were she here, able to speak English, and not a fictional character. But then again, when you cared for a dormitory full of girls, let alone a campus full of dormitories full of girls, and boys, something was always not right. The dramas, crises, drugs, self-harm: Webster College was an eternally unfolding disaster under her own personal aegis.

Then the phone rang.

A moment later she was out of the house, pajama bottoms still on, feet shoved into her furry snow boots. She'd thrown on a Webster sweatshirt and her parka and left her own door ajar behind her, purse and phone abandoned on the hall table. She was moving fast. She wasn't hanging around. She couldn't understand what he'd said, but that wasn't a good enough reason to wait. Peter Rudolph had made the call. He sounded terrified.

The fire truck was pulling up as Naomi reached Billings Hall, and overhead smoke was twisting out through the shattered window on the third floor. She tried to tell herself that smoke was a good thing, or not as horrible a thing as flame would be, but then she saw the flames too, and smelled that indescribable smell of modern plastics melting. Dust and papers, wood and wood laminate, a telephone, a computer, all of it a single burning soup. She couldn't make words. She found Peter Rudolph with the firemen.

"No one's in there, right?" was what she ended up asking first.

"Someone's in there?" one of the firemen asked.

"No. No one. I hope. I don't know." She sounded hysterical. "How bad is it?"

"This is President Roth," said Peter Rudolph inanely.

"That's your office?" said the fireman.

She looked up, as if she needed to check. "My office," she said. It smelled so terrible. She didn't want to take the air in. Out on the Billings Lawn she could see people emerging from their tents.

The lights on the fire truck hit the façade of the administration building. It looked absurdly pristine except for the top floor, which also looked weirdly normal, except for the smoke and the flames. There were more flames now, or else the same number of flames but from an additional window. How did any of it make sense?

"I didn't hear anything," she said to Peter Rudolph.

"No, you wouldn't," said the man standing a few feet from them. He had a cell phone to his ear and seemed to be running things. "Not that kind of a bomb," he said, and it was the first time anyone had used that word. She thought she might throw up. That revolting chicken stew. How it had congealed around her spoon. It was all inside her now, solid, begging for escape.

"Wait, what?" Peter Rudolph asked. "You know that? How do you know that?"

But the man with the phone was gone. He was with the others. They had turned on the hose and angled it up. The water shot high onto the roof of Billings Hall and then into the window. Her window. Her office. The indignity of it was what she couldn't get her mind around. All that water, hissing across her desk, into her chair. The leather blotter she'd pretty much destroyed only hours before. The chair that tipped back. The portrait of Josiah Webster in the conference room next door. Was that gone, too?

"What happened?" she asked Peter Rudolph.

"Campus Security got a call from the alarm company, just after three. The smoke alarm sent an alert. They called the fire department and I called the police. Then I called you. Then I came over myself."

"Good." Naomi was shivering. That seemed like the correct order.

Already it seemed to be slowing. Already the new smell, the smell of water, was mixing with the older terrible smells, making a different terrible smell. Could that have happened so quickly? Water in, fire out?

"It's working," she observed. It seemed miraculous, despite what was generally known about fire in combination with water. Behind her, cars were arriving, though they weren't cars.

A stocky man stepped out of the first van and walked straight for the front steps, already filming. Peter Rudolph did nothing.

"Hey!" yelled Naomi. "Get back from there!"

The man turned his camera in her direction. She wanted to tackle him.

"Sir?" It was Patrick Hogan. "You need to move back *now*. Get back to the sidewalk."

The cameraman complied, but slowly and walking backward to preserve his shot of Billings Hall. Another van arrived, and the first of the students from the encampment crossed the road.

"Keep back!" Patrick Hogan was taking charge, she saw. "Everyone back on the sidewalk. Let them work, please."

The men, three of them, were going inside now. They would be working their way up, checking to be sure that no one was in the rooms they passed. Naomi, who was full of fear about so many things, was not afraid of that. A few minutes went by, and a first-floor window sash was raised, an arm stuck out and a thumbs-up given. A few minutes later, the same thing happened on the second floor.

The next wait was longer: five minutes, or eight. Then the fire chief, the one with the cell phone, the one who'd said it was a bomb, signaled to the others and the hose went slack. Smoke and ash seemed to fall from the window ledges. It was all over but the cleanup.

"I need to call someone," Naomi said when she had calmed down. Actually she needed to call a bunch of people, but Will Rennet first, and then poor Mrs. Bradford, who'd unwisely let it be known on a number of occasions that she was an insomniac and likely to be up at all hours. "Will they let me inside?" she asked Peter Rudolph.

"No idea."

"Can I go inside?" she called after the fire chief as he passed. He stopped and looked at her as if she were out of her mind.

"Uh, no. No, you may not."

"But I need..." She petered to a halt. Actually she wasn't sure what she needed, but she did want to know whether Josiah Webster's portrait was all right. "Listen, can you just tell me how bad it is?"

When the men came out they gathered around her, and incredibly it turned out to be not that bad, at least in terms of the physical damage. Not too much bang, mostly smoke, said the man in charge. "Not that kind of bomb," he told her. "Like I said." It had been in the middle of the floor, away from the furniture. It had been small. It was early to say any of this, of course, and none of it was to be taken as official information, and naturally there would be an investigation, but he'd been in the first Gulf War and he'd seen a lot of incendiary devices. What they were dealing with, in his opinion, was a pretty simple item, not the kind to make anybody dead, just enough to ruin the curtains and scare the crap out of you. Of course, if it hadn't been caught, the building would have gone up eventually. He shrugged. Then he was called away.

Patrick Hogan stayed with her, which she appreciated, but when she asked again if she could go inside he looked at her as if she were mad.

"Until they clear it, absolutely not."

"I just want to see if anything can be salvaged." She was thinking about old Josiah Webster. She was thinking of the outcry if that portrait had been destroyed.

"It will have to wait till morning."

Instead they walked over to the Webster Inn, where the night manager kindly showed them into the dining room, turning on the light and even bringing them coffee. Hogan began to work on his report. Naomi, who was still in her pajamas, was grateful not to have to look him in the eye.

"Any thoughts?" he asked.

"I'm sorry?" She'd been stirring sugar around and around her Webster Inn mug.

"Thoughts. Is this connected to Sojourner Truth Hall?"

"House," she corrected. "Sojourner Truth House."

He did not apologize. It was the middle of the night for him, too.

"Somebody bombed my office," she said with wonder.

"Looks that way," said Hogan. "Any thoughts who?"

"Oh my God," Naomi said. This was catching up to her, after an hour's delay.

"It is disturbing. Has there ever been a bombing at Webster College?"

She tried to think, but the synapses refused to fire. The '60s? Not at Webster. The '70s, which had been like the '60s everywhere else? She didn't think so. Not even over the Indian symbol. Not even over poor Luther Merrion.

"I'm not sure. But I don't think so."

"Well, then, I'm sorry this happened to you."

He said it without affect, and Naomi was certain he didn't, personally, feel sorry about this, or have empathy toward her. But it still hit her hard. Something had actually happened here. The office of the president of Webster College had been bombed. *Her* office . . . had been bombed.

"Kinda getting through now, isn't it?" he asked, observing her carefully.

Naomi nodded. "Kinda."

"If I didn't know better I'd say you were maybe in shock. Which is understandable."

Oh, good, she thought.

"But it's better to talk about it now. Sometimes if you can articulate an idea before you have a chance to decide it's a bad idea, it turns out that wasn't a bad idea at all."

She tried very hard to understood what this meant, but gave up.

"For example, who did this?"

Naomi stared at him. "Are you kidding? I don't know."

"Who's angry at you? Not only at Webster. At you."

"Take your pick." She rolled her eyes. "Have you seen the press? I'm the Mephistopheles of higher education. I tempt the unsuspecting students of the world with the dream of a progressive university, then I give them Kent State."

She saw that he was confused. She hoped she didn't have to explain Kent State to him.

"So the students are angry."

"The alumni are angry. Liberals who have no connection to Webster are angry, because this place was supposed to be the Oberlin of the east and I turned it into a war zone. Right-wing loonies are angry because Webster exemplifies what happens when we stop telling the students what to learn and how to learn it. My daughter is angry at me for supposedly telling the world that our victim professor may not be the martyr she thinks he is."

His eyes widened. "Your daughter? Could she be responsible for this?"

Naomi sat up straight. She suddenly felt very calm. Very calm. She hadn't felt so calm, so sure, in months and months, not since before the first tent pole had been shoved into the earth of the Billings Lawn. It felt so sweet, that certainty. She couldn't stand the thought of losing it again.

"No. Hannah didn't do this," she said to Patrick Hogan. "The person who did this was Omar Khayal."

CHAPTER SEVENTEEN

THE POINT OF
LOOKING CLOSELY

Omar was gone. Omar had left in the night, the night of the "incendiary device" (as the Billings Hall bomb was officially termed), and no trail of him had been found since then. Like many an object of fascination before him, Naomi observed, this young man from Bureij had known how to make an exit, and as the weeks miraculously passed without a trace of him she began to feel as if some bell jar of woe that had long been descending over her was now being just as gradually lifted. Air came in. The clean air of Webster, Massachusetts, her home.

As for her office, the early word from the fire department was that the damage looked worse than it actually was, a concept she did not fully understand. (How could something in plain sight look worse, or for that matter better, than it actually was?) The carpet was ash and the walls scorched. The old desk was half charred and half pristine, but was a write-off (a shame—Naomi had always liked that desk) and the shredded leather blotter, bizarrely, had been mainly spared (though she threw that away, too). The Hitchcock chairs and her own wooden chair on the far side of the desk would also require replacement, and most of the class banners and Webster pennants, a collection on loan from the college archive, could not be saved. The old Drunkard's Path quilt, one of the last things she still had from her time in Goddard, New Hampshire, was likewise gone.

But the building, Billings Hall, and its inner and outer structures had come through this indignity of ash and smoke in winning form, and she was elated. Smoke had barely entered the outer office (Mrs. Bradford had not lost a single one of the plants she kept on the window ledge) and the conference room had also been spared, though Josiah Webster's portrait was sent to the college art museum for a checkup. No, she would not have to go to the Webster alumni with the heartbreaking news that this most Websterian of Webster structures must be condemned, nor to the board with a request for millions in reconstruction. A few weeks working out of the president's house and twenty grand or so in cleanup and furniture replacement and she'd be able to put this particular chapter of the larger ordeal behind her. Except, of course, for the small matter of having been firebombed in the first place.

The item in question had been, the fire chief informed her, a not uncommon device, consisting of a plastic vessel filled with gasoline and a piece of clothing serving as a wick. Typically the plastic bottle was a milk jug, but in this case the arsonist had used an oversized water bottle that bore the Webster College crest, and the clothing was none other than that classic "Webster College—The Harvard of Massachusetts" T-shirt. The incendiary device had burned for about fifteen minutes before the gas fumes escaped and caught fire—plenty of time to open the window, shut the door, descend the stairs, and disappear into the night. Naturally the nonexistent security cameras in Billings Hall helped not at all.

Patrick Hogan went looking for Omar Khayal, but he was not to be found in any of the expected places. Sojourner Truth House had, overnight, been handed back to its actual tenants,

and while there were a number of hangers-on hanging out
in the common rooms and even in the disinfected basement,
the more public faces of Webster Dissent had vacated the
premises. Hannah returned to Radclyffe Hall and Chava went
home to the Bay Area, where she began interning at a website
devoted to student activism. Nicholas Gall continued to teach
his two classes: the final two classes in his Webster College
career, Naomi fervently hoped. He claimed not to know where
his protégé had gone, though he was happy to let it be known
that he himself had been offered a position at a traditionally
black college in Georgia. Back to Rabun Gap, in other words,
to inspire a whole new cadre of disenfranchised students and
continue his important academic work on Lowe Stokes and
"The Mountain Whippoorwill."

Most wonderful of all, however, was the slow but undeniable
unshackling of the Stump. One by one by one the tents were
folded and taken away, their stakes pulled up, even the trash
gathered and disposed of. On a Monday a few weeks after the
Billings bomb there might be patches of mud visible between
the lean-tos and shelters; a few days later the patches were more
common than the tents. The flock was moving on, and as it did
the media trucks, too, took off. The Webster Inn emptied of its
unruly tenants. The emotional temperature cooled even as the
days warmed up and slouched toward spring. And though Naomi
knew she had done nothing to deserve it, she felt triumphant. It
was ending.

Hannah, though nearby, maintained her distance, and Naomi
knew better than to turn up at Radclyffe Hall a second time,
asking to see her. She could only imagine what her daughter's
thoughts on the arson had been, or how it must have rattled
Hannah to know that the very Hitchcock chair she'd sat in during their argument would be consumed by flames only a few
hours later. That kind of thing could disturb on a very deep level,

and as her maternal confidence returned to her, Naomi decided it was best to let Hannah initiate her own approach.

Given the fact that she had recently survived a very targeted act of violence, the Webster College trustees were giving her what she hoped was sincere support. President Naomi Roth was a victim now—a clear victim of a violent act. And though Omar Khayal had never once been publicly named as a suspect in the fire, the general feeling was that some loose cannon attached to or in sympathy with Webster Dissent had been responsible, which cast that responsibility in the general direction of the group but at no specific individual. Naomi, stunned by her reprieve, wasn't looking a gift horse in the mouth. She watched in grateful wonder as the various participants in this baffling episode drifted away: the Webster students returning to dorms and classes, their guests from other institutions departing for their own campuses, the educationally unaffiliated dispersing, more than likely, to their next points of conflict. Nicholas Gall and Omar Khayal had made some insidious mischief at the college, but now Gall was going, Omar was gone, and one day soon, when actual sun pushed away the last of the Massachusetts spring, sunbathers would return to the Quad and sunrise yoga would return to the Stump, and all would be as it had been before in the queer and evolved and beautifully creative world that Webster was. She had kept her chin up through a nasty bit of intended harm. She hadn't betrayed her own ideological standards. And she was still here. And the threat was passing. Her office, indeed, was getting a fresh coat of paint.

Best of all, the Native American Gathering was now imminent and represented, Naomi dared to believe, the best possible antidote to that plague of ill feeling (and bad publicity) Webster Dissent had cast upon them. She had made sure that there were no other significant activities on campus that weekend, claiming the slot between the Persephone Festival and Welcome Webster, the weekend program for admitted applicants. Francine, emerging from her cave only a week or two earlier, had been pleased to announce that their successful applicants hailed from forty-nine states and thirty-one countries, and that the average GPAs and test scores of this group had not seemed to suffer at all from the barrage of negativity in the media. Webster, once again, had the fifth lowest admit rate in the nation, and their yield was only a sliver behind Yale's and Princeton's. Naomi could not help feeling some vindication.

The Native American Gathering kicked off with a welcoming cedar ceremony at the First Nations Center, led by two Lakota graduates and their daughter, a current senior. After this, and an invocation from the college chaplain (a hippie Episcopalian of impeccable counterculture credentials) and a more official greeting from two members of Robbins Petavit's advisory committee, the entire group of nearly two hundred attendees walked over to the dining hall, a wing of which had been given over to them. There was wine, and better than usual Webster Dining Services food, but Naomi was elated to note that neither of these seemed as interesting to the alumni as the sheer fact of one another. From Josiah Webster's time to Sarafian's and beyond, no one had ever made this gesture to the ethnic constituency most publicly identified with the school. Men and women all over the hall were moving around the tables, greeting one another and talking excitedly. She sat beside Petavit, content to say little, fascinated by the intertribal rituals of linkage and distinction going on all around her. Two people could seem to belong to the same tribe, but membership in different bands meant that they were as far apart as Ashkenazi and Sephardic Jews. Others would introduce themselves as cousins but look nothing alike. ("We're all cousins," Robbins said, laughing, when she mentioned this later.) Many of the attendees, especially those from earlier classes, wore clothing and jewelry that clearly signaled their Native American status; others looked indistinguishable from other Webster graduates; if you didn't know, in other words, you'd never know.

Later there was a mixer in the cellar pub at the inn, and it turned out that Robbins wasn't the only Webster student to have spent memorable evenings in its old pine-paneled booths. After the first hour the party looked like any Webster reunion, and Naomi, waving to Robbins, thought it was safe to peel off. She walked home across the Billings Lawn, keeping to the pathway between two large areas of reseeding, and felt a trill of joy at the thought of that new grass. The Stump itself seemed flatteringly lit by the half moon overhead, and the stars were out and bright. She went to bed an hour later, happier than she had felt in months.

In the morning she had breakfast with Robbins at the Webster Inn. He, too, seemed pleased and also surprised by how nicely the weekend was unfolding, and he told Naomi that he and some classmates had taken a very late walk down to Webster Lake and spent a couple of hours on the boathouse dock, catching up and having the kind of heart-to-heart you can only have with people who've seen you at your most imbecilic. "For that alone I'm glad we did this," he said, making short work of his scrambled eggs and sausages. "But you know what? I think today's going to be really memorable."

Even as he said it, even with his clear elation, she had felt a chill.

"Me too," she said bravely.

She had nothing to do but listen until the last panel of the day, a discussion with current undergraduates which she'd be moderating.

The program began with a talk from Robbins, telling again the story of how Webster College had ended up in the middle of a Massachusetts forest. The main characters of this tale, familiar as they might have seemed to Naomi, came newly alive in Robbins's narrative, supplemented by visuals from the college's art collection: Josiah himself, his 250-year-old image saved from incineration, and the other Josiah, his Nipmuc protégé, and also his actual son and heir Nathaniel, and Samuel Fairweather, the wealthy whaler who'd made Nathaniel choose between his father's legacy and his own worldly ambitions. From there it was a two-hundred-year hyperspace leap to Oksen Sarafian. And here they all were. "My hope for today," said Robbins in conclusion, "is that we can come to recognize that Webster does indeed have a place in the Native American landscape, and an important role, though it's a role Josiah Webster wouldn't recognize and might not understand. He intended his namesake school to change the Indians who attended it. We were supposed to become 'civilized,' which meant Christian, and we were supposed to bring Christianity back to our homes so that more of us could be changed. But in fact it hasn't worked out that way at all. We are the ones who've changed Webster."

There was applause. Naomi was sitting in the back, an open notebook on the flip-up armrest, but she hadn't written anything down. She had grown a tiny bit uncomfortable during the talk, though not because Robbins had done anything wrong. She was trying to remember their first meeting, that lunch at the Webster Inn. He'd eaten a burger and drunk iced tea. She hadn't felt a thing. She was sure of it. Well, she wasn't really sure of it. Not at all. At any rate, she wasn't sure of it now.

Just under eight hundred Native students since Sarafian's inauguration in '66, Robbins was saying, with more than one hundred fifty tribes represented. Since 2000, between thirty and forty Native students had matriculated each year.

"I really believe that Webster is a place where Native culture can thrive, which is so wonderfully ironic given that the whole point of this place was to kill that very culture. And before we go any further I'd like to express my gratitude to President Roth for conceiving of this gathering and frankly forcing me and the others onto the committee."

They all laughed. They turned to Naomi and smiled and raised their clapping hands but she didn't want to be looked at. She didn't want him to look at her. How old was Petavit, anyway? Had they ever established this? Not younger than her, she was sure. But not much older, either. She was relieved when that was over and the first panel began.

Six men from the early years. They were an odd group, neatly divided between tribal representatives and attorneys, the former with long hair and dressed in jeans, the latter attired for court. Petavit, who was moderating, introduced them by name and tribal affiliation, and by the year that they'd matriculated at Webster. None of them, it would quickly become clear, had actually graduated, at least not from Webster College. The first to speak had arrived as a freshman from the Pacific Northwest, alerted to the college and its newfound interest in Native applicants by the father of his basketball teammate, an alum. He'd come in the fall of '69, delighted not to be in basic training but otherwise at sea. Inside of three months he was floundering, academically and socially, and had all but moved up to Worcester, where he had a girlfriend who worked at the Webster Inn. "And basically," said the man, whose name was Thomas Dark Feather, "for the next couple of years I'm dropping in and then dropping out. And you know, they were always okay with me coming back, which now I look back on and think that's kind of amazing. But I kept wanting to try and they kept saying what do you need to make it work? Like, tutoring? Or a single room? But I didn't know what I needed, and finally I gave up and went home. I did go to the community college in Ashland, Oregon. But I didn't blame Webster for what happened. I just never got my feet under me."

Not a promising beginning, then, but Naomi imagined it

might have been worse. The first women at Webster had had their dormitories surrounded by drunken men in the middle of the night, calling for the "co-whores" (their favored term for female students) to go home. The first openly gay students in the '80s had had their meetings secretly recorded by writers for the *Heritage Review*, Milton Russell's odious gang. For the most part it sounded as if these early Native students had not come in for outright opposition, only clueless neglect. Of the others on the panel, two had transferred to four-year schools close to their homes, one had left education entirely after completing half of his Webster degree, and two had limped in and out of the college for years, finally finishing credits at their state universities, where they'd also stayed on to attend law school.

Still, the lack of ill will shown by Thomas Dark Feather was echoed by the others. It hadn't been Webster's fault, was the general feeling; the school had tried to do something good, however uninformed it might have been on complex tribal issues and the weight of Native history, particularly when it came to Indians and education. Naomi found herself very moved by this lost first batch of Native students at Webster, this sacrificial pancake on the griddle of Sarafian's noble intentions. That all six panelists appeared healthy and engaged in meaningful work was, of course, not inconsequential, but she couldn't help feeling that the college owed them a bit more than airfare and a weekend at the Webster Inn.

When the discussion turned toward the Indian symbol in the following panel, that general benevolence only continued. In fact, she was quite surprised to learn, the first Native student arrivals at Webster had not unanimously been in opposition to the Webster Indian, an image that might have been drawn from a John Ford Western. This caricature Indian had been attending Webster games for decades before it first appeared on an official college document, but its having been grandfathered into the college culture didn't make Webster any less culpable. The story Naomi had always heard, and that Robbins had confirmed, was that Native students confronted Sarafian after their very first football game, and firmly requesting that no Indian mascot should ever again emit its deeply inauthentic war whoop in front of a crowd. This was not untrue; the meeting had taken place, and one participant on the panel, a Legal Aid lawyer in Montana, had actually attended it. But feelings about the symbol had not by any means been unanimously held. "I know it was a problem for some of the others," the man beside the Legal Aid lawyer explained. He'd identified himself as Hopi/Navajo, and he was a drug and alcohol counselor at a reservation facility in New Mexico. "But for me, it was kind of a part of the history of the place. I thought of it as a tradition, and tradition was something I'd been brought up to respect. So even though I knew people were organizing about it, and some of my friends were organizing, I never joined. I guess I wasn't ready to be that militant at that time."

The man to his left took the microphone. "My feelings were, yeah, this is important, and it was annoying to see kids who weren't Indian dressed up like somebody in a Western, and we were just starting to talk about how Indians were being portrayed in movies." His name was Roger Vasquez, and he built commercial real estate in Tulsa. "But at the same time, I remember thinking: Aren't there a lot more pressing issues for us going on? Not just nationally but also at Webster in particular. Like I had this anthropology class where the professor would come in dressed up as a Plains Indian, and we'd walk into the classroom and he'd be sitting there cross-legged on the floor. We were supposed to ask him questions and he'd answer them as a Sioux, and the point of this was to say something about how hard it was to talk to people who were from a different culture. I was kind of horrified by the whole thing, actually. He was doing this 'silent Indian' act, which is a big cliché about us, and I was very, very offended by it, but my friends didn't want to do anything until we'd gotten rid of the symbol. So yeah, there were a lot of us who were totally focused on the symbol, but some of us were just, you know, 'What an idiotic thing.' Just stupid crap, but we weren't that worked up by it. Now I think that Webster was kind of behind the curve on social change in general. But from what I can see now, on campus, eventually you really caught up. This is my first time back and I really just can't believe it's the same place."

Naomi smiled. So not every Native student was enraged by what was waiting for them at Webster. Perhaps not every Webster alum had rent his garments over the symbol's loss, either. Everything was grayer than you first believed, when you looked closely. That was the point of looking closely. She realized, all of a sudden, that she was missing her own academic work.

After lunch, which she ate beside Petavit but mainly with her back to him (he was being monopolized by a widely built man in a green ribbon shirt), they returned to the conference hall for the afternoon sessions. First came a look back at the Native American studies program and an evaluation of its current status, chaired by Francis Kinikini and resolutely positive. The program had been important since its inception in the '60s; and was now routinely ranked in the top two or three undergraduate programs nationally. It had six faculty members, four of whom had dual appointments with other departments, in anthropology, environmental studies, history, and English. She had nothing to fear from this panel, and used the time to go over her own notes for the panel she herself would be moderating to close out the formal portion of the gathering.

These were current undergraduates, a group she'd handpicked to talk about life as a Native student at Webster today. They comprised two young women, a freshman Chippewa from Minnesota named Millie and a Shinnecock senior called Lila from the ancestral patch of land now more commonly known as the

Hamptons. The two boys were Lawrence Yona-Rusk, a Cherokee from Oklahoma, and Joe Driggs, who was Seminole and from southern Florida. All four of them, she saw, had dressed for the occasion in clothing that did not really distinguish them from other Webster students. The girls were both in jeans and zip-up sweatshirts (one said JUICY; the other WEBSTER WOMEN'S CREW) and the boys in button-down shirts, but unbuttoned over T-shirts and not tucked in. The Seminole, Joe, had a First Nations Center hat, but that was the extent of their sartorial Native identification. Naomi wondered what it meant, then decided it didn't mean anything.

She introduced them. They nodded as they were described, looking forward. The Shinnecock looked nervous; the others seemed pleased to be in front of a crowd. "Before we begin, a small piece of information we're pretty excited about." In the current admissions cycle, she announced, the college had offers out to more than ninety Native American applicants. If every one of them said yes—which was unlikely, but still possible!—Webster would have a 5 percent Native enrollment for the new class, roughly five times the national rate for four-year institutions and a record for Webster itself. Which was amazing, really, given where they'd started. Over in the college cemetery behind the chapel, she told the room, Samuel Fairweather was probably howling in his grave.

Weirdly, nobody laughed.

Which also didn't mean anything, she told herself. But her thoughts were already rushing ahead.

They started at the far end: The Cherokee had turned down a lacrosse scholarship at Oklahoma State to come to Webster, a move that confounded his parents. He lived at the First Nations Center and captained the lacrosse team, but he was far and away the strongest player on the team, which was currently in eighth place in its central New England league. In the summers, he said, he traveled the festival circuit with some cousins who had a stall that sold books and music. He would probably major in government.

The girl from the Hamptons did not participate in First Nations activities at all, and after the freshman week welcome reception she hadn't set foot in the place. The previous fall she'd been to Florence with the art history department, and she hoped that her post-Webster life, which was now imminent, would mostly consist of advertising, or PR. Millie, the Chippewa girl, was pre-med and a cox for the women's eight. Her main concern, she said with a thoroughly straight face, was organic chemistry. "Passing it *and* understanding it." This panel was the first non-homework and non-rowing-related thing she'd done since before Christmas, she said, to general amusement. Lawrence Yona-Rusk had been in Naomi's freshman seminar on Second Wave feminism. He hadn't said much in class, but his papers were solid, and even showed some curiosity about the politics of protest and change. He'd said at the time that he wanted to write novels.

"I'm wondering," said Naomi when Yona-Rusk had finished, "what it's been like, listening to these older alumni. How do you relate the Webster they describe to the Webster you're attending?"

They looked at one another. Only Joe Driggs had been there earlier; the others hadn't been sufficiently interested, or were busy.

"Yeah, it's kind of an interesting question, because on one hand that stuff about the professor dressing up like a Native, and the Indian symbol, that couldn't happen today. No way would somebody do that, I mean not even on Halloween or something, any more than they'd dress up like a Nazi. Webster students, like, pride themselves on how sensitive they are. And they *are*," he insisted, as if the audience were challenging him on this point. "Like, for example, we have these days where everyone eats what the typical African eats on an average day, which is like fourteen hundred calories. And there's tons of sensitivity training when the freshmen get here. Cultural sensitivity, religious tolerance, sexual harassment training. But you know, it's hard when there's an endemic issue at the institutional level."

Naomi looked over at him. She couldn't be sure she had heard him correctly, but she was suddenly terrified to ask him to repeat what he had said. Joe Driggs sat, nonchalantly scanning the audience.

"Uh...would anyone like to comment on what Joe just said?"

"I mean," said the Shinnecock, "like, I'm kind of fortunate because I always attended, like, a regular school. I actually went to boarding school in Connecticut, and I know my tribal side, which is super important to me, is something I can choose to display or not display, so I've really made decisions about when I want to be Lila from Southampton or Lila the proud Shinnecock through my mom's side. And I haven't been, like, that involved. But have I felt threatened here in some ways? Absolutely."

"Threatened?" Naomi said. She couldn't stop herself.

"I wrote this story for my creative writing class last year," Lawrence Yona-Rusk jumped in. "It was about this teenaged boy who tries to kill himself. And he's not an Indian, he's just this normal teenager who lives in a cul-de-sac in anywhere suburbia. And my professor spends half the class trying to explain why the story doesn't work because I haven't been honest when I wrote it. Because if I'd been honest this would have been a Native kid on a reservation, with alcoholic parents and a wise old grandparent who wants to do a smudge ceremony or something and bring him back into the fold of his people. And I said, 'Hey, would you be telling me this if I weren't Native American?' Like, are we only legitimate if we're excavating our own ethnicity every single second? Because, like, that means Winston Burberry the fourth from Charleston over there better start writing about plantation life before the War of Northern Aggression, because if he doesn't he isn't going to produce anything worth reading."

At this, all four of them laughed. Naomi knew she'd gotten lost, but exactly when had that happened? She was backtracking frantically, but they were moving on without her.

"The problem," said the Chippewa freshman, "is that Webster has like two centuries of impacted racism. You don't just flush that out even in a couple generations. You can overlay it, and it's obvious to me that there's been a lot of effort in that direction, but we're walking over it all the time. We're walking over all the people who weren't allowed to be part of Webster for hundreds of years. And we're walking over dead Native people."

"Oh, wait," said Naomi. "I don't think that can go unanswered."

Someone in the audience had raised his hand. She called on him, immensely relieved. He was a man in his thirties. She'd met him the night before, in the dining hall, one of the twenty or thirty Petavit had introduced her to. He was from somewhere in the south, a physician. Or, no, a researcher. Drugs.

"I'm curious," the man said, sounding so eminently reasonable. "What's your take on the student protest we were hearing about this winter? Was that about racism?"

"It was about a professor in the anthropology department," said Lila, the proud Shinnecock. "Nick Gall. I had him freshman year and he was amazing. But he got turned down for tenure, and they tried to say it was because he'd plagiarized."

"Who said that?" someone in the back asked. Someone who hadn't raised a hand.

"The board or someone. They kind of leaked it then they denied they'd done it."

"And they got rid of the kid who was leading the protest," Lawrence Yona-Rusk said. "He was a Palestinian kid. His whole family was murdered by the Israelis, and he got himself to America. The whole thing was peaceful, but they kicked him out anyway."

"That is not what happened," Naomi said. She said it into the microphone. She hadn't meant to.

"And don't forget the basement of the Sojourner Truth House." Joe Driggs was leaning forward. "I belong to the community at Sojourner. I have black forbears also. There were escaped slaves who took refuge with the Seminole, I'm sure you know. So I identify as black also. And the fact that this could happen at Webster just made us sick."

"What happened?" said the man in the green ribbon shirt.

"Somebody wrote the N word on the walls of the basement," a voice shouted.

"In shit," said Joe Driggs. "And of course the campus police didn't do anything."

"They don't know who did it," Naomi said lamely. She was reeling. "Can I just say"—her voice rose—"that we've gone through something very difficult these last six months. What happened at Sojourner Truth does not represent our values or our students' values."

Her eye fell on Petavit. He sat in the front row, one leg crossed over the other. He was folding and unfolding a plastic straw in his left hand. He looked grim.

"But see, that's the thing." It was the man who'd spoken on the Indian symbol panel. The one who'd told the story about the professor dressing up as a silent Indian. "By default, if the incident takes place at all it's indicative of somebody's values, and that somebody is part of the Webster community."

She shook her head. "That was never established. The police never identified a suspect. And this is a safe campus. We keep our doors unlocked a lot of the time. Anyone could have gotten into that basement and...committed that crime. Believe me," she said fiercely, "no one wishes more than me that they'd arrested someone. I was appalled by what happened. And the house was full of peaceful protesters at the time. It was an affront to them and to me."

None of them believed her. Not one of them.

"So, basically," said the Chippewa girl, the pre-med cox who hoping to pass organic chemistry, "the situation is that we have this historically homogenous place, and then suddenly it undergoes a conversion and it *looks* different, and I'm not saying it *isn't* different, but under the surface the pace of the transformation is a lot slower. So, like, Webster admits women, but those women come from the same socioeconomic class as the men always have. They're the daughters of Webster graduates and the sisters of people who already go to school here. And the black students are really well educated and come from professional families. And the ones who come from overseas, even poor countries, are from the upper classes, and they blend right in with the old kind of Webster student. There aren't that many poor people here, in other words. And if you're poor, whether you're Native or not, that's the permanent underclass here, and they look at you, like, you should be so grateful to be here. So, like, when I was deciding between Webster and the University of Minnesota my grandma said, you know, do you want to stay where it's a normal thing to be a Native person or do you want to go to this elite school in the East where you're going to be this exotic creature? And I guess I wanted to have that whole Ivy thing, like the classic American college, but I'm just not happy. So I'm going to finish up the term and go back. I'm starting junior year at Minnesota in September."

Naomi stared at her. *Are you crazy?* she wanted to yell, but she stopped herself. The room broke into applause.

CHAPTER EIGHTEEN

A BIT OF A MYSTERY

That night there was a knock at her door. Naomi had been sitting on the long couch in the living room, drinking a glass of red wine. She knew who it was.

He was standing on the front step, holding the classic red plastic cup. There'd been a cookout under a tent down at the river: planked salmon and corn and potatoes, a hodgepodge of simulated Native dishes the dining hall thought they could manage. She had skipped the whole thing.

"I'm sorry," he said. "I looked for you."

"Yeah," she said. She was standing, holding the door open.

"I'm revisiting my wild college days," he said, holding up the cup.

"How's that going?"

He grinned. He was maybe a tiny bit inebriated, but she didn't know him well enough to say. "Oh, not too bad. The quality of the beer is a lot higher than I remember."

"I had them order the good stuff," she said. She still hadn't made up her mind.

"I'd like to talk, if you're willing."

Naomi hesitated. She was, she discovered, willing. She

stepped back into the entryway and he came in. He was carrying his satchel, old leather with a long shoulder strap. He put it down on the stone floor.

"I never saw the inside of this place," he said, looking around. "Sarafian lived here, right?"

"Right. All my noble predecessors for the last century. It's too big for one person, but I figured I should just relax and enjoy it. It won't be forever," she said. And then she thought: *truer words*...

"Can I have a tour?"

She led him around the ground floor. To the kitchen, where she gave him a glass of the same red wine, and the living room, and the parlor in the back whose glass windows overlooked the garden. The college landscapers had been in that week, planting annuals. She'd asked them: no orange. She'd never liked orange. But she always asked them that and they always forgot. Maybe they had no idea what they were planting.

At the foot of the stairs, she waved a hand. "Like I said, it's way too big for one person."

"Didn't you say you had a daughter?"

"Yes. Hannah. She was here with me while she was in high school. She's a Webster sophomore now."

"And lives...where? In a dorm?"

"One of the houses on Fairweather. Radclyffe Hall."

Petavit grinned. "'And that night, they were not divided.'"

"Ah." She had to admit, she was surprised. "I see you know your lesbian classics."

"Isn't that what a liberal arts education is for? Impressing women?"

Naomi tried not to react. From this odd exchange she had taken one thing only: *He wants to impress me.*

They went into the living room and sat. She had been here for an hour, at least, on this very couch, trying not to think about him. Now he was here.

"I wanted to say," began Petavit, "that I was very surprised by what happened. And I am very, very sorry."

"Not your fault," she said, not looking at him. "I suppose I didn't think it through."

"You thought it through. But what we sometimes forget—well, I forget it a lot—is how badly young people need to feel their specialness. And one way they feel it is to transmute any kind of discomfort into outright oppression. That kid in his creative writing class, maybe he didn't have the best teacher in the world, but he wasn't being oppressed. And I haven't spent all that much time at Webster in a couple of decades, but I'm very sure that girl from Minnesota wasn't being ostracized because she's a Native student. Or poor." He paused. "She did say she was having trouble in organic chemistry."

Naomi sighed. "Yeah."

"I imagine it's got to be pretty intense at a place like Webster, if you're going pre-med. I didn't get through organic chemistry, myself."

She took a sip of her wine.

"Not to compare myself. But what I mean is, maybe it's a way of her saving face. I'm going home to be with more people like me, where maybe it'll all be a little easier. You see?"

Naomi nodded. She did see.

"I think, what I'm trying to say is, you tried to do something good. That's the important part."

"Yep. Just like Josiah Webster. Good intentions, all the way to hell. But I guess it's better to have tried and failed..." She smiled weakly.

"Oh, I wouldn't say it's a failure. Down there in the tent people are talking and laughing. It's a beautiful thing, very meaningful. They're having fellowship. They have strong feelings for Webster, too. And this speed bump, it's not a referendum about Webster. It's just part of the—"

"No, please!" Naomi groaned. "Do not say 'journey.'"

He looked chagrined. "Actually, I *was* going to say 'journey.'"

She smiled. "Well, I'm sorry then."

"Hey, we're Native people. The journey is important. And we take the long view most of the time, because we've been here a good long time. Webster College is still pretty young at two and a half centuries. It's going to keep changing long after we're gone."

To her own surprise, this affected her. She thought about it, in silence, looking not at him but into her own wineglass. She didn't drink red wine very often. It had been there, in the larder, and she'd needed something.

"So, cheer up."

Naomi glanced at him. "It's been a rough few months. It's been the hardest thing. I still don't understand it. And my daughter isn't speaking to me."

Petavit nodded. Naomi was shocked. She could barely believe she'd said any of it out loud, let alone with Robbins Petavit in the room. She didn't know him. She didn't know him at all.

"Would you like to tell me?" he asked.

That was about nine thirty, not later than ten. She sat with him and told him every bit of it, though not what Hannah had said in their last meeting, the night of the firebomb, which would have been too much. It would have hurt too much. Sometime around midnight he took her hand. It terrified her, but she didn't pull it back.

"How old are you?" she asked at one point.

They were exactly the same age, it turned out.

Naomi must have fallen asleep first. Robbins had found a blanket in one of the closets, but they were still in the living room, still on the couch. Neither of them said a thing about going upstairs; it had been agreed upon: this, but not that. Here, but not there. She had loosened her clothes but hadn't taken them off. No one had touched her for years, she realized. At

least, not like that. When she woke up her head was on his thigh
and he was sleeping, half reclined against one of the cushions.
The phone was ringing.

"Yes?" His legs jerked under Naomi's head. She sat up.

"No, it's okay. I'll get it."

The phone in the hallway was old, a heavy Bakelite thing
attached to the jack by a cloth-covered cord. It emitted a distinctive metallic ring, utterly unlike the tone of a modern receiver.
Not many people had this number, but the ones who did were
almost certainly calling because something bad had happened.
She climbed to her feet and moved toward it. *Fast and faster*, she
thought, but the truth was she didn't move fast at all. The truth
was she didn't want to know.

"Hello? This is President Roth."

It was Peter Rudolph from campus security, but there was
nothing wrong, he told her. Not at Webster.

"I don't understand," she said.

A police detective from Hartford, Connecticut, was trying to
reach her. There was a Webster student down there. Possibly a
Webster student. Who needed to be identified.

She closed her eyes. "Identified?"

"He was calling from the medical examiner's office."

"Who is it?" she asked stupidly.

Peter Rudolph paused. "They don't know. They need someone
from Webster to identify him."

Him? She could have wept. "Him?"

"It's a male. College aged. He has a Webster ID. Are you willing to go?"

There was a tall grandfather's clock in the hall, across from the
phone table, a gift to the college from some grateful graduate a
hundred years earlier. It wasn't exactly accurate, but it was accurate enough. Three forty in the morning.

"What does the ID say?" she asked, bracing herself.

She could hear him breathing. From the living room next door, she could also hear Robbins breathing.

"It's Omar Khayal," Peter Rudolph said. "I mean, that's what the ID says. Of course, it might not be him."

"I'll go," Naomi said. She wrote down the address, then she hung up the phone and stood, just stood, for another long moment. Did that matter, that she was still standing there? How could it matter, if he was dead? But then, how could Omar be dead?

"What is it?" said Robbins. He was in the doorway.

"I need to go to the medical examiner's in Hartford."

"Is it a student?"

"Former student. He actually..."

"Wait," said Robbins. "You don't mean...I've forgotten his name. The boy who was in charge of the protest?"

Quite unexpectedly, Naomi started to cry. "I don't believe this. In Hartford? What was he doing in Hartford?"

"I'm driving you," said Robbins. He looked very awake and very sober. "Where are my shoes?"

"You don't have to." She wiped her face. "This isn't your responsibility."

"I'm driving you. You know where to go?"

She looked down at the pad she'd written on. There was an address. "Yes."

"All right. Do you...maybe a different shirt?"

The shirt she was wearing had lost a button. It was not something to wear to a morgue. She had never been to a morgue. She went upstairs and put on a different shirt, a white shirt with all its buttons, and black pants. Then she took off the black pants and put her jeans back on and put on a black sweater over the white shirt. Her hair was loose and halfway down her back. Her mother had once told her that once a woman reached forty she had to cut her hair short. Her mother had also said that when hair started to go gray it must be dyed, and then gradually, at some undefined point in the future, allowed to become gray again. It was unseemly not to do these things. Naomi reached back and touched her long gray hair. *I am unseemly*, she thought. She had been unseemly for at least fifteen years. She had been unseemly for all of her adult life. But how could Omar be in a morgue in Hartford, Connecticut?

They drove in Robbins's Subaru, southwest on 84, rarely see-ing other cars, a straight shot to Hartford through the night. Naomi didn't say much, except to thank him, repeatedly, for what he was doing, until he asked her to stop.

"I can't believe this," she said instead. Then she said that repeatedly.

"Did you know where he went when he left school?" They were reaching the first East Hartford exits.

"No. The police wanted to talk to him about the firebomb in my office, but they had no idea where he was. I think they looked at Nicholas Gall's place in Georgia, and his own town in Okla-homa. Well, not his town. It's where he applied to Webster from. But they couldn't find the family he'd been living with. Beyond that he could have been anywhere. And he wasn't a formal sus-pect, just someone they wanted to talk to. Because of me," she said with a sudden, deeply guilty pang.

"You thought he was responsible for the firebomb."

"No! Well, it occurred to me. But . . . nonviolent. That was his whole thing. He was post-violence. His father and brother had been killed in the West Bank. He refused to be a suicide bomber. Some American who worked for an NGO helped him get refugee status here. It was all in his application essay. Very powerful essay."

"I imagine," Robbins said quietly. After a moment he asked, "When was he expelled?"

"He wasn't expelled!" She hadn't meant it to sound as nasty as it did. "Where'd you hear that?"

"From the kid on the panel today. Yesterday. I mean, 'kicked out' was what he said."

"Well, he was not expelled. We were putting him on academic probation because he'd done no work at all in the fall semester. He didn't show up to a meeting with me and the dean of students, and then he gave the press some story about how we were kicking him out, we'd thrown his stuff out on the sidewalk. Never. I'd have been happy for Omar to go away for a semester and then come back and get serious about his work."

"With the emphasis on 'go away'?"

Her face felt hot, even in the cool car. The indictment, though mildly spoken, and probably not even intended, was still there. It simply reminded her of what she already knew. "I can't believe this," she said again.

The Hartford County medical examiner's office was one of a half dozen nearly identical buildings on a municipal campus in West Hartford. They drove around for a few minutes, trying to read the signs in the darkness: ANIMAL CONTROL, PUBLIC HEALTH. They found it on their second circuit, an unremarkable single story the color of sand, with a door that slid open at their approach. Inside, a drowsy security guard sent them downstairs to an appropriately grim corridor. There was no one there except down at the end, a maintenance worker on one of the wooden benches.

"Should we ask her?" Robbins said after a moment.

Naomi looked down the corridor. The woman was leaning back against the wall and had her eyes closed. She looked as if she were trying to take a nap.

"No."

They stood in silence for a few minutes. Somewhere in the building, not far away, a conversation could be heard, muffled and not easily locatable. "Do you want to sit?" Robbins said finally.

"No."

She walked to a door, the nearest door, and knocked. There was no answer. Naomi moved down the corridor toward the dozing maintenance worker, knocking and calling "Hello?" as she went. At the third door her knock was answered.

"I'm sorry," she told the man who answered. He was slight and nearly bald, though with very full blond eyebrows—an arresting combination. "I wanted to let someone know we were here."

"Did someone call you?" he said, not unkindly.

"Someone called security at my college. Webster College. They called me. I'm afraid I didn't get the name of the original caller."

Even as she said this it struck her as the height of idiocy. Why on earth hadn't she asked for a name?

"Detective Miller?"

Naomi shrugged. "I'm sorry. I was asked to come to this address. I was told that a student from Webster College was . . . I mean, I was asked to identify him. I'm the president," she said, feeling like a total fool.

"Okay." He nodded. He wrote down her name on a form on a clipboard. "Just give us a minute, we'll bring you in."

He disappeared back into the room. Robbins, behind her, asked, "Do you want me to come with you?"

She shook her head. "It's okay. Thanks for the offer. I'd better do it alone."

But that's not exactly what she was thinking. What she was thinking, selfishly, was that she didn't want him to see her as she did this. If she were going to lose control, if she were about to say something about how she felt, which was that she was somehow the cause of this, whatever *this* turned out to be, she couldn't bear for him to witness it. Robbins took a seat on the nearest bench. Naomi stood, steeling herself, her jaw set. A moment later the door opened again.

"Naomi Roth?"

It was a black woman in her thirties, forties. A bit on the short side, more than a bit on the stout side. "I'm Detective Miller. I called your campus security office."

Naomi shook hands. "You spoke to Peter Rudolph."

"Right. I appreciate your coming down. Bad phone calls in the middle of the night probably aren't a nice part of your job."

"No." She offered a weak smile. "But they *are* part of the job."

"Want to come through?" The woman held back the door. It was steel with a frosted glass insert. On the other side, Naomi found herself in a chamber with a table and two wooden chairs. Hitchcock chairs, ironically enough. The far wall of the chamber had a curtained window. She supposed she knew what was on the other side of that.

"I'm thinking we should get the hard part over first? Then we can talk."

"If it's him," Naomi said quickly, deploying the last of her magical thinking.

"I'm sorry?"

"If it's him. It might not be him. And if it's not him, there won't be much to talk about, I'd imagine."

Detective Miller was watching her thoughtfully. "Him being...?"

"Omar Khayal," said Naomi. "I mean, that's why I'm here, right? Because he... because this person had Omar's college ID? But he could have found it. Or... stolen it?"

"Let's not get ahead of ourselves," Miller said. She sounded very calm, and not unsympathetic. "We'll talk afterward."

Naomi felt herself nod. The detective gestured to the side of the room with the curtain. There was an intercom on the wall, and she pressed the button: "Louis, we're ready."

No, we're not, Naomi thought.

Another button operated a pulley overhead. It made a gentle clicking sound.

In the next room, the bald man with the blond eyebrows—
Louis, presumably—stood behind the steel table, and the person
on the table (the body, she corrected herself), who was bare from
the hips up, draped in a green cloth from the hips down. Narrow hips. A small tattoo on the right one; she couldn't see what
it was.

"Mrs. Roth?" said Detective Miller.

Ms., she almost said.

"Do you know this man?"

Did anyone know this man? He had arrived, emerged, and departed. His hair had always been long—well, always. For Naomi
"always" had been from October of last year until two months
ago, and that wasn't much of an always. Now it was short, very
short. Almost military, with a carefully etched shadow beard. His
fragile frame seemed fuller, puffier, as if he'd been well fed, at
last, and the eyes—she couldn't see them. They were closed, on
the other side of the visibly grimy glass, in another room. Were
they the same dark, limitless eyes? She had been persuaded by
those eyes, their ancient sadness. He had experienced so much
of the awful world. Among his classmates, so tended and nur-
tured, so principled, so willing, he had worn his story like a
magical cape. But Naomi couldn't see his eyes from where she
was looking. He was almost unrecognizable, but he was recognizable.

"Yes, that's Omar," she said.

"I'm very sorry," the woman said perfunctorily.

"Yes, it's terrible."

"Could I just ask you to spell that name?"

Naomi looked at her. "Omar? O-M-A-R."

"And the last name?" She was writing.

"K-H-A-Y-A-L."

"Like the poet," Detective Miller observed.

"What?"

She smiled, unaccountably. "'A Jug of Wine, a Loaf of Bread—and Thou.' You know, the Rubaiyat."

"Omar Khayyam? No, that's different." But not so different. Now there was something she hadn't thought of for months: the nearness of those names. That line about the jug of wine, it was a celebrated come-hither, almost a joke. But not to a Webster undergraduate. Nobody read Omar Khayyam today; if they knew his name at all it was because they mixed him up with Kahlil Gibran. For a while in the seventies, everybody quoted *The Prophet* in their wedding services.

"Did he have a middle name?"

She tried to remember. She was thinking about his application, which she'd read in her own bed at the Stone House. *Sometimes people ask me what it was like to grow up in the middle of a war.* Naomi closed her eyes. Had there been a middle name? Arabic names had multiple parts. They linked back to ancestors or places of origin, like South American names did, so even people from humble backgrounds sounded aristocratic. Not at all like American names. "I don't remember a middle name. But I remember the town he came from. It was Bureij." She spelled it. "In . . ." *Gaza*, she'd been about to say. But under the circumstances Omar deserved otherwise. "Palestine."

"I see. Can we talk a bit?"

Mercifully, Detective Miller closed the curtain again. They sat in the chairs. The woman placed her clipboard on the table between them.

"I'm sorry we don't have coffee yet. Couple of hours they come in and make a pot. But I don't think either of us know how the machine works."

"It's okay," Naomi told her, though she would have liked a cup of coffee. The day, outside, was getting ready to begin.

"I'll be honest with you," the woman said. "To me, this young man is a bit of a mystery."

Join the club, Naomi almost said. What she said instead was "We were looking for him. The Webster police couldn't find him after he left campus. I never thought I'd see him again, and to tell you the truth, I wasn't unhappy about that. But why he's here, just an hour away..." She shook her head.

"Why were the Webster police trying to find him?" the detective asked.

She tried to keep it straightforward. Omar had been the leader of a student protest. It had been a peaceful protest, mainly. But there had been some incidents on campus that had not been peaceful. "Maybe you heard about it?"

Detective Miller had not heard about it. That was almost a relief, but it also meant she had to explain.

"My office, back in February, was bombed. Just a little bomb, the kind that starts a fire. Luckily the damage wasn't bad, but Omar left town that day. So obviously they wanted to talk to him. I thought...well, I don't know what I thought. He'd come to us from a town in Oklahoma. But he wasn't there, and anyway that wasn't his home. He'd just been staying with a foster family there when he applied to our college. I think home was probably Palestine, but he couldn't go back there."

"Why not?" she asked.

"Well, he was recruited by...I can't remember if it was one of the groups we hear about. Hamas or Al-Qaeda. Or someone else. He was supposed to blow himself up on a bus or in a market. But he came to America instead. I think he felt he couldn't go back. He would be killed. And his family were gone in any case."

She nodded, but said nothing. She was waiting for more.

"His father and brother were killed by Israeli soldiers. There were photographs of them on the street, trapped in the crossfire. The father was trying to shield the little boy, but they were both shot. Do you remember those photos? I can't remember exactly when it was."

Detective Miller looked pensive. "I think I do."

"Yes. And then his mother died. So he had no one."

"I see."

"No family. But he met some American NGO employee who helped him immigrate, and a couple of years later he came to Webster. He was..." She wanted to say something nice about Omar, something respectful. He had abandoned his academic work. He had refused to engage in consensus building, or to find common ground, or any of the euphemisms that had served so many other agitators so well. Instead, he and his baffling mentor had nearly destroyed the college. "He was a very good writer," she said, thinking of that application essay.

"He wrote about his childhood, then?"

"Well, he didn't like to speak about his childhood at all. Not in public. But he did write about what had happened to him in his application essay. I read that," she said, a mite defensively.

"You read every application essay? There must be thousands."

"No, our admissions department does that." It struck her as odd that they were discussing college admissions. Even here? Even in a morgue? People were so fascinated. Possibly Detective Miller had a child in the zone. Was Naomi about to be told of some civic-minded high school junior, first in her class and bound for the heights? Likely to apply to Webster? "I asked to see it. I was curious about him."

"Because of his story."

Naomi frowned. She must have meant his *history*. It was only a subtle difference. "Yes."

"And as far as you know, there is no reason why Omar should be here in Hartford, as opposed to somewhere else."

There was no reason. There was, overall, an absence of reason.

"No. I'm completely at a loss."

The woman nodded. She set down her pen. "Well, I want

to thank you for coming here. I'm sure this wasn't fun, getting called out of bed."

Not technically bed, Naomi thought. But no, it had not been fun.

"I hope we can call you if we have more questions."

"Of course," Naomi said. She got to her feet. She was weary. She felt that now. "Was it a busy night here?" she asked, she didn't know why.

"Quiet," the woman said. "Just this one case. Usually, a Saturday night, it's more, unfortunately. I don't know how familiar you are with Hartford. The suburbs are quiet, but the city itself has some very serious issues, you know."

She didn't know. She didn't know much about Hartford, despite having spent the past twenty years living in its general proximity. Hartford was a place where highways intersected. You drove through it on the way to New York or New Haven or Amherst. Or Webster. It was known for insurance companies, and Wallace Stevens, and the Atheneum. She'd been to a play in Hartford once.

"Unfortunately, not a peaceful place. I grew up here, and I love it, but there are gangs. *Gangs*, plural. Drugs and gangs."

"Oh, I'm sorry." Naomi didn't know what to say. She didn't really want to say anything. She wanted to leave.

"The Latin Kings, and a new one, Los Solidos. It's a plague."

"Yes, it must be. Well, I'll head back, then." It sounded wrong, like she was personally trying to escape from warring thugs. "I mean, if it's okay."

Detective Miller held the door for her and Naomi returned to the corridor. Robbins was still on the bench, looking at something on his phone. She sat beside him and closed her eyes.

"It was him?" he asked quietly.

Naomi nodded.

"That's so terribly sad. I'm sorry, Naomi. Are you all right?"

She nodded again.

"Did they tell you what happened to him? How he died?"

She turned to him, stunned. It had never occurred to her to ask. What was the matter with her? Wasn't that why people came to a medical examiner in the first place? To find out exactly that? "Shit," she said. "I can't believe I just did that. I mean, I can't believe I didn't do that. She didn't say a thing, just about how dangerous Hartford is. Drugs and gangs. But nothing about Omar."

"Well, you'll find out eventually, I'm sure," Robbins said. "They'll figure it out. I mean, I suppose they will."

Naomi sighed.

Down at the end of the corridor, the woman stirred. The maintenance worker.

"Do you want to go?" said Robbins.

She wanted to go, more than anything. But she kept looking at the woman on the other bench, because she couldn't figure out what was happening down there. The maintenance worker had sat up but then fallen back against the wall. She seemed to be shaking. She wasn't shaking, Naomi realized. She was weeping. "Wait," said Naomi.

She walked toward the woman, who was small and round and dark: Latina. Her gray hair was bobby-pinned flat against her head, and into a coil. The maintenance uniform she wore was dark green and had a red-and-white patch on the upper arm that said HARTFORD HOSPITAL. Naomi approached her.

"Can I help you?" Naomi said. A ridiculous question, but there was no one else here to ask it.

The woman turned to Naomi. Her face was wet but the expression blank. "Do I know you?" she asked. She had an accent: Spanish.

"No, no, I'm just here...for something. I just thought, do you need anything? Are you all right?"

"My son died," the woman said.

"I'm so sorry." Naomi sat beside her. Again, she didn't know why, only that she couldn't stop herself. "What a terrible thing."

"They came to get me at my job. I work at the hospital. When they brought him in. But he was gone already."

"Oh no." She looked up. Robbins was standing in front of the other bench. He was watching. "Can we ... are they taking care of you? Is there someone we can call?"

The woman shook her head, very slowly. "Just my nephew, but he's at the hospital. They brought him in with my Eduardo, but he is going to be okay, the doctor said."

"That's good. That's good." She was afraid to touch the woman. She was afraid to say the wrong thing. As far as she could tell, anything was the wrong thing. "Were they in an accident together?"

"I told Eduardo not to go out with his cousin. I told him. Rafael was in some bad thing. He was always in some bad thing. I couldn't stop him. But they were so close. Not like cousins. Like brothers."

That didn't sound like an accident. Gangs and drugs, the detective had said. It was terrible.

"But Eduardo. Eduardo was going to college." The word *college* wrenched something deep inside of her. She wailed, bent forward, into her own hands. "He was a smart boy. He wanted to do good in life. He said, 'Mama, I can study.' He was a good boy."

"Of course he was," Naomi said. But really, was he? Maybe this woman didn't know her son all that well. Maybe he'd been out there with his cousin, doing whatever bad thing his cousin was doing. Drugs and gangs. *Gangs*, plural. Just another Saturday night in Hartford.

The woman wept on. Naomi felt useless. Finally, she placed a hand on the woman's shaking shoulder. There was no reaction. Robbins had moved a step closer.

Parents knew so little, even when they'd hovered over their

kids, every second of their lives. Even when they'd ferried them from swimming to Brownies to the SAT tutor, monitored their homework and overseen their college applications. They dropped off their sons and daughters that first day of freshman year, hauling massive Bed Bath & Beyond bags and laptops and duffels full of clothing, and then they left these perfect strangers behind and drove home to their depopulated houses. Parents never believed their kids were capable of such subterfuge. If something went wrong, if the student was caught selling a joint or buying a term paper off the internet, they thought it was something Webster had done, some metamorphosis brought on by the college's famously permissive mores. Naomi had sat with parents after disciplinary hearings, listening to them explain that Fiona or Dashiell could not possibly have done what they'd been accused of doing, what they had been found guilty of doing. *Not my child*, they said, even after the student had admitted an infraction or there was clear proof. *Not my child.* These perfect girls and boys, the curious scholars and open-hearted citizens of their college essays—they had gone off to a place like Webster and become changelings, new and strange, made-up people who could barely look their parents in the eye.

And this one, Eduardo, who would never look his parent, his mother, in the eye again. What had he hidden from her?

The door to the viewing room was opening again. Naomi looked up to see Detective Miller step out into the corridor. She felt embarrassed to be seen this way, giving comfort, or trying to give comfort, to a stranger. She was supposed to have left by now. She was supposed to be on her way back to her own life, duty discharged, and not so very touched by the death of a college student, a *former* college student, one of thousands enrolled at Webster. And yet here she still was, inserting herself into the worst night of this poor destroyed mother's life. *Who does that?* Naomi thought.

A human person does that. Another mother does that.

"I see you two have met," said Detective Miller, unaccountably.

Naomi looked up at her.

"Oh," said Robbins. He had his hand against his forehead, pressing it, as if he had the most terrible headache. "Oh, no. Oh, Naomi. We should leave."

"I don't understand," she said. But she took her hand from the shoulder of the mother of the boy named Eduardo, who was the only case at the Hartford morgue on that atypically quiet Saturday night in April.

CHAPTER NINETEEN

VERITAS

Over the next week, as the Webster lawns began to give up their daffodils and hyacinths, Naomi watched the Omar story hatch and bloom. She had informed the people she had to inform—the trustees, the Webster police, and Dean Stacek—but otherwise she intended to say nothing to anyone. The truth about Omar was as incendiary as any bomb he might or might not have set, and when it emerged, as it obviously would, she wanted it not to come from her. At any rate, it didn't take long.

A week after the night drive to Hartford, Mrs. Bradford took a call from Laurence McAfee in the press office. A reporter from the AP was asking for an interview related to the death of Omar Khayal. Did the president know anything about this?

Naomi asked them to decline the request. Decline all requests.

Then there was a grace period of three days, and then the thing exploded.

Out on the Quad they gathered in a kind of mourning scrum, first distraught and then, when the rest of it emerged, stupefied and paranoid. It was some kind of frame-up. It was some kind of besmirchment. The fate of their brave and beautiful Palestinian boy was so unexpected, so appalling, that it could only point to some far-reaching conspiracy—and yet, the other part of the conundrum kept tripping them up. *Omar had been eliminated! Omar had been silenced!* But...well...he hadn't been Omar, he'd been someone else. Some other person, who had made an entire life for himself, and offered it to the world in a bouquet of all the right things: loneliness and war and loss and exile and wandering and the power of those simple ideas, fairness and justice and peace.

But, at the same time, *Omar had been gotten rid of!*

They ricocheted back and forth, roiling and arguing and holding one another in their honest grief. Naomi didn't blame them. She'd spent days doing a version of the same, and nights unable to sleep as she braided together and pulled apart the two boys, Omar and Eduardo, Eduardo and Omar. They had had nothing to do with each other, those two, apart from being the same person.

Eduardo Sombra, the only son of his grieving mother, had been killed in the crossfire between the Latin Kings and Los Solidos in Pope Park, a place you didn't want to go walking at night, not if you knew anything about Hartford, Connecticut. His cousin Rafael had also been shot, as had four other young men, but all of these were either handcuffed to their beds in Hartford General or had been released to the custody of the police. At issue in this particular incident were half a kilogram of crack cocaine, two kilograms of powder cocaine, and ten pounds of marijuana: a very normal subject of dispute in Pope Park and the surrounding neighborhood, where Eduardo had spent his entire life before arriving at Webster. He had been a bright boy who loved to read books; this she gleaned from an obituary posted on the website of the *Hartford Courant*. He had played baseball on a local team, and spent summers working in the bodega of an uncle, Luis Aritza. He left behind a mother, Dolores Sombra; a sister, Luz Sombra; and many cousins in the Hartford area. At the time of his death, the obituary noted, Eduardo Sombra had been attending college out of state.

It was a waste, of course—a terrible waste. That went without saying. But there were other things that could be said, that someone ought to say, like the fact that it was also a lie and a crime and a crazy sad story. Eduardo, at the end of the day, had fooled everyone, including hundreds of young people who cared deeply about him—as Naomi, truthfully, had not. She thought of all those open-hearted kids in the parlor of Sojourner Truth House, gazing up at him, adoring him, wanting to comfort him and do meaningful things in tribute to him. She thought of how the cameras had loved him and the microphones had loved him, and how his story—his *story*—had inspired so many people.

The little boy who'd been shot in the Gaza Strip that day, sixteen years earlier, had had many siblings, according to Wikipedia. His father had survived.

The American who worked for an NGO, foster homes in Wisconsin and Texas, the public library in Arkoma, Oklahoma, where Omar had read about Webster College, so far away in the green forest of central Massachusetts, and sent out his humble request to join its welcoming community of scholars, artists, and activists—where had any of it come from? And did the fact that none of it was true mean that Webster was somehow also untrue? Or otherwise diminished?

Around and around she went, baffled and bitter and disconsolate, but she couldn't make sense of it. Eventually she realized there was no point in continuing to try.

The media trucks had returned, but this time there was no encampment of young people, eager to speak. Sojourner Truth House was now occupied solely by its legitimate tenants, and even Nicholas Gall seemed to have gone quiet. Perhaps this sudden dearth of interview subjects and the lack of an obvious person to blame had an impact on what happened next, as the story, slowly, then quickly, began to turn in an entirely new direction. If Omar—Eduardo—himself could not be made to answer for his subterfuge, then someone else must be responsible. The college, yes, but in particular its admissions office, which had given this con artist a place at one of the most competitive institutions in the country, in addition to a full-ride scholarship, thereby depriving an applicant who had *not* lied about every single thing in his application. This was a crime, obviously. And like any other crime, someone must have committed it.

Suddenly no one wanted to speak with Naomi Roth, the college president. Now the only interview anyone wanted was with Francine Rigor, Webster's dean of admissions, and they weren't bothering to go through the press office, and the callers were worse than the worst of the rejected applicants' parents, Francine reported. She had no idea what to do with them. People were turning up on campus tours and in Q&A sessions with her staff, asking for comments from anyone who could be made to sound like an official admissions office source. In the meantime, an ancillary story about elite colleges not bothering to confirm the credentials of applicants was swallowing up the entire affair.

Still, Naomi sat tight, and she advised her friend to do the same, assuming that in time the strange case of Omar Khayal would metamorphose again, and this time set off in an entirely different direction: psychopathology in teenagers, the effect of violent communities on high school students, the seductive iconography of the Palestinian experience and rhetoric...who knew what it would be? But then Milton Russell wrote an email to the Webster board, expressing the strongly held belief that Dean Rigor should step down immediately, given the fact that her office had admitted and awarded a full scholarship to an applicant with shockingly dubious credentials, which she had not seen fit to check.

When Naomi saw that, she called the college attorney into her office.

It was decided that the two of them, Naomi and Francine, should hold a press conference the next day, in the admissions office lounge in Service Hall.

"And may I ask why, after months of not talking to the press, we're suddenly holding a press conference?" Naomi asked. "I thought we were meant to be silent and dignified."

"Silent and dignified is usually a good policy," said Chaim Wachsberger, "but what really matters here is that we state and uphold college policy. Before, the issue was the confidentiality of the tenure process, but this is general admissions policy we're discussing now, not private information. I'm assuming that Harvard or Columbia or Podunk wouldn't have been any more likely to catch the fabrications in Mr. Khayal's application. It seems obvious to me, but apparently this is something that has to be explained to people, so we'll take this opportunity to explain it."

After he'd gone, and she was through with her phone call to Francine, Mrs. Bradford knocked gently at her office door and came in with a letter. "I'm not sure what do with this," she said, handing it over. She looked up at the painting the art museum had sent over: Webster College in 1788, three of the original buildings, the green that would eventually become the Billings Lawn, and overhead the massive elm trees. "It's such a shame about your quilt," she said. "I did like that quilt."

"Yes," Naomi agreed. "It was beautiful."

"Was it from your family? I never asked."

"No." She smiled briefly at the thought of her mother, Rachelle, or her grandmother, Judith. Neither of these women had been terribly domestic. She could not remember either one of them holding a needle. "It was from a business I once ran in New Hampshire. A group of local women making quilts and embroidering things. It was a mail-order business. Remember mail order?"

"Of course I do. I still get my socks from the Vermont Country Store catalogue."

"That's a fun one," Naomi agreed. "We're doing a press conference tomorrow afternoon, in the admissions lounge. FYI."

Mrs. Bradford nodded. "I'll give Leanne a call and see if they need anything from us."

Once she'd left, Naomi sat in her new chair (in truth, all but identical to the old) and looked at the wall where her old Drunkard's Path quilt had hung. The women who'd sewn it came roaring back to her, more clear, more sharp than before the fire, before the textile itself had been reduced to char. Their names and stories and grievances, the childish ways they had made one another suffer, even as they'd sat together and joined their hands to create something as illogical and lovely as a patchwork quilt. She wondered which of them were still alive and which were dead, marveling again at the fact that she had only removed herself by a distance of a couple of hours, and still she had never gone back. The quilt had kept them all with her, she realized now, and she was glad it had burned up.

The envelope in her hands was addressed to Naomi Roth, Billings Hall, Webster College, Webster, Massachusetts, and was from the bursar of Stanford University. It contained a tuition bill. She sat with it for a long while, then she took out her cell phone, photographed the bill, and texted the picture to Hannah with a single question mark. That was about as much as she could handle. It wasn't today's problem, maybe not even tomorrow's. She had to get through the press conference first.

The following afternoon they opened the lounge to the media-credentialed curious. Naomi and Francine took two wing chairs at the far end of the room and sat, doing a final pass on the statement Francine had prepared and waiting for the room to fill. Speaking before crowds was a part of Francine's job, and she did it well, but Naomi knew she didn't exactly enjoy being in front of people. School visits, alumni gatherings, and NACAC conferences—she gave off a relaxed but slightly geeky affect and did what she could to avoid personal encounters, the bane of many an admissions officer. She had dressed, for this occasion, in a quiet brown suit offset with a gold circle pin, and brown leather boots that might have shown very little of the leg of a shorter woman, but given Francine's height revealed the knee and several inches below it. She was fidgeting with her watch as Naomi read the statement again.

"It's going to be fine," Naomi said quietly.

"No, I know. It's just, we hate to get caught out like this. I mean, as it says in the statement, it does happen. It happened at Harvard and Yale and it happened at Princeton. Probably many other cases we don't know about."

"And you're telling them that," Naomi said.

"But I mean, now they'll say it happened at Harvard, Yale, and Princeton, *and* Webster. Makes me mad."

Naomi looked at her. "All right, but...mad for later. Sad for today. This is sad. Remember what Chaim said."

Chaim had said that they were not to be led too far from the fact that someone, a young person, was dead. And if it got heated, they were supposed to remind people of that: It was a tragedy. Nothing else was relevant.

"Okay." She nodded, looking glum.

"It's going to be fine," Naomi said.

"You said that already," said Francine testily, and it was the testiness that made Naomi remember the other conversation, the one in the student center. Neither of them had raised the subject again since that night, but now Naomi did.

"How is Sumner? Did his situation get resolved? The one you told me about?"

"Oh. Yes." Francine was watching the people come in. The space had been designed for prospective applicants and their parents, to look over the school catalogue and various Webster publications as they waited for their tours or interviews. The walls bore gleaming photographs of Billings Hall, the modern student center, the chapel, the boathouse on the lake. There was even an artful study of the Stump, looking—to anyone who didn't understand its Websterian significance—merely like any other stump in the world. On the far end of the room, outside the double doors that led to Francine's office, was the desk of Leanne Gall, Francine's assistant and the unfortunate wife of Nicholas Gall. She'd been no warmer to Naomi on this occasion, but now, of course, Naomi understood why. The two women, after a mutually frosty nod of greeting, had not looked at each other. "The board met," Francine said. "They renewed his contract for another two years. He'll retire then."

"Two years!" Naomi said. "That's wonderful news. He must be very relieved. You both must be."

Francine nodded. "Yes, it's a relief."

"You were so worried. I was sure it would be fine. Sumner is so devoted to Hawthorne. They'd be crazy to lose him."

"Should we start?" Francine said abruptly. "I think we should start."

Naomi looked at her. "All right," she agreed. "So, I go first, then you, then questions."

"I hate this dress," said Francine.

Then why did you wear it? she thought, before she could stop herself.

"No, you look really nice," she said instead.

Naomi got to her feet and spoke briefly. The entire Webster community was grappling with this student's sudden death and all of its implications. Obviously, the person they had known and respected as Omar Khayal had hidden much from the college and from his friends at Webster, and it was understandable that questions should have arisen. She and Dean Rigor would be happy to respond to those questions insofar as they did not violate the privacy of this or any other Webster student, or member of the community. But first Dean Rigor would read a statement.

Francine did not get up. She read from her chair, without looking at the men and women in the lounge or reacting to any of the cameras.

"First," she began, "we want to extend our profound sympathy to the family and friends of the student who died a few days ago in Hartford, Connecticut. We knew him as Omar, and we respected him as a gifted student and a kind and bright young man. I personally had a number of conversations with him when he first arrived at Webster, and I had very warm feelings for him.

"Given what we now know about Omar," Francine continued, "naturally I have gone back and reviewed the application he submitted two and a half years ago, and when I did, I could only conclude that I'd be inclined to admit anyone who submitted such application. Of course you're wondering why I couldn't tell that the essay was fiction, and that the entire persona Omar created in his application was fraudulent. I suppose I might have if Webster had an entire department of investigators, evaluating every application. We don't, and neither does any other college in the world. Not only would that necessitate an application fee of several hundred dollars, it would also send the message that we don't trust the students who fill out those applications, the teachers and counselors who write recommendations, or the schools that send transcripts. That is not the world we live in, and it's not the world we want to live in.

"Having said that, if something in an application jumps out at us, we might follow up with a phone call to a guidance counselor, but otherwise it's rare that we would verify a grade or check something a student's essay or recommendation has referenced.

Like most American colleges, Webster has an honor code, and because our relationship with the student begins with the application we consider that code to be in effect. In other words: We trust our applicants. That is our philosophy, and while it won't protect us from an applicant who sets out to be deceitful, it reflects our own principles, and the kind of academic environment we choose to create here at Webster.

"With this incident, Webster joins the list of colleges who have been defrauded in this way. Because while the vast majority of our applicants are honest and principled, there will always be people who prefer to mislead and obscure. We will never be entirely able to prevent this behavior, or even to identify it. But we'll continue to evaluate applicants to Webster according to our own integrity.

"Once again, we are deeply saddened by what has happened to Omar, because whatever else he may or may not have been, he was a human being and a member of our community.

"Now, if anyone has questions for either of us."

They only wanted to talk to Francine, though. Maybe they were like everyone else in America, eager to grill the dean of admissions of a highly selective college while she, more or less, couldn't refuse. They went for her, at least as avidly as any proud parents at a cocktail party who found themselves suddenly introduced to an Ivy League gatekeeper. Naomi, half amused, half relieved, sat in her wing chair, listening to her friend field the expected questions. Would the college change its procedures to prevent another "Omar" slipping through? What would have happened if "Omar's" deceptions had been discovered while he was still enrolled at Webster—would he have been expelled? What message did it send to potential applicants when someone could make up an ideal candidate out of whole cloth and do an end run around legitimate and truthful kids?

"He claimed to be the brother of a Palestinian boy who was

murdered in the Gaza Strip, an incident that was photographed and seen all over the world. You didn't even attempt to verify that?" said a woman in the back. She was having some difficulty keeping the umbrage from her voice.

Francine looked at her mildly. "Neither did you," she answered. "And last time I checked, verifying a story was something journalists actually *were* expected to do. As far as I'm aware, not one of the writers or broadcasters who interviewed Omar did basic fact checking on the person they were talking to. Besides, Omar was very vague in his application essay when it came to this incident. He alluded to something traumatic that happened to his father and brother, but didn't include specifics. Those details"—she smiled sadly—"seem to have been...added later."

"As was the incident in which he declined to participate in terrorist activities," Naomi chimed in. She wanted that on the record, too.

They had more for Francine, of course. How much of a scholarship had Omar received? Was there an institutional bias toward students who claimed oppression by Israel, and would she please share her personal views on the Middle East conflict? Did Webster College welcome returning veterans and make any concession for their service? They drilled on like a chorus of jackhammers.

Naomi was proud of Francine, who never lost her cool, not even when the questions had already been addressed in her statement. Her friend was nailing it, and why not? She'd done nothing wrong and had nothing to hide.

"President Roth?" It was a young woman up front. Not college young, but young. "A question for you? This situation with Eduardo Sombra wasn't the only allegation of dishonesty Webster has been dealing with this year. A couple of months ago a source close to your board of trustees gave an interview in which he suggested that an African-American professor who'd been denied tenure was guilty of plagiarism. Are you concerned that, between these two incidents, one involving a student and the other involving a faculty member, Webster is going to become known for academic transgression?"

Naomi's eyes had gone instantly to Leanne Gall, but she made herself look away. She did not want to answer this question at all, and especially not with Nicholas Gall's wife looking on. But she couldn't see how to get out of it.

"If that happened, I'd be terribly sad, because it really wouldn't be fair. Academic dishonesty is a pervasive problem, and I'd be surprised if there were a campus anywhere in America that hasn't had to deal with it. You know the motto of a certain pretty good college over in Cambridge—*Veritas*, right?"

There was a bit of gratifying laughter. Not much, but a bit.

"Unfortunately, having 'truth' in their motto didn't prevent them from admitting a student who'd plagiarized virtually every word he wrote in his college career, including his academic work, his application materials, and even a poem he won a writing prize with. This happens, in other words. If people are motivated to lie, they're going to lie. But honesty—whether it's academic or personal—it's the bedrock of everything we do. If we gave that up that ideal, I don't think there'd be anything left to teach."

"Well, we know what Eduardo Sombra did," the young woman said. "What we don't know is what the professor, Nicholas Gall did, or didn't do, to be denied tenure. And since the two of them were close, I do think it's pertinent. At the very least I'd like to hear whether the professor knew about Sombra?"

Again, Naomi's vision was drawn back to Gall's wife, who sat glaring back from her desk. Today she wore another of her African cloth shirts, a jarring lavender and black.

"It's not that I don't understand your curiosity, but the privacy of the tenure process, I'm afraid, has more weight, far more weight, than your wish to know the details. As for what Professor Gall knew about his protégé, you are going to have to ask him."

If you can find him, she thought sourly. The previous week, Gall had failed to turn up for his classes. Professor Kinikini had let her know this in an email. He had asked an adjunct to finish up the last few weeks of the term, and left it at that. The department was no more eager than Naomi, it seemed, to have Gall back in a Webster classroom.

"If there are no more questions about admissions..." Francine said. She got to her feet optimistically. "I'd like to thank you for coming. We have copies of my statement at the door, if you need them."

There were a few stragglers, hoarding questions they didn't want to share with their colleagues, but both Francine and Naomi were firm in declining to answer. They did this without even looking at each other, like a practiced, synchronized team, and soon they were alone with Leanne Gall at the other end of the room, still seated, still glaring.

"That went..."

"All right," Francine said.

"Better than all right. You were very, very good."

She shrugged. "Years of angry parents wanting to know why their kid didn't get in but the kid's awful friend did."

"Well," Naomi said, "you should thank every one of them, because you came off as calm and virtuous."

Francine gave her a tired smile. "Are you saying I'm not *naturally* calm and virtuous?"

"No, you are. You are. But these are trying times. Anyway, maybe we'll get lucky now, and they'll go away."

"Maybe." She nodded. "So. Walk this weekend?"

"Love to. Let's go to Wells State Park. We haven't been there in a while."

"Okay, good. I need to go call Sumner. He wanted to know how it went."

Naomi gave her friend a quick hug. She felt light. She was so ready for it all to be over.

Francine walked through the lounge, stopped at her assistant's desk and said something to Leanne, then went into her office and closed the door. Leanne never took her eyes off Naomi.

There was no other way out of the room, which was annoying. Naomi was trying to hold on to that lightness, that optimism. Already it was leaking. She started to walk toward the door. She didn't get far.

"I don't appreciate the way you were looking at me," said the voice, so icy it made Naomi wince.

Right back atcha, she wanted to say.

She would have to pass within a few feet of Leanne's desk.

"I wasn't looking at you in any particular way," Naomi said. "That must have been uncomfortable for you to listen to."

"Uncomfortable?" the woman said. "You think?"

"I'm sure you were fond of Omar."

"Like you give a fuck about Omar. Like you give a fuck about anything but yourself."

Well, that gets right to it, thought Naomi. She stopped in front of Leanne's desk. It was either that or stalk out. Instantly she knew she'd made the wrong choice.

"I just meant...I'm sure this has caused a lot of upheaval in your life."

"You mean the part about how I have to pack up my house and move? Or the part about how somebody on the board, like maybe you, decided to tell the world my husband was a criminal and that's why he got fired."

So many ways to go, thought Naomi: the leak that hadn't come from her, the plagiarism that wasn't technically criminal, or the fact that denial of tenure wasn't strictly the same as being fired. But her heart wasn't in any of them.

"Where is your husband?" she asked instead. "He didn't show up to teach last week."

Leanne looked annoyed, as if this were an inconvenience to *her*.

"Nick went down to Georgia. I have to take care of the move while he gets ready to teach in the fall. Back to Rabun Gap. But my family's up here."

"I'm sorry," said Naomi, surprised to note that she did feel some actual sympathy. "He put us in an impossible position. Like I said over there, honesty is everything. It's the bedrock."

"Oh, what bullshit," said Leanne Gall. "You people. It's one thing if someone like Nick does what you say he did, but then *she* does what she does and you all look the other way. You think what she did isn't as bad?"

Naomi felt warm. She was standing about six feet from Leanne. Her legs were suddenly immoveable.

"I don't understand what you mean. If you have something you want me to know, you'd better say it."

"Oh, okay," Leanne said with rich sarcasm. "You want me to? I'm happy to. Your friend who's so *calm* and *virtuous*? Ask her how she put the daughter of her husband's boss on the waitlist, so the two of them would have some leverage when he was about to get fired. And then ask her how she took the girl *off* the waitlist in exchange for him keeping his job. You think that board of his just gave him a new contract when they were about to fire his ass? They just had a last-minute change of heart?"

Naomi, numb, couldn't say a thing.

"No, they did not. I heard the two of them on the phone. She just wanted to accept the kid, but he thought it was better if they put her on the waitlist. That way they had more control. So he got a new contract and the boss got his daughter in. On the exact same day. I went home that night and I looked it up on her Facebook. 'I just got into Webster!' She posted it a couple hours earlier. You know we're probably not going to the waitlist at all this year, except for her. You think that's okay, madam president?"

Naomi wanted to shake her head no, but she couldn't feel her head at all.

"Well, I don't. So next time you go preach about honesty and the bedrock of the institution and all that crap, you keep it in mind." She got to her feet. Naomi had never seen her upright—always Leanne Gall had been seated at the desk outside of Francine's office. Now she rose and Naomi's gaze rose with her. She was tall, epically tall, and radiated command. She stood with regal stillness for an excruciating moment, then took her purse from the back of her chair, offered a disarmingly pleasant smile, and walked unhurriedly from the long room, closing the door behind her.

Naomi didn't move. She couldn't move, because she knew it was true, and knowing it was true broke her apart. That and understanding what had to happen next. For the longest time she stood, steadying herself in the empty room, concentrating on remaining vertical.

Francine was on the phone when she went in, with her elbows on the desk, nodding her head. She looked up at the sound, and didn't react right away. "Hang on," she said, but not to Naomi. "Hang on. Naomi's here." She straightened a bit. "I thought you'd gone."

"No," Naomi said.

The two of them looked at each other.

"Oh," Francine said at last. "Oh yes. I see." She put the phone to her ear again. "Sumner, I need to speak with Naomi. I'll call you back. No. No, I don't know. I don't know." And she placed the handset, very gently, into its cradle, looking at it intently as if daring it to move. Then she looked at Naomi. "All right," she said.

"Is it true?"

Francine closed her eyes and let out a long breath. Then she opened them again. "You know it is. You wouldn't be here if you didn't."

"Well, knowing it and believing it. Two different things. I can't believe it. I can't believe you would do something so..."

What? Asinine? Or merely appalling?

"Naomi, we were in a terrible situation. We felt very desperate. And this applicant, she was fine. A strong student and an athlete. She's going to do very well at Webster. There's no loss here."

"Oh," Naomi sighed, "but there is. Plenty of loss. The fairness of the process, even just the intention of fairness. That's an untenable loss. I'm amazed that I need to explain this."

But she didn't need to explain it. Naomi saw that on Francine's face, and Francine knew everything that Naomi knew, probably more. She knew that she was no longer the dean of admissions at Webster College. Already, that was over, and so much more besides.

"I let your daughter in," Francine said suddenly. "Hannah's great, but they're all great. You know that. But I let her in, instead of others. Was that fair?"

She felt so tired. She wanted oblivion, horizontal and total, and now.

"Probably not."

"And how is that different from this?"

"It probably isn't," Naomi said. "But it doesn't matter. If you want to fight, I'm willing. I can do that, even in public. After this year I could take on anyone. But I hope you'll go quietly. That would be better."

"For *you*," Francine said bitterly.

"And you. And Sumner. And also this girl who's coming to Webster in the fall. She doesn't need to be humiliated. But if you want, as I said, I'll take you on. I'm fully capable of that, it turns out."

Francine seemed to sink into her chair. Her hands were on the desktop, palms flat. She turned her head away.

"What am I supposed to say about this?" Francine wanted to know.

Naomi sighed. "I'll leave it to you. 'Personal reasons unrelated to recent events at Webster' should be enough."

"People are going to assume I was fired because of Omar."

Under the circumstances, Naomi thought, that was a gift.

"And I suppose this is you speaking truth to power. *The principle your whole life is organized around.*"

Naomi started. There was loathing in the way it was said. She had never suspected. She shook her head sadly.

"No, I don't think I can do that anymore. As you pointed out to me, I'm the power. This is me speaking power to truth."

Francine couldn't look her in the eye.

"I'm leaving now," she told her friend. "If there's anything else you want to say to me, say it now, because this is the last conversation we're going to have."

But Francine had nothing to say, so Naomi left her to not say it.

CHAPTER TWENTY

THE ENTIRE POINT OF A COLLEGE EDUCATION

The reseeded grass seemed to be off to a decent start. Naomi walked slowly across the Billings Lawn. The sprinklers were just winding down, and she caught the end of the spray from one near the Stump, but, strangely, it wasn't unwelcome. In a few weeks the seniors would undertake their final Webster ritual here, assembling on the eve of graduation to smash clay pipes against the flat surface of the old stump itself, reenacting a scene of good-natured collegiate destruction that supposedly went back to Josiah Webster's days. It was another myth, probably, but after a long enough time it had become as good as a truth. For all she knew every single thing she'd ever thought of as a real event had started out as some kind of story. Once those hundreds of students and their hundreds of parents and siblings and friends had swarmed this spot to smash their pipes and then, the following day, collect their degrees, the poor lawn would need yet another generation of grass seed, and another period of care. It was the least of her responsibilities.

When she got to the Stone House she found her daughter on the steps, reading a book, mindlessly rotating a plastic cup of iced tea on the top step. Hannah looked up only when her mother blocked her light. "Oh, hi," she said, genially enough.

"Well, hello. Did you forget your key?"

"No, I have it," Hannah said. "I just . . . it didn't feel right to go in."

"That's funny," Naomi said. She sat beside her daughter on the top step, but not too close. She didn't want to push her luck. "I mean, it's your home."

Hannah turned and looked up at the edifice: its baronial dimensions and massive blocks of stone. The late sun hit her jaw and neck and one end of that sculpted clavicle where her shirt was loosely buttoned around her neck. Sometimes Naomi failed to see how lovely Hannah was, and sometimes she got reminded. That whole beauty thing—she'd been so militant about evading it when her daughter was young. She got annoyed whenever someone, well-intentioned, called Hannah "pretty" to her face. "Pretty" was the patriarchy. "Beautiful" meant no one expected you to achieve, and Hannah had so much to achieve in the world. But here her child had gone and grown up beautiful anyway, despite Naomi's efforts. It was out of her hands. She needed to make her peace with it.

"You know what's strange?" said Hannah. "I never thought of this as home. I know I lived here for years, but it's the president's house. It wasn't ours."

"Well, I get that. But I loved living here with you." She was surprised to hear how sad that came out sounding. "You want to talk about it?" Naomi asked, after a moment.

Hannah drank the last of her iced tea, then set down the cup. "I applied for the transfer last fall. I'd been thinking about it for a while. I meant to speak with you about it, but . . . well. You know. I was angry with you. And now I'm angry at myself."

Naomi was feeling strangely calm, as if she'd imagined this exact conversation and now it was simply being played back. The actual lines had undergone a rewrite, but the scene was more or less intact. Hannah was leaving. The rest was noise.

"Why should you be angry at yourself, Hannah?"

Hannah looked away, out over the Billings Lawn where the disappearing sun was throwing back reddish light onto the grass and the Stump. There was a boy on the Stump now, cross-legged, facing west. Even seated you could see how tall he was, and how thin. He had hair that was probably blond, but in that light it, too, was red. He was hunched over something on his lap.

"I thought I knew him. It took me days to believe any of it was true. I kept thinking it had all been manufactured somehow. Someone just put Omar into this other person's life, and walked him into a shootout, just to get rid of him. Or he was somewhere else in the world, but this person in Hartford had his ID for some reason. I was trying to come up with some solution that would explain everything, but they just got more and more convoluted. And then I went down to Hartford, to the funeral."

"You did?" Naomi was surprised.

"Yes, with some of the others. And I saw his body, so I knew it was him. And I saw all the people in the church who were grieving over Eduardo Sombra. I couldn't get my head around any of it. I still can't."

Naomi nodded. "I know."

"Why did he do it?" Hannah said. "I mean, why not apply to college as himself? He could have gotten in, here or somewhere. It was all so unnecessary."

"Not to him, I guess," Naomi said sadly. "But I can tell you right now, you won't get an answer. I'm sure a lot of people have a lot of theories, but that's not the same as the truth. I don't think there is a whole truth. Even if Omar were here and you could ask him: *Why did you make all this up? What did you want from us?* He probably wouldn't be able to answer."

Hannah seemed to shudder. "I'd gone on television and talked about his childhood. I talked to journalists about how he'd refused to carry a suicide bomb. That's a lot for me to handle."

"And so unfair," Naomi reminded her. "And not your fault, at all." She thought for a moment. "Do you think... did he do those things?"

Her daughter turned to her.

"My office? And even... that basement?"

Hannah shut her eyes tight. "I don't know. I hope not. But... everyone was away over the winter break. I was in New York. He was with the Galls, that's where he was spending those couple of weeks. And by the time we all returned the basement was there, that's how we found it. Which only means it isn't impossible, though, believe me, even that I couldn't get to right away. And the night of the fire, we had a meeting at Professor Gall's house. We were working on a statement about institutional openness. Then we all said good night and everyone left. I went back to my room and some of the others were sleeping out or at Sojourner. All I know is, that was the last time I saw Omar. The next morning he wasn't on campus, and he didn't get in touch with me, or anyone. So, I mean, what I'm saying is that if someone showed me evidence it was him, I'd probably accept it. And the basement... it could have been anyone, and that means it could have been him. It doesn't make any sense, but it could have been. That's as far as I can go, I think."

"You have an open mind, in other words."

"Yeah. Open mind. The entire point of a college education."

She'd said it with sarcasm, but Naomi smiled. "It kind of is. I mean, consider the alternative."

They sat in silence. Hannah moved closer. She draped a long arm over her mother's shoulder.

"Why Stanford?" Naomi asked. She was happy under the weight of her daughter's arm. She never wanted to move.

"I don't know," Hannah said. "I wanted something really different. Different part of the world. Different frame of reference. Maybe I wanted to be atypical in my setting." She smiled. "I'm kind of generic here, you know."

"Nothing wrong with that," said Naomi. It came out sounding a tiny bit defensive. "Generic Webster is a great kid."

"Yeah. But if it's all you know, how can you tell if that's who you are because it's really who you are, or because you never actually gave it serious thought? And besides: California! California's gorgeous!"

"And three thousand miles away!" Naomi said. She was no longer even trying to censor her tone. It was really hitting her now.

"Yeah. But it's time for me to leave." Hannah smiled at her, though sadly. "You know that."

"Wasn't it time for you to leave two years ago? That's the way most people do it. You could have applied to Stanford then. You could have applied anywhere."

Hannah shook her head. Her truncated hair looked nearly gold in this last light. "I should have, I guess. But...you know, I didn't think you were ready."

Naomi stared at her. Then, somewhat to her own surprise, she started to laugh.

"It's funny?" her daughter asked.

"It's hilarious. I have raised the most empathic child on the planet. Obviously! Everybody else is tearing out the door. They can't get away fast enough. But not Hannah. Hannah stays behind to keep an eye on Mom."

"Well, someone has to." She smiled. "You can't be left alone. Who knows what you'd do? Speaking of which, I hear you've got a boyfriend."

"Who told you that?" Naomi asked.

"My friend Millie. She was on your panel at the Native American thing? She said there was a definite something between you and the keynote speaker. I was skeptical, obviously."

"Obviously?" Naomi said. "Thanks a lot."

"She also said he had a certain...appeal. For an older guy. So it's true?"

Naomi shrugged. "Could be. We've met up a few times. We went to Sturbridge Village a couple of weeks ago."

Hannah looked mystified. "Sturbridge Village? Like where you go on elementary school field trips? That's a date?"

"Well, *date*. We're too old to go on dates. But he's a history professor. It's hard for historians to resist a 'living history' installation. Half the time they're getting excited about some obscure tool or bit of ephemera, the other half they're railing about things the museum got wrong."

"Well, it sounds just fab," Hannah said with glorious sarcasm. "I'll leave you to it."

"Come on. He's an interesting man. He's kind. I like him. I think you'd like him."

Hannah was giving her a maddening smile, tight-lipped, as absurdly proud as any mom watching her kid perform some deeply ordinary feat for the very first time. Then she leaned her head against Naomi's shoulder, and Naomi, full of this sweet and melancholy thing, closed her eyes. She was concentrating on the last warmth of the sun before it fled, and the sound that was now coming across the Billings lawn. The boy on the Stump was playing an accordion. Hannah, beside her, was listening, too. "I know that song," Naomi said.

But she didn't. She couldn't name it. Something about the waves? Something about a hot air balloon? "'On a Flight Above the Ocean'?" she suggested.

Hannah laughed, clear and light. "'In the Aeroplane over the Sea.'"

Naomi nodded. Yes, that. Her daughter moved closer.

"It's pretty, though," Hannah said, after a minute. Her eyes, apparently, were not closed. "Whatever else you can say about Webster, it's pretty here. I got to grow up in a beautiful place."

Naomi nodded. What else could you say about Webster? Just now, she couldn't say anything, but the next time she did there would probably be tears. That thing you dread, after all, when it comes, if it comes, it doesn't matter how unsurprising it turns out to be; it is still that thing you dread, and it has still happened. She'd had a little reprieve, Naomi saw, but now it was here. The thing. This thing: Hannah was leaving. Hannah had grown up and she was leaving, and Naomi had no sympathy for herself, because the whole fact of it was so very ordinary. But it was everything, too.

ACKNOWLEDGMENTS

In the spring of 1999, my second child arrived hot on the heels of my second novel, *The Sabbathday River*, which related some extraordinary events in the life of a woman named Naomi Roth. The little boy grew up, and I wrote other books about other characters. I thought I was finished with Naomi Roth. I wasn't finished. A few months after *The Devil and Webster* is published, my son will leave for college. I really do think I am finished with Naomi Roth now. I will miss both of them, though perhaps one more than the other. So goes the ordinary life of a novelist, a mother, or, in my case, both, but of course I also know how extraordinarily fortunate I've been.

I am grateful to Ragdale for a fellowship that enabled me to make significant headway on this novel. I thank two college presidents, Debora Spar of Barnard College and David E. Van Zandt of the New School for Social Research, who fearlessly allowed me to peek beneath the veil of their demanding jobs.

A certain tale about plagiarism was itself plagiarized, or at any rate *borrowed*, from the late Frank Kinahan, who told it to me a quarter century ago. It was just too good not to.

I am ever thankful for my wonderful agent, Suzanne Gluck, and my loyal, brilliant editor, Deb Futter, and everyone who works with them; I can't convey how lucky I feel to be in their care. Thanks to my parents, sister, husband, daughter, and son, and to my friends Lisa Eckstrom, Leslie Kuenne, Elise Paschen, Elisa Rosen, Sally Singer, Peggy O'Brien, and most especially Deborah Michel and Laurie Eustis.

And to Jack, who left us during the writing of this novel. *Beloved accordion boy, good-bye.*

ABOUT THE AUTHOR

Jean Hanff Korelitz was born and raised in New York and graduated from Dartmouth College and Cambridge University. She is the author of five previous novels, *You Should Have Known*, *Admission* (adapted for the 2013 film of the same name, starring Tina Fey, Paul Rudd, and Lily Tomlin), *The White Rose*, *The Sabbathday River*, and *A Jury of Her Peers*, as well as a novel for children, *Interference Powder*, and a collection of poems, *The Properties of Breath*. She lives in New York City with her husband, the Irish poet Paul Muldoon, with whom she recently adapted James Joyce's "The Dead" as an immersive theater event: *The Dead, 1904*.

If you would like to invite Jean Hanff Korelitz to your book group please visit www.bookthewriter.com.